The Eve's End

STEPHANIE M. MATTHEWS

paperback ISBN 978-0-9953132-4-8
e-edition ISBN 978-0-9953132-5-5

To everyone who has ever felt out of place:
You are not alone.

For it is hard to speak properly upon a subject where it is even difficult to convince your hearers that you are speaking the truth.

Thucydides, *The Peloponnesian War*, 2.35.2

I found a therapist four weeks after I got back to Brussels. She told me to write down my thoughts to help my recovery. So, here I am. Acknowledging in writing that on Christmas Eve . . . I don't even know what to say. The person I knew myself to be is no more. I don't recognize myself. Nicholas freed me from that monster, but that monster ruined me.

Year 1

June 8: Therapist says the writing is helping. Funny. I can't write a word without a couple drinks first. Nefas won't leave me alone. He's in my thoughts. He's on the street . . . I'm scared of the dark, a stranger in my own life. Everything around me is foreign and uncomfortable. She said I should try to "write around" the event which means writing about . . . what? Belgian waffles?

Year 28

November 19: Dominic visited me in a dream. Told me to go back to the village. At Christmas. He had me go back once already nearly twenty-one years ago to help those people. It was summer then, yes, but everything changed for the village on that trip—and for Nefas. Previous entries record how poorly I reacted to being there, and there's twenty-one years of written proof here in this journal for how little that trip changed anything for me. I don't care what I'm supposed to do when I'm there this time. For Dominic to make me go back at Christmas . . . God. Nefas is going to be . . . I don't know . . . expectant? If I go, I might not come back. I haven't told Jordan yet but there's no way he's coming with me.

Last entry was thirteen months ago. I was just starting to get used to these long, peaceful stretches.

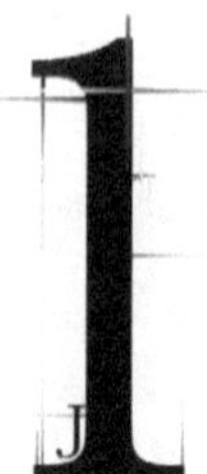

"The gates to the portal of Hell were open." The masterful storyteller captivated his small audience using nothing but his voice to tether even the youngest listener to his every word. The outdoor air was crisp, and the bustle of the small Belgian village was not enough to distract as his eyes grew wide with warning. "They were never supposed to be opened, much less opened and left unwatched, and yet"—he paused, letting his next words hang—"the two cold metal doors were both opened and unwatched." He caught the eye of each member of his growing audience, inviting them deeper into his story. With them on the cusp of suspense, he smiled crookedly and forged ahead.

"The gates to Hell were meant to be forgotten in the same way that the villagers meant to forget what they held: a terrible gift born from an ageless struggle between light and dark, life and death. The doors were unadorned except for splattered dirt and garbage that had collected along their base where the summer winds and the passage of time buried what the villagers did not wish to remember.

"It was on that cursed day that Adrien Jandreau and André de Boer walked past and saw daylight shining between the gates. And so begins our tale.

"They should've listened to the heart-stopping sound of the gates' metal chain clanging against its keep in the late-morning breeze. The blood-chilling sight of la Rue through those cracked gates should've been warning enough. But neither boy listened to those ominous warnings." The storyteller dropped his voice, and against the bustling background noises of the Christmas market, his audience crowded in closer.

"Only one person has the authority to open those gates: the Monsieur. Most of their names have been lost, but first in our memory was Maria Peeters. Then it was Lars Drechsler. At that time, it was Iakob Courtellemont, and on that day, in the lonely part of the village where Adrien had been teaching André parkour, Monsieur Courtellemont was nowhere to be seen.

"'Monsieur must be inside,' André said uneasily to his friend, believing no other explanation possible.

"To which Adrien wondered out loud, 'What if something other than Monsieur opened those gates?'

"A breeze picked up, swinging the gate open even wider, the loose lock and chain clanging once more.

"'It's none of our business if Monsieur is in there or not,' André said at last, then suggested going home for lunch.

"But Adrien hesitated. For all the tales of evil, there lay the greatest opportunity to become a living legend: to actually walk upon la Rue. Stories circulated of people who'd snuck in before on a dare, but none could be proven, and no one had gone all the way inside to find out where la Rue went. The opportunity to tread upon the doorstep of Hell and live to tell the tale was more than Adrien could resist. But he wasn't brave enough to go in alone.

"'We should poke our head inside,' Adrien said, 'and call for Monsieur. If we don't find him, we'll come back out and lock the gate.'

"Adrien's plan was a dangerous one, stupid even, for it was no mystery of *who* lay behind those gates. If that *who* was on this side of Hell on that particular day . . . well, none could know for sure. A cold sweat broke down Adrien's spine as he said with words much too hurried, 'Five minutes. In and out. We go in, make sure Monsieur is or isn't there, and we're done.'

"André looked at Adrien like he was mad, and adamantly refused.

"'C'mon, it's the middle of June.' Adrien taunted, trying to make himself sound braver. 'The scary stuff only happens on Christmas Eve.'

"André shifted his eyes between his friend and the old gate. Another breeze rose up and the gate creaked open even further so that the two friends could easily see the narrow, bricked street that lay on the other side. Adrien was about to recant of his suggestion when André caved.

"'It's June,' André agreed. 'La Rue is like any other street this time of year, right?'

"Neither of them immediately moved. It was as though they were waiting to see who would be the bravest, or most foolish.

"Adrien knew he had to make the first move.

"He took out his cellphone and began recording their trip to the portal of Hell. They'd be the first to prove their journey. The tension on that bright day was as tight as the string of life that the Fates were about to cut. Adrien's knees felt weak, but he set out toward the gates, André following close behind.

"'Monsieur Courtellemont? You in here?' André called out, having not yet breached the threshold. 'Iakob, you forgot to close the gate behind you!'

"André and Adrien exchanged nervous laughs before Adrien fully pulled open one of the gates, the hinges protesting under their own weight. Before they knew it, the friends were standing on la Rue itself looking down the thin, plain street stretching out before them.

"The two smiled bravely at the phone, giving a thumbs up. 'Here we go,' Adrien said to the camera. 'Where no man has gone before.'

"'Be back in five,' André added.

"Perhaps Adrien Jandreau should have made the same promise, for André de Boer came back out with the phone but Adrien did not return.

"Having escaped la Rue, André managed to find Monsieur Courtellemont and Adrien's parents in the village and gave them a stumbling, babbling, soul-chilling account of what had happened. They wasted no time racing to la Rue in hopes of rescuing Adrien.

"No one knows exactly what they found on that street. Some say they found nothing at all. Some say they found Adrien's body frozen to the ground, encased in ice and immovable, and there it still lies today. Others say that his parents met the Devil himself and made a deal with him to get their son back. If they did, it was a deal the Devil did not keep, for a week later the whole Jandreau family was found dead in their home. It was a grim reminder that Death does not negotiate. Monsieur Iakob Courtellemont went mad with guilt and no one knows where he is today, or if he is even alive.

"As for Adrien Jandreau, he does not let us forget him. On cool nights when the breeze is blowing just right, and the sound of a chain clanging against a metal door can be heard, he can be seen wandering the streets, calling out to his parents to help him. What happened to his cell phone, who holds it now, or where it's hidden, no one knows. But that is the story of the Jandreau family who once were."

The storyteller stopped and took a deep bow as his audience applauded. Receiving the praise humbly, he proceeded to beseech them to recompense his art. He spoke quickly before too many people slipped back into the Christmas market where vendors in wooden stalls and booths were fighting for patrons' attention and hopefully deep pockets. Coins clinked into the busker's open case to join a few bills as parents herded their children. One little boy and his mother approached the storyteller together. When the storyteller saw the two coming, he dropped to one knee.

"He wants to ask you something," the mother said, coaxing the boy to speak up. It was a short struggle, but the boy found his voice.

"Why did you tell such a scary story? Christmas isn't for scary stories."

"No?" The storyteller asked. "What's Christmas for then?"

"Presents!" The boy blurted out, a shy smile breaking onto his face. "And Mémé's chocolates. And sledding. And Jesus's-s birthday."

"And what about the choir? Do you like listening to them sing on Christmas Eve?"

The boy nodded and pointed his mittened hand to behind the storyteller where the small gothic basilica rose high above them like a wise, old sage.

"In there, Maman and Papa have their Christmas party. They go to the basement with the other adults and older kids. They say one day, when I'm old enough, I'll join them."

A wave of sadness flashed across the storyteller's face as he looked up at the mother who nodded in affirmation. They both knew that "party" was a deeply naïve understanding of events, though the boy was too young to understand. The storyteller, not wanting to ruin the boy's day, brightened again and responded cheerfully.

"Well, let me tell you why I tell ghost stories at Christmas time. It's because . . ." He took an audible breath and began to sing a jolly melody that made the boy and his mother smile. He sang of Christmas parties and caroling in the falling snow, and of telling scary ghost stories—

"It's the most wonderful time of the year!" The boy belted out, giggling.

"Thank you," the mother told the storyteller as she guided her son away, dropping some money into his case.

From her seat at the restaurant patio not far away, Fae Norris-Peeters watched as the pair wandered off to finish their day's activities. She heard the mother say to her son, "the Jandreau family are a part of this village's history. The story you heard probably isn't true, but we shouldn't forget them."

"Did they really all die, Maman?"

"They really did. It's an unsolved crime."

"What's an . . . unsolved crime?"

Fae sighed. She was tired of sighing, but it was an outlet and she needed it. Dominic had asked her to return to this watershed village, and there were some people whose requests couldn't be ignored.

Turning her attention to her empty coffee cup, she motioned over the waiter who was tending to her and the others who were taking advantage of this bright December day. She ordered another coffee with a double shot of Grand Marnier. There weren't many things that drove her to drink anymore, but that story represented everything that could.

The crisp air filling her lungs kept her thoughts sharp while the patio heaters kept her warm, though there would always be a chill to this place. Decades may have passed since her nightmare here, but there would never be enough time for her to be OK being back, to bring her to a place of ease. As cute as this little village was, Fae would never let herself be charmed into a sense of security. How this place had changed. A Christmas market! Maël, her second cousin and one of her closest friends, had kept her updated as village life progressed over the years, but it was still hard to fathom. Hell had frozen over to get her back here for Christmas, and frozen Hell never looked so idyllic.

"Hell's graveyard" she'd once called this village. Sitting at her table, she watched a new generation wander around the market that had taken over the basilica plaza. Some of the booths were topped with striped canvas. Others, with evergreen boughs. Christmas lights strung across the aisles and around each booth were turned on, but in the afternoon sun they had little effect. There were stacks of soft pretzels so high they threatened to fall over, handmade ornaments hung from displays, and candle powered mobiles spun gently around. And, of course, there were the Nativity sets: molded-chocolate Nativities; wool-knitted, blown-glass, and gingerbread; wood-carved and leather-stitched ones too. The village had developed a reputation for being the place to find the most unique Nativity displays. No doubt that contributed to the large crowds. Only two days before Christmas Eve, the market was full.

The people here were so much more welcoming and friendly than how she'd first known them. New life had taken root. No longer did it feel like a graveyard, but rather, it felt . . . normal. And that openness felt out of place, like an untouched flower in the middle of no-man's-land: a thing that shouldn't be.

The waiter returned with her spiked coffee.

"Merci." The French rolled comfortably off her tongue, helping to take her focus off the resurfacing memories. She let the coffee refocus her thoughts on her newest work project that lay open in front of her. It was a facelift for Vancouver's Pacific Central Station, and it was starting to stress her out. There were too many cooks in the kitchen, and it was a perfect reminder of why she preferred to work for the private sector. The city had bent over backward to secure her services though, and it had been too good an opportunity to walk away from.

With her fingerless gloves on, she worked on another round of proposals, updating them with the new requirements. She quickly lost herself in her work and was surprised when a soft alarm she'd set alerted her to the time.

With practiced proficiency, Fae packed up her conservative work space, paid her bill, and wove her way through the Christmas market to the Basilique de Notre-Dame du Seigneur for what she desperately needed to be an insightful meeting with a priest who was too often better at trying her patience.

———————————

Fae wandered the perimeter of the basilica's sanctuary, her thoughts silent, her emotions calmed. Unlike the village outside, very little had changed inside this place, the stalwart stone icon that it was. Yes, the wooden pews were now padded in a kingly royal blue, and she spotted artificial lighting hiding in the corners but these were the superficial observations. In all the ways that mattered, this Gothic-Renaissance hybrid was the same.

Closing her eyes, Fae took a deep breath and slowly let it out as she ran her hands over the pews' rounded wood endcaps and across the cool stone of the pillars. This basilica was the oasis in the turmoil. She let her imagination fill in the quiet of this holy space with the sound of the gorgeous Christmas choir.

"Madame Peeters?" The questioning voice came from behind her, and Fae let her hands casually drop to her sides. Turning around, Fae greeted the elderly priest, Cuvelier, who embraced her warmly. She reciprocated his action but not the same fondness he showed her. He'd gone more or less bald since she'd last seen him, and he hadn't given up his thick rimmed glasses. He was thinner too, though he still seemed sturdy on his feet. "Did you travel well?"

"I did. Thank you. Other than the squished legs, it was perfectly uneventful."

"Wonderful." Cuvelier smiled, wrinkling his aged face. "Shall we?" He extended his hand showing the way to his office and Fae fell into step beside him.

He led her down the hallway to the right, opposite the hallway that, so many years ago, had led her down into the crypt. *Find the baby* . . . Fae put a hard mental brake on that memory. She wasn't here to relive the past.

Cuvelier's office was modernized with painted plaster walls and LED lighting. Tidy bookcases of theology texts lined the walls, interspaced with busts of people Fae didn't recognize. Taking off her coat, she sat down in the armless chair across from his sparse desk.

"You know," Cuvelier began amicably, "I wasn't surprised when Maël told me you'd be returning to us this year. When I'd first met you, I'd said to myself, now there is a young woman who will mean something special to this village. And the Lord confirmed it in my spirit. I had hoped that you'd return sooner, in the spirit of your grandmother. But all in the Lord's timing, not ours. He does know how to confound the wisdom of men!"

Fae smiled politely. "Your lack of surprise shows just how great your faith is," she said as kindly as she could. "I'm not my grandmother, and I didn't come with any plans to take her place; Maël is holding the job just fine. I don't want to take up too much of your time," Fae said, not knowing how much Maël had confided in Cuvelier. The reality was that Maël wasn't holding the job of Monsieur "just fine." He wasn't made for the role, he didn't want it, and even though he rarely spoke of it, she could tell it was a heavy burden for him.

"I'll get right to the point. The truth is, I don't know why I've been told to come back, and you're one of the few people who might be able to fill in the blanks. As you can imagine, I would really like to know."

Cuvelier nodded slightly, looking thoughtfully down at his desk. He folded his hands then returned his attention to her. "The first time you came to us, your grandmother asked you to come. Then, a few years later, we asked you back to help us. We asked, but it was your friend from the choir who brought you in; what's his name again?"

"Dominic. But he's not so much a friend; I'm more his assignment." That was something Cuvelier should know.

"In both cases you were asked here for a purpose. Now, you return to us a third time. Who dragged you onto the plane this time?"

Cuvelier looked amused with himself, but Fae smiled, fighting down her rising offense at being talked to like she was a child. As if all her reluctance to come back to this hellhole village wasn't born from an extreme, survival-based aversion. The smile she held continued to mirror Cuvelier's oblivious friendliness.

"It was Dominic. I boarded the plane myself," she clarified. "But unlike last time, he wouldn't tell me why I had to come."

"Then maybe," Cuvelier suggested in his priestly voice of wisdom, "you aren't supposed to know."

That wasn't the answer Fae was looking for and she'd already considered it. She pressed. "Have you seen anything, or heard, or dreamed anything, has *anything* happened that might indicate . . . I don't know, a change in the . . . arrangement . . . with *him*? Considering the role I played in bringing that arrangement about last time I was here, maybe my return has something to do with it. Has there been unusual activity around the old entrance to la Rue, maybe?"

"Has Nefas been making trouble?" Cuvelier asked, unceremoniously clearing that elephant from the room. He looked at her sympathetically, but his sympathy was muted by the sound of *his* name. Spoken aloud, in this village, it felt like jagged ice being driven through Fae's heart.

Fae plastered on another fake smile.

"The simple answer is no," Cuvelier said. "I haven't heard nor seen anything that would indicate that this year would be different from any other. Then again, I don't keep tabs on Nefas' activities like Maël does. Ever since Nefas was confined to his pit, he has stayed there, and his grim mirror reflections have stopped. Everyone here has adapted well to hiding in your underground hall on the Eve, and for all that I know, this year's Eve will be the same as every other. The choir will sing the night away to welcome us out of the Gift, meals shall be eaten, wine drunk, children will play—"

"Yes, but that can't be the case; otherwise, why would Dominic make me come back? Don't take this personally, but I have never wanted anything to do with this place. When I tell you that Dominic made me come back for *Christmas*, I can't emphasize enough the effort he had to put in. There has to be *something* out of place. Something unusual." Fae was squeezing her fingers tight hoping Cuvelier's memory would jog with anything useful, but while she pressed him for information, an oblong vial on his desk made itself known to her. She took closer notice of it. No more than five inches long, maybe two in diameter, it was held horizontally in a simple wooden cradle. The glass was thickly clouded making it look very, very old. Capped in wax, it was tightly sealed.

Cuvelier didn't seem to notice her shift of attention. "Ma chère, despite our freedoms with Nefas caged and muzzled, the Gift still takes us over. La Rue, though hidden by your skill, still exists. We always live with a certain level of unusualness."

"Like the ghost of Adrien Jandreau," Fae offered, still taken by that vial.

"Exactly. I've never seen the ghost myself and have my doubts. God holds the boy and his family now, but—"

"I'm sorry, can you tell me about this vial?" Fae asked, leaning forward to get a closer look.

Cuvelier stalled with the sudden change of topic but didn't seem too bothered. "This?" He picked up the vial between two fingers. "It's an old piece that's been in the church for, well, likely forever!" He gave a jolly little chuckle. "There's no history telling where it came from or who it first belonged to, but it's become something of an unofficial mark of this church's priesthood that gets passed on. It was analyzed back in the 1930s and again in the 1980s for any significance, but obviously nothing of interest was found or it would've been taken by researchers, I suppose. Maybe if the cap was opened, but we don't want to do that."

Cuvelier offered the vial out to Fae and she delicately took it from his fingers. "If you're so interested, why don't you take it with you? Study it. I just moved it to my desk yesterday from storage after a strong feeling arrested my spirit that I needed to put it out again. Just make sure to bring it back before you leave, or I 'unofficially' won't be priest anymore!" He winked with his joke, but Fae wasn't interested in encouraging his weak humor.

"Thank you, of course." She carefully turned the smooth glass over in her hands. There was definitely some sort of powder inside. An old spice jar, maybe? Sand?

"Are you hungry? Have you had lunch yet?" Cuvelier pushed himself up from his desk, knees cracking along with him. "I always eat mine so late and can never find someone to share it with."

Fae couldn't help but smile at how little this man had changed, just like his basilica. After all this time, she honestly still had very little to talk to him about over a late lunch. "I have eaten, thank you. But I'll walk with you outside."

The old priest nodded and the two of them grabbed their jackets, Fae gently placing the vial deep inside a pocket.

"How long will you be with us this time? I've heard you have a family now?" Cuvelier asked as they made their way back into the sanctuary.

"No longer than I have to be, and my family didn't come. I wouldn't let them."

"What are their names?"

"Jordan's my husband. Bailey's my daughter. She's eighteen."

Cuvelier kept the small chat going until they reached the back of the basilica. He opened the door for her as they both exited to the renewed sounds of crowds, music, and shopping.

"I promise you," he said, stopping beneath the archivolt that had the story of this village carved into it, "if I do notice anything out of place, or learn anything, I will tell you."

"Thank you," Fae said, holding out her hand to shake his. "Anything to help provide some insight would be very appreciated."

As Fae descended the steps back into the heart of the Christmas market, she stuck her hand into the pocket and held the vial. Something had changed since going inside the basilica. The atmosphere seemed different somehow, and she had the unsettling feeling that someone was watching her.

He knew she was back.

Katie Windsor rolled her car up to the guard booth protruding from the village wall, lowering her window and the volume of the rap song she'd been listening to at the same time. She didn't know who the artist was, but he sounded German and the music was good enough, so she'd kept it on. Stopping in front of the little window, she waited for the guard to state what he was looking for. For a little village in the middle of nowhere Belgium, it was strange to even have a checkpoint. Classic little-man complex.

"Bonjour, hallo."

Please speak English, please speak English, please speak English . . . "Do you speak English?" Katie crossed her fingers.

"Yes, of course," the guard said, and Katie let out a small sigh of relief. If forced, she could make broken conversation in French, but she'd never gotten very good at the language.

"Valid ID s'il vous plait."

"Can I ask what this is for? I'm British."

"It is standard for any visitor coming in or out."

She handed him her driver's license, which he took and scanned into an old machine. He skimmed over some information for a few drawn out seconds before asking her, "How long will your stay be?"

"One night."

"What is t'e purpose of your stay, if you do not come to listen to our famous choir on t'e eve of Noël?"

"Work. I'm a photographer. Trying to wrap up a project before Christmas."

The guard's face brightened with interest. "What do you photograph?"

"A bit of everything. For this project, a lot of buildings. Someone suggested that I should come here. Does the name Fae Peeters mean anything to you?"

The guard shook his head.

It'd been a long shot.

Katie was on contract to photograph some of the more iconic Europeans structures of the last one hundred years by any of a shortlisted group of architects. She'd gotten a tip while in Reims that there was a private project here by Peeters, who was on the list, and Katie was keen to find it. The potential for a bonus was worth putting off Christmas break by a day.

The guard handed her license back with a welcoming smile. "Do you have a room to stay in?"

He was a guard and a travel guide? Katie did a quick check in her rearview mirror to confirm no one else was behind her. Considering the size of this village, she alone must've constituted the traffic jam for the day.

"No, this was a short notice detour. Do you have a recommendation?

"We have deux choix. Bed and Breakfast, also, an 'otel. I will show you." He reached back into his booth and pulled forward a piece of paper on which he circled two points. When he showed it to her, she almost laughed as it was a hand drawn map that looked like it had been photocopied about forty times too many. She hadn't even gotten into the village yet and the rural amazingness of this place was almost too much. "The 'otel is closest and most easy to find. It is very close to t'e train station. The Bed and Breakfast is over 'ere and buried in our little streets. It is very nice."

Katie took the map but had already decided the hotel would be best. The easier the better, and she could expense it anyway. "Merci."

"Merci." The guard gave a little wave as he slid shut his window, and Katie rolled up hers, turning the rap music up again. She set off into the cute little streets, the unmistakable sound of tires rolling over uneven paving stones welcoming her in. Everywhere she looked the village was alive with Christmas. Naked strings of light bulbs were strung across the streets. Golden angels hung from historical lamp posts, store fronts wooed customers with their holiday delights. . . not to be too distracted while driving, Katie put her focus back on the map. She was nervous about navigating without a voice telling her where to turn next, but she was up for the challenge. Holding it above the steering wheel, she began looking for a roundabout near something that looked like . . . a tank, maybe?

———————————

The hotel was a converted three-story house making it stand a story higher than most everything around it. It was renovated to be modern and comfortable, which was a relief given the low expectations set by the photocopied map. Across from the front desk was an open lounge with a fireplace and a lovely decorated Christmas tree popping its branches into the hallway. A brilliant choir sang from hidden speakers creating a charming atmosphere. One other patron sat in the lounge playing chess against himself, but otherwise it was quiet.

A young man behind the desk smiled a toothy grin beckoning her forward as though he'd been waiting for her. "Bonjour, hallo."

"Bonjour, do you speak English?"

"I do. How can I help you?"

The young man, whose spotless golden nametag said his name was Frédéric, spoke with almost no accent, and while he was setting her up with a room, a well-dressed older woman came out from the back office and began rummaging about on the desk.

"Perfect," Frédéric said with a large smile when everything was processed. He reached behind to an old board where only two remaining room keys hung in a grid—a nostalgic and somehow appropriate tradition in this otherwise modern setting. "Room 3A will be—"

The older woman stopped her rummaging and interrupted him in hushed

French. She flicked her eyes up toward Katie before reaching back to the key rack and grabbing the other key.

"I apologize," the woman said, also with barely an accent. "The heater in 3A hasn't been fixed yet. Room 2B will serve you very well." She flashed a well-practiced smile leaving Frédéric to pick up where he'd left off detailing the rules of continental breakfast, internet access, bike rentals and other relevant details.

"Is there someplace where the public-records are kept? A library?" Katie asked.

"Yes, yes, of course. Our library is quite close, very easy to walk. It is closed for the rest of the day but will open again tomorrow at ten o'clock until thirteen-hundred."

"And what's there to do around here at night?"

Frédéric's smile grew from professional to genuine. "Our Christmas market has its last night tonight. Follow the spires of the basilica and you will find it."

Katie thanked the man, and as she pulled her key off the counter, she knocked over one of the shepherds in the sizable Nativity scene placed on the counter. "Oh, bollocks, I'm so sorry," she apologized, being quick to right the piece. Frédéric waved her off but the older woman eyed her carefully before returning to the back office. The Nativity was really attractive, if that was an appropriate word for a religious icon. It was handmade from raw wood, the barn tall like the narrow Belgian houses. Real straw covered the floor, and all the characters were hand painted. The whole thing was about two feet high and she felt sloppy for having hit something so noticeable. "It's quite lovely," she said, to help smooth things over.

She headed up the stairs with her suitcase, and as she rounded the first flight, another person came into the hotel. Katie wouldn't otherwise have been interested except the woman looked familiar. The woman looked up having noticed her standing halfway up the stairs, and in that moment, Katie realized who the woman was: none other than bloody Fae Peeters herself. She looked just like the photos Katie'd seen while doing her background research. What were the chances? The tip that Peeters had a project here just got that much more credible.

Instead of doing the rational thing and calmly going back down the stairs, introducing herself and her purpose, Katie was seized by sudden embarrassment as Peeters kept an uneasy eye on her. She quickly shuffled up and out of sight to her room, rationalizing her unprofessional mad dash the whole way. Peeters was an important person and probably didn't want to be bothered by some random photographer.

In her room, Katie continued to wrestle with herself while unpacking, struggling between feeling like an idiot having lost that imperative first impression and feeling like it was better this way. She hadn't been prepared to introduce herself anyway. It was only a couple hours ago that she'd been finishing up in Reims when an old professor-type stranger with a fedora had begun talking with her as they both waited for a bus. Their small chat revealed a shared admiration for the work of Fae Peeters, and he'd mysteriously asked if she'd known about this village, which of course she didn't. With hidden adventure in his voice and a gleam in his green eyes, he'd suggested it would be well worth it if she came here to find the little-known project of Peeters'. Being only a few hours away, Katie decided there was no harm in investigating the professor's claim. She'd hoped to find the project tonight so that she could be on her way home to Reading, England, first thing tomorrow morning. But with the library closed and having only people from the street to question, that didn't look likely. Unless she somehow ran into Peeters again.

Katie stepped into her tiny bathroom, nicely decorated in tile, and took off her favorite accessory, an imitation rose-gold watch, to wash her hands. With her hands still wet, she ran them through her blonde hair, fixing it, assessing her reflection. It wasn't great, but she was only going to check out the Christmas market anyway and ask some people about the Peeters project. And if she did run into Peeters downstairs again, she'd be ready this time. Adjusting her knitted scarf around her jacket, she grabbed her purse and trotted back downstairs. Peeters was gone, but if she was staying in this hotel too, then Katie was hopeful that she might run into her again.

Once outside, Katie followed the basilica spires, as instructed, through the winding streets. Night had quickly fallen, so the spires acted like a beacon, and with the light flow of foot traffic headed in the same direction, it didn't take long to find herself deposited into an open plaza surrounding the basilica. Compared to the Reims basilica, or any of the other famous churches in Europe, this one reminded her of a little terrier acting like a much bigger dog. Small but mighty, the church was quite wonderful, and she couldn't help but smile. This village was so photographic.

Dickinson-styled singers sung a cappella, greeting people into the market, their songs riding on top of the buzzing crowd. Katie found herself slipping into her inner child as she strolled between the booths. There were only fifteen or so spread out in short rows, but each had something different and unique to offer, so it was hard to simply walk by on the excuse that someone had the same thing two booths down.

She bought a little wood plane with a spinning propeller for her young cousin and was smelling some soaps when she noticed down the way a man who looked exactly like the professor from Reims. Katie was pretty good at remembering faces, and with the fedora, she didn't doubt his identity. If he was from this village, then it made perfect sense that he'd known so much about Peeters, which meant he could also show her the Peeters project and save her time. Katie set off after him.

The professor hadn't seen her, and he moved with purpose through the crowd. She didn't know his name and yelling "hey!" into the open to snag his attention would be too awkward. People were getting in her way, as though everyone in the entire market had flooded to this very place, their armfuls of packages bulging intrusively. She struggled through as fast as she could without being obnoxious, and thankfully, the professor's recognizable hat kept him in sight. She followed him through the market to its end where he headed into one of the streets, which was dark and lonely in contrast to the bright joyfulness of the market. She felt confident of finally being able to catch up with him when behind her she heard an, "excuse me?"

Katie turned around and found an attractive Indigenous woman with long, black hair and a warm complexion looking at her with expectation and holding out a wallet.

"You left this at one of the stalls."

Katie looked down at the wallet, confused, then back to the woman. She spoke English with an American accent, which only added to Katie's disorientation. ". . .What?" Katie quickly checked her purse and found her wallet missing. Her confusion was swiftly replaced with gratitude as she took it back. "Oh my god, thank you! I'm usually not so careless." Putting her wallet back in her purse, she nodded her thanks again and turned back to her pursuit of the professor. He was gone.

"Do you need directions somewhere?" The woman asked. "You look a bit lost and I'd be careful of the streets if you don't know where you're going. They can be hard to navigate, especially at night."

"A real maze, huh?" Katie asked, disappointed.

"Something of the sort," the woman smiled. "I can go with you, if you'd like? It would definitely be safer."

Katie shook her head. "No worries. I was trying to catch up with someone, but I lost him." Katie turned back into the market, the woman going with her.

"If you haven't gone by the wine vendor yet, he's giving free samples," the woman suggested with a wave before disappearing back into the crowd now rapidly unclogging.

Well, Katie thought, it was too bad about the professor, but now she had two people to keep an eye out for. As for right now, there was wine calling her name.

3

When Fae had first returned to the village nearly twenty-one years ago, the experience was stressful, to say the least. The same survival instinct that would keep her out of piranha-infested waters also tried to keep her from going back inside the village. The meeting she was to attend could *only* be held inside the walls, and she wasn't allowed to call in, so she'd stayed the night in a nearby town. Maël had been her chauffeur, and he alone had seen the panic attack that seized her as they drove through the village's gates. There had been an immediate and overwhelming sense of welcome from Nefas that washed over her like tar and feathers, and it'd taken Maël an hour to help her breathe normally again. Then it'd taken the rest of the morning for her to calm down enough to be a functional human being. That trip had been seven years after she'd experienced the Gift, and it had been seven years too soon.

This time, Fae was stronger. And, she was determined to prove that she was wasn't afraid of Nefas. She had wanted to arrive on Christmas Eve, but of course all the flights were full. So, here she was on December 22nd with all the time in the world to wonder what would be left of herself as a person in three days' time. To help with that anxiety, and having correctly assumed that Cuvelier wouldn't have any answers, she'd set a meeting with Maël and Elise to pick their brains, and she'd asked for it to be held in Elise's hotel; *the* hotel that had marked the start of everything. It was there that she'd first met Nefas and where she'd first decided to trust him. The meeting was going to be another big step on the ladder of overcoming the past and reclaiming her life.

Elise had maintained the hotel well, having continued Mrs. Lemmens' renovations since she'd taken over ownership. It looked every bit as pristine as Fae remembered Elise herself being.

As Fae made for the hotel's front desk to meet Elise, she noticed a young lady standing on the stairwell looking back down at her. Caught staring, she quickly turned and disappeared upstairs thumping her suitcase behind her. In any other place, Fae would've thought nothing of it. But here, it was like watching a young version of herself hauling up those stairs, so innocent to what was about to happen. It was chilling déjà vu.

She turned back to the front desk. "Bonjour," Fae greeted a well-manicured young man; he didn't have a chance to respond. At the sound of Fae's voice, Elise popped out from the back room smiling warmly.

"Elise, ciao," Fae came around to politely embrace the other woman. She was still a sharp dresser and had let her hair go gray, which made her look as no-nonsense as she had ever been.

"A sight I thought I'd never see again: you back in my hotel."

"That makes two of us," Fae said.

"Follow me. I have a private room we can talk in." Elise showed the way behind the desk and Fae followed.

Of all the people Fae could've imagined being alone in a room with, Elise would never have been one of them. As a result of her last trip here, she and Elise had been forced to communicate, and it was enough to start the process of them understanding each other more honestly. They would probably never get to the point of exchanging Christmas cards, but at least they didn't hate each other anymore. And now here they were, in Elise's back office, being pleasant.

"Maël should be here soon," Elise began as the two sat down. She motioned toward a plug-in kettle and Fae nodded. "How did your meeting go this afternoon?"

"Cuvelier's best suggestion was that I'm simply not meant to know why I'm here."

Elise gave her a flat look of not being impressed, and Fae couldn't have agreed more.

"Seems to be a reoccurring theme with me, right? I'm worried that something is going to change in Nefas' arrangement."

Elise gave a simple nod of understanding.

"It could be a good change," Fae said, trying to stay positive. "Maybe new terms will restrict his influence even more. I don't know. It's just a feeling, an apprehension."

Elise sat down. "Maël will probably be told this by the time he gets here, so let me get you up to speed. A young British woman was flagged at the West gate, plans on leaving tomorrow. She's here doing photography and asked the guard if he knew who you were. She checked in just before you arrived."

Fae frowned.

"Frédéric was going to give her room 3A so I changed it. I didn't like how that was going."

"No," Fae agreed. "You did the right thing." It was two days before Christmas, and someone was here asking about her? Then was given the same room where Nefas had first met her? Fae didn't believe in coincidence, not when it came to this village.

The kettle came to a rolling boil and clicked off.

"How would she know to associate you with this village?" Elise asked.

"I have no idea." Fae got up to pour the tea. That woman had no reason to be here asking about her, and the fact that she was couldn't be ignored. She was a photographer, so Fae's thoughts instantly went to who might've betrayed the secrecy of her work. The group of potential informants was small, and none would have any reason to give away her involvement.

The walls of the office were starting to feel thin, and the need to escape began itching at Fae's insides. Maël needed to hurry up and get here.

Fae poured the water into their cups and Elise settled in her chair with a reassuring calm. "Let's wait for Maël before we discuss anything further."

Fae nodded and they sipped their tea in silence having nothing more to say on their own.

Maël arrived shortly, a garlic-scented wave ushering him in. He was a thicker man than he used to be, but not fat, and while his hair had receded a bit, it hadn't entirely betrayed him either. He'd grown it a little shaggy giving him a younger look.

Maël quickly put down paper bags, which were the source of the garlic scent. Fae jumped up into his hug, and Maël kissed both her cheeks. "You're looking so good, beautiful!" he said in her ear.

Short of Jordan being here with her, Maël was everything she needed right now. "And so are you, handsome," she said.

"I know," he said with a wink as they separated. "I missed lunch, so I brought an early supper for us," he announced, undoing his jacket. "Kabob and fries!"

"It's so messy," Elise said with a twinge of disapproval, "and you've stunk up my lobby."

"Those Christmas trees are still fresh enough to mask any odors, and"— Maël pulled out a disposable knife and fork with a flick of his wrist and handed them over to Elise, who was still not impressed—"I planned ahead."

Elise rolled her eyes but took the utensils. She doled out the foil wrapped kabobs and opened the container of fries to share while Fae shuffled a few things on Elise's desk to make an appropriate eating surface. Fae was pretty sure the one stipulation Maël had for moving back to the village and taking the job of Monsieur was that a kebob restaurant had to be opened. The man was mildly obsessed.

They small-talked while they ate and Maël complained about having to go into the office, which was where he'd been. He still worked for the government but had been allowed to set up a remote office when he'd moved back. Despite all the advances made with remote office technology, sometimes bosses still wanted people to physically be in the same place. Though, to hear Maël talk, this wasn't one of those times.

Elise was the last to finish eating, and with the sound of her garbage hitting the bottom of the trash, the three of them settled into their meeting.

"Fae," Maël said, all business, "tell me again what Dominic said to you."

"He told me, 'the time has come,' which could mean anything. I've had a thought about that though; there was no terminal date given for the arrangement, correct?" Fae looked at Elise and Maël to confirm and they shrugged. "When I agreed to design the façade to cover la Rue, and the hall to hide everyone when the Gift takes you over, I became intertwined with your village. It's a fact Dominic emphasized when I agreed to get involved. It was me who shut la Rue and separated Nefas from you, and he won't forget or forgive that. Maybe Nefas being confined to his pit isn't forever." Fae nodded at Elise, circling back to their earlier conversation.

Elise looked at Maël. "Have you gone over Marc's report?"

He shook his head. "Not yet, but you're going to tell me I should've."

"It was marked as important," she said, a bit shorter than was necessary. It made Fae wonder if Elise had ever gotten over being disqualified as Monsieur Drechsler's successor, but maybe Fae was judging Elise too harshly. Elise quickly filled Maël in on the young British woman named Katie Windsor.

"How did she know to come here looking for you?" he asked.

Both Fae and Elise shook their heads.

"Nefas has been muzzled to near impotence though, so why would it matter if a girl had your old hotel room?"

"It's the symbolism of what that room was to me," Fae said. "He's muzzled to *near* impotence."

"He knows you're here," Maël said. "And he can still send messages."

Fae nodded. "He knows that we, and that I, would find out about Katie Windsor. He wanted her to have 3A because he loves to mess with me." Forcing herself to talk about all this was not sitting well with the food she'd just eaten. Nefas knew she was here, and somewhere, he was waiting for her, waiting for Christmas Eve when the Gift would come and when he'd have the liberty to come for her. Fae forced herself to exhale slowly through her nose.

"Maybe this Katie Windsor is meant as a distraction," Maël offered, leaning forward.

"For what?" Elise said. "Distract from an unknown bad for an unknown good?"

"Maël," Fae turned to him, "is there still a camera watching la Rue?"

"Yeah. Outside of some normal creepy stuff, it's been pretty quiet."

"Do you mind if I watch the tapes?" It was a terrible idea, honestly, one that did not help relax her rising anxiety, but she couldn't wait around for two days not having any idea what she was going to be thrown into.

Maël raised his eyebrows in question. She knew what he was thinking, back to the panic attacks. "In principle, no . . ."

"If Nefas wants us to know something, he'll leave a note on his door. It's a start. Maybe I can notice something you wouldn't know to look for."

Maël tilted his head, rubbing his eyebrow. He took a deep breath. "OK. But I'll watch them with you."

"Do it during the day," Elise said. "Trust me."

The meeting didn't last much longer. There were no real facts to work with, and the value of fearful, or overly optimistic, guesses was small. With all the talk of the Gift, Fae's thoughts were starting to cloud over, and her ability to remain in this hotel was weakening, so she called it to a close. She said goodbye to Elise and left with Maël, with whom she was staying. She'd wanted to stay outside the village again, but Jordan had insisted that if she was going to come back, then she was going to stay with Maël and his family, a position Maël had seconded. Their argument for being surrounded by people who could help her was practical enough, and she couldn't disagree.

Getting into Maël's car she checked her messages and found one waiting from Jordan.

Haven't heard from you all day. How are you?

She wrote back, *Still alive, so that's good.*

It only took a minute for Jordan to reply. *How about everything else?*

Fae wasn't sure what to say. She'd never been able to truthfully tell him what had happened to her here. How she'd innocently come with the itinerary her grandmother had set to meet extended family and to get a Christmas present. How that "present" was revealed to be the Gift, an annual occurrence where Nefas—sin and death incarnate— competed for both soul and life. She'd only survived because of a baby she'd named Nicholas. The Gift was designed as a brutally honest experience for visitors to learn the realities of the supernatural world around them, and to choose between life with Nefas or life with Nicholas. Nefas could show people their dead soul through a mirror's reflection, and his essence—in the form of a green, parasitic blob—turned all the people born in the village into those same dead souls. It was their "gift" to warn against choosing Nefas.

Fae's problem was the same as this entire village's: no one would believe her story of a supernatural being trying to force her into dark submission. She'd kept the details of her experience vague but summed them up as a cult incident and a rape. In no way did she want to detract from actual victims of such situations, but they were similar enough that her recovery process was what she needed. The deceit passed in her therapy sessions, and Jordan was able to accept that she had an ugly past, allowing them to create a life together without too many questions. When she told him that she was coming back to face her demons, he naturally thought figuratively but was still reluctant to let her come alone. Only when Maël promised that there was no more cult activity had Jordan relented.

Tell me. We agreed.

It's not easy, but I'm a survivor.

It was another minute before his next message came through. *Don't fear. It will kill you.*

Yes. It would. She'd told Jordan Dominic's words knowing that he'd keep them for her when she needed them most, and she was happy to read them now. She let Dominic's life-saving phrase bounce around her head as Maël's car bounced through the uneven streets.

Fae began to realize what she had to do tomorrow. She had to prepare herself for whatever was coming. She had to face the last of her fears now, before the Eve, while it was still safe, which meant that she had to go to la Rue even though its entrance was now camouflaged with her covering façade. She looked over at Maël and predicted what his reaction was going to be when she told him and decided not to do it when he was driving.

As they drove, there was an unmistakable peace in the village. It suggested a normalcy so far removed from her present realities, and she began to wonder how Nicholas was going to play into everything. He was the other half of the

Gift, and nothing could happen with it that didn't involve him.

We're on the way home. I'll call when I can.

What was she going to tell him though? Jordan thought everything was in the past and had no idea of the reckoning that was waiting for her.

She should ask for him to pray some grandmother-inspired prayers. God knew she could use some right now.

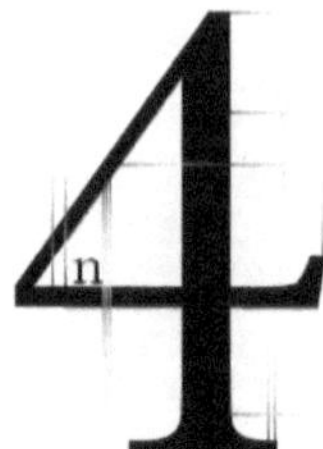

Henri Meyer's forearms were screaming at him in warning. He held himself flat against the wall almost five meters above a moderately padded concrete floor. There were only another two, maybe three, handholds left before reaching the top of the rock wall and then he still had to come back down. His forearms didn't have enough strength left to do both.

It was against the rules to be this high without a harness, but after Henri had learned about free solo climbing, he'd made a deal with the owner of the rec facility, Levi. After Henri signed his life away in waivers, Levi reluctantly allowed him to practice free soloing so long as no one was around to see him do it, usually after hours. Today was extraordinarily slow. Otherwise, he'd be climbing with full equipment, and that harness was looking pretty good right now, five meters below. So was the thick crashmat nearby that he should've slid beneath him but hadn't.

Henri's fingers and toes were cramping. If he made a last push, he could get to the top but then he'd double his risk of falling from even higher. Or, he could admit his weakness, grab hold of that attractive, bulbous blue hold a little to the right, and get down before his muscles quit. He should've been smarter about this.

Henri's right hand started to slip from its hold and his calf was shaking. He needed to get down. At that exact moment of decision, his forearms quit and both hands lost their grip. He tried to jump toward the crashmat.

"Henri!"

Henri heard Levi yell his name as he fell, his mind screaming that this was going to hurt. Everything was a blur as he managed to land mostly on the crashmat, registering a dull pain in his ankle.

"Henri, Henri! Are you okay?" The middle-aged owner of the facility was bending over him, his trained eye scanning for obvious injury.

"I'm good," Henri said carefully, shifting one knee under him then another. His ankle was the only part that had hit the thinner mat. He'd have a bruise, but he could put weight on it. "My arms gave out on me. I—"

"If you can't judge your own strength properly, you're in the harness from now on, or you boulder like everyone else. No higher than the red line. I'm liable for you, waivers or not, and I'm not going to have you break your body in my gym."

"C'mon, Levi-"

"You promised me you wouldn't be stupid. What I just saw was uncontrolled and stupid."

"Better in here than on a mountain."

"Henri."

"Come on, there's no thrill with a harness."

"Thrill? Henri, you're bored. Dissatisfied, anxious, something, but it's not a thrill you're after."

Henri carefully rolled out his ankle as Levi watched.

"When did you move back here?" Levi asked. "Two years ago?"

"Two and a half."

"When did you start harassing me to let you free solo?"

Henri had to think about it for a second. "Ehhh, six months ago?"

"Only one month after you started climbing. You've always had a good head on your shoulders, Henri, even as a kid, which is why I took the risk and let you do this in the first place."

"Nothing's changed with my head or shoulders." Henri said, a smile in his voice. It did little to lighten the mood.

Not amused, Levi nodded at Henri to follow him, their feet sinking into the mat as they left the walls behind. "How's it going with Josie?"

"Fine," Henri said with an easy, honest shrug. "She isn't distracting me, if that's what you mean."

"Maybe she should be if it'd get you thinking again. Climbing that high without the proper mats beneath you? Common sense, Henri. Take a break and figure yourself out. I don't want to see you on my walls until the new year, and then you're gearing up, or never again."

Henri frowned as he dropped himself onto a bench as Levi walked back to his desk. He took his time undoing his climbing shoes, popping them off to the instant satisfaction of freeing his squished toes. The shoe was tight by design, giving the foot optimal contact and grip with the wall. Thanks to Levi's sentencing, the shoes felt like a wistful metaphor for his life in this village. His feet could be sprung free, but he was cramping up inside the walls of this place. He could leave the village whenever he wanted; he hadn't been born here and didn't suffer the Gift. But Josie . . . Josie was tethered.

He was still taking his time closing his chalk bag and wiggling out his toes against the cool, concrete floor when a balled up, orange t-shirt landed at his feet.

"You forgot this at my place."

"Or, was it a calculated excuse to come back over and collect it?" Henri didn't try to hide his smile as he picked up his crumpled shirt and lifted it to his nose taking a deep, exaggerated sniff. "Mmm. Tropical breeze."

"I was aiming for your face." The brown-haired wonder that was Josie laughed. She shook her head and came over.

Henri stood up and walked toward her, meeting her halfway and kissing her lightly in greeting. "Ready to lose?"

"I was going to ask you the same thing. You're tired and weak from climbing. Advantage goes to me. Tonight's the night, I can feel it." She smiled at him, but it wasn't the kind of smile between people who love each other. It was the kind of competitive smile that said, see you on the other side, loser. And Henri fell in love all over again.

"Levi," Josie called out to the proprietor, re-doing her ponytail as she wandered over to his desk, "how was he tonight? Getting better?"

"Sure," Levi said. "He took a rough landing on his right side, so try to exploit that. Then make sure he ices down when you're done."

Henri's eyes grew wide and he tried to catch Levi's gaze to get him from saying anything more, but the older man wasn't watching for Henri's direction. Josie didn't know he did free soloing.

"A fall, huh?" Josie looked back at him not in the least concerned, sizing up his right side, zeroing in on his ankle. She turned back to Levi and again Henri tried to catch his attention, motioning him to not say anything. Levi noticed him this time and shook his head in disappointment.

"Make sure to ask Henri all about it. Did he mention that he's taking a break for the next couple weeks? Doing a little muscle recovery."

Josie looked at him in mild surprise. Henri smiled, forced to go along with whatever Levi said. "Yeah, Levi and I talked about it, changing things up."

"Well, let's start by getting on the court."

"The basketball is already waiting out there for you guys."

Josie came and picked up Henri's hand, and he let himself be pulled out into the rest of the renovated warehouse where, among other things, there was a half-court for basketball. His forearms were stiff, his ankle was tender, and he suspected his win streak was going to be over.

Henri stood in the middle of the court patiently dribbling the ball waiting for Josie to make her move. They were staring each other down, both with dwindling energy but neither willing to give up. He dribbled the ball to keep time as they both caught their breath. She made a move for the ball. He changed hands. She gave him a dirty look, bumped him off the ball, and took off for the layup. The ball hit the rim, circled it, then rolled out to the sound of her groaning, but she was quick to grab the rebound. She did a quick turn to pop it back in, but Henri got in her way and blocked the shot. She got to it first again, and with another shot, the ball rolled in over the rim and fell back to the floor with a victorious bounce.

"That's two points you can't have, you criminal," Josie said, walking past him for the reset of possession. She glistened with the effort of their matchup, which was a superficial distraction from what really mattered: the three-pointer he needed to tie.

"Criminal? I haven't even been convicted, much less charged," Henri said as he dribbled back up the court.

"Well, the media has you pegged," she said. "Your life is ruined, your boss doesn't trust you, and your landlord doesn't want the negative attention." They checked the ball to each other putting it back into play. "You're best off starting a new life in Iceland where they don't know your name."

"You're coming with me into exile though, right?" Henri asked as he tried to dance around her. She stayed with him the whole way. She might not be able to shoot well but she was fast. "I could secretly be really rich."

"How do you feel about Australia?"

Henri took the three-point shot and it fell short, hitting the net below. She grabbed the ball, took her own shot, missed, and he snagged the ball. This time it went in. Two points.

"Will you let me wear one of those outback hats?"

"Mmmm . . ." she considered with a sly smile, "consider it a negotiation point."

"Hey, you two!" From courtside Levi waved to get their attention. "Get off my floor."

"What time is it?"

"You two are the last ones in here, that's what time it is."

"It's eight," Josie said, coming off the court and tossing her towel into the laundry bin.

"What's the score?" Levi asked.

"Forty for me, forty-one for Josie," Henri said, stuffing his shoes into a bag. A small, magnetic white board hung crookedly from a metal stud and Levi adjusted the two numbers written there.

"She's catching you, Henri. Better step up your game."

"My parents asked you over for supper," Josie told Henri as they headed outside, zipping up their jackets as they went. He grabbed her mittened hand in his and they walked side by side in the cool winter night. He'd left his car at his workplace, so they walked in that direction. There wasn't much in this section of the village. Much of it had been abandoned for a long time, and it was only within their lifetime that it had started to be revived. An air of abandonment still lingered. "You can shower at our place."

"Are you sure you don't want to shower and eat at my place? If we ever get to the supper part," Henri said mischievously. That earned him a punch to the arm. "But I say that so innocently."

"You can't lie. Stop trying," Josie said, laughing.

She knew he was joking, of course. He liked his supper too much to miss it.

Josie began talking about something she'd read earlier that day of interest and Henri let her talk not really paying attention to what she was saying but loving the sound of her voice.

According to his older sister there'd been a collective cry from all the mothers of the village when he and Josie had gotten together. He didn't believe his sister, and he didn't believe his niece either who said her friends also cried; they were now all thirteen. The apparent hope that the mothers had for their daughters was short sighted, however, as he'd made no secret that he'd wanted to leave and not come back. The first day he could, he moved away for university and then he happily stayed away as he got a job and a built a life for himself. He hadn't looked back until the tech company he was working for folded and the cool job market forced him to move back in with his parents. It was then that he got to know Josie beyond her being just a girl he knew from school.

"Hey," Josie pointed ahead to where one of the sparsely placed streetlamps lit up the side of a building. "The newest theory is that that's where the entrance to la Rue used to be; Julia told me."

"Where the light is highlighting the wall?"

"Mmhmm."

"Nope, it was further up, up there by the mechanic's. Victor told me."

"Who told Victor?"

"Who told Julia?"

"Well, maybe it should be right here," Josie said, pointing immediately to their left.

There was nothing where Josie pointed to suggest anything special, simply the plain brick of a building. It was at a T-junction and was as good a place as any to pin where la Rue had been—if there really had been such a street.

Josie continued, "We'll say we know for sure it's the entrance because we saw the Jandreau ghost come through the wall. He was actually quite a nice guy, even introduced himself. The tragic, misunderstood ghost."

Henri laughed. "A misunderstood ghost who introduced himself on his way to drag someone down into Hell with him?" As soon as he said it Henri knew he'd forgotten himself in Josie's laughter and the joke fell flat. He let it. Some things were never funny, and two days before the Eve, dragging people into Hell was not funny.

They walked on. Henri took his turn talking of his uneventful day to help change the subject when the loud sound of an impact behind them made them jump and turn around. He expected to see something had fallen from a roof, but instead it was a man who'd come silently up behind them. Josie startled, letting a little laugh of embarrassment escape.

"Nothing like the talk of ghosts to make people jumpy," the man offered. He looked unkept with a worn-out hood pulled over a dirty baseball hat, his eyes hidden beneath. His hands were stuffed in his pockets making him look colder than he should've been. The only thing that gave him any sort of identity was a short ponytail that hung down beside his neck.

A few loose stones fell to the ground behind him as though disturbed, and instinctively everyone looked backward to find the culprit. There was nothing but shadows.

"Hope I didn't scare you," the man said as a few more pebbles came down. "Don't mind me."

Henri and Josie walked on, the man hanging back a few feet to give them their space. It would've made more sense if he passed them, but, whatever.

In the quiet Josie began singing softly. She'd be the first to admit that she wasn't very good, but she liked to do it and Henri was no judge either way. She'd recently added a couple new English songs to her Christmas playlist, and she kept getting the words and tunes mixed-up. It was cute. Resting merry gentlemen and wondering while wandering—they were poetic songs that fit her vocal range as much as they did the night.

They continued past the same naked trees that had always been there, and the same uneven stones in the same spots; the same businesses and homes with the same flower baskets hanging outside their windows. At Christmastime, the boring gained colorful costumes of lights and glitter. For Henri it was a cover-up. For Josie it was comforting familiarity, and he wished he could see it with her eyes. In it she found the peace she needed to get through the season. He could only see yet another year where he was still living inside these walls not growing his career or his life.

"Josie," Henri began, his fingers toying with the fuzz inside his mittens. "This year you should spend the Eve at my place." He'd been holding back the suggestion for months.

Josie stopped singing and he felt her deflate beside him. "Henri, not tonight."

"Last year we had a plan. This year, we can make it happen. My place is just outside the walls. It's the best option—find out if it's possible for someone with the Gift to be on the other side."

"No. And no one is going to try because it shouldn't be done. We have to be on this side of the wall to protect the world out there." Wanting that to be final, she began singing again.

"If no one tries then we'll never know," Henri pushed back. This was a theoretical discussion they'd had before, but this close to the Eve, it was anything but. Was the person freed from the Gift once outside the wall's confines? Did nothing happen? Knowing could change everything.

Henri slowed to a stop and he slid his hands down Josie's jacketed arms to hold her hands in his. They'd stopped near a streetlamp, and the mellow light beaming down transformed her brown hair into deep amber. She was beautiful. "People have been outside the walls before for the Eve and we haven't heard of anything bad happening," he said. "Maria Peeters and her husband left years ago, Iakob left—"

"No news doesn't mean good news. Do you really want to lock me in your bathroom all night? What if I released something I could never forgive myself for? Maria, her husband, and Iakob—they all had special places in relation to the Gift. How do we know—"

"We don't," Henri said quickly, trying to hide his disappointment. Despite all their daydreaming conversations over the last year, her opinion about actually going through with their Eve plan clearly hadn't changed. He couldn't blame her. "You deserve to be free of this mess of a Christmas. We *all* deserve to be free of it." He stopped himself before he started ranting, resetting. "What if I can find one of the choir singers when they arrive and ask if it's safe to try?"

He held his breath. She was thinking it through; he could see her thoughts running. If only she could imagine her life unrestricted by the Gift, like how he saw it, then maybe she'd see beyond these village walls to another life where this place could be forgotten.

With a heavy sigh she squeezed his hand and walked away toward his car, now within sight.

"No one from the choir is going to tell you that," she told him. "And the Gift isn't something you experiment with and only risk one or two people; *everyone* could get hurt. If *he* gets released from these walls? We were born into this curse, we have to stay here; it's easier to accept that than fight it." Josie paused but kept walking. "It's fun to dream about life without the Gift. It helps to escape reality. But I can't leave on the Eve. It's not worth the risk."

"All I'm asking is to find out if the risk isn't as big as we've been made to believe. I mean, what happened before there was a wall? There's reason to ask questions. If you don't want to get involved, I won't guilt you into it. I just don't want you to suffer without cause."

"I know. You're sweet like that." Josie flashed him a wistful, sad smile. "It's not me I'm worried about."

Henri nodded and let the conversation die. The psychological, even physical, strain that the Gift put her and the rest of the village under was something he could never fully comprehend. To have Nefas' essence transform them from human to corpse, to lose all control to Nefas' whims . . . to have the tortures of Hell forced into their minds . . . They could never be normal. It wasn't fair that they had to be prisoners in their own homes because of a couple hours every year, and it wasn't fair that he couldn't do anything about it.

They reached the car, and before he climbed inside, she told him, "Come here." He met her at the hood, and she wrapped him in a deep hug, letting her head rest on his shoulder. Henri hugged her back.

"Hey, this isn't my final answer forever," she said. "I want to see what a normal Christmas looks like too. I want to travel the world, see all the Seven Wonders, miss our flight and run after our train, do all that crazy stuff normal people do without caring if it's July 24th or December 24th. And I want to do it with you. You just have to let go of this for a little while, OK? Maybe something will change. Things have changed before."

Henri hugged her tighter, kissed her cheek. It wasn't OK, but this close to the Eve, he agreed. He had another year to help her find her courage, meaning one more year to wait to find out the truth. Or, to find someone else.

Over Josie's shoulder, Henri watched as an outline of man passed them by, his hooded profile suggesting the stranger who'd run into them earlier. The man ignored them and walked listlessly with no arm swinging or bounce of stride as though trying not to disturb even the air around him. Henri felt sorry for him. Maybe he was already depressed about the coming Gift.

Josie squeezed him, then let him go, and Henri's thoughts left the stranger. It was time to take her home.

Fae was in the middle of a frivolous dream racing ponies through a mall against Jackie Chan when she heard Dominic talking to her. His non-descript English accent was as memorable as picking strawberries in a warm summer rain, and the sound of it called her out of one dreamy adventure and into another. He was saying something about the weather, about a coming snow. The more he talked the more he came into focus, and she realized that they were sitting on the wharf of a lake with night coming on fast. Even then, she didn't really see him so much as her memory filled in his details. He was calm and relaxed, and he'd traded in his white winter jacket for a green polo, which complemented his premature white hair. It was striking against the twilight. Seeing him again sitting beside her, both their legs dangling over the rippling, black water of the lake, was as pleasant as it was concerning. Dominic didn't stop by for friendly visits.

"Fae? Fae, are you listening?"

When he called her name, everything came into clarity and she knew that this wasn't just a silly dream. He was there, inhabiting her dream, and everything he was saying was making sense. He'd been talking of a storm, but it wasn't snow, and the falling night was about five hours too early.

"I'm listening," she said.

"How have you been, Fae?"

She stared off across the lake to the outline of a darkening forest against the pink and purple sky. "I survive. That's what I do."

"The time has come. You have to return."

She didn't have to ask where. She was already back in the village; why was this dream repeating?

"I won't go back there," she said, letting the dream play out. "I can't. It'll be Christmas, how could you ask me to go back?"

"You always have the choice, Fae."

"Do I, though?" She glared at him. "Why would I do such a . . ." She tried to find a diplomatic way of saying what she wanted to express but struggled to find a word to adequately described her feelings. So, she swore before saying, "stupid thing like that?" She apologized but it wasn't because she was sorry.

Crickets chirped on the shoreline. "You are only one character in a larger story," Dominic said. "If one person doesn't do their part, then the whole story suffers. You need to go back."

"Then tell me why."

"The time has come."

"What does that mean?"

"Nicholas, your victory, goes with you always."

"You'll meet me there, right? Dominic!"

He smoothly stood up and walked back up the dock, his image fading as he went.

She hadn't even agreed to go. "Give me an answer! Dominic! Tell me!" And then he was gone.

When Fae awoke, she didn't swear at Dominic like she had the first time she'd had the dream, or the second. This time she was annoyed. Why had he spoken as if she wasn't already here, like he was still trying to convince her to come? Maybe because he knew she had no interest in "doing her part" unless it included sitting safely inside the Notre-Dame du Seigneur all Christmas Eve.

Last night she'd told Maël about going to la Rue. He was no happier with that than when she'd asked to watch the surveillance tapes, but he'd recognized the value of it. He'd refused to let her go alone, which was fine; she was going to ask him to come anyway. Maël wasn't just emotional support, he was also the Monsieur, which gave him a position with Nefas. So, with a cold dread, and with Dominic's voice echoing in her mind, Fae got up, worked through a banana, got into the car with Maël, and together they drove to la Rue. He tried to encourage her by telling her she was being strong like a general presenting for battle. She appreciated his effort, but the analogy was unrealistic. She was going to la Rue with no fight in her, just a desperate need to face her fears and then retreat as in-control as she could.

In the terrible span of time between when they left Maël's house and when they arrived at their destination, Fae forced herself to focus on the structure of the village, processing her observations in audible mumbles. She still really liked the fine examples of Mosan-style architecture on display, which she'd enjoyed during her first visit here. Back then the village had been a place untouched by time, but she was happy to see that it had allowed itself to grow. Even the dead area around la Rue was being reclaimed with family businesses, and a recreation center no less! But it was also like building beneath a dormant volcano: the danger was in forgetting that there was still a danger.

"I'm not seeing many Communion settings at the doors or windows," she observed.

"A lot of people have stopped putting them out because they're not necessary anymore," Maël explained as he came to an empty four-way stop at which he barely slowed. "They didn't want the constant reminder, and I decided not to make an issue of it. Businesses are still big into making displays with it though. Pierre's Chocolaterie had a good one a while ago. They put a small chocolate fountain on top of a larger wine fountain so that it looked like the chocolate was being turned into wine. The bread was put on fondue forks. The year after that they began the Communion contest."

"A contest?" Fae couldn't hide her distaste. "Really?"

Maël pursed his lips and made a grunting noise. "The village council voted to make it a thing partly to keep the tradition alive without having to say why it existed in the first place, and as a community bonding activity. I gave my opinion, but since the Gift was hidden in the hall, the Communion wasn't necessary anymore, and I didn't have the final say." Maël shrugged. "Between you and me, Fae, honestly, I don't have the kind of authority that Drechsler had."

Fae shook her head. To create a silly decorating contest out of something that had been so life- and property-saving was cheapening. The fact that Maël had clearly been outvoted on the issue made Fae wonder who was on the council because Elise wouldn't have been happy about it either.

It was just another example of people who should've understood better, and it made her thoughts wander. It'd taken a couple years after leaving this village before she'd resigned herself to seek help from the Church. It'd felt like a betrayal of her well-earned principles, but therapy couldn't take the fear away, and she'd never forgotten the purity of peace that this village's basilica had brought, a peace she'd desperately needed. Whether in Belgium, Germany, or back home, she'd found a sense of security in church buildings, but the people always found well-intentioned ways to make her feel isolated. She found some true friends there, yes, and she stayed for them, but she never apologized for providing an accurate metaphor for what sin and death were really like, no matter how many times she was passive-aggressively invited to a Bible study for beginners. Even so, they always thought her description of the baby was beautiful like a poem, but then would easily move onto the next beautiful poem, or song, or testimony after a few "amens". Nicholas deserved better.

Maël soon found a parking spot on the side of a street a block away from la Rue, thus marking their arrival. Fae could see it directly ahead, a plain, blank wall of painted brick, a seamless patch between two buildings. To an unknowing eye the façade did not exist. This was her first time seeing it finished.

She felt Maël looking at her. Then she heard him asking if she wanted to go through with this. She nodded. He came around the car and opened her door, then guided her down the street.

La Rue was the heart of the Gift and the place where Nefas had nearly taken both life and soul from her. She could see him now, waiting in his pit, behind the iron door that was behind the black door, all hidden behind her façade. He was smiling to himself, waiting for her . . .

"Fae?" Maël asked, concerned. "You don't have to do this."

She shook her head. "He's not going to haunt me to my dying breath, Maël." Fae took a deep breath and kept walking down the street like, she supposed, a general going to battle. "Even in the unending shadows of death's darkness, I am not overcome by fear." She recited a poetic version of the famous Psalm. "Because You are with me in those dark moments, near with Your protection and guidance, I am comforted." Yet, Fae was only marginally comforted.

Arriving at the façade, Fae stood as boldly as she could in front of what looked like nothing. It was a calm morning with some foot traffic giving life to the street, but Fae's isolated world was reeling. She rubbed her sweating hands together, taking long breaths through her nose and slowly exhaling through the mouth, forcing herself not to blink as she stared the façade down.

There was no sign of Nefas. She couldn't even feel him. With nothing to see and nothing to feel, Fae started to feel a twinge of hope.

With a nervous little smile, she looked at Maël. First yesterday going inside the hotel, and now this, all with no panic attacks. She was so close to the façade she could reach out and touch it.

Fae's phone buzzed to life in her pocket, but she ignored it. It was probably Jordan checking in. It went silent after a couple of rings, but then she quickly received a follow-up message buzzing her phone, then a second message, and a third, and then Maël's phone came to life too.

"Elise?" Maël asked as the two of them checked their messages.

"Maybe she learned someth—" Fae didn't finish her sentence. The messages were all from the same unknown number, and she only had to open the first one to know that she didn't want to read the rest. "Maël . . ."

He must've received a similar message as hers.

"Get to the other side of the street, now." Maël grabbed her arm as they raced across the street.

Once there, Fae didn't stop.

The texts were from Nefas. They had to have been. He'd been patient knowing that she'd come to him, one way or the other. She'd been so confident that she could go to his doorstep and nothing would happen other than a stare-down of her fears.

Her heart was pounding, and she looked back over her shoulder at the façade, half expecting to see green fog pouring through and ushering Nefas out. Whatever Dominic wanted from her, it wasn't worth it. She was leaving and going back home.

"Who's your message from?" Fae demanded, Maël keeping her pace.

"It's an unknown number. I shouldn't have let you come. You need to stay away from this place."

"What did it say?" she asked with another shoulder check. They were almost at the car.

"It says, 'Our secret is getting out. There is so much to share.'" Maël offered the message for her to see but she waved it off. He continued. "My village—"

"He doesn't have the authority anymore," Fae said, no longer as sure of that as she was five minutes ago. "I'm so sorry, if I hadn't come—"

"No." Maël reached out and calmly grabbed her arm, slowing her. He pulled her around a corner, out of view the façade. "Nothing that has or will happen is your fault. Do you understand that?"

"This has to do with the arrangement. Read them." Fae shoved her phone into Maël's hands, and she took off again towards the car, this time, not looking back.

Maël carefully read the messages out loud as he followed. "I knew you would come back. You've always been my favorite."

She set her jaw and kept walking. "Read the next one." She hadn't read any of the other messages yet.

"The gifts I gave you have kept on giving. This year, I give you the world." Maël looked at her.

"The next one."

"I know what you've done against me, Fae Norris-Peeters, but I still love you, like worms love a body in the ground."

Like worms love a body in the ground. Those had been his parting words to her when she'd first left this horrid place. And now he welcomed her back with them. She sealed her decision. "Delete them," she told Maël. "I'm leaving on the first train out. You don't have to drive me to the airport. I'm gone."

She saw from the corner of her eye Maël flicking his finger around erasing the messages, and as he handed the phone back, his own rang. It rang two, then three times before Maël dared to look at the call information. Fae realized she'd stopped walking.

"It's okay," he said quickly. He showed her the ID but she didn't know who it was. He took the call, said a few acknowledgements, then hung up. "Our British friend from yesterday went to the library this morning. She's found out a whole lot more than she should've been able to."

"What did she find?"

"She somehow gained access to the r28 recording; that's our meeting about the arrangement. She watched it from the library, but that shouldn't have been possible. Those files were encrypted, never put on an internet linked computer . . ." Maël's voice faded out. "Your secret is getting out," he mumbled. For the first time ever, Fae heard Maël swear. "I'm going to get someone to the library to pick Katie up. We'll meet them at the village hall." As they got to the car, Maël leaned on the roof looking across at her. "Fae," he pleaded, "please don't go home yet."

Fae stared at him but didn't reply. In fairness, he didn't really want to be the Monsieur, but he couldn't ask this of her, not after those texts.

They climbed into the car, the tenseness between them following.

Maël shot a text off to his contact and Fae sighed. There wasn't going to be another train for another couple hours anyway. "Let's go meet Katie, your latest candidate for the Gift." How Maël interpreted that statement she had no idea, and quite frankly, she didn't care.

Katie was the first one to the library that morning. She'd managed to sleep in, take a lazy breakfast, look for her misplaced watch— again, which she decided to report as missing to the front desk, and she'd still arrived before the library opened.

An older gentleman came and unlocked the doors. "Bonjour," he welcomed her, holding open a second set of doors. "Puis-je vous aider à trouver quoi que ce soit?"

It took a second for Katie to figure out that he was asking if she needed any help. "Ah . . . no, merci."

The library was about as big as she could've expected. Four short aisles of double-sided shelves, an open corner in the back for the kids, and a modest Christmas tree with a Nativity scene underneath. One computer station sat underneath the windows, which was where Katie went directly, not surprised to see an out of date machine waiting for her. A USB stick poked out of one of its ports. She woke the computer up and a pop-up notification greeted her saying that the upload was complete. She closed it out and made a mental note to hand the forgotten USB to the librarian when she left. Making sure the automatic translation program was running, Katie opened the intranet and started her search for blueprints and newspapers, anything that could have Peeters' name on it. A couple of minutes of searching yielded nothing of use. The town records held no mention of a Fae Peeters, and the last name Peeters only showed up in pre-WWII records. She simply found nothing to supplement what she already knew.

She'd previously read a short biography of Peeters that had given an overview of her and her design philosophies and inspirations. It was something Katie liked to do with her subjects, human or not: read their history. It helped her understand how to get the best shots. Peeters often talked about classical beauty and providing spaces of empowerment and freedom by controlling natural light. Whether inside or outside a Fae Peeters design, you felt something. After photographing four of her designs already, Katie hadn't quite figured out what that "something" was, but empowerment and freedom was a good start.

As for Peeters herself, she was born and raised in Vancouver, Canada, and earned her master's from the University of British Columbia in their Brussels campus which had been formed jointly with Belgium's KU Leuven's Faculty of Architecture. There she was able to work under Bruno Gesell to complete her degree by being part of the team that redesigned the side of Ghent's city hall that had taken the worst of a terrorist attack. When she graduated, Gesell had introduced her to the owner of a blooming new architecture firm in Berlin that specialized in repurposing, sustaining, and preserving historical buildings. While there, Peeters was part of a small team that split into a new department dealing with new builds rather than repurposing, focusing on the historical designs the firm had become famous for restoring.

Peeters became the only North American and the only woman asked to join the elite team of three others who led the design of the European Union's massive and impressive Art and History Centre in Zürich. It was hailed as the modern Library of Alexandria for research and preservation, and the eyes of the Western, if not the whole, world had been on it. Her work on the Centre cemented her winning the Pritzker Architecture Prize, the so-called Nobel Prize for architects, becoming only the sixth woman to ever do so. Peeters had gotten into trouble for being caught off the record saying to an unknown person that she was glad the facility hadn't been built in Rome, but a genuine apology and some make-good initiatives made the incident disappear. The Centre had been, and continued to be, a huge success not only from a place of academia, but also for tourism as the building looked like the glory of the Ancient world reborn with modern flair. Peeters eventually moved back to her home in Vancouver and there she partnered with an Egyptian architect to start her own firm where she remained to this day.

All in all, Katie had to admire Peeters, not only because she had been so successful, but because from everything she'd read, Peeters seemed like a genuinely decent person. In an industry where edgy and unique got the attention, Peeters stood out by tapping into the timelessness of the past.

Katie closed out the intranet and was about to head out when a lone file on the desktop caught her eye. It was simply titled "r28 Arrangement," and curiosity made Katie open it. She figured it was the file that had been uploaded from the USB. What kind of files did people in a place like this leave on a library computer? Probably details of some woman's floral arrangement hobby.

The file contained a single video with the same naming convention, "r28_Arrangement," and the date from nearly twenty-one years ago, which really pushed Katie into watching it; twenty-year-old fashion waited. Katie did a quick look for the librarian, found him sitting at the desk organizing some papers, and double-clicked the video. The translation program asked if she wanted the audio subtitled, which she did. Audio began piping over the speakers and Katie quickly paused it to dig out her vintage earbuds from her bag, plugging them into the computer.

The camera was aimed at a round, multi-purpose table in the middle of small room. Six people were settling in around it: two young women, a young man, a middle-aged priest, a suited older man, then one other Katie could only see by the top of his white hair. If he shifted or moved at all, he'd be off screen completely.

With everyone now seated, one of the women began speaking in French and Katie read the subtitles.

"For the record, I want to be clear that the position of Monsieur has not been filled from Iakob Courtellemont's departure and this meeting is without that representation. For the purposes of this meeting, Maël and myself have been selected to jointly stand in. Bourgmestre Verhulst and the priest, Cuvelier, are both participating as village representatives as well. Fae, Dominic, let's begin."

Katie's interest suddenly perked and she leaned in closer to study the other woman. Though the angle was bad, she recognized her as a much younger Fae Peeters. Katie smiled at her luck and was now completely invested.

The young man identified as Maël spoke next. "To start we're going to give a quick background so that we're all on the same page. Four years ago, four friends from Germany visited us in March asking questions they only could've asked if they'd known something about the Gift. Monsieur Drechsler and Iakob discovered that the friends had gotten hold of satellite images from some back-water internet site from a previous Christmas Eve. Their questions were satisfied easily enough, but they showed us that what we fear the most, the Gift being found out, was on the verge of coming true. Since then, we've had a local man monitoring the internet as best he can. One of his earliest discoveries was from an astronaut on the ISS who'd posted photos 'tracking' Père Noël. If you zoom in on the high-res photos, you can see a little, bright green spot that was us. It would only mean something if you knew what you were looking at, but the point is, we can't control people looking in, and nothing can be truly deleted from the internet."

The first woman spoke again. "Last year we were able to stop a drone flying by, but we have no ability to control satellites and the growing popularity of Google, or other information magnets from taking aerials and making them public. Conspiracy theorists, alien lovers, ghost hunters, they're never taken seriously, but if they come looking for something, they will find it."

Maël picked up the presentation again. "Governments are getting quicker at jumping on anything that could be considered a threat or an unknown. If their intelligence wants to take a little spot of unexpected green light on the map even half-seriously, they will come to investigate."

The woman again. "Our wall isn't enough to keep the Gift hidden anymore. Even if we lock ourselves in our homes and black out the windows, it's all for nothing when the Gift takes us over and Nefas does what he wants with us." The woman paused. "I predict that in five years the village will be out of our control. This is why we're all here: Dominic has come to give us a solution."

Fae now turned to the white-haired man beside her who wasn't fully on camera. She spoke in English as an aside. "I didn't think this kind of thing was in your job description."

"I do as I'm asked," Dominic said simply. He had a bit of an accent and Katie thought it sounded a bit like he came from Lancashire. "I'm here for them as much as I am for you. You all need someone you can trust." Dominic switched to French as he addressed the group as a whole, and Katie looked back to the subtitles. "If the Gift is seen without context, it will serve the purposes of Nefas rather than being a demonstration of warning about him. The Gift must continue to be a warning as was promised to Nefas' first victims very long ago."

The old bourgmestre was not happy with that. "You're telling us the status quo is our solution?"

"Georges," the priest calmly said, "he isn't finished."

The bourgmestre settled back in his chair, but he wasn't done. "God knows what we have to go through every year, doesn't he? And for what? To hide ourselves behind a wall so we won't be seen? There's no warning about Nefas in the Gift anymore. It's hideous torture. Take it away."

While the other members of the table had stayed quiet, Katie could see that none of them were thrilled about this development either. Whatever this "Gift" or this "Nefas" was neither sounded like a good thing. Maybe they were code words. Katie began to question if she should be watching this video at all. She looked over at the librarian again and saw he was still engaged with his organizing, paying her no attention.

Dominic calmly continued as though the bourgmestre's frustration hadn't fazed him at all. "The choir will return every year to sing through the darkness and to welcome the true Gift on Christmas morning. Nefas, however, will be severely restricted, which will allow you to protect yourself and this village from the outside world. On Christmas Eve he'll no longer be allowed outside his pit, and he will have no ability to show people the condition of their soul through mirrors. You, though, will still be taken by the Gift to stand as that warning to anyone who does find their way here to visit."

There was a pause around the table. It was Fae who broke the silence first, speaking French this time.

"Has Nefas been told?"

"Yes, he has," Dominic replied.

"And how did he take it?" She asked with a little snap.

This time it was Dominic who took his time responding. "Have you heard about the string of unexplainable church fires across Spain and Portugal?"

"Spain and Portugal aren't even close to here."

"His feelings on the matter were very clear, trust me," Dominic said, but he gave no more away.

"Thirty-seven people were killed in those fires," Maël said in sad amazement. "More injured."

"Nefas has been given his new boundaries and he will stick to them," Dominic said. "What you do beyond this is up to you."

The first woman pinched her lips and set her face as she brought the conversation back. "Getting rid of the Gift entirely was obviously what we wanted. Hoping for one thing, we expected another, and planned accordingly." Pulling out a binder from beneath the table, she didn't have a chance to say more.

"I'm happy for all of you," Fae said. "I think this is a good time for me to take my leave and let you happy people get to the planning for your happy, potential-filled future." She pushed back her chair and was about to get up to leave.

"Fae, this is why you're here," Maël said, stopping her. "The fact that Dominic had you come to provide consultation clued us in that the Gift probably wasn't going to go away." Fae halted her departure and she and Maël exchanged a long, silent negotiation across the table. "This is the part where we say how much we're going to need you."

Fae's resignation was unmistakable. She slid back into her chair.

The unnamed woman opened the dialogue again. "Based on the possible outcomes, we'd developed a couple ideas on how to go forward. This one was our best all-around option." She tapped the binder in front of her. "Fae, you're the only one who is both qualified and trustworthy enough for the job."

"I'm not interested in pre-amble, Elise. What do you want from me?"

"Fine." The woman now identified as Elise opened the binder and flipped a couple pages in. "We need you to design an underground containment facility large enough to hide and hold everyone with the Gift. And, we want you to make the entrance to la Rue go away."

"I design museums, Elise. Libraries, banks, civic buildings. You should look for someone who knows something about fallout shelters."

"We aren't asking for a favor. You're worth a very reasonable compensation." Elise folded her hands on the table. It was hard to tell Fae's response, but Katie thought Elise looked insulted.

"Thanks," Fae said, "but the whole European Central Bank doesn't have enough money to bribe me to willingly put myself in Nefas' way." Fae's voice was getting louder and it wavered with breaking emotion. "While you have your Gift one *night* a year and move on, I've had him haunting me for the last seven *years*, stalking me, threatening—" she paused. "And now you're asking me to build you a Batcave, to put *myself* between you and *him* by hiding away your corpse bodies, which he still thinks will be parading around outside? He just killed thirty-seven innocent people because he can't come out and play anymore. What else do you think he'll—absolutely not." Fae sharply stood up, looking at everyone in the room. "Congratulations on securing a cage for your hell dog." And then Fae left the room leaving behind an awkward silence.

"I should . . ." Maël offered as he pushed his chair back uncertainly. "Or, Dominic, maybe she'll be less likely to murder you?"

The priest cleared his throat. "Angry enough to pop a baby's balloon and steal its lollipop."

"Does she know about the Jandreaus?" Elise asked.

Maël shook his head. "No, and that's not going to make her feel any better about what we're asking her to do either."

Maël and Dominic both left the room and the camera kept running. Katie skipped ahead past the resulting dead air. When they finally returned, the time stamp showed that almost an hour had elapsed. Fae came in closely behind the two men and sat back down.

"I'll design the underground shelter for you," Fae stated, "and I'll hide la Rue so that it looks like it was never there. I'm going to need an engineer to work with, and I hope you understand how much the construction is going to cost. Going underground isn't cheap and it makes for a big construction site. You'll have to come up with a convincing cover story."

The bourgmestre spoke up, now also calmer. "Our ancestors sacrificed to build a beautiful basilica to celebrate a beautiful truth, and then they sacrificed to build a wall to protect the people. Now, it's our turn to sacrifice and build an underground hall to protect both the beautiful truth and the people. We can negotiate your compensation as soon as you're ready to draw up a quote."

Fae sat unspeaking for a few drawn out moments, flipping a pen up and down on the table. She stared at everyone in turn before taking a deep, stabilizing breath. "Keep the money. You'll need it for the construction costs. There's only one location for this hall that will do what you need it to."

Someone tapped Katie on the shoulder and she startled, scrambling to close the video before they had the chance to see what she was watching. It made her look even guiltier, she knew, but only if they had a reason to suspect. The person who tapped her came around her shoulder, a university aged girl with a pompom winter hat, the smell of cold air still clinging to her, fresh from the outside.

"Excuse me, are you Katie Windsor?"

"I…" Katie did a double take back to the screen. Nothing but the open file on the desktop. "I am," she said. It was always concerning when someone you didn't know came looking for you by name. Katie's thoughts were still with the video as the girl introduced herself saying something about Fae Peeters and being able to help. Katie caught sight of the librarian looking at her, a cell phone now in hand.

"Come with me, and I'll show you. No one really comes here interested in the name Peeters, but I'm sure if Maria was still alive, she'd be happy to know."

The girl had a friendly, helpful air about her, and Katie didn't have any other leads, so despite not knowing exactly what she agreed to, she logged off the computer and packed her things. Passing off the USB stick to the librarian on her way out, she followed the girl outside.

She'd understood little of what had happened in that video, bad people and bad things. What she did take away was confirmation that somewhere in this village there really were two more Peeters' designs that had otherwise been unknown: a façade and an underground hall. The opportunity for a bonus cheque suddenly rose from a simple chance to a very real possibility. She'd worked with her current employer on contract before and they were generous in bonusing extra work, though, not in a happy, "keep up the good work" kind of way. More in the way of encouraging aggressive competition. She almost didn't take this contract because of not wanting to feel like she was competing against their other contractors, but the job market was still slow and she had bills.

Depending on how Peeters designed it, a bunker-styled hall could be brilliant. Katie started imagining a grand cavern playing in the shadows of its own forest of embellished pillars; a completely unrealistic imagination, but a fun one. The pictures she could get in a place like that! She could only hope that whatever this girl promised was going to be helpful.

Katie's new friend walked her to the village hall, which, she cheerily explained, was really more of a multi-function, multi-administration building. To give it some distinction, it had a handsome row of huge, glass-sheathed porch lights running its length between its two stories. Her friend greeted the woman at the front desk saying that they were there to meet with the Monsieur about the Peeters project. The lady gave some simple directions and Katie's concern that she might be in trouble lessened. Taken to an empty room, her friend told her to wait there. Then she left, closing the door behind her.

Katie sat down in the loveseat rather than the armchairs at the head of the room. All were made from the same mass-produced gray woven fabric. In front of her was a large, mirrored window and Katie was impressed this village had one, assuming it to be the result of boys wanting their toys.

A couple of minutes passed. Maybe she was in trouble after all? It was no use worrying about her situation, so she made good use of the mirror by realigning the part in her hair and flattening some of the stray strands that had been freed by winter static. Then she let her eyes wander the room looking for anything remotely interesting without success. She was about to pull out her phone when the door opened with a distinct *click*, and a man just on the other side of middle-age strode in.

"Bonjour, Katie." He gave a welcoming smile and extended his hand to her. Rising to her feet, she returned his firm shake.

"Bonjour." They sat down, she on the couch, he in one of the chairs. He had a kind face with his graying hair falling over the top his ears. He wore well-fitting jeans and a quarter zip sweater, an ageless outfit, and he gave an impression of instant likability.

"Welcome to our quiet village," he said in lightly accented English for which she was grateful, both for the purpose of communication and as a guilty pleasure. "My name is Maël Dupont, and I'm probably the best person to help you with what you're looking for. I hope that asking you to come here is OK? It is a good place to talk." He smiled nicely and Katie found herself wanting to relax, but the fact that his name was the same as the man from the library video forced her concern to linger.

"You're here looking for Fae Peeters' work, is that right?"

"Ah . . ." she stalled, then nodded. "Yeah. I'm a photographer. My current project is photographing the work of a shortlisted group of architects. Peeters is one of them."

"We're home to no beautiful buildings 'ere, only our basilica, and that is much older than Fae Peeters. What did you expect to find?" It wasn't a harsh question.

"Honestly? I don't know. I was in Reims yesterday and a man there suggested I come here." Katie shrugged. "He sounded like he knew what he was talking about, so I took a chance."

Maël raised his eyes with interest. "This man, he didn't tell you specifically what you were looking for?"

"He didn't, no. He spoke like it was my secret to find, kind of like a treasure hunt."

"And what did he look like?"

"Black fedora," Katie said easily. "On the short side, a bit of a stomach, maybe thirteen or fourteen stone," she tried to recall. "I thought I saw him last night at the Christmas market, so maybe he's be a resident here? Smart looking, scholarly type; real professor vibe. Oh, green eyes. Like really green, not gray-green or anything. I remember because they're so rare. Do you know him?"

"Mmm. Maybe." Maël shifted his weight. "You came 'ere to find a Fae Peeters design?" Maël took the conversation back to where Katie wanted it. She nodded. "Have you learned anything 'elpful in your hunt so far?"

Katie wanted to tell him about Peeters' façade and hall so he could help her, but if she said anything about them, then he'd ask how she knew. She caught a quick glance of her reflection in the mirrored window. It faded out for a flash and then it came back just as fast. It was weird. She must've imagined it. Or, maybe it was a flaw in the reflective surface.

Well, she rationalized, Maël looked like a man of some importance. The library was public, and who knew what kind of monitoring software was on that computer. Or, what that librarian saw over her shoulder. One of those two probably alerted Maël to her seeing that video. Denial would only further remove her from innocence. "I found out this morning that Peeters has two projects here."

"Two projects?"

"A façade that hides a street and an underground hall. I don't know where either are." Maël pursed his lips with a nod. The way he did it triggered perfect déjà vu from the recording. She now had no doubt. "Are you . . . You're the same Maël who was in the video."

"What video?"

This was definitely the same man who sat around the table disheartened by thirty-seven dead in a string of serial arson attacks. This wasn't an interview for her sake. It was an interview for his. Pulled from the library by a stranger, brought to a small, mirrored room, made to wait, and now being pleasantly questioned by a man in charge . . . Whatever hope she had that this meeting was to benefit her quickly gave way to sobriety. She was in trouble.

"It was named r . . .82 Arrangement? I really didn't understand what was going on in it. It was just sitting alone on the desktop. I had no idea what it was."

Maël smiled kindly. He uncrossed his legs and comfortably leaned forward.

Now they were on the same page. Katie shouldn't have seen that video.

Maël remained pleasant and Katie tried to keep herself relaxed. So much for rule number one of not self-incriminating, but she couldn't help herself.

"Did you watch the whole video?"

"Almost. I was interrupted before it finished, thank you." She groaned internally. She sounded like she was thanking this man for the pleasant opportunity to wrongfully watch his confidential file. That's how interrogations always started, wasn't it? With polite conversation?

"Other than information about a hall and façade, what else did you learn?"

"There was a problem with unwanted visitors because of aerial imaging. There was a big concern with a person who . . ." Katie shook her head trying to think of a way out of this. A mystery man with a funny sounding code name who was linked to a major unsolved crime was not a conversation she wanted to be involved in. "It was a serious sounding discussion. I think the subtitles may have dropped off for part of it. I really didn't know what was going on." A bit of lies, a bit of truth. The whole recording had been a conversation out of context. "Is this village some sort of family mob hub? The Belgian mafia?" Katie laughed with forced levity, trying to take some of the pressure off. But then she swore. What if this was actual mafia activity? "You know what, forget I asked that. I don't want to know."

Maël laughed lightly too. "There are no mob ties 'ere, maybe to your disappointment," he said. Katie exhaled with a nervous laugh. He was trying to keep her at ease, and she was grateful for that. Sadly though, she saw her chances of being given direction to Peeters' works, or even meeting the woman herself, slipping away, and with it, her bonus. "When you came from Reims, what did you *want* to find?"

That was a good question, and she thought carefully before she answered. "I was hoping to find something I might've missed. The man spoke of a little-known project by Peeters, so it could've been anything, a gazebo even. I really didn't have extraordinary expectations." Katie shrugged.

Maël nodded and leaned back into the chair. "What do you think of Peeters' work?"

Thankfully, they were moving beyond the video. "It's beautiful," she said.

"It's special. When I was photographing her work, I watched locals and tourists come by, and they didn't just look at it, they interacted with it, with their eyes and their emotions. Other architects design things that are impressive, or interesting, and elicit reactions, but not necessarily emotion. And she can do it on any scale, from the EU's incredible Art and History Centre to, well, a gazebo. She's revitalized the majesty of Classical architecture in the face of the popularity of minimalist metal, glass, and concrete."

"You've spent some time thinking about this."

"I have," Katie said firmly. "I want to make sure everyone who sees my photos get to feel as if they were seeing the subject in person. Peeters deserves recognition for what she's given to the world."

Maël smiled and nodded, a wave of a thought crossing his face as though he was remembering something. He politely excused himself, promising to be right back.

As soon as he'd gone, Katie slumped back letting her head bounce off the stiff padding behind her. Was he going to bring the police to arrest her or some tea to continue the discussion? As she figured it, the best thing that could happen now was for her to sign a non-disclosure and then be asked to leave.

This was the last time she was ever going to take mysterious advice from a stranger, professor or not.

On the other side of the mirrored glass, Fae was watching Maël question the English girl. Still caught up in Nefas' texts, she kept expecting the girl to slide off the couch, glide over to the glass, and stare her down while speaking things only Nefas would know. But rather than finding Nefas in disguise, Fae found a genuine young woman who was completely oblivious to the part she was being drawn into playing in this Christmas Eve drama, a drama that was supposed to have been all but shut down.

Katie couldn't have been much more than twenty-five, not much older than Fae when she'd first come to this village. She had shoulder length, straight blonde hair, dark eyes, a cute face, and converse sneakers, jeans, and a patterned long-sleeve shirt rounded out her look. On the outside at least, Katie appeared average.

Keeping half an ear on the conversation going on, Fae flipped through the intel Maël had requested be gathered on visitors who'd indicated that they were staying for Christmas Eve. The notes were handwritten by his volunteers and not presented in any official way, but they were informative.

There was an old man from Liège who'd driven as far as his old car would take him and was suspected to be a recent divorcé. There was a mid-aged couple from Dallas who were described by the note taker as simply "American" and were the only ones staying at the Bed and Breakfast. They hadn't been shy about their directive "from the Lord" to come to this village and speak the sweet name of Jesus to reclaim what the Devil had stolen. What the couple meant by that exactly, the report didn't say. The last group was two families from Brussels. One was Spanish, the other German, which made them likely to be European Union employees. They'd been short on conservation, so there wasn't much recorded about them except that they were four adults and three kids.

That made a lot of visitors for a little village with no real Christmas Eve attractions other than a choir whose existence only spread by word of mouth. Like Katie, these people could be here to play a to-be-determined role in the drama, or maybe they'd truly stumbled onto this place for a Christmas holiday. It was something Fae had no interest in finding more about.

She continued to listen to the interview with increasing awareness, and when Maël left the room, she had a deep suspicion why.

Maël came into the observation room seconds later. "Have my minions found anything d'intéressant?" he asked once the door closed, slipping into Frenglish.

"Maybe," Fae said, still not over Maël asking her to stay rather than letting her run far, far away. They were both being selfish. "There's one couple of interest from the US, but you've had more experience with this than me."

Maël gave a shallow scoff and came further into the room, looking through the window at Katie. She was just sitting, waiting.

"You 'eard, I'm sure, that you have a fan?" He nodded at Katie.

"Did you tell her all fan requests have to go through my agent?" Fae sighed, pinching the bridge of her nose. "Who brought her here, Maël? Who was that professor character?"

"I'd love to know too." Maël leaned against the back wall. "What do you think?"

Fae shook her head, unsure. "The green eyes raise a warning flag that it could be Nefas, but I've seen him with blue eyes or even no eyes." She shrugged, letting her arms fall to her sides. "Either way, someone got her here, and that means she's probably not going home for Christmas Eve. She just doesn't know it yet."

"What does your instinct say?" Maël pressed, looking at her earnestly.

Fae suspected he was driving at whether or not to tell her about the Gift—and extending the choice that came with it—and he didn't want to make the decision alone. Fae's annoyance with him lessened and she sighed again.

"That her professor is Nefas. But I'm the most biased person to ask."

"I need you to be biased, s'il vous plait. I want to be generous with the Gift like your grandmother was. I've shown the Gift before, it turned out fine, but this is different. One mistake here and I could be giving Nefas everything he wants."

"Hey," Fae gave him a light shoulder bump, "you still pray?"

He nodded. "But I remember Iakob and . . ." Maël drifted off as he rubbed the stubble on his face, working his jaw, holding in whatever was threatening to come out. Fae didn't know what to say. Thankfully, he spoke again before she had to. "I agree. We should move forward under the assumption that the professor is Nefas. I'm going to put some eyes on her." He paused for a while longer then said again, "If she does stay for the Eve, I'll have her in the Notre-Dame du Seigneur long before eleven o'clock, well before the Gift comes. If it was Nefas who brought her here, she'll be inside the basilica and out of his reach.

"Will you show her the Gift?"

Maël hesitated.

"Plan to show her then, so you're prepared," Fae helped him out. "Who can be her handler?"

"I 'ave someone who has shown le cadeau before, Chantal."

Fae nodded, and she watched as Katie stood up from the couch and came closer to the mirror, fiddling with her hair again. "You think I should go in there and meet her." Fae finally said, getting down to what probably really inspired Maël to interrupt his interview with Katie.

"How many fans do you honestly have under the age of thirty years?"

"Can architects even have fans? We really only have critics." She was hardly in the frame of mind to be doing autograph signings and making small talk. But before she could say anything more, both she and Maël looked quizzically at Katie on the other side of the mirror swaying back and forth, side to side, her facial expression somewhere between disgust and amusement.

"What is she . . .?"

"It's a mirror," Maël said quickly.

Fae swore. The two darted for the neighboring room, any doubts put on hold.

While Katie waited for Maël to return she fiddled idly; she was trying not to look bored, having resolved a couple months ago not to default to the internet at the drop of a hat. The world was meant to be noticed rather than ignored. She felt awkward though, doing nothing but waiting, so she got up and wandered over to what she still suspected to be a one-way mirror. No doubt Maël was on the other side now. If he was observing her, then she'd make sure he saw nothing more than an innocent woman from Reading, England fixing her hair who was of no threat or concern.

As she was moving hair strands around, she could have sworn that her image flickered, like it had earlier. She stopped moving. Nothing else in her sphere of vision had flickered, only her reflection. She frowned, blinked a couple times, and went back to what she'd been doing. But then her reflection wavered again, and Katie scrunched her eyelids, flexing them as though she were trying to wake herself up. But it wasn't that her reflection blurred or went out of focus as it would if her eyes were tired. Her reflection actually wavered, fading in and out.

Thinking again that she must've caught a flaw in the reflective surface, she swayed to the left, then to the right, trying to see if she could notice a difference. Maybe there was a projector somewhere running an interactive program with her reflection? Katie looked at the ceiling, then along the surface of the window for something that would validate her projector theory but found nothing.

Again, she swayed to the left, then to the right. Forward, backward. And then, ah! She tripped the program or found the fault in the surfacing, whichever it was, as her reflection wavered again. The glitch lasted longer this time. She watched with growing amusement as her image distorted with her movements as though she were looking at herself in one of those fun house mirrors. Leaning forward, her forehead grew to a bulbous proportion, then backward elongated her body. Back and forth, left and right produced similar results. Then suddenly it all changed. The whimsical distortions of her body snapped to that of a meatless body, and the sudden switch in imagery convinced her that this had to be a computer program. Her proportions were normal, but she'd lost all her substance and she looked like she was starving to death. Her shoulders and clavicle bones protruded grotesquely from beneath her shirt, her skin sallow and sickly. Katie flinched at the repulsive sight, staring into her own sunken eyes. Disturbed but amused, she brought her boney and knobby hands up next to her nearly fleshless face. This easily bested any image filters out there; this was flawless.

Intrigued, Katie wanted to find out if there was in fact someone on the other side of this window. She leaned in closer to the mirror until she and her skeletal reflection came together. And then, when she was only an inch away, her corpse-like reflection winked.

Katie jumped, but she wasn't sure if she jumped because of her reflection's autonomy or the sound of two people entering the room.

"Katie, is it?" None other than Fae Peeters herself came through the door followed closely by Maël, the dull clip of her boots purposeful. Both Peeters and Maël cast wayward eyes toward the window, and Katie followed suit, giving an accusing glare at whoever was behind that program, having fun at her expense.

"I'm Fae Norris-Peeters." Peeters extended her hand, and Katie found herself shaking hands with of one of the top architects in the world, thoughts of her winking reflection pushed out of the way.

"Katie Windsor. A true pleasure."

"Katie," Maël began with a smile that hid no small amount of pride, "I'd like to introduce you to my second cousin."

Peeters carried a professional command of the room, no doubt earned from presenting and arguing with leaders of all rank and file. Her dark brown hair was pulled back into a simple ponytail, which, based on her age, might've been dyed but Katie didn't care. Small, golden ball studs decorated her ears complementing her green V-neck jumper that looked so comfortable Katie was immediately jealous of it. Jeans and expensive-looking heeled boots completed the image of humble success.

"What are the chances that we'd be in the same remote place at the same time?" Peeters asked with a friendly tone, offering Katie a seat beside her in the other chair. Maël put himself on the couch where Katie'd been sitting before.

"Fairly small," Katie agreed.

"I figured that if you were going to come all the way out here, I deserved to meet you. Maël tells me that you've been able to fill out my resume a bit more than what's publicly available," she said with a hint of a smile that kept Katie in limbo about whether or not she was unhappy. "Congratulations."

"Thank you," Katie said, hoping to encourage a positive interaction. "I stumbled on that information by complete accident. Sometimes we just fall into things!"

"Sometimes," Peeters nodded, though she didn't look convinced. "So, not to overwhelm you," she continued, "but what can I do for you?"

"I…" Katie's mind raced. "I…you'll have to forgive me," she apologized nervously, "I hadn't expected to actually meet you. Now. But, um, in a perfect world, I'd love to see this façade and hall. I'm photographing the work of top architects, so both these would be brilliant to include."

Peeters exchanged a glance with Maël. "I'm honored, but there is a security reason for why both of those remain off the record."

Katie's face fell, though Peeters hadn't actually refused. "I understand," Katie said, "but if they need to remain off the record, I can agree to that. I'd still love to see them."

Peeters considered a moment, exchanging another look with Maël, then nodded. "How would you like to sit down later today? Will you still be around?"

If she wasn't going to get the shots, she should go home. But on the other hand, she could learn a lot from someone like Peeters. "Sure, yes. That would be lovely." There was an airport not much more than an hour from here, so she could meet with Peeters and still be home late tonight. She liked the idea.

"An early dinner then. Maël, what do you suggest?"

"Try the Luxembourg," he offered. "The same street as Café Noir. It's good for food, drink, and will stay open later than t'e other places."

"The Luxembourg, then? At five o'clock?" Peeters asked.

Katie agreed, though she'd expected that "later today" was going to mean early afternoon. There might not be a flight out in the evening, but she couldn't say no now. Still, she couldn't help but ask one more time about those two projects. Fortune favored the bold, after all. "Would you mind, you don't have to answer, but would you mind telling me, completely off the record, what the purpose of your façade and hall are?"

Maël and Peeters started to speak at the same time but Peeters won out. "There was an abandoned alley that was no longer safe which needed to be covered, and the hall is for short-term storage. They're not architecturally interesting in any way, and not having them on record keeps the bored kids away."

It was an easy enough explanation. The simplicity of it, however, didn't match the strong, negative reaction of the Fae Peeters in the video, nor did it address how that guy with the code name fit in. But Katie left those questions alone; she was already on thin ice.

Peeters nodded and stood up. Katie followed suit, and, for whatever it was worth, was happy to see that she and Peeters were about the same height. In a meaningless way, they had something in common. "I'll see you at five o'clock tonight at the Luxembourg then."

"Brilliant. I look forward to it," Katie said, putting her jacket back on.

"Oh, and Katie," Peeters said, catching her before she left, "small villages like this one have lots of little quirks and . . ."

"Personality," Maël suggested.

"Yes," Peeters agreed, "personality that bigger towns and cities don't necessarily have. Depending on how traveled you are, it can either be fun or a bit . . . off-putting. If you see anything that seems strange or unusual, feel free to ask me or Maël, and we can give you some background."

The word "off-putting" made Katie think of her missing watch, but that could happen anywhere. She thanked them both again and left, going down into the lobby and escaping into the gray, overcast day.

No non-disclosures, no stern talking to. She was luckier than a leprechaun.

Fae fell back down into the chair and looked at Maël at a complete loss.

"You could've asked to do lunch rather than supper," Maël said, back in French, guessing her thoughts.

Fae rolled her eyes. "Yes, but I couldn't remember what the train times were." Fae shook her head. "It doesn't matter. I'll leave tomorrow. Besides, I promised your boys some Lego building time while I was here."

Maël laughed. "I saw they had drawn up a schematic, which I've never seen them do before. I think they're trying to impress you."

Fae smiled. "Drechsler had a drawer full of confiscated cameras," she said. "Do you still do anything similar?"

"If Drechsler wanted your puppy he could have it with the right look. I can't seize people's phone, and I can't legally order searches of phones or cameras at the gate," he said, also sitting back down. "Katie didn't seem as interested in the r28 video as I worried she might've been."

"It's not her business and she knows it. Regardless, do any of your people know where la Rue is? Whoever you have watching her, they need to make sure she doesn't go near it. If she does try, it'd be another indication that Nefas is behind her professor."

"I have someone I can call on. Which leaves just one question." He looked at her with expectancy. "Do I extend the Gift to her, or do I try to let her leave?"

"You should throw her out of here as far as you can and let her live her life." Fae took a deep breath. "But, if Nefas brought her here, then he wants her. And if she does leave, he'll either find someone else to take her place, or he'll get to her outside these walls and she'll be helpless."

"We need the choir."

"We need Nicholas," Fae added. "I don't know. Maybe Nefas didn't bring her here."

"In which case, the only reason she would be brought here is to have the Gift."

"Full circle."

The two of them were once again left staring at each other.

Maël ran his hands through his hair with a heavy exhale. "OK," he said. "Make Katie the offer to let her see the hall tomorrow on the Eve. That'll put her safely inside the basilica in case Nefas is behind all this. Tell her as much or as little as you want, and we'll go from there. It won't be the first time this village rides on faith and hope alone."

Fae nodded and wished she could tell Maël that this was the right choice. Katie leaving was full of risks. Katie staying was full of risks, especially if she was going to receive the Gift. She'd have to go outside the protection of the basilica, find Nicholas, and bring him back. Or, at least that's how the Eve used to play out before the arrangement. She didn't know if that was still the case.

Maël drove her back to his house and even though she was mentally done with this village, she couldn't stop thinking about Katie and her own reason for being asked here. Which brought her thoughts back to the strangely fascinating vial that the priest let her borrow.

"Do you know anything about the small vial of powder that Cuvelier has?" Fae asked as Maël drove.

"That small glass bottle?" He shook his head. "Wow, I'd forgotten about that. Yeah, when I was young he told us kids wild stories about what it was to make us laugh. I finally asked him seriously and he told me it's just a valueless artifact."

"He told me the same thing. I was interested in it, so he let me take it to look at; it's in my room now."

"Well, if you have any divine revelations about it . . ."

"I'll let you know."

8

Henri's father had to run an errand and had taken Henri's car. Henri couldn't help but notice his departure was conveniently timed to coincide with when his mother discovered that the milk was all gone, and the lack of milk was a crisis that threatened to ruin the entire Christmas feast—if his mother was to be believed. It was a problem that wouldn't wait, so it was up to Henri to save Christmas dinner by going to the grocery store on his bike. He could say little else than "yes, maman" and repeat after her exactly the type of milk and brand of coffee to buy because no mother could ever have a grocery list of only one thing.

The streets were busy by village standards, with bikes, cars, and pedestrians all running around, and full of people finishing their shopping. Some would still travel to the nearby towns and cities tomorrow, but most wouldn't risk something happening and not being able to get back in time for the Gift. With the whiz of his tires in his ears, Henri quickly peddled along the street easily passing the slower, cautious cars. He saw Theo and Isabelle Magnette dealing with their toddler having a bad day and gave Theo a sympathetic wave of good luck as he sped by.

A flash of movement and a panicked shout in front of him and Henri squeezed down hard on his brakes. He swerved, trying to miss the man popping out from between two parked cars, fighting to keep his bike from skidding out and crashing. A vehicle behind him slammed on its brakes with a squeal. Henri managed to get control, planting his feet on the ground, adrenaline racing. As much as he wanted to yell at the man for not being more careful, the same argument could be thrown back at him, so he bit his tongue. The man was standing between the two cars having jumped back between them in time, a look of surprise frozen on his face.

Seeing that everyone was all right, the car behind Henri drove off. Henri was about to pedal off too, but he recognized the pedestrian as the same stranger from last night who'd popped up behind him and Josie. The short ponytail hanging over his shoulder gave him away.

"You OK?" Henri asked. A trapper's hat with its ear flaps hanging over his cheeks and cheap sunglasses created the man's look.

"Yeah, all good," the man confirmed. "Hey, you're the guy with the girlfriend last night, right?"

Henri nodded.

"I was hoping I'd see you again. Walking behind you, it was hard not to overhear your conversation. You two aren't the only ones thinking about Christmas outside these walls. Got a couple of minutes?"

Did he? Yes. But anything to do with the Gift wasn't a normal conversation starter. He'd thought it weird that this guy didn't pass them last night when he and Josie were obviously taking their time, and now he wondered if it was intentional. Henri *had* promised Josie to walk away from the subject, but . . . Henri quickly ran through all the scenarios where agreeing to this conversation might be an actual cause for concern. This guy was . . . different, but not concerning. At worst Henri would have an interesting story to tell, and this was a great excuse to put off the grocery haul for a couple minutes longer. "Sure, why not."

"Let's go inside where there's fewer ears, then."

Fewer ears? Henri stalled. The Gift wasn't party conversation, but talking about it wasn't forbidden either, unless this man was a visitor who knew a little something and was trying to bait him into talking. He looked borderline homeless. No, Henri decided, he wasn't a visitor. He shrugged his agreement and, after resting his bike on a nearby lamp post, led the two of them into the Luxembourg two doors down.

A restaurant and bar on two floors with a beer and wine cellar in the basement, the Luxembourg was really the only locale that provided something resembling a night life, while its warm environment welcomed all ages. Henri led them to sit at the bar, where three rows of brightly colored liquor bottles were on display in front of them. The radio was coming through ceiling speakers playing something repetitive but catchy.

"Menus or just drinks?" the bartender asked, coming out from the back. Henri didn't recognize him. He looked early twenties maybe, like the kind of guy who could make friends with anyone. The arms of his plaid shirt were rolled halfway up and his face held a couple days of uncertain growth that helped to cover the small imperfections still lingering from the teenage years. He looked like an average guy except that his eyes were almost erupting with an excitement for life that Henri was not used to seeing.

"Just drinks," Henri confirmed. "Coke for me."

"Stella."

The bartender nodded and grabbed the appropriate glasses for the order.

"I'm Alex," the stranger said. "Probably a good place to start."

"Henri. Look, sorry for out there. I wasn't paying attention."

"Don't worry about it," Alex shrugged. "We're having a drink now, so it worked out."

"Nice watch," Henri observed, trying to make small talk while the drinks came. It looked delicate, like something his sister would like. "Rose gold?"

"Bronze." Alex said quickly, pulling his jacket sleeve down and crossing his arms, hiding the piece from sight.

"I didn't think watches were made out of bronze," Henri wondered aloud.

"It's just a watch."

When the bartender came back with their drinks, Henri stopped him before he left. "You new?"

"Yeah!" The bartender's face brightened. "Been here about a week." Henri heard it then, his accent had some German inflections. He must've been from the East. "The owner of this place is an old family friend. He mentioned needing some short-term help and I figured why not?"

"Why not," Henri agreed though he was bewildered why anyone would willingly come to this place. "Are you going home for Christmas?"

"No. It's part of the contract. But I hear there's an incredible choir who sings all night on Christmas Eve?"

Henri gave a short laugh. "They're pretty good. I'll see you in the basilica tomorrow night. Don't be late. And, welcome to our little village."

"Thanks man. I'm Max, by the way." He stuck out his hand and Henri gave it a quick shake while introducing himself. Max next offered his hand to Alex, but the older man didn't make a move, like he wasn't sure if he wanted to take it. He slowly gave in though and their handshake was long, almost awkwardly so, and even though Alex hadn't taken his sunglasses off yet, Max didn't break eye contact. Henri had seen similar things when two guys were sizing each other up, but this wasn't hostile; Max looked like he was on the verge of bringing it in for a man-hug.

"It's great to see you," Max said as they broke the handshake.

"Let's sit somewhere else," Alex suggested, grabbing his drink. "This stool hurts my back."

Henri followed Alex upstairs.

"So, what did you want to tell me?" Henri asked as they took their seats. They were the only ones up here.

Alex finally removed his sunglasses, letting the plastic frames bounce on the table, wiping his eyes. "Yeah, so, like I said before, I couldn't help but overhear you with your girlfriend last night, how you want to experiment with leaving on the Eve." He took a deep drink from his beer. "I can trust you, right?" The question sounded rehearsed, like a cliché from movies and books when shady guys wanted to get something off their chest, or to be a snitch.

Henri went with it. "Of course, sure."

"Good. Because my whole family and I could get in trouble if this got out to Monsieur."

And now, playing his part, Henri gave the cliché response of confidants and to-be victims. "What about me? Will I get in trouble if Monsieur learns I'm even talking with you?"

"You'll be fine. If there's any bounce back, feel free to name me. I can handle it."

"Really," Henri said, sitting back, no longer playing along. "A no-strings-attached scenario where only you get in trouble." He took a drink of his Coke. "Listen, if you're going to ask me to sell drugs or something, I'm going to report you."

"Drugs? No, drugs are for—" All of a sudden Alex held up his hand for silence and cocked his ear to listen to the radio. The station was a local one a retiree ran as a hobby. It was actually a pretty decent station, and it had local news, which is what caught Alex's ear.

"A report of the Jandreau Ghost having appeared last night has been made. One witness reported that they allegedly heard the apparition though did not see it. The location and time of the reported appearance have not been disclosed."

Alex dropped his hand. His lips curled into a half smile, though it didn't reach his eyes, and Henri thought Alex was about to start mocking the story. "What do you think about the ghost? Are you a believer?"

"I haven't seen it or heard it." Henri said. "But people have recorded audio of what they say is the ghost crying out, and you can't live in this village and not believe in the supernatural." Alex took another deep gulp of his beer and Henri pressed again for the point of their conversation. "So, if it's not drugs, what's the deal?"

Alex leaned over the table hugging it close with his body. "Every Eve my wife, myself, and my young daughter get out of here. We escape the walls, leave behind the Notre-Dame du Seigneur and all the crap that happens there, and celebrate Christmas Eve normally like the rest of the world. There's a hunter's lodge about thirty kilometers away in the forest. It's not much, but it heats up good and makes for the best Christmas decorating, so my wife says. I told her about you and your girlfriend last night. We want to invite you to join us." Alex leaned back and cleared his ponytail from his shoulder, crossing his arms as though he'd done enough to impress him.

"But you weren't born here. Otherwise the Gift would still affect you?" Henri asked.

"No. We're both natively born here, so we're both affected by the Gift, and guess what? We don't change into corpses or release the spirit of Nefas or nothing. Thirty kilometers is the range of the Gift."

"But how do you get out? Absences don't go unnoticed and the gates are locked."

Alex smiled again, but it was hard for Henri to read what kind of smile it was. His eyes were completely stoic and detached from what he was saying. "There's a hole in the wall."

"I don't believe it."

Alex pounded his hand on the table with enthusiasm. "Exactly! It's perfect and it's how we've been sneaking out for six years, seven tomorrow. On the north-west side there's a line of young pine trees and a patch of ivy growing up the wall," Alex said. "That ivy hides the hole. Who knows how it got there, but I found it, and then I made it big enough to get through. It's easiest to find from the outside, so sometime today go out and find the hole then follow the alley to the other end where you'll see where the entrance is. Tomorrow night we'll meet you outside the wall at ten-thirty. I pre-park the car outside the walls in the morning." Alex gulped his beer, now almost gone and started to get up to leave.

"Hold on," Henri said, stopping him. "I didn't agree to anything."

"You wanted to get your girlfriend out of here on the Eve? Prove to her it can be done? I've told you how to leave. You know where to find us if you want to come."

"They'll know I'm missing. What about next year? I'll have time to make an alibi." Henri couldn't believe he was actually giving this unbelievable story a second thought.

Alex shrugged. "Maybe we'll get caught this year and Monsieur will close the hole. Or, maybe you and your girlfriend will break up because she doesn't want to risk anything and you want to risk it all. You wanted a chance. This may be your only one." Alex finished his beer with a final chug. Putting his sunglasses back on, he got out of the booth a little less than stable on his feet. "See ya, Henri. Hopefully." He clopped heavily down the stairs, a guiding hand on the wall. "North-west side," he called over his shoulder. "Pines and ivy."

Henri heard Max say a goodbye but couldn't tell if Alex said anything in return.

Left with his Coke and an opportunity, Henri rolled the glass between his hands, the condensation making his hands slide smoothly against its sides. There was something weird about Alex for sure, but someone didn't just make up lies about the Gift. Henri could easily validate or disprove enough of Alex's story ahead of time, so there was no purpose to lying. And if Alex wasn't lying, then he had to be telling the truth. Which meant that not only had Alex and his family done an incredible job keeping their secret undiscovered, but Henri's experiment of going outside the walls would be low risk. It had already been proven possible. And Alex did have a point: every year could be the last.

Henri took one last drink then trotted back downstairs where Max was waiting for him with his bill.

"That much for a Coke?"

"Your friend said you were covering the bill."

Henri groaned. He'd been had for a free beer.

"I'd be careful about that guy," Max offered as he took Henri's payment. "I knew him when he was younger. I'm not sure if he recognized me because I've obviously grown up a lot too. But there's something about him."

"I noticed. You don't trust him?"

"I wouldn't get caught up with what he says without a second opinion; a heavenly second opinion."

Henri gave Max a quizzical look. "That's high praise for your thoughts."

"I didn't mean mine," Max said, laughing. "But why not."

"Why not," Henri agreed, putting his wallet away. He found himself rather liking this guy. "I'll sit on it. See you around." Henri waved goodbye and headed back out into the overcast morning.

Back on his bike and headed toward the grocery store, Henri tried running through the grocery list his mother had given him, but all he could think about was being at a wood shack in the forest with Josie on Christmas Eve.

Even though she had told him repeatedly to stop thinking about it.

9

The immediate result of Katie's meeting with Maël Dupont and Fae Peeters was that Katie now found herself without any plans for the afternoon. She thought of trying to track down that professor, but she didn't need him anymore and she didn't want to give the impression that she was still snooping around. She instead decided to take her time wandering the village, visiting the shops, and taking photos. At the very least, she could pick up a couple small presents for her friends, and more urgently, get some lunch.

It didn't take long to find a deli that seconded as a sandwich shop, its front facing windows full of monstrous rounds of cheese and fat legs of smoked meats. The shop was busy, though, and her stomach was growling. Beside the deli was a produce vendor that looked to have a small self-serve. Her heart told her to wait for the sandwich, but her head reminded her of the many sweets waiting back home, so she resigned herself and went with the self-serve.

Her urbanite expectations were that there'd be some hot options she could eat on the go, but she quickly discovered she was wrong; everything was cold. There were cold cabbage rolls, cold fish, cold chips, cold pickled vegetables . . . And with a humorless woman behind the counter watching her every move, Katie felt obligated to buy something. As the only table inside was occupied by two old men doing crossword puzzles, she took her cold, unappetizing lunch back outside.

Stabbing at her food, she ate as she strolled the streets. Like the night before, she decided to follow the church's spires to the plaza and hoped the purposeful destination would help distract her from her disappointing meal.

She stuffed mouthfuls of pickled eggs and cold potato patties in her mouth until she finished, arriving at the church plaza soon thereafter. It was now almost empty of the market vendors except a few who were still packing up. Seeing the crates and boxes being packed with toys and decorations was a sight that marked an end, like hauling the Christmas tree to the pavement, only prematurely.

Tossing her garbage into a nearby rubbish bin, Katie took out her camera and started looking for something to shoot. The most obvious subject was the church, but she didn't want to miss the action of the market clean-up and jumping right to the church felt like dessert before the meal. With its deeply Gothic front, the church looked like the black sheep of the family in an otherwise quaint village of pointed roofs and painted bricks. It made Katie wonder if this church was the lone survivor of a once-booming medieval town devastated by the Black Plague, or maybe the Prussians, leaving only a church and a humble remnant who would survive to become this village. It wasn't a likely history, especially since her theory combined most of what she remembered from all her history classes. The truth was probably closer to a rich philanthropist wanting to build a church.

But regardless of how the church got here, it clearly remained central to village activity. And thinking of human activity, she decided she should call her parents and tell them she'd be home late. She took the shots she wanted of the tear-down, capped her camera, and pulled out her phone.

She called her mum, but her dad picked up. He kept the conversation appropriately short before passing her over to her mum, who gave full vent to her frustration over not having Katie home for Christmas yet. By the time she was done getting upset, she'd jumped right into telling about her Christmas work party, and it was another forty minutes before Katie could hang up.

Katie had sought warmth in a café during the call and was more than ready to get back to her goal of checking out the church. Leaving the café, she crossed the plaza and came into the church's shadow, feeling it invite her in like a kindly old butler opening the door for afternoon tea. *Well,* she thought, *don't mind if I do.*

She was about to start up the stairs when she was surprised to see the professor walking toward her, a calm smile of recognition on his face.

"Bonjour et bienvenue to my village! I see you did take my advice."

"I did, thank you," Katie said. "I've actually already had a run-in with Fae Peeters. I'm going to meet with her later, so it worked out wonderfully."

"Non, non, ma chère, I must t'ank you for listening to me." He shouldered up the collar of his jacket and began wandering away from the basilica, forcing Katie to follow him. "You will now be able to divulge to the world the true inspiration for the unparalleled talents of a woman we both admire, yes?"

"True inspiration?" She didn't understand. "I'm not going to see her work. It's closed to the public."

"T'is is not true," he said dismissively. "You will be able to see both before you leave, trust me."

This morning that promise would've made Katie's day, but now she was more comfortable letting sleeping dogs lie.

He continued. "Were you able to learn anyt'ing about her secret projects?"

"I know that they're still secret," Katie restated carefully, wondering what he knew that differed from Peeters' earlier statements.

They came into the mix of people packing up their stalls, but the professor didn't pay them any notice. He kept walking without deviance, forcing people to go around him while Katie found herself side-stepping boxes and mouthing words of apology to those trying to load up their lorries and boots of their cars.

"Not'ing else?" He looked over at her. It was the first time since they'd begun walking, and he looked directly into her eyes. Making eye contact was like a blanket had been ripped away, and Katie now saw him as though for the first time. He wasn't rudely walking through these working people, their purpose secondary to his. He wasn't just an academic. He was a great leader of minds, one who had earned respect and knew how to command it. She saw it so clearly and knew it so suddenly that she didn't know how she could've missed it earlier in Reims. She knew she was staring into his gaze, but she was a bit awestruck.

"I know everything there is to know about this village," he assured her, breaking his eye contact and his intensity. "You can talk openly and not worry."

Katie felt compelled to be perfectly honest with him, as though to prove her loyalty, which was an excessive response, and she wondered why she wanted to react that way. She was still sensitive about mentioning anything too specific from the r-whatever video, so she forced herself to suppress that desire of wanting to please and impress him. "I know both projects were built maybe twenty years ago," Katie said. "Peeters said one's a façade for security, the other is underground holding. Both sounded rather utilitarian."

The professor smiled fondly. "Ah, oui, she can be 'umble like so. It may cost her one day, but for now, it is a nice part of her personality. But no matter, her work is flawless, like her soul, and it should be recognized."

A pile of pine boughs lay in the middle of their path, someone having laid them out neatly for collection. The professor walked over them, sending an invigorating wave of fresh pine scent into the air. The woman whose boughs they were shot the professor a dirty look and Katie hurried to catch up with him, purposefully going around the boughs.

"I don't recall if I ever got your name," Katie said, once she was at his side again.

"Did you say you were meeting Peeters t'is evening?"

"Mmhmm." Katie nodded.

The professor stopped short and Katie skidded to a halt beside him. His eyes danced with spark. "Excellent! Very good."

"How do you know her, if I may ask? Was she a student of yours?"

"I will show you where you can find her façade, so you can see it for yourself ahead of your interview. It is in a public street. People see it every day without knowing." The professor's eyes snapped onto something over her shoulder, and instinctive curiosity caused Katie to look behind herself as well, but he called her attention back, speaking quickly. "It would seem we are going to be interrupted. 'Ere, before I leave you."

He pulled out a wrinkled paper map from his pocket, just like the one the guard gave her yesterday, and drew a path of travel through the streets to the edge of the village. He confirmed that she was comfortable with the directions, then promptly left with barely a farewell.

Perplexed and feeling a little empty, Katie looked behind her to see who, or what, could've chased off such an elite man. There were only three people behind her, none of them paying her any attention, though she did recognize the woman from last night who'd found her wallet helping someone dismantle a wooden booth. The woman looked up from her job, and, seeing Katie, waved kindly, power tool in hand. Katie returned the wave.

Well, Katie thought, shifting her attention to her next afternoon adventure, she would have to find out who this man was before she left, at the very least, his name. Until then he'd simply be "Professor." Still buzzing with the feeling of being in his presence, his insistence that the façade was innocent would make his directions wasted if she didn't at least walk by it. She'd come back for the church. She oriented herself and set off.

It took her about twenty minutes of walking to arrive where the façade was supposed to be. Nearly every window and door she passed paid tribute to Christmas in some form or another. Nativities were by far the favorite decoration, and there was a repeated theme of wine and bread, from whole bottles and loaves to plastic cups and slices. Sometimes it was left on the steps, while other buildings integrated into other existing decorations. Peeters had said that the village had quirks, and these displays certainly fit that statement.

The façade was supposed to be at the edge of the village, maybe only a block away from the village's outer wall. She was to look for a T-junction and then, give-or-take, it should be directly in front her. It was supposed to be between two buildings, but Katie had no way to find it exactly; the whole length of unbroken, painted brick wall looked exactly the same. And now Katie understood Peeters' dismissal of it; there was honestly nothing to see. She snapped a couple urban street shots, then crossed the one-lane street to get closer.

She took a couple more photos on this side and searched for something interesting to feature. Looking around, then up, she saw in the deep overhang what looked to be a large hole. Or maybe it was just a deep shadow cast by the sun, it was hard to tell. It wasn't what she was looking for though, so moved on.

She spent another couple minutes there, then decided that she was done; she was ready to go back to that church and finally look inside. Putting her camera away, her phone suddenly began ringing. She fished it out and frowned. Well, that didn't happen very often: an unknown number.

The phone kept ringing.

Cautiously, Katie answered. "Hello?"

There was silence on the other end of the line.

"Hello?"

Some crackling static, then a male voice.

"Kate?"

"Hello? Who's this?"

"Kate! It's Ed!"

Katie grinned. "Ed, you twit, what happened to your regular line?"

Her longtime friend laughed on the other side. "My phone broke. Some drunk bloke fell on it last night, so I'm borrowing a mate's. I saw you're in France?"

"I hopped into Belgium yesterday, some small-pot village you've never heard of. Where are you?"

"France. I thought we could head home together if we're on the same side of the country."

"Yeah, of course."

She talked with Ed a little longer, laying groundwork for a meetup if everything worked out. In the background, Ed's mate began asking for his phone back, so he promised to call her back later. Hanging up, she took a silly photo of herself with her phone to send him. It turned out exactly how she wanted it: just embarrassing enough to make him laugh. She and Ed had been friends long enough that anything less would be a letdown. Deciding that sending her parents a nicer photo might take the edge off not being home yet, she found some good lighting and struck a nice pose. It was then that a man walking by noticed her and came over with a helpful smile. Katie groaned; she hated when people offered to take pictures for her. They usually didn't do a good job, but it was rude to refuse so it was a waste of everyone's time.

The man wore cheap sunglasses underneath a flappy-eared hat pulled down low. An oversized jacket bundled him up while a ponytail hung over his shoulder. He flipped it away as he held out his hand for the camera.

Katie begrudgingly handed it to him and waited for his OK before smiling, but it didn't come. The poor man fumbled around the screen until he finally looked at her apologetically and said, "Dieu, je ne connais pas cette technologie."

"Ah . . ." Katie's mind scrambled for the translation, aided by the way he helplessly held the phone out to her. "Ici." She showed him how to snap the photo mystified that this middle-aged man didn't know technology that had been mainstream for years now.

He took a couple shots, muttering "belle femme," then handed her phone back looking rather satisfied.

"Merci," she thanked him, expecting him to move on.

"I know . . ." he said, struggling heavily with his English, "un bel endroit pour la photographie. It is . . . many cool." He smiled expectantly.

He was offering her a nice place to take pictures, but she didn't feel like giving him any reason to stick around. He smelt like a cave.

"I . . . take you?"

"No. Non, merci," Kate told him, shaking her head to emphasize. "I don't have the time at the moment."

"Time?" He looked up into the sky, visibly squinting. "Time? Il est quatorze heures," he said, wiggling his hand in approximation.

"No, yes. Um, no. I have to go. Je m'en vais."

He nodded, then pointed to the village wall behind her. "Behind wall . . . a . . ." he didn't know the next word and began making hand motions to help.

"A . . . door? An opening?" Katie guessed, and he jabbed his finger at her in relief.

"Oui, an opening. Un bel endroit, many cool. Inside t'e door. Belles photo."

"Before I leave, I will go and look. OK?"

"And t'is opening, t'is door . . . ahh . . . utter half of façade."

"The façade?" That surprised Katie. Peeters had made her believe the façade was a secret held close. Either Katie got the wrong impression, or Peeters had underestimated how much people liked to talk.

"Oui, la façade." He pointed to her camera. "Utter half, many cool." He smiled and nodded, readjusting his hat.

He had piqued her interest. Just not enough to go with him.

"Thanks. Nice meeting you, monsieur. Merci, au revoir." She waved him off.

Thankfully, the stranger took his leave. And so did she, flipping through the pictures he'd taken. She didn't get past the first one before she stopped dead in her tracks and did a hard double take at the wall she'd just been standing in front of. She flipped through the next couple of photos, looking back at the wall after each one and feeling more and more uneasy. Going back to the same spot, she ran her fingers against the bricks as she went, looking for anything that would suggest that this was something else other than just a boring wall. Was there a projector across the street? She saw nothing. Nothing that would give the trick away.

"Hey, hello?" She didn't talk too loudly, not wanting to draw attention. There had to be someone watching, or listening, someone behind the projection or . . . some sort of technology that had photobombed her. How many boys-with-toys purchases did this place have? "Hey, bonjour? Whoever you are . . ." An older couple holding hands walked by and gave her an awkward sideways look. She decided to walk away, swiping through the pictures again.

The man had taken seven photos, and in each one, something different was written on the façade behind her. In the first picture, in what looked like dripping red paint, was written the words *My beauty in your soul.* The next photo, even though it was taken a fraction of a second later, had completely different words—*This will end*—written in the same dripping red paint. Then in the next photo, *I.* And the next, *am.* Then, *here* and *my runaway queen.*

It was the last photo, though, that really made Katie uncomfortable. While there was no writing, it looked like the picture had been double exposed.

She'd seen examples in her grandmother's picture box. A double exposure was the only way to explain how a man was photographed behind her. He was blond haired and blurry from being caught in motion. In a T-shirt and stylish vest, he looked quite handsome despite the blur, and he'd been caught looking directly at the camera. Katie had been standing no more than two feet in front of the wall, and yet a strange man had gotten behind her within a fraction of a few seconds and she never noticed? What was going on?

Katie was getting a creepy feeling about this place, and she was happy to leave it behind without a second thought.

10

As far as Henri was concerned, the notch he'd chopped into the tree had been done with all the skill of a perfected art. Specifically, an art that had been passed down from father to son for generations and which was now being evaluated by the demanding eye of his own father. There really wasn't much substance behind the Meyer family secret of tree felling, but that wasn't an opinion he was allowed to hold. His father was going to ensure that the cherished skill would survive him.

"Can I give a helpful hint?"

Henri let a well-placed chop of the axe fly strong into the condemned evergreen, then pulled it back out with a deft jerk. "Sure." He loved his father, but by the time all his helpful hints were given, he could've had the tree down.

"Make the top cut deeper. The weight of the tree will make it fall faster."

"I'll remember that. Thanks, Papa." He stole a quick look at the tree hunting party standing to the side and saw Josie keeping her eye on him even as his mother went on about the dog's health problems. He winked at her, then continued to deliver death strokes to the tree until a satisfying cracking sound of snapping wood ended the hunt.

The two boys from the village who'd tagged along for the adventure bolted in on the downed tree. Veronique, his thirteen-year old niece, tried to grab them, yelling to be careful of the open blade, and to get off the tree before they shook it naked.

"Ver, let them play."

"Uncle," Veronique stopped her chastising duties and crossed her arms. "*I* was never allowed to jump on the tree."

With that, Henri defaulted to his older sister, Elena. She gave the boys her best mothering look and told them to get off the tree. Veronique smiled with justified satisfaction.

"Another successful hunt," Josie said to Henri, breaking away from the group with a smile that could put the world on hold, "and my boyfriend takes the kill. I don't get to see you be the outdoorsman often enough."

"How often would you like to see it? I'll make it happen."

"I'm sure," she said with a tease before turning her attention to the fallen tree. "Veronique, help me bind this thing."

"I'll get sap on me," she said, looking at the tree with distrust.

"If you do, I'll let you stick it in your uncle's hair."

Josie flashed him a devilish grin and Veronique was sold, kneeling with the roll of string at the ready. His father hovered, offering all his Meyer family advice on tree binding, while his mother and sister continued their detached oversight of the whole process. The boys started to wrestle.

Henri carefully wiped down the axe's blade as his father coached on how to lay out the string and push down the boughs. Then his father tested Veronique on the special tree-tying knot which could survive being dragged through a warzone, if necessary. By the time they were prepared to start the third string near the top of the tree, Veronique was whining for him to just let them do it on their own.

With the tree now bound and ready to be dragged back to the car, Henri's father gave the nod to the boys to help him do the dragging. They jumped at the request and practically started running away with it, its needles leaving soft scratch marks in the thin veil of snow. Their shouts echoed through the forest as they tried to run with the tree bouncing along behind them.

Henri's parents and sister headed out after them at a much more relaxed pace while Ver began singing a popular new remix of "Vive le Vent." She was a good singer, her talent born in her younger years. She'd been convinced that if she could sing well enough, she could join the Christmas Eve choir and wouldn't have to go downstairs when she was old enough for the Gift. But she'd been old enough last year, and her voice hadn't been able to save her.

Rather than following right behind, Josie kept Henri back until the group disappeared ahead of them. "I want you to myself for a bit," she said, admiring the axe slung over his shoulder.

She hugged his arm as they slowly walked back up the trail, listening to the crunch of their boots, the stillness of the air, and the dissipating sounds of the talking and singing up ahead. This was one of the things Henri missed when living in the city: the ease of escaping into the tame outdoors. In the city, ten minutes would get him stuck in traffic. Ten minutes here, and he escaped from it all.

They broke through the tree line, and on the horizon below, Henri could see the train heading north. It rolled past their station without slowing. No one was leaving today.

This forest, Henri thought as they left it behind, was the same forest that Alex had told him about earlier that day. Somewhere in it was a hunter's lodge decorated for Christmas waiting to receive the same three people as last year. And maybe two more? In theory, Josie could go there and come back again without anyone knowing. Henri would have to make an excuse as the group who waited out the Gift inside the church wasn't big enough to hide his absence. If everything went well then next year, maybe, Ver could go too.

Henri hadn't told Josie yet, but he had a second job interview in January with a bio-tech company based in Paris. If he got the job offer, he couldn't say no. He'd get his career back with a good enough wage to make for a decent life in the city. Paris was close enough that travel back home for Christmas wouldn't be difficult, but he hadn't found it in him to mention the job to her yet, and last night's conversation didn't help.

Josie leaned into him and kissed him on the cheek as they walked. "What are you thinking about?"

"You."

"Before I kissed you, silly."

"Us."

She smiled at him. "You felt so far away."

"I was just thinking."

"Want to think out loud?"

No, he didn't want to. But not saying anything wouldn't save this afternoon from spoiling either.

He must've taken longer to wage the debate in his head than he thought because she moved her arm to around his waist and hugged him in encouragement. Well, he thought, he was going to have to tell her sometime.

"I ran into a guy this morning, almost literally. He told me that every year he and his family leave the walls on the Eve and spend it in a hunting lodge in the woods not far from here, thirty kilometers out. The Gift doesn't follow them. They escape it." Josie dropped her arm away and Henri braced himself for exactly the type of conversation he didn't want to have.

"What's his name?"

"Alex."

There was pause. "Why did he tell you that?"

"The guy who was walking behind us last night after basketball? Same guy. He overheard us talking."

There was another pause, longer this time. "How do they get out?"

"He told me the north-west wall has a hole in it, hidden by a hedge of trees and some ivy. They park their car outside the wall in the morning, then leave through the hole after the gates have been shut."

"Do you believe him?" Josie looked up at him, her gray eyes almost blue in this light.

"Yes. No. I don't know. He's got a little girl. He wouldn't put her in danger."

They walked a little while longer until the sound of the boys' shouting reached their ears. There was a sharp drop in the trail down to the road where the car waited, so they were still out of sight. Instead of continuing forward, Josie led them to a nearby stone wall, and they sat down. The stones were frozen, uneven, and an edge poked into the back of his leg.

"I know I asked what you were thinking," Josie began. "I'm grateful you told me, but you were thinking about everything I'd asked you to forget. *Please*, Henri. I can't go with you outside the walls. If leaving was possible, Monsieur would've told us. Or Cuvelier."

"Would they though?" Henri asked, reluctantly committing himself to the conversation. "Other than Maria Peeters' husband and Iakob Courtellemont, you can't tell me that no other person born here, in the entire history of this village, has been outside the walls for the Gift."

"That is what I'm telling you," Josie urged. "Because if you had to go through the Gift like we do, you'd know. There's zero room for experimenting. You'd understand if you knew what it was like having *him* in your head, what it feels like having your body rot around you. We *die* every year!"

"I know!" Henri bit his tongue. He started again, more calmly. "I know. And I've asked others to tell me what it's like, but all I get is metaphors. So, for the last two years I've gone down to the hall. I know what's at risk—"

"You've never told me that." Josie said. The edge was gone from her voice.

"I think the choir is getting nervous about me going down so often." He tried to smile but it was weak. "It's . . . it's not an easy sight to see." A short breeze picked up, and while Josie readjusted her hat, Henri put his face into it, letting the chill air nip his cheeks. "Most of us who've seen the Gift only have the stomach for it once, and then everyone pretends like nothing happens down there. I dunno. I'm lucky I can still sleep at night."

"Then I guess that's the difference between you and me."

"You have to get away from here, Josie."

"You have to stop."

He could see the frustration welling in her eyes as she blinked hard and looked off into the distance.

"I don't want that to mean anything . . ." she said, "like, like an ultimatum or something—"

"Why would you even go there?"

"I . . . I can't let you keep going down this road. Nothing good is going to come from it."

Henri brought her in close. His intention to justify why he was still thinking about this by telling her about the Paris interview suddenly felt like incredibly ill-timed, so he kept his mouth shut. It was nicer to live in a fantasy where the potential of her agreeing to move to Paris still existed.

"The Eve is less than twelve hours a year," he said. "Twelve hours won't be enough to break us." Then Henri remembered an earlier thought. "What about . . . would you consider—"

"Henri." Josie warned him as she sat back up.

He held up his hands asking for some extended patience. "What if I can find someone else who'd be willing to go to the hunter's lodge with me? I trust Antoine, or Victor, if I can get him to stay sober. There'd be no risk to you or to—"

"There's every risk!" Josie burst. "I'm not going to leave with you, so stop trying." She stood up sharply and locked him in a firm stare. Tears were coming to her eyes. She didn't cry easily, and Henri didn't take their emergence lightly. "It's not just me I'm worried about, it's . . ." She stared at him hard, and Henri could tell she was fighting herself as much as she was ready to fight him. "Because . . ." She started again, "Because if you keep trying to figure out a loophole in the Gift, you're going to die."

"What? Babe, no, I won't die from—" He stood up to comfort her, but she stepped back uninterested, cutting him off.

"No. I'm going to tell you why, and you're going to listen." She wiped her eyes with the back of her mitten. "About a year ago I started having a reoccurring dream, the most real dream I've ever had, and don't you dare say anything about it being 'only' a dream and nothing more."

"I wasn't—"

"This was a warning, honest to God."

"I believe you!"

Another glare. "In the dream I'd decided to try and leave on the Eve with you. We were going to go to Paris, and I waited on the steps of the Notre-Dame du Seigneur while you went to the gate to unlock it for us. I waited, and waited, and waited, Henri. For so long I waited for you, but you never came back. I cried for God to bring you back and then I saw that the village had swallowed you whole. A green shadow hovered over your seat in the basilica where you would've—should've—been sitting . . . He took you Henri. You were trying to get around Nefas and he took you. And that's why you have to stop this. Maybe not forever. Maybe when I stop dreaming it . . . I don't know." She took a deep breath and looked up into the sky. "Henri, you have to promise me. The power behind the Gift is so dark, and it gives you so many thoughts and feelings that aren't even yours. Henri . . ."

He brought her into a hug, holding her close. "I promise. No Christmas lodge. No great escape. I promise." And he meant it.

The fact that they were going to Paris in her dream was enough to give him pause. The timing for telling her the news kept getting worse. He continued to hold her as he tried to come to grips with this stake in the coffin of his dreams until Veronique's voice carried up and over the hill, bored and impatient.

"Josie! Uncle!" Her head popped over the rise and she sighed dramatically when she saw them. She looked right at Henri and said, "Maman says that if you don't stop making out with her you're walking home *and* doing all the dishes for the next two days. By yourself." With the message delivered, Veronique promptly turned about and went back the way she came, calling over her shoulder, "we've been waiting, like, half an hour for you two, and that's after the tree was loaded!"

That made Josie laugh, and Henri had to laugh too. There was nothing like a teenager to change the mood. Josie began to clear the tears from her face.

"It's not fair," Henri said lightly. "We didn't even make out and we're still getting in trouble for it."

"Well," Josie said with a small sniffle, "there's still plenty of hours left in the day."

Back at the car, the boys were already packed in the hatchback for a free ride back home. Henri and Josie squeezed into the back seat along with Elena and Ver. The car was chatty and loud, and Josie was squished into sitting both on him and beside him, responding to his mother's conversation only when she had to.

Henri paid little attention to the women's conversation or the bantering of the boys or Ver watching something on her phone. His thoughts were empty. His eyes and ears were empty. Like his father driving, he became lost to everything except the passing landscape, happy to reside in nothingness for a couple minutes. It was safer that way.

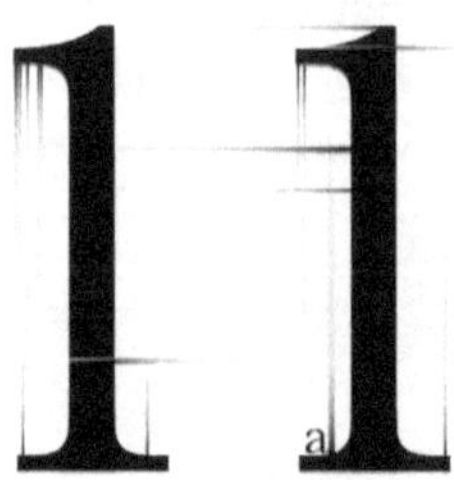

Fae rubbed her eyes with heavy fingers, letting her head fall into the empty space behind the office chair. The thundering sounds of Tchaikovsky's *1812 Overture* were pouring into her ears, the current song on her randomized playlist; it provided the anti-soundtrack to the la Rue surveillance videos. Knowing firsthand the dark mind behind everything she was watching, it was the music's job to prevent, or at least lessen, the creep which scraped at the base of her skull as she watched the days and nights speed by in fast forward.

The camera trained on la Rue's façade was more than enough to capture the message Nefas wanted to keep alive: he might be handcuffed and his corpse family hidden underground, but he was not to be forgotten. Like a helicopter's blades moved the air around it, so too did Nefas' presence create a storm around him.

Fae didn't specifically know what she was looking for, so she decided that the last two years would provide enough video to scour through, including last night's footage as Maël had suggested. Based on their conversation with Katie that morning, Maël wanted to learn more from the visitors firsthand, so he'd asked Elise to take his place as Fae's tape-watching support. Together they were currently watching the conclusion of what was a two-month span of small wildlife dying in collective groups at the mouth of la Rue as though in offering. Earlier there'd been a foggy night from March that both Fae and Elise had to skip over. The timestamp was around 2 a.m. when the fog started to move and swirl about as though someone was walking through it. The autonomous movement continued until the fog began creating faces. Seeing one or two could be dismissed as the brain finding familiarity in the undefined, but dozens of crisp, unique faces in various states of anguish could not be so easily dismissed.

Fae reached for her glass of water, but when she tried to drink, her stomach closed off. She set it back down.

"Do individuals keep track of everything that happens?" Fae asked, as Elise reached for her water as well.

"Maël could tell you more accurately of our, and his, record keeping habits, formal or otherwise," Elise said. "The generation who remembers la Rue is smart enough to ignore what happens as best they can. The younger generations call the area haunted, but not everyone believes it is. A few years ago, our version of a sheriff had to get involved with a couple of teenagers who wanted to find out if la Rue really existed. They drilled holes in legitimate walls but didn't find the façade."

"We're designed to fear the unknown, but it still attracts us." Fae shook her head. "What psychologists wouldn't do to get their hands on some of you."

"What I wouldn't do to stay out of their hands," Elise said humorlessly. "Nefas inserts himself into that space between fear and thrill. It's why he's so dangerous." She flashed a quick, helpless smile, and stretched her arms out with a crack. "Ever since the r28 arrangement we've done our best to bury and filter the Gift to allow more people to live as normal a life as possible. I'm dreading the day when that decision will catch up to us."

They continued to watch a little longer until the next song on the playlist began playing and Elise actually cracked a laugh. It was the first time Fae'd ever heard Elise laugh.

"What?"

"This playlist."

"This playlist," Fae defended herself, "has been highly randomized to help change up the brainwave frequencies while watching this footage; to help disassociate the visuals from emotion."

Elise laughed again. "It's only that 'Do-Re-Mi' turned into Axl Rose singing about that sweet child of mine, and now backstreet is back."

"Wait until the Bavarian yodelers turn up," Fae offered. In truth, there was an actual possibility of yodeling being on the playlist.

Elise calmed herself with a few last escaping sounds of amusement before she returned to her resting face of polite professionalism, maintained even when there was no need to keep such form.

The rest of the October and November footage was quiet, minus a few cars stalling in the same spot. But as the nights continued to grow longer, the first snows and winter rains began to fall, and the timestamp sped closer to Christmas Eve, Fae slowed the speeding footage down. The night of what used to be Nefas' big parade of himself as the lord-of-all-desires alongside his family of corpses was not something she wanted to see. It was, however, not something she could rush through if this viewing party was going to serve its purpose.

A reimagined rendition of "In the Hall of the Mountain King" took over the speakers. It was a version that smoothed over the iconic staccato bars for an unnerving affect, and Elise moved to change the song but Fae stopped her. She could make it through this.

Nefas' show began early in the morning of Christmas Eve. A golden retriever trotted by with something drooping from its mouth, a toy maybe. Soon thereafter it trotted back the way it came still holding onto whatever was in its mouth. And then it trotted by again, and so it went for about five minutes back and forth until finally the dog dropped to its haunches and sat next to the wall shifting its head nervously about, whatever it held swinging from its mouth. It didn't sit there long before it gave a sudden jump of surprise and ran off limping, leaving the object behind. The delivery completed, Fae and Elise both recognized it for what it was: a doll.

It wasn't until later in the day when a group of adults walked by that one of the women stopped and arranged the doll so that it leaned up against the façade. The woman couldn't have known to do it, but the doll's face was aimed directly at the camera. It was an old doll with disheveled hair, and the face was losing its paint. As night fell the light from a nearby streetlamp saved it from the consuming darkness.

At one hour to midnight, about the time when the Gift would start coming to life, one of the doll's arms began to slowly slide up the wall. It moved so slow and so smoothly that Fae didn't notice it right away. She waited until she heard Elise startle before she bumped up the speed of the video. At the faster speed, it was much easier to see that the sick little abandoned doll was waving at the camera, up and down, up and down.

The words from Nefas' texts earlier that day flooded back into Fae's memory, and she tried to focus more on the music as she began to feel really disquieted. The doll's face was changing while it continued waving, its platonic smile beginning to spread across the width of its face. Its eyes steadily grew larger like two ink spills, the corners of the grinning mouth reaching up and meeting the edge of the eyes. Fae was about to turn away from the screen, not trusting herself to keep watching, when the camera feed was suddenly interrupted. The digitized image froze and distorted, glitching and seizing. It lasted for a couple of seconds before the image stabilized. Fae swore, turning away from the screen. A shadowed figure was standing in the street.

"It's not him. It's OK." Elise said softly. Fae nodded, having just as quickly come to the same conclusion. Nefas was barred from coming out. It wasn't him, but she still had that gross feeling in her stomach. Fae changed the song to something poppy and with lyrics she could sing to as she forced herself to look back at the video, ready at any second to leave the room entirely.

The figure in the street began to wander away out of camera shot and only then did Elise quietly explain. "The Jandreau ghost. He still looks for his family to rescue him. They're all dead."

"I've heard the story."

The Jandreau ghost wandered back into camera, his mouth moving in what looked like a repeated call; no sound came with the recording to know for sure. He then disappeared back up the street again.

"It happened only a few years after you, maybe a year and a half before the r28 arrangement," Elise said, only loud enough to be heard over the music. "It devastated all of us. The survivor, André de Boer, said the two of them had gone in as far as the pit. Iakob broke after that. He hadn't even had the job of Monsieur for a year and he took full responsibility for losing Adrien and his family. Why Nefas went after Adrien's family too, no one knows."

The doll was still waving, its face now a completed, disturbing image of evil, and the dark shadow of the ghost of Adrien Jandreau continued wandering around. At some point the ghost had picked up some mittens to wear.

"Iakob knew Nefas like the rest of us," Elise said sadly. "He knew better than to blame himself, but he still couldn't handle it. As far as anyone knows, nothing like that had ever happened before. Iakob left the village, and I believe only Maël has managed to contact him."

"I'm sorry," Fae said genuinely. While Fae had never met Iakob, she knew that he'd been a close friend with Maël. Maël had never mentioned why Iakob had exiled himself, just that he had. Other than Elise, who wasn't able to take Drechsler's position after he died, only Iakob had willingly agreed to take on the role. And that alone was enough to speak for the strength of his spirit before it was broken.

But that's what Nefas did. He broke people. And then kept what was left for himself. And once something is broken, the fracture lines never go away. That was why Elise could never be the Monsieur and why Fae was scared to death of being here. Nefas had broken her too, and he knew exactly how and where she'd been broken. If she ever encountered him again . . .

Between those thoughts and what she was seeing on screen, Fae began to feel light-headed. *Deep breaths, Fae. Deep breaths.* She steered her thoughts to Nicholas, who was the one who'd helped her escape Nefas. Physically, Nicholas had been a baby, but he was Nefas' biggest weakness; Nicholas overrode Nefas. But still . . . deep down Fae was concerned. She knew where Nefas was, could feel him waiting for her, but Nicholas was . . . well, absent. She didn't even know how, or if, he would be here for Christmas Eve.

Remember, fear will kill you in this place.

Fae cleared her throat. She was leaving tomorrow and none of this mattered.

The Jandreau ghost came back on the screen and, staying in the shadows as best he could, picked up the doll and looked up at the camera. He said something that Fae couldn't make out, and Elise didn't have any better luck. The screen crackled again, the digital image scrambled for a couple of seconds, then the image was restored and the Jandreau ghost, and the doll, were gone.

"That's pretty convenient timing again," Elise said.

"Yeah." Fae's heart nearly stopped as a thought hit her. She let out a slow groan and stopped the video on what was now an empty street. "Elise, how far into la Rue did you say those two boys went?" The horror of her thought dropped a heavy brick in her stomach.

Elise frowned. "André de Boer said they found themselves at the pit itself."

"When I was here for the Eve, why did you choose the pit as the place to trap me?" Fae pressed, then quickly added, "I'm sorry, I don't mean to bring up the past. What I really want to know is what your understanding of the pit is. What do you know about it?"

Doing a poor job hiding her discomfort, Elise said, "the pit was always as much myth as anything. There are many stories, but few facts. I found out from Drechsler that the pit was kind of like a door between Nefas' world and ours, that the escaping earthly gases could affect memory. I admittedly made a lot of assumptions about what Drechsler told me and my own research on Earth's gases. The idea was for those gases to affect your short-term memory."

Fae's poker face to this first-time insight must've been non-existent because Elise's own expression hardened.

"You asked and I told you honestly, not because the stupidity of it has passed."

"I'm sorry," Fae said, only to move the questioning along. "The past is the past," she said, as much for her sake as for Elise's. Fae got out of the chair and walked to the window. "The boys went into the pit," she clarified.

"Yes," Elise agreed. Her phone began to ring just then, and she excused herself.

Fae went back to the security footage, no longer interested in Christmas Eve, and fast forwarded the video looking for another instance of the feed cutting out.

The Jandreau boy had gone into the pit. And then was never seen again. His family brutally murdered days later. And yet his "ghost" still came out.

The Jandreau ghost came from the pit.

No. Adrien Jandreau came from the pit.

Of course he did. Because Adrien Jandreau was still alive. Nefas was keeping him alive, buried in the pit.

January, February, and March of the next year, the current year, sped by as Fae focused on looking only for the video to scramble again. There! The timestamp read April 28th, just after three in the morning. The video feed cut out and Fae slowed it down. The same digital scramble happened as before, cleared, and then Adrien appeared on the screen as if out of nowhere. He walked off and didn't reappear for twenty-two hours. Which meant that Nefas allowed him day trips into the village. Why? To torture him with his lost life?

When Adrien came back, he was sporting a new jacket and Fae rewound the video back to when he first appeared and ran it frame by frame. She saw nothing so she did the same thing for when he disappeared. And there, in the scrambled image, she found exactly what she didn't want to see. She stopped it as soon as she saw it, staring at the image. In the middle of the scrambled feed was a fraction of a second that hadn't been perfectly disrupted. Frozen on the screen was a blurred, but unmistakable, image of Adrien Jandreau scaling up to the overhang in her façade.

Adrien was very much alive.

Fae pursed her lips, a rush of tears flooding into her eyes. They were tears of anger as much as they were of complete devastation for Adrien. "You monster," she said, letting a hot tear fall onto her cheek. She could imagine the dark grin of satisfaction that was probably on Nefas' face right now as he thought of her finding out his little secret.

She heard Elise finishing up with her call, and she hurried to grab a screen shot for Maël before shutting the video down. She had what she needed, and Elise shouldn't know about this before Maël.

Elise came back in and took one look at Fae then back at empty screen. "Are you okay? What about the pit and the boys?"

"Do you know why Maël suggested looking into last night's footage?"

"There was a report of the Jandreau ghost making an appearance . . ."

"God." She took a second before trusting herself to speak. "I need to talk with Maël first." Elise understood. "I'm done," Fae confirmed as she made sure the system was turned off. "I'm meeting with our English friend tonight, and I promised Maël's boys some Lego time beforehand. I need a couple minutes to collect myself. Thanks for staying, Elise. This can't be much easier for you to watch."

Elise put on a brave smile. "Anything for the good of my home."

Fae smiled back, and thought wryly, *that same attitude was half the problem twenty-eighty years ago.*

12

The bartender put a square cocktail napkin on the worn bar in front of Fae, then the squat, clear glass followed.

"Cranberry and," the bartender said in French, pausing for dramatic effect, his eyes full of hidden surprise, "ice. It's on the house."

Fae had to smile as he winked at her. It was actually the perfect drink, considering it was non-alcoholic and she was sitting at a bar. But now that she had it, it was exactly what she'd wanted. She'd made a good choice letting this young bartender surprise her.

"Thank you." She took a drink, the tartness rushing over her tongue. It tasted good.

"You're not from here," the bartender said, and Fae shook her head as she took another drink. "Neither am I. I'm Max."

"Fae," she said, nodding her head in greeting. "What brought you here? Parents move?"

"I'm helping out for a bit." He nodded to the bar space that he currently inhabited and flipped a bottle of Vodka in the air as he put it away. "Where are you from?"

"Canada. I'm visiting a relative."

"Oh?" The young man looked interested but then received an order of drinks and excused himself. He expertly grabbed one blue bottle from the shelving behind him, then drew a few draughts, poured some wine. He was fun to watch, Fae thought. He wasn't a professional, city-style entertainer, but he was confident in his movements, and he clearly enjoyed what he was doing.

He also reminded her of someone. She'd seen it as soon as she sat down. She couldn't place him though, and that made her watch him even more closely. He was of average attractiveness, kept his black hair well cut, and had naturally tanned skin which gave him a Mediterranean vibe. His constant facial expressions said as much as his mouth did. Black jeans and a fitted plaid shirt that reminded her of home rounded out his image. It was a welcome mystery to distract her from the day she'd had. Max caught her studying him, but she knew her expression was neutral, so she didn't mind. When he was finished with the order, he came back over.

"Do you want another one?"

Fae looked down at her almost-empty glass, the ice cubes swirling around on the inside like a carnival ride. "Better not. If I'm not careful, I'll be tipsy before my dinner partner arrives." She tipped back the glass finishing the last traces of juice before pushing it away. He gave her some club soda anyway.

"I know I'm probably not the kind of person you want asking life questions," Max began, leaning on his side of the counter, "but, I'm pretty sure psychiatrist is part of the role of a bartender, am I right?"

Fae raised her eyebrows, then took a chance and switched to speaking English. "Did you learn that by watching re-runs of *Cheers*?"

Max laughed and responded in English as well. "I spent some time in Montréal and Boston." He switched back to French. "You look kind of stressed."

She personally would've used a stronger word like "neurotic," "traumatized," or even "unstable," but "stressed" was accurate enough. "The holidays can be pretty different around here."

"I noticed. The last couple of days, wow, it's all over everyone's faces. I thought little villages were supposed to be relaxing."

"Has anyone told you about what the holiday traditions are around here?"

"Should they have?" Max scratched the back of his head and laughed, the sound light and cheerful. It caught Fae's ear, and she wondered again why he looked familiar.

"Probably. You should ask someone else though. I'm not the best person to tell you."

He accepted that answer and began wiping down the counter around them. That's when Fae noticed a unique necklace rolling around on his chest where the buttons at the top of his shirt weren't done up. "If you don't mind me asking, what's around your neck?"

Max fingered the woven hemp string and pulled out a small vial that could contain no more than a few ounces. "What do you think it is?" He dangled the vial from his finger and brought it closer so she could take a fair guess. It looked strikingly similar to Cuvelier's vial, almost exactly like a smaller version of the same thing actually.

"Is it sand? From a vacation?"

"A popular guess!" He smiled in approval. "It's dirt. As in the 'we're all dust of the Earth' kind."

The sound of the front door opening, and a draft of cold air rushing in, announced Katie's arrival. Her cheeks were flushed as she scanned the room looking for Fae.

"Looks like the other half of your party is here." Max nodded his head toward the door. "Go ahead and seat yourselves. I'll make sure the waitress finds you. Upstairs has been reserved."

"Thanks. And thanks for the drink."

He nodded with acknowledgement and Fae slid off the stool, waving at Katie as she met her coming in. Who *did* he look like? It was in his eyes, that much she'd managed to isolate. They held her attention like a fascinating painting.

"Katie, hi." Fae put on her best professional smile, confident in her ability to keep the two sides of herself separated for an hour or two. It was the one side embroiled in the anxiety of knowing that Nefas was waiting for her and knowing that a dead man was actually alive versus the real Fae Norris-Peeters, the person she'd fought to keep alive these last decades of her life.

She'd gotten pretty good at compartmentalizing.

"Hi." Katie smiled as Fae Peeters found her from the bar. Katie began to offer her hand in a shake, then thought better of it having already met this woman once today, but felt rude taking it back, so she offered it again with an awkward laugh.

"Don't worry," Peeters told her, playing Katie's fumble off coolly, "it's informal tonight. Here, there's a table by the window."

Grateful, Katie followed Fae's lead, navigating around the tables and chairs. The Luxembourg was a comfortable place, Katie thought. It wasn't dark like a pub, but it was lively enough to be one.

As they both took their chairs Katie began to ask, "So, you live in Vancouver," but then Peeters also began to say something at the same time, and both stopped in deference to the other. *For the love of King and Queen,* Katie thought with a painful sigh. She made herself laugh lightly and opened the napkin on her lap.

"Why don't you tell me more about this project you're working on?" Fae suggested. She'd changed clothes since that morning, still jeans but now a fitted, brown long-sleeve, perfect for any occasion. Katie couldn't help but like her even more. She had every right to be the kind of person who wore only designer turtlenecks and didn't know how to drink beer from the bottle. But she didn't come off like that at all.

"Can we start with how you'd like to be called?" Katie asked.

"By any portion of my name," Peeters told her, flipping open the menu. Katie did the same. "'Fae' gets us to where we want to go faster though, so if you're OK with first names, go for it."

Katie nodded her thanks, and it was with a new-found sense of ease that she began telling Fae about the contract she was working on for a coffee table book. She told her about her employer and how she almost didn't take this job because of them. Then she told her about how she'd studied marketing but was a coffee barista to support her photography. Fae appeared interested in what Katie had to say, so she kept talking, and it was only when Fae was half-done her food that Katie realized that she'd done all the talking. Not wanting this to be one sided, she started to ask her own questions and soon they had a flowing conversation.

Katie discovered, with no surprise, that Fae had deep chasms of knowledge and insight.

"The thing about natural light," Fae was saying, "is that it makes people happier. It can make any space look more alive, feel freer. But light needs to be harnessed to help achieve the purpose of the space. If you just let in as much light as possible without a purpose, you've really only created a fancy fishbowl. Humans want to feel secure, free, and alive, so it's my job to harness this gift of natural light to let people feel all of that. If they feel free, they can be creative. If they feel safe, they will let themselves be challenged. I aim to remind people of who we are as humans by showcasing the very qualities that brought us to where we are today: tenacity, inquisitiveness, mercy, strength, love. If I can do that with a building, these places where we can spend up to sixty or seventy percent of our day, then I've created something where we're free to unleash our human potential."

It was another world Fae lived in, Katie thought as she listened to her answer each question. The well-practiced person Katie had met at the door had come alive with a deeper energy that could only come from someone talking about their passion. Even though Fae joked that architects were the starving actors of the engineering world, there was no doubt that she loved what she did. Katie had finished eating, but that gave her more time to listen without distraction.

"I read somewhere," Katie said, "and I'm going to get the quote wrong, but you said something like, if all you're doing is taking lines from paper to reality, then a great opportunity has been lost to encourage the human race toward greater potential." Fae nodded in recognition of the statement as she took a bite of food. "That kind of makes you an optimist, doesn't it?"

Fae took a moment to finish her mouthful before shaking her head. "I'm a realist. I put all my positivity into my designs to prevent me from becoming a pessimist." She smiled. "Every building has a purpose, but creating a building purely on function is flat. As a photographer, you know that a building can have a life of its own and is its own type of art. Not all art is pretty, but all art conveys a message. Modern art, and so modern architecture, can be interesting and impressive, but to the wrong audience it can also be thought of as unrelatable and cold. It gives people something to look at, but not everyone will feel something because of it. What I've found is that a more universal art expression is found in the past, a past that is already part of who we are as a human race, and so is identifiable and comfortable to everyone on some level."

"Do you think that you're a bit of a lone crusader in your approach though? I see a lot of buildings going up and most of them are either built cheap, or as a statement piece like modern art."

Fae thought the question over for a minute as she finished her plate. "It used to be," Fae said, putting down her fork, "that a building of any significance was supposed to tell a story. It could've been how great a personal achievement was, how great a god was, or how important the city was, whatever. Today, resources are more abundant than ever so the stories architecture is able to tell should be greater, but instead, the opposite had happened. People are no longer interested in telling universal stories, and it's a small tragedy. I don't think I'm a lone ranger, but I'm not in the majority. I'm sure there'd be a lot more of us if the demand were there."

"Is that what you want your legacy to be then?" Katie asked. She hadn't meant to turn this meeting into an interview, but it had certainly turned out that way. Fae didn't seem to mind, and Katie was really interested in what Fae was telling her. "You're one of the few architects, who I know, who have really brought the 'classical' back into neo-classical design, if I'm using that term right? Everyone has tried to replicate the beauty of the Greeks and the strength of the Romans, the Americans especially. Your designs don't only retell those stories though, they emit emotion of their own. How do you do that?"

This time, Fae's thoughtful pause was longer. The sounds of the Luxembourg faded back into Katie's world and she realized that the patrons had gotten a bit louder since they'd sat down. The background music had been all but drowned out.

Very simply, Fae said, "To share emotion you have to know what triggers it. What I do with my job is as much about inspiring as it is about defying. Maybe that's one of the reasons I come off as an optimist?"

"Is that . . ." Katie hesitated. "Is that something you could elaborate on?"

Fae shifted her gaze out the window into the street. A man was trying to walk his dog; it was doing more peeing than walking.

"I was always drawing as a kid," she started, giving her attention back to Katie. "I started drawing houses because I thought that if I could control the area where I lived, then I could control how I felt, and how other people felt and acted. It was like playing with a dollhouse, but the house was more important than the dolls. Whenever I got stuck some place I didn't want to be, I imagined myself somewhere that could make me feel different, or make someone act different than they were, and then I would draw it."

The waitress came by to clear away their plates and ask about dessert. Katie waited to see if Fae was going to order anything.

"Do you have mixed fruit?" Fae asked in French.

"Oui. C'est très bien."

Fae nodded, indicated two orders, and the waitress left.

"So, tell me, Katie, how was your afternoon?"

"Good." Katie nodded. "I did some shopping, went inside the church. I did run into the professor again," Katie added on excitedly. Fae raised an eyebrow. "Oh, no, never mind though. I didn't tell you about him. It was Maël."

"The man in Reims who told you to come here?" Katie nodded. "Maël told me that someone suggested you come. You saw him again?"

"I did, outside the church. We crossed paths, and, you know, I didn't see it in him before, but he's amazingly inspiring. It was like I could see into his eyes, not poetically, but actually, and, blimey." Katie struggled to find the perfect word to describe the man who should be let free upon the world like a Socrates or a Hawking. "Some people you just have to get into their presence to understand how exceptional they really are."

Speaking openly about him stirred up the same unexpected sense of loyalty that Katie had felt earlier that day, and she felt elevated, purposeful even. "You wouldn't happen to know his name, would you?" Katie asked, knowing it was a long shot. "Do you know the professor I'm talking about?"

Fae shook her head. "I don't know that many people here. But tell me more about him. It sounds like he's quite the person. What's his subject?"

"You know, I don't know. I'm not even sure he's a professor, but I have to call him something," Katie admitted. "I was hoping to find his name to see if he has any books or something online I could follow."

Fae smiled lightly but it wasn't hard to see that she was only being polite, and that irritated Katie. She didn't know why, but the fact that Fae didn't share her fascination with the professor was almost . . . offensive? That was a harsh word, but it felt right.

"He must've had some interesting things to say then?"

Katie wasn't entirely sure what to say. Should she tell Fae about going to the façade? It *had* been a public area, and she really wanted to know about those photos. Whatever Fae had meant by this village having "personality," they qualified.

"He told me where to find the façade," Katie said casually.

Fae fumbled the spoon she'd been toying with and it clattered to the table with a loud noise as it hit the water glass. "I'm sorry," she apologized, resetting the spoon away from herself. "That's OK. We just generally don't want people to know about it."

The waitress came back with two glass bowls of mixed fruit soaked in citrus juice. She set them down and walked away, but Katie didn't pick up a spoon to enjoy the sweet medley. Neither did Fae.

Katie inhaled deeply. "Do you know if your façade's been enhanced?"

Fae frowned. She picked up her spoon and casually began picking at her fruit but not eating. "What do you mean?"

"Well, some cities and large companies have projectors that run interactive programs for the fun of people walking by."

Fae nodded her understanding of the technology.

"Has anything like that been installed here? On that façade, or in the room where we were this morning? The mirror in there was changing my appearance, making it waver and . . . you know, change."

"Not that I know of. It seems a bit out of budget for a place like this. How was your reflection changing?"

"I looked like, well, death," Katie said with a forced laugh. "Something any quality program or app could do. I swear it winked at me."

The passion that had charged Fae earlier was gone, noticeably so. The lights overhead dragged her face down; she traced the rim of her desert cup with her spoon. The motion was calming to watch, though Katie had a feeling there was very little calm in the action itself. Katie found herself fingering her phone, which she'd put beside her in anticipation of showing Fae what was on it. She locked eyes with the older woman, an air of expectation hanging between them, and Katie didn't have to be asked to show what she had.

She found the first picture in the sequence of photos and handed the phone over to Fae. As she looked, Katie explained.

"I was taking some photos of myself to send to my parents. A man passing by offered to take some for me, and I couldn't say no." Katie watched as Fae slowly looked at one picture after another and her expression became absolutely unreadable. Katie didn't know what that meant so she kept going, speaking a little faster. "There was nothing on the wall behind me when these were taken, or before, or after. If there's a projector or interactive screen, then that explains everything, except for the bloke with the poor humor who programmed the thing."

Fae came to the end of the photos and gently handed the phone back.

"This qualifies as a small village quirk; doesn't it."

"Yes." The corner of Fae's mouth twitched. "You'll have to excuse me a moment. I need to use the washroom." She got up and disappeared to the back of the restaurant.

Katie looked at the time. They'd been here for well over an hour, and the group in the back corner had gotten louder. She opened the pictures again and flipped through them slowly, one at a time, trying to understand. The only thing that bothered her was the questions these pictures left her with. What was going on in this place? And did she want to be part of it?

She picked at her fruit and wished she remembered more of the video she'd watched in the library. The man with the code name was one of the reasons they'd been meeting in the first place. Peeters had been clearly distressed in that video. Maybe that handsome blondie who'd photobombed her last photo was the delinquent hacker and also owned the funny code name? She was on the edge of something much more complicated than what she'd signed up for, and as long as she wasn't going to get in trouble, that was kind of exciting, in a forbidden sort of way.

13

The slightly intoxicated young woman coming out of the bathroom stall didn't wash her hands, and she'd barely cleared the bathroom door before Fae threw herself back against it and flipped the deadbolt locking herself inside, alone and shaking.

". . . forty-four, forty-five, forty-six . . ." Light-headed, heart pounding, she felt like throwing up. She could barely breathe; the world was spinning. Fae gasped, the air being sucked in sounding high pitched to her ears. Nefas, he was . . . Nefas had . . . another high-pitched gasp as her lungs strained.

The bathroom floor. It had patterns of ceramic tile—pasty yellow, light blue, white. Somewhere in the random mix there had to be a logical pattern. She had to find it. ". . . forty-seven, forty-eight, forty-nine, fifty . . ." Her counting got faster, not slower.

Two yellows, a white, a blue, another two yellows, a blue. That wasn't it. Her knees were shaking violently, and she slapped her hands over them so she didn't collapse. "Fifty-one, fifty-two . . ." Two blues on diagonal. No, that wasn't it either.

The shaking creeped upward and reached her stomach, replacing her insides with a tumbling rock. Her core tightened, intensifying her shaking until she was almost convulsing. "Fifty-three! Fifty-f-four! F-fifty-f-f-five!"

She couldn't stop shaking, her body wouldn't stop. She collapsed to the cold tile floor, her hand landing in a small puddle.

"Oh, God!" She closed her eyes and curled in on herself. "J-J-Jes—" *Just breathe, just breathe. Breathe . . .*

She managed to suck in a deep inhale, but she couldn't let it out properly and began choking.

"Jesus!" *Breathe in . . . breathe out . . .* She could do that, she could breathe. *In . . . now out.*

"He's been contained. He can't get out. He's not allowed out." Somehow he'd managed. ". . . Fifty-six, fifty-seven . . ." No, no. He could manipulate and distort, he could use avatars, like Katie's professor, but he hadn't gotten out. "He's not allowed out. The arrangement."

He'd been looking directly at her in the picture. He'd called her his queen. He hadn't forgotten a thing. He was waiting for her and wanted her to know it.

Fae's stomach started heaving. *No, no, no, no. Please don't throw up. Please don't.*

Her insides tightened again ahead of another convulsion. She gritted her teeth against it and groaned, "C'mon!"

The fact that he'd even dared to come so close to breaking the rules only emphasized the immediacy of Nefas' intentions. Of course he wanted Katie, but Fae was his prize. She was going to be his queen, enthroned atop a pile of destroyed bodies and dead souls. When she'd left him, she'd left him nothing but embarrassment for his efforts, and he'd never let her live in peace for that decision. Fae was Maria Peeters granddaughter, and it was Fae who was supposed to be the one to build him into streets and plazas across the world.

Remember, fear will kill you in this place.

Breathe. In. And out. Fae managed to stop convulsing, but her knees were still twitching and shaking, and her body was so tight and contracted she didn't dare try to unfold herself. Warm tears fell down her face, leaving cold trails before hanging off her chin and falling onto her jeans.

My beauty in your soul. This will end. I am here, my runaway queen. And then he looked at her. She didn't need a picture to see those eyes, to feel them drawing her down into his void, so deep that time and space meant nothing, that light was a memory too foreign to recall. The void was so intoxicating it satisfied every deep craving she didn't even know she had.

Her heart was pounding in her throat and her stomach lurched hard again. She groaned down into her chest so her voice wouldn't echo off the empty walls.

"Fifty-eight."

Her insides began to relax a bit.

"Fifty-nine."

Another deep breath.

"Sixty."

A few more deep breaths and her seized muscles loosened. A shudder of release rippled through her and she slowly unfolded herself to sit back up.

Fae rested her head against the door, exhausted. Her eyes fell shut and she remembered the choir. The most beautiful singers ever to grace the earth, their voices could bring both tears and strength. What she wouldn't do for just one member of that choir to come and sing to her now.

From her position of hiding, crumpled on a public bathroom floor, Fae had to face the irony that she'd come so far in proving that Nefas wouldn't rule her life anymore only to end up here. Like this. And she knew she couldn't walk out of this bathroom with fear-stained tears shadowing her cheeks. She had no strength in her at the moment though, so she focused on simply breathing.

It took a few minutes and someone rattling the door to get in, but Fae found it in herself to struggle to her feet and hobble to the sink, stretching and easing out all the tension from her joints. Her knees were tight, but they would support her.

The reflection that stared back at her over the water sodden sink was rough. The pot lighting seemed to deepen the lines in her face, and she thought she looked every one of her years plus another ten. Her eyes were tired, her hair had gone wild like a bad case of bedhead, and her lips had dried.

Smoothing down her hair, she sniffled and set her jaw, staring deep into her reflection. "I dare you to try." With her palms leaning on the rounded edge of the counter, Fae waited for something to happen. "Come on, do it," she challenged. Or mocked. "You can't, can you?"

Her image wavered and flickered for a blink of an eye, but nothing changed. There were no skeletons or corpses waiting for her in the mirror. "My soul's not dead anymore. You *can't* control me!"

And then in a flash, Fae saw herself in her mind's eye breaking the mirror with the nearby garbage can. The glass splintered on the counter and into the sink, sharp pieces scattering on the floor. She picked up one of the larger pieces and walked out of the bathroom. Passing the diners and the drinkers, she marched back to her table, and called Katie's name. Katie turned around and Fae slashed at her throat leaving a dark red gash across her neck. There was cathartic release as she watched Katie's eyes grow wide, blood pumping through her fingers that were clutching her throat. Fae smiled with deep satisfaction.

"That's not my thought!" Fae snapped, ripping herself out of the dark vignette. It was no more her thought or desire than had been the time when she'd imagined suffocating her neighbor and then sleeping with her neighbor's husband. It was one of the many things Nefas had suggested to her over the years, each experience so extreme it fit Nefas' nature that he'd thought them funny. She didn't know how he could keep dropping ideas into her head. They were like ripples from his void, that drug-like mental state he'd breathed into her and had somehow been able to keep haunting her with; they were like ripples that continued even without their epicenter.

"You're that interested in Katie?" Fae stared back into her reflection, wanting to pierce through the divide separating herself from *him.* The fear had shifted so seamlessly into defiance. Thanks to her younger years of flashing the middle-finger to everyone and everything, Fae knew what was going to come out of her mouth next, and she could already feel the regret.

"You can't have her."

There was nothing else to be said or done. Fae unlocked the door, tidied herself up, and sent a message to Maël to pick her up. The thought of falling exhausted onto her bed was consuming as she walked out of the bathroom and navigated her way back to the table where Katie was waiting patiently.

"I'm sorry to keep you waiting," Fae said taking her seat, the fire from her challenge still burning. "I had to take a call." Conveniently, their waitress walked by, and Fae flagged her down for the bill. "Something's come up I need to handle right away, so I'm going to have to call this. I have the bill, don't worry about it."

Katie looked like she was going to protest, but Fae stopped her. "Maël and I would like to offer you the opportunity to see the underground hall. You really need to see it in use to understand the design. You won't be able to photograph it, but," Fae added quickly, seeing the hesitation on Katie's face, "I think you'll be able to appreciate it." Fae felt a little guilty for the misdirection, but she was more focused on keeping Katie out of Nefas' reach than being perfectly transparent. "I know you were a bit nervous this afternoon about how and why these projects exist, but I promise no mafia or terrorist syndicate is involved." Fae smiled with a tease. "The only downside is that because of the type of storage the hall is used for, I can only let you in late on Christmas Eve, so you would have to exchange time with your family for this. It is a place that means a lot to this village; it will change you."

Katie laughed, no doubt thinking she was still teasing. "My parents really want me home . . ."

Dominic, Fae thought quickly, *you and Nicholas had better come through tomorrow.* "It's nothing beautiful, but like we talked about before, it has an important message to tell."

Katie took her time, a consideration for which Fae was glad. Christmas with family was always a bit sacred.

"This is a once in a lifetime chance?" Katie asked.

Fae nodded.

"I'll catch the first flight out in the morning and be home before brunch. Maybe I'll have a run-in with Santa along the way."

And just like that the wheels were set in motion. If Nefas had his eye on Katie, then Fae would make sure she didn't get the chance to know him. She hoped that Maël hadn't had a change of heart about wanting to show her the Gift.

"Why don't you give me your number, and I'll contact you tomorrow with details for the site visit. There's a local woman named Chantal who's experienced in telling the history of the village who will meet you." Katie agreed and as they exchanged numbers Fae continued. "It was the right thing to show me those pictures. If it helps, your welcome to this village is pretty tame. My first visit, they tried to kill me," Fae told her in a did-you-know kind of way. It was such a ridiculous claim; there was no way Katie would believe her, so Fae felt OK with the revelation. The way Katie laughed, Fae knew she didn't suspect anything other than it being a joke.

"Lovely," Katie responded, and Fae could've thought she was sharing afternoon tea, not trading veiled truths as dry humor to a girl who Death himself had zeroed in on. "Seeing scary pictures seems like a good deal."

"It'd be best to stay away from the façade too. New faces stand out and there's no need to draw attention to the site." Fae paid the bill and the two of them stood up, put their jackets on, and got ready to part ways. "And let's try to find out more about your professor," Fae added. "See if I can't help you learn a bit more about who he is."

Fae had no doubt she could help Katie learn a whole lot more about her professor.

Katie promised she could find her way back to the hotel, so they said their goodbyes. With Katie gone, reality started to sink in about what she'd done by positioning herself between Nefas and Katie. Max called out a farewell as she left, but she was too overwhelmed to give him much of a goodbye in return. Once outside she slowly paced back and forth while she waited for Maël. The night felt off, wrong, misaligned. Like the world was disjointed.

Maël pulled up to the curb and opened the car door for her from the inside. Cozy warm air from the heaters welcomed her in.

"How'd it go?" he asked.

"We need to go to the Notre-Dame du Seigneur."

"That well."

Fae barely gave a nod as she settled in for the short drive.

Peaking above the roofs of the village, the six spires of the basilica were lit from below in alternating red and white lights, lighthouses to her soul. They couldn't get there fast enough.

"Nefas is showing up tomorrow night."

Maël cast her a long look sideways as he accelerated into the streets. "Sounds like you've learned more than I have today."

"Did you learn anything interesting? What of the Texans?"

He shook his head dismissively. "They know nothing about the Gift. I have no idea if they're going to be helpful or not. They kept asking me when the best time is to go to the EU headquarters to pray for America."

"What did you tell them?"

"A three-hour drive north to pray for Europe was acceptable at any time provided they could do it in at least two European languages." He paused for dramatic effect. "They asked if American English and British English counted as two different languages."

"I'll believe you," Fae told him.

Maël chuckled and, as he stopped at a stop sign, looked over at her. "They're honestly nice people." Fae could only shake her head. His attempt to lighten the mood faded away.

"We have eleven visitors not including yourself," Maël said, refocusing the conversation. "The most we've ever had for Christmas before was a family of three. Now, the two families from Brussels are interesting. I played tour guide for them briefly. Nice, but private; they're here together. One of them is connected with EU Foreign Affairs, the other with Regional Affairs. They're here because they found a travel blog advertising the most unique Christmas experience in the world and are understandably confused by the lack of tourism to support such a claim. They gave me the website, and while it initially looks legit, it's an amateur site. I reverse-image-searched the author's photo and it's stock. Only a dozen posts, the last one being from August, and with the exception of our village, it only covers large cities that are easy to write about."

"And no idea who's behind it?" Fae asked.

Maël shook his head, and Fae didn't ask about whether or not he'd decided to invite them to witness the Gift too.

Arriving at the plaza, Fae couldn't help but marvel yet again at the little basilica. Its three Gothic portals and doors were still lit in candy red, casting dramatic shadows, while the Renaissance body of the church was as bright as the stars and moon. The mash-up of styles was the fascinating result of a generational feud between builders, and while it was beautiful during the day, it was captivating at night.

They crossed the plaza and went up the stairs and under the archivolt, the story of Jesus' ascension to heaven depicted on the right side, and a much darker story of redemption on the other. She didn't have fond memories of the piece and refused to look at it as she hurried inside, unable to resist a quick shoulder check, fighting that being-stalked feeling. The door's evergreen wreath softly banged against the door as Maël gently clicked it shut behind them.

The basilica was empty. A few low burning candles still wavered on, sputtering from the stirring air as the two of them passed by. Low wattage lights around the outer walls gave enough light to navigate by, but otherwise the basilica was wrapped in shadows. Fae led them randomly to sit in the middle of the pews.

It was so quiet. She could hear her heart beating and the wind pushing against the paned windows outside. It was safe in here. Nefas wasn't allowed inside, couldn't see her. If she closed her eyes, she could fall asleep right now as carefree as a puppy in a blanket.

"Maël, there's something I never told you that you should know." She spoke quietly not wanting to disrupt the silence. "I didn't tell anyone before because I was never sure if it was real or if it was just Nefas messing with me. And, and if it was real, there's nothing anyone could've done."

She stopped before saying anything more. She just had to get this over with.

"When I was captured in the pit, there were other people in there with me. Other bodies. Buried deep in the gravel. Nefas somehow kept them alive, buried for his use, whenever, or if ever, that might be. I uncovered one of them, a German soldier from World War II. When Dominic came to get me out, Nefas made the soldier fight him. There were other people in there too, below me, grabbing my ankles and trying to pull me in. I don't know how many."

She managed to look over at Maël, wondering what he was thinking, not really wanting to know.

When he did speak his emotion was sheathed. "I have the responsibility to keep the people of my village as safe as possible in all things concerning the Gift. You should've told me Nefas has a storehouse of human beings stolen away for his private purposes." He frowned. "Even if you thought it was only a trick, you should've told me."

"I'm sorry. I don't even know if Drechsler knew," she said quickly, hoping to lessen the revelation. "Though, that man knew more than he would ever tell. The thing is, I don't think Nefas can preserve them past their normal lifespan. When I first uncovered the soldier he was young, the age he would've been in the war. Within minutes he'd aged to an old man, the age he should've been if he hadn't been buried. Nefas could have dozens of missing and unaccounted for people in that pit, and because they'd die within minutes of being uncovered, he just keeps them there. Not dying and not living."

Maël frowned even more, the deepening shadows making him look so severe. "Why tell me this now?" he asked. "His parasite can't use dead people." As soon as the words left his lips, Fae saw the dread of realization come over him. "Adrien." He shook his head almost as if to beg her not to confirm his suspicion. "What was on the footage?"

Fae pursed her lips. "I noticed . . . something. When the Jandreau ghost appears, the video scrambles." Maël shifted in his seat to look at Fae more directly, nodding agreement. "I slowed the video down, and in one of the instances, for a split second, I saw Adrien jumping up to the top of the façade. He must've made a hole or something, but I can almost promise you that Adrien Jandreau is not dead. Nefas is keeping him alive, buried in the pit, and he's let out whenever Nefas wants."

"Fae," Maël said, "he could've been saved years ago if—"

"No," Fae told him firmly. "How would you have dug him out? That pit is like quicksand. Even if you helped him escape, Nefas would've found someone else to take his place. Everything has to be a choice with Nefas, no matter how strong-armed and deluded that choice is. He probably had Adrien's family murdered as part of the process to force him to stay."

"They should've been protected."

"I don't know why they weren't. But this cause and effect makes the most sense."

Maël nodded shallowly. "I've always suspected there was something more behind the ghost, the video scrambling all the time. I never saw anything when I looked, but I didn't expect . . ." Maël let his head fall. "I don't know what I expected. Iakob should be told. He was one of my best friends, and I haven't heard from him in ten years."

Fae hated Nefas so much.

"Let's make sure I'm right first."

They put their attentions elsewhere for a while then, taking in the spectacle of the light and dark playing out on the pillars of the basilica, and the ceiling with its soothing pattern of white rosettes in golden squares.

"People believe the ghost is just one of Nefas' haunting tricks," Maël soon said. "They live their lives without another thought." Even though he spoke softly, his voice still carried in the open space. "Now they're going to learn that he's not a trick after all." Maël turned and faced the front of the basilica, leaning his elbows on his knees and keeping his eyes forward. "There's more though, isn't there? Your supper with Katie. My people couldn't find her until midafternoon."

Fae nodded, and she turned to face the front as well. She rested her arms on the back of the bench, and let her head hang wearily between her arms. She spoke to the ground, which allowed her to speak at a more normal volume. "She saw that professor again this afternoon. He wouldn't give his name, and she knows nothing about him, but she's bewitched. It's Nefas."

"One of his, what did you call it?"

Fae rolled her head up and rested it on her arms, looking horizontally at Maël. "An avatar. I don't know if that's what it should be called, but it fits. He told her where to find la Rue." She paused before she kept going. "While she was there, a man passing by took some pictures of her like a good citizen helping a tourist. Nefas left a message in those photos, writing on the façade behind her. He said . . ." Fae took a deep breath and powered on. "He wrote, 'my beauty in your soul. This will end. I am here, my runaway queen.'"

Fae wasn't sure what Maël would think of the last part because he didn't know the type of relationship Nefas had manipulated her into, but he didn't react one way or the other. He just kept listening. "In the last picture Nefas left an image of himself. He was looking right into the camera."

Fae had barely finished before Maël sidled over and she sat back into his hug, so thankful for someone she could talk to.

"How did you react?"

"Badly." Fae studied her hands, spinning her wedding ring around her finger. It made her wonder how she was going to talk to Jordan next time he called. "Katie did see her soul reflected in the mirror this morning. She believes everything she's seeing is because of computer programs and projectors."

"Each generation to their own."

"I got mad at him, Maël. He can't have her. I told Katie to stay for the Gift." She pulled herself out of his side hug and shifted in the pew to look at him directly, not afraid to show how she felt—at least, in here. "I think it was a huge mistake. I can't be here for the Gift, I just . . . I have no idea what Dominic was thinking."

"That you're ready for this."

"Maël, she thinks a creeper with a computer is messing with her and that her professor is some sort of Ghandi. You thought I had a problem wrapping my head around the dangers of the Gift? At least I knew something unnatural was going on."

Maël ran his fingers through his hair. He was quiet for a couple moments. "When all of this plays out tomorrow night, most of us will be locked up downstairs and there's nothing we can do once the Gift comes. I'll tell Cuvelier and Chantal, but we'll have to be careful who knows. Whatever Nefas is planning, you're part of it. I *need* you to stay. Please."

She stared at him hard, her anger spiking. She got up and walked away, leaving Maël sitting there alone, probably just as scared as she was but for different reasons.

The pillars that divided the outside aisle from the nave were large enough to make her feel separated from her troubles, and Fae slouched against the backside of the stone, needing the moment to herself. She found herself in front of a simple wooden table covered in a light-colored cloth. A hand carved Nativity sat on top.

The Nativity was everything to this village. That baby, more specifically, was everything, and to her as well. He was her Nicholas. He'd saved her from Nefas, and it was Nicholas who'd allowed her to get this far in life without losing herself to Nefas. She needed to keep reminding herself and believing that silence on his and Dominic's part since arriving didn't mean that they were abandoning her. It only afforded them the opportunity to show up fashionably on time.

Though early would be nice.

After that ominous encounter with Nefas on the train when she left this village for the first time, Fae had prepared for the worst. She'd barely slept and never with the lights off. There were no mirrors to be found in her life and she refused to look in any reflective surface, even a pond. When nothing happened during those first weeks she'd started to hope that her student life would return to normal. But it didn't. She was in the drafting room late one night in February with only the janitor to share the evening with when she both heard and saw him at the same time.

His voice was like ocean waves on a rocky beach and was as enjoyable as being dropped into an ice bath and stabbed with a hundred needles. He wandered past the drafting room door.

"I've missed you."

He'd waited in the hall for her to finish, then calmly accompanied her home, sitting beside her on the bus, then leaving her outside her apartment. She remembered very little of that walk home, having long ago suppressed the memory of it. He'd waited for her again the next afternoon, looking different, but the horrendous chill he gave off was unmistakable.

From then on, he'd kept waiting for her to walk her home after her lectures, internship, drafting hours, or drinks with friends. He was always there, always looking different, but unable to hide who he was. Fae didn't remember what she said to finally make Nefas leave, but he did. At least for then. What started that February night began an endless siege of Nefas trying to get what he thought was still his: her.

The frequency and intensity of Nefas' attempts to interact with her decreased over time. The problem was there was *always* a next time. A voice in her ear. A face in the crowd. And every time he showed up, he asked the same thing, as if he honestly wanted to know: What happened to Dominic? Where did Nicholas go? Nicholas had snatched her away from Nefas once and continued to protect her by his name, but where Nefas wouldn't leave her alone, it felt like Nicholas had. She hadn't seen him since that first Christmas Eve. And even now a black thought pulled at her: had the time finally come when the threat of Nicholas was no longer enough to hold Nefas back?

It was the echoing ripple of the void that fueled her doubt. Even though Nicholas had taken it out of her, Nefas still used its shadow to give her a poke. Like the idea of slitting Katie's throat. Sometimes the ideas were less insane and much more tempting, and she'd considered what would happen if she ever acted on of those thoughts. Would her actions void Nicholas' protection?

She had to get rid of every trace of the void once and for all. She couldn't go home tomorrow. Even if she still didn't know where Nicholas was.

Fae focused back on the Nativity in front of her. Baby Nicholas. The name Nicholas meant victory for the people. She had to believe that he would be so again. For her and for this village.

Maël came up beside her. His face was grim.

"I'm sorry," he said, joining her in watching the Nativity.

"Something positive has to happen from all this . . . right?" Fae looked at him expectantly. This was, without a doubt, one of those times when the responsibility of the Monsieur weighed heavier than he would ever let her, or anyone, know. It wasn't fair. But what in life ever was?

"We don't put our trust in a sadistic god, Fae. Otherwise, what are we doing?" He reached forward and adjusted the Joseph figure, which was out of place. "Everything our God does is for a good purpose, and if it's not, then he isn't behind it. Sometimes that good means asking more from us than we could ask of ourselves."

They continued to stand in front of the Nativity a while longer before they were both ready to go, and then they left the basilica behind knowing that tomorrow night they would both be there again but for very different purposes: Maël, to die. Fae, to survive.

As she closed the door to the car and buckled in her seatbelt, she let her tired eyes rest on the Basilique de Notre-Dame du Seigneur, hoping against hope that she was going to be able to spend Christmas Eve in the midst of the choir's song, hidden safely within the walls of the basilica.

Tomorrow. It seemed so foreign, so unknown, and yet she would wake up in the morning and it would be there.

Maël put the car into reverse, and as they pulled away from the Notre-Dame du Seigneur, she saw a tall man with white hair and a white winter jacket walk outside and stand at the top of the stairs watching them drive away. Dominic. It was Dominic. He was here.

She was too tired to be outwardly happy to see him again, and his presence doubled as a harbinger of what was to come. She kept his sighting to herself as she let her eyes close, the rolling sound of the car against the paving stones lulling her into a partial sleep. They'd be back at Maël's house shortly, and she was going to need every last minute of sleep, so she didn't waste it.

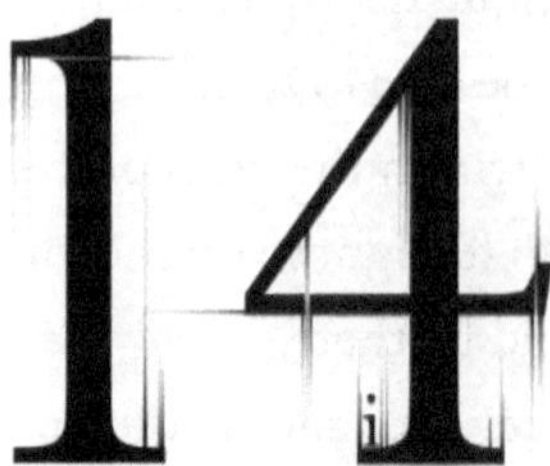

Henri had grown up seeing all sorts of Christmas Eve traditions. Everyone in the village had their own way of coping with the dread of the coming Gift, trying to keep themselves sane for as long as possible; some were healthier than others. But as far as coping mechanisms went, Josie had one of the best.

In a quiet side street beneath the shadow of the basilica, Henri sat on the edge of a drained shell-shaped fountain, his legs wrapped protectively around Josie who was leaning back against him. They were laughing at videos of cats being jerks and puppies being dorky, their furry cuteness muting out the coming darkness. Henri nuzzled her neck as they watched and every couple of minutes she would twist around and kiss him in turn. It was as much Josie's happy place as it was his.

Henri hugged Josie closer as they watched a Doberman sulk at a fist-sized kitten sleeping in his bed. She turned around in his hold to face him, the plight of the Doberman left unresolved. Her breath was warm against his skin in the damp air, and he was eager to do whatever she needed to take her mind off what was coming.

Josie pulled her head back to look Henri in the eyes, her fingers running through his hair. She stared deeply into him and Henri marveled. Here, honestly, was his other half.

"God, I love you," she murmured before leaning in to kiss him, her lips tickling the stubble on his face.

And it was then that he thought, not for the first time, that he should ask her to marry him.

"What time is it?" she asked, tracing his jawline.

He checked. "Just after nine-thirty. When do you have to go?" She turned back around in his hold so that he again held her from behind.

"In a couple of minutes." They started watching the videos again, dogs who couldn't catch things, but she wasn't paying much attention. The doors to the hall were opened now, and the villagers were being divided between those who went in and those who didn't. "Ever make a promise you wish you could take back?" she asked.

"You won't feel that way soon. This girl you're meeting . . ."

"Ellie."

"Ellie needs you, her first year with the Gift, too embarrassed to have her parents with her. She asked you to be with her because she looks up to you. You'll show her how to be strong." Henri returned his attentions to her neck, but she arched away.

"Can I tell you something?" Henri's response was muffled but she continued anyway. "Sometimes I wish you'd been born here too." Henri stopped what he was doing. "Then we could go in and out of the Gift together, holding hands like the sweet, old couples do. Knowing that in the morning I don't have to search for you upstairs in the crowd."

"You always know where to find me. On the left at the fourth pillar."

"You're too literal sometimes," she said, turning in his arms to face him. A smile pulled at her lips. "Now, shut up and gave me something to remember you by."

Henri did as he was told.

Their farewell was cut short when Henri's phone began ringing. It buzzed and vibrated, and they both very willingly ignored it until it rang back again twice in rapid succession. Unable to ignore it forever, Henri fished it out and saw that Veronique was the one to blame. He showed the ID to Josie.

"Why did you take so long to pick up?" Veronique demanded when he answered. He had the urge to tell her how equally irritated he was at being interrupted, but she didn't give him the chance. "Unbelievable. Where's Maman? I've been trying to get a hold of her and Papa. I thought the signal shutdown already happened. You need to come and get me."

With the greatest of pains, he indicated to Josie that she had to give him some space. "Why aren't you with your parents? Where are you? Do you know what time it is?"

"Yes! Why do you think I'm panicking? The Gaudets haven't come back. They said one hour, one hour to watch Lou, and that was two hours ago. You're the only one I could get ahold of!"

Henri stood up. "Ver, the gate is already closed, why did you wait so long?" Josie looked at him with concern and he could only shake his head.

"I told you, I've been trying to reach someone for the last hour! I can't walk that far to the gate carrying Lou, he's too heavy. The Gaudets must have his stroller in their car."

"Didn't someone try to get hold of you before they closed the gates?"

"I don't know," Veronique said sharply, like she was explaining something to him for the fiftieth time. "I couldn't get a hold of anyone, so how could they reach me? It's not like anyone came knocking at the door like they should've! Useless guards. Besides, don't you think the Gaudets would've gotten the same message?"

Henri paced a few steps before turning around, looking at Josie sitting in his place, hair so soft he could still feel it through his fingers, a little tussled. . . *Focus!* He looked at the time again and saw that his last five minutes with her were up anyway.

"OK, I'm on my way. Call the North gate. Tell them you're still outside and that I'm coming. They'll probably be pretty mad, but tell them to call Monsieur if they want. I'll do the same in case you can't get through."

"Thank you so much. Hurry!"

The line went dead, and Henri went back to Josie. He tucked her hair behind her ears, and she looked worriedly at him. "I don't like how that sounded. There's something off." She kissed him with finality, tampering with his priorities. "You need to go."

Henri rolled his eyes, not at her, unable to help himself. "The Eve is always 'off.'"

Taking her hand in his, they left their little spot, the urgency of Veronique's call forcing them out. They exited onto the main road and then into the plaza, which was coming under a layer of fog. It did nothing to lessen the growing unease.

Though still early, small clusters of people were starting to make their way into the basilica, either through the basilica upstairs, or through the back door and into the crypt directly. Others hung back not ready to commit themselves quite yet. Henri took Josie to the back door and hugged her close one last time. There was a very old prayer that his mother used to send him and his sister to bed with every night, and this was now his Christmas Eve tradition to Josie. "May the Lord bless you and keep you. May you find his bright face shining on you." He decided to adapt the rest. "Remember that his peace calms your soul and protects you from fear. You never walk alone."

"Henri." Josie clutched his jacket in her fists. "Come straight back with Ver and that child she's watching." She stared at him intently. "Drive dangerously if you have to. Just do whatever you have to to get back here as fast as possible. Something's really off, and not in the normal Eve kind of way. I have a weird feeling."

"I'll make it back," he promised.

She still held his jacket. "Find your sister, or her husband, they can't be far. It's . . . it's like I can't let you go."

"Josie," Henri looked at her earnestly. She wasn't like this, was never clingy. Was her dream really plaguing her that badly? He noticed a girl hovering nervously nearby, and he figured it had to be Ellie. "There's a kid over there who needs you to help her through tonight. And Ver needs me. I'll see you in the morning, by the pillar." He backed away, Josie letting his jacket pass through her hands until he was out of reach.

He hated leaving her like that, but neither of them had much choice.

He'd parked a block away, and as he jogged, he fumbled around for a number to the North gate. He tried calling it. Busy. Hopefully, that meant Ver had gotten through. He didn't know if the gate had ever been opened once it had closed, but the guard couldn't refuse. Henri jumped in his car, revved the engine to life, and called Monsieur, just in case.

This stupid village, Henri thought once he hung up with Maël. He sped through the streets, annoyed, angry. He had to balance his driving with the need to not run over anyone walking to the basilica, which only annoyed him even more. In any other place in the world this situation wouldn't even be a thing. He growled out his frustration as he decided to ignore an empty four-way stop.

The Eve posed the greatest internal conflict for people like him who didn't have the Gift, who weren't born here. They were helpless as nearly everyone they knew was taken over by the great, mysterious Nefas. Meanwhile, they got to experience the safety and peace of heaven itself through the choir, which for Henri at least, wasn't enough to overcome the guilt of watching his friends, or Ver, or Josie, disappear into that hall. He tried to relieve the guilt by finding out as much as possible about the experience, but no one wanted to share much.

The Gift was supposed to be a demonstration of good against evil, light against dark, but if no one saw it anymore, what was the point? Monsieur, Cuvelier, the bourgmestre—they all knew how to hide the village's open sores so well that no one from the outside world would know anything was wrong. The only demonstration was that of the choir preaching to itself—literally and figuratively. Sure, there was always that one person every ten years who stumbled into the freak show, but the ROI wasn't enough to justify keeping the Gift around.

Because of *one* night a year, this village could never become famous for producing a great athlete, or artist, or business mogul. He'd always told people that his hometown was Gennevaux rather than here. It was a place so small most people hadn't heard of it, and if they had, there was little to talk about.

Henri arrived at the North gate in the same bad mood the guard was in. They had a standoff about whether or not he was going through the gate, and in the end, it took a second call to Monsieur and a promise to be back in twenty-minutes before Henri finally won. The drive to the Gaudet farm was about ten minutes and he called Ver to tell her he was on his way and she better be ready.

The car bumped hard as it hit a pothole in the unmarked road. Henri grimaced thinking of his shocks, but he didn't let up the pedal, his memory more helpful than his headlights in navigating the bumps and holes. Thankfully, the fog noticeably lessened as he left the village behind. His drive was marked by Christmas lights on an outdoor tree, or a lit Nativity at the end of a driveway, and he turned corners blindly based on distances from this Nativity, or that row of bushes.

The Gaudet's was the fourth house and the third field and he braked hard in the semi-circular dirt driveway, inadvertently sending a spray of mud and small rocks toward the front door. Leaving the car running, he jumped out. Veronique was waiting for him and she met him halfway, baby—almost toddler—Lou in her arms, his travel bag dangling from her shoulder.

"Let me take him," Henri said, not giving her the option as he took the boy. Relieved of her burden, she stopped and began fixing the bag, double checking the contents of one pocket, stuffing something else in the rest of the way. "Come on!" Henri urged from the car. "You should've checked all that already."

Veronique glared at him but had the sense to jog the rest of the way to the car, slipping into the back seat, doing up her seatbelt, and opened her arms to receive the boy. Seeing that the two of them were secure, Henri hopped back in and took off, a little more carefully this time.

"Are you mad at me?"

Henri looked into the rearview mirror. Ver was eyeing the back of his head while trying to calm Lou, who wasn't settling.

"I'm annoyed," he said. Lying to teenagers was always counterproductive. "I'm annoyed at the situation though, not you."

"I'm sorry for making you come and get me."

Henri sighed internally, making every effort to guard his emotions. "It's not your fault. It's just a bad situation. I'm glad you got hold of Claude at the gate."

"He was really rude."

"You were asking him to break the rules. Monsieur had to talk with him directly before he even let me out to get you." The drone of the engine filled the car, and now that they were headed back toward the village, Henri began to calm down. "Why did the Gaudets need you tonight? That's really last minute."

"They needed to go to Rochefort for whatever reason and Lou's car seat broke when they were putting it in."

The fog had gotten thicker again coming back into the village, and the light from his headlights danced on the water particles in front of them. He slowed down even further, which was probably closer to the expected speed limit. His caution immediately paid off as part of the road had crumbled leaving a deep rut dropping into the ditch. He smoothly swerved around it.

"Hey, someone else got stuck outside too," Veronique observed as she looked out the window. "Maybe it's the Gaudets? Slow down."

Henri was already slowing down, looking toward the village wall. Someone was running toward them out of the foggy darkness, waving their hands to get their attention, and it wasn't either of the Gaudets. It was that man he'd met yesterday, Alex, and he was coming from the north-west side of the village where he was supposed to be hiding.

Henri had every inclination to keep driving as though having never seen Alex. There was too much that was questionable about him, and for a man who was supposed to be keeping his Christmas Eve getaway secret, Alex was drawing a lot of attention to himself.

"Uncle, stop!" Veronique demanded and Henri instinctively did.

Maybe Alex really did need help.

Alex approached the driver's door, his trapper's hat still covering his head, his mess of a ponytail swishing back and forth as he jogged. He'd lost the sunglasses. Henri locked the doors.

"I know this guy, Ver, don't worry."

"Then why did you lock—"

"For Lou's sake," he said quickly, hoping that would stop her questions.

Henri rolled down the window, and Alex nodded toward the backseat. Henri shook his head. No, she didn't know about the great escape. Alex leaned in like a curious kid.

"I figured your car would be the only one out here."

"Do you need a ride back in?"

"Your girlfriend has been trying to get a hold of you. Something's changed. She told me you were out here and to flag you down on your way back."

"See!" Veronique jumped on Alex's information with a pure sense of validation. "I told you the phones weren't working properly!"

Henri ignored her. He studied Alex hanging off the door. He had an earthy, dusty smell coming off him. How would he have run into Josie? And what could've possibly changed since he'd left that she *had* to reach him right away? "What did she tell you?"

"She's not telling me anything. It's for you only. Come on, I'll take you to her."

"Why didn't she come with you?"

Alex put his hand on the door handle as though to open it for him. "I told her to wait."

Josie wouldn't have done that. If she had to tell him something so urgently, she would've outrun this guy.

"There's still enough time to get everyone back to the basilica," Alex said. "Come on. You'll see what we talked about at the same time."

Lou was getting fussy, and Veronique was digging blindly through the bag. "What did you guys talk about?" she asked.

"Nothing," Henri said. He heard her unsnap a container lid. Lou grabbed at it right away.

"Maybe your house caught fire?"

As if his running imagination needed any help right now.

Alex laughed and dipped his head towards the backseat. "No, I don't think it's that. Who's the baby?"

Alex was eyeballing Lou with too keen an eye.

"The Gaudets' boy," Henri said.

Alex nodded, though if anything, Henri thought he looked disappointed. "Look, it'll take five minutes. If you don't trust me, whatever, but I'm telling you, your girlfriend is waiting for you, and not exactly patiently."

"Uncle, we don't have a lot time to get back to the gate. Claude—"

"Thank you," Henri said sharply, the tug of war playing hard on his thoughts.

It was the nagging thought of *what if* that was eating at him. What if Josie really did have some really important, time sensitive thing to tell him? What if she had left Ellie, or had brought Ellie with her, to track him down knowing he'd be coming back through the gate? It wouldn't be impossible for Alex to have run into her.

"C'mon," Alex said. "We could've been there and back by now. Your house could be burning down." He winked back at Veronique, but Henri didn't see any glint of a friendly tease that should've accompanied such a gesture.

Frustrated, Henri rolled up the window and ripped the keys from the ignition and Alex stood back. Henri turned in his seat to Veronique and handed her the keys. The girl's eyes grew wide.

"What time do you have?" he demanded.

She fumbled to find it amid her coat, the child, the bag, and everything. "Ah, 10:15."

"Damn. This is getting close. Ver, if I'm not back by 10:25, drive to the gate without me. Drive right to the Notre-Dame du Seigneur. You'll have to take Claude with you."

"I thought you said not to worry!"

"Buckle Lou up in the back, drive slow, and careful."

"I've only driven once! And that was with Papa telling me everything!"

"There's no other cars around, you'll be fine." He put the keys into her limp palm and got out.

"Why not bring them along?" Alex suggested.

"No," Henri said firmly. Alex shrugged; like a teenager who didn't care.

Henri began the run through the fog, his feet crunching in the crystalized snow pellets that hadn't melted. Alex kept up, taking the lead once they got to the hedge growing in front of the wall. He took them through it and then pulled away the ivy growing up the wall revealing a small, roundish hole, as advertised. It was pitch dark inside, a place void of any light, and a stale, cool air wafted out.

"Where's Josie?"

"Inside with my wife and daughter. Follow me." With surprising athleticism,

Alex hopped through the hole and Henri heard his feet tap down on the other side.

Henri steeled himself and ducked into the hole, his sense of sight completely and immediately erased.

"Alex?" It definitely sounded like an enclosed space.

"Straight ahead. Path is clear."

Cautiously shuffling his feet forward, Henri's eyes adjusted to being blind. He only went a couple feet before Alex touched his arm to let him know where he was.

"How can you see in here?"

The sound of heavy hinges being turned came directly in front of him, and a luminescent green light shot out from around all four edges of a door.

"Because I exist here." Alex swung open the door the rest of the way revealing a wall of green fog swirling restlessly. It didn't escape over the threshold.

Henri bolted back for the hole but ran straight into Alex who moved to block his way. From the light of the green fog Henri saw a tear slip from both his eyes.

"I am so sorry."

Grabbing Henri by the jacket, Alex flung him through the door, then followed, slamming the door shut behind them.

Henri stumbled into the fog, feet skidding until he stopped, frozen. He didn't even want to breathe. The fog had an independent movement, gliding over his head, swirling down his legs. A deep sound like that of distant bees buzzed around him.

He was here. The one whose name was barely uttered. The keeper of death and the birther of sins.

Henri's heart was beating with the urgency of tribal drums. His breaths were short. He frantically wheeled around to escape and saw Alex, who stood motionless. Lit in the green luminescence, his eyes looked as lifeless as ever. Henri made a grab for the door handle, but something unseen pushed him back before he could touch it.

"Alex? Alex, you need to let me out . . ." But maybe Alex *was* Nefas! Henri defensively backed away from both the door and the ponytailed man.

Henri searched madly through the thick fog for an escape. Why was it so hard to breathe? Like trying to breathe with a forty-five-kilogram weight on his chest.

There! Another door on the other side of the room. Henri charged for it and ripped aside the cold, metal slide lock with both hands. With a grunt of panicked effort, Henri yanked open the door and rushed forward.

The floor suddenly disappeared beneath him and Henri fought to not fall headlong into a hole, his arms waving wildly. He stumbled backward, saving himself, and sprinted back the way he'd come. He had to get out!

That would be unwise.

A voice, unlike anything he had heard before, spoke to him, tickling the back of his neck. A voice so confident, so perfectly pitched and harmonious with his own mind that he stopped running and let the last bit of his momentum thump him harmlessly against the exit door. He turned back around to face the green fog. He couldn't find his breath.

That voice hadn't been Alex's.

Run, run, as fast as you can. . . The voice swirled around his head, first on one side, then on the other. The buzzing was ongoing while the fog began retracting, forming itself into a denser, oblong mass. *You can't catch me . . . I'm Henri Meyer.*

Like a magician appearing out of his own smoky curtain for a big reveal, the shadowy shape of a man solidified behind the condensed fog. With two steps, it broke through and came into existence before Henri. The vapor trail that broke away with him was absorbed into his body while the remaining fog dispersed, giving its light to the otherwise lightless space.

"Hello, Henri," the form said. "I can see that introductions aren't necessary." He stepped closer, slowly circling him, looking him up and down. Henri could do nothing but stand there, paralyzed.

The form reached down and gently touched Henri's hand, trembling as if the moment of touching was almost more than he could bear. The form flinched, catching his breath in a gasp at the touch, and then closed his eyes with a little smile. "It's been so long . . ." he said, exhaling with a sound Henri didn't want to entertain. "Not as soft as she was though."

Henri couldn't let his eyes off this apparition, this thing, now a handsome man, standing with so much hubris in front of him. Every nerve in Henri's body was shaking like they were all wanting to run away from him.

"You can't keep me here."

"Can't I?" The form looked taken back and then laughed. "Maybe introductions are needed." He laughed again, darker this time, and the light from the vapor which had been reflecting off his eyes disappeared as the sides of his mouth twitched. "You, Henri, have a virgin soul, an alive soul. A rare combination to come to me. I very much intend to take it from you."

"You have to let me go," Henri said. Squeaked. "Nefas. It's my choice. Let me leave."

The man nodded. "It is your choice, isn't it." He turned on his heels, hands folded behind his back. "How vain and presumptuous of me to forget. Adrien, open the door."

The name caught in Henri's mind and he did a double take to the poor man Henri had known as Alex standing in silent obedience. Adrien *Jandreau*, Adrien?

"Oh, my dear Henri. Confused?" The green glow came back to Nefas' eyes as he smirked.

"But . . . but he died." Henri looked back at Alex. "You died."

"Clearly he didn't," Nefas said. "His family did though. I taught him how to play fetch, then told him how to catch you. The Gaudets are fine, by the way. I had them convinced that their boy was already at the basilica so they didn't bother going home.

"I'd asked Adrien to bring me two new friends, you know. Stay with me and you can bring the girl in, pick up where Adrien failed."

Nefas strolled around to where Adrien was standing and fixed his ponytail for him, then nodded toward the door. Adrien laid his hand on the handle and began to open it, deliberately, as though waiting for a last-minute change of orders.

Henri made a charge for the door, ready to force it open.

If you leave, Josie will never be free of the Gift.

Henri stopped.

"You're thinking you might have to leave Josie behind for a job," Nefas said, looking at him, green light playing in the shadows of his face. "How conditional." He smiled through cynically curved lips. "How can you think you're the man she deserves when you're not willing to be there for her when she suffers?"

Henri had to escape. He couldn't listen to this. And yet, he was tethered to the spot.

"Let me give you a taste of the Gift you've been wanting; it will be your Christmas present. But, if you'd rather leave, then I won't give you this present and I'll keep Josie for *every* day of the year."

"That's not possible."

Nefas moved quickly, pinning Henri against the door. Adrien leapt out of the way. Nefas was taller than Henri by a head, and he leaned down. "It is possible. Because I decide when to . . . come out."

"You can't—"

"You've wanted nothing more than to help her be free, but I'm the only one who can hold back my Gift. Don't bite the hand that feeds you, Henri." He backed off and turned away.

Seeing his opportunity, Henri raised his hand behind him trying to find the door handle. Nefas stopped, his back still turned.

"You're still thinking about leaving." He turned back around. "Good for you. Unfortunate though." He returned to Henri until their bodies were only inches apart.

"I don't think you fully understand what you're about to commit your girlfriend to."

Henri couldn't meet his eyes. He stared down at the ground. He felt so small, and weak . . . he had to leave.

Nefas' dark voice penetrated beyond Henri's ears and mind and straight into his soul. "First, I cut off their light." With a snap, Henri found himself in complete blackness. Nefas had his full attention. "Then their darkness I fill with perfect worlds, worlds where we can be together."

As Nefas spoke, Henri found himself in a gray, ashy, forest. He was seeing again but not with his physical eyes. The trees were well spaced. There was no place to hide, and he needed to hide. There was a snaking line of gray people, submitted and spiritless, curving through the trees, leading into a dilapidated shack. They were all ragged and broken, nearly lifeless with defeat, making them almost indistinguishable from each other. Nefas' voice followed Henri.

"In a stale breeze the songs of demons come."

On command, hellish shrills and haunting screams came wafting in from a distance. Human cries grew, coming out of the shack. Those standing in the line didn't flinch. He could see through the walls of the weathered shack to where the systematic processing of those condemned was taking place. Everything inside was metal and plastic. People without faces in blue plastic aprons were holding various instruments and needles. They were extracting these peoples' souls. The people cried, they shook, they begged. Henri yelled against it all, but the sounds of the people were in his head, and they couldn't be drowned out.

No one was coming out the other side. A chimney billowing thickly suggested why, with ashes falling from it like snow. Henri looked down to where the ash was settling on his shoes and he suddenly found himself caught inside the shack, head strapped to one of the cold, metal sanitarium chairs.

Nefas continued his narration. "Sometimes I give them a choice to be with me. And sometimes they die. Over and over again."

A blinding light shone into Henri's eyes and he shouted, fighting the plastic bonds holding him down. He squinted hard, and a featureless face came into view that eclipsed the impossible glare.

He was standing in the middle of a crowded rave. Penetrating sprays of laser lights cut through the stage fog, and people with wildly colored hair and black-lit neon clothes were pushing him in every direction. He was barely standing as it was, and he didn't just feel like throwing up, he felt like he was on the verge of dying. A foamy saliva drip slowly ran out of the corner of his mouth, and someone beside him was rolling up his shirt sleeve, tapping on his vein. A needle pricked his arm. *You've got one more in ya!* Someone shouted at him. No! No more! It was fire in his veins! He had to get it out! Scraping numbly at his arms and neck, he was drawing blood. Above all the noise he heard laughter. That diabolical laughter of—

"Nefas."

As fast as it all began, it was over and Henri was back in the chilled room with Adrien, the glowing vapor, and . . . *him.*

"Yes," Nefas smiled darkly still inches away. "Me. And imagine not hours of my playhouse but a lifetime."

Henri shook his head. "No," he said, weakened from the experience.

Nefas took a step away. "Celebrate Christmas Eve with us, Henri, and I'll free your girlfriend. I'll show you how to live life on the edge and I don't mean climbing up and down a wall. I know what you want."

Henri had fallen against the door, hearing, but only half-listening, his ears ringing, the echoes of his own yelling crowding his thoughts. He heard "show" and "life," and to that he agreed. Show what, he didn't know, but showing meant that he could *do* something.

Nefas looked at Adrien. "You're about to have a half-brother. He'll be everything that you aren't."

Adrien had no reaction other than to quickly glance up at Henri before looking back down again.

Nefas snaked one of his hands to the back of Henri's head clutching tight a fistful of hair. Henri jerked against the hold.

"I lost someone once," Nefas told him quietly. "I loved her from her first breath. I took my time with her, and she left me. I won't make the same mistake twice." Nefas leaned down and kissed Henri on the forehead, a trail of green vapor exuding from his parted lips. "Getting all of me at once may be . . . shocking." Nefas leaned in again and kissed his cheek. "And, Henri? I lied about keeping your girlfriend. I could never keep her past the morning. She's not mine to keep. But you are now."

When Nefas finished speaking, Henri saw himself face to face with Josie, her eyes dancing. "You trusted me, Henri," Nefas said, in Josie's voice. "I'll never forget it." With a little blow, green vapor eased out of Nefas-as-Josie's mouth and entered Henri's orifices, a cool stream of air being forced into him.

Henri tried to shake his head. "No…" But it was too little and too late.

Nefas-as-Josie let his free hand roam upward clamping down on the side of Henri's neck. With his peripheral vision, Henri could just see a growing green glow emanating from Nefas' fingers. Five sharp pinches at his neck jerked his head as an impossibly cold burn pushed its way inside him. Something was forcing its way into his body. Josie's lips met his, the vapor proceeding them, and he sucked it in, his pain and choking smothered by the lips covering his.

And then it all went black.

16

Lemmings. Little gerbil-like, suicidal fuzzballs popularly known to run off a cliff to mass death. Fae had learned that it wasn't actually dumbness that killed the lemmings, it was their inability to effectively navigate their migrations. They simply ran into perils they couldn't overcome. But that was nevertheless how Fae imagined the villagers as they went one by one down into the basilica's crypt: like lemmings falling off a cliff. Sitting alone in her pew, Fae watched as they passed in front of her, filing into the hallway on her left and then out of sight. From that point on, she mentally tracked their journey and, based on their pace, predicted when they would reach the wrought-iron gate at the top of the stairs. Then, *drop*. To their death.

It was a cynical thing to imagine. These people were unable to change their fate. They were all white faced, teary eyed, afraid. Some came holding each other tight, others came noticeably drunk. Most came with a quiet resolve. They'd done this routine for most of their lives, and there was a steely hardness that came with having to endure the same brutal thing over and over again. But Nefas had the ability to make anyone feel fear, and no amount of exposure could condition that away. And like the real lemmings, these people didn't so much blindly fall to their deaths as they just didn't have any another plan. They'd tried. They'd gotten Nefas locked up, and themselves too.

The night was wearing on fast toward eleven o'clock, and what had simply begun as a trickle of people was now a steadily moving crowd. As the villagers grew in number, so did the choir. Fae didn't notice them slipping in alongside the villagers at first. Like their presence, their singing also began unnoticed until Fae suddenly realized that she was surrounded by notes of pure, beautiful, warm emotion. They wandered through the pews and up the aisles, singing with the perfection of a people born with the same song on their lips.

One of the villagers broke out of the anonymous migration and came to her with a hesitant smile. He introduced himself as Julien, the once-teenager from Café Noir who'd been there when she had her first encounter with Lars Drechsler. Fae stood to greet him as he told her he was glad the rumor was true that she'd come back. After quickly introducing his family, he continued on his journey, down the hallway, and fell off the ledge.

Among those arriving, Fae also saw the choir director. She was a young woman sporting an unstyled mohawk. Her mentor was young as well and wore clumsy looking glasses, an out-of-style dress, and a small plush panda backpack. The enthusiasm she was showing the world couldn't cover up the fact that genetics had robbed her of a fair start in life. Both looked like the kind of people society tended to dismiss too quickly, though if that was the reason for them being chosen as the choir director and mentor, Fae had no idea. Theirs was a deeply personal journey.

Fae stifled a yawn and pulled out Cuvelier's mystery vial from her pocket. The curvature of the glass caught the flame from the nearby torch in an almost mystical way. She hadn't learned anything more about the vial, but she'd brought it with her so she wouldn't forget to return it. Closing her eyes, she let her tiredness have its moment. She'd gotten practically no sleep last night. After unloading on Jordan as best she could, and checking in with Bailey, she'd ended up going downstairs to work on the Central Station project where she'd found Maël's office light on and him shut inside. They burned the night away like that until his wife and two boys had woken up.

The cushion beside her compressed from someone sitting down, and Fae opened her eyes to the sight of a white-haired, white-jacketed man smiling conservatively.

"Hi, Fae." He spoke calmly, a characteristic she needed in spades right now.

"You." She couldn't help smiling and leaning over to give Dominic a hug. She'd been cradling the terrifying possibility that he might stay away, but her hope had come through.

"I'd appreciate it if you didn't swear at me this time," he said, letting her go.

"It wouldn't do much good anyway."

She could see him trying to hide his amusement.

Dominic may not have looked traditionally tough, but it was the quiet ones that always had to be watched out for. Without him having put himself between her and Nefas that night decades ago, she wouldn't have survived long enough for Nicholas to get involved. He alone knew every detail of that night and with him alone could she be perfectly transparent.

"He knows I'm here," she told him, wasting no time. "He's waiting for me, and he's going to try and get me back."

"I know," Dominic said. "A corner is going to be turned tonight. Everything will be decided and transitioned."

As was typical, he offered no clues in his expressions to provide more meaning, so Fae pressed with her best assumption. "The r28 arrangement?"

"Couldn't last forever," he confirmed. And now you have your role to play."

She shook her head. "Does it involve leaving this pew? Because I'm not going anywhere near that door. Not with him out there."

"Unlike last time, you know who Nefas is. You're not powerless against him."

"What do you mean, 'not powerless against him'? What do you expect me to do?"

"What do you expect of yourself?" Dominic nodded a greeting to one of the choir members passing by as he answered. "Nefas has been biting at your heels since day one, and since arriving here, you've had mixed results trying to face your past." The way he looked at her, she knew he was aware of everything that had happened yesterday. "You're in the unique position of having once been on Nefas' side and now you're on Nicholas'. Because of this direct connection to both Nefas and Nicholas, you're like a bridge to both worlds; an ambassador."

An ambassador? It was everything Fae could do to not jump to conclusions, anger and panic rising quickly.

"An ambassador," Fae said, trying to keep her voice down, "figurative or not, is a hell of a job to assume I'd be OK stepping into. And don't say anything about it being my part to play. I am *not* going to meet with him for any purpose. You know what risks happening if I did."

Unable to say anything more without regretting it, Fae turned her attention to an older woman helping her husband hobble toward the hallway, his foot in a boot brace. Their grandkids followed behind but were refused access by a woman standing at the hall entrance. They weren't old enough to take the forced separation well. Someone hurried out from the pews and, to the grandparents' obvious gratitude, gently took the kids away.

"What did you mean that everything was going to be decided and transitioned?" Fae asked. The choir was loud enough to prevent their conversation from being easily overheard. "If the arrangement couldn't last forever . . . Does Nefas know?"

Dominic nodded. "There are endings he's planned for," he said. "Others he hasn't. He knows the arrangement is done, but what happens next? He's going to try and force his idea through. Tonight, beginnings and endings are made, including yours," he said, bringing his point back. "You're a bridge between two worlds."

"Dominic . . ." Fae wasn't sure if she was trying to warn him or plead with him, but whichever it was, she didn't have a chance to express it. A man broke off from those headed downstairs and came toward them. He had a shaved head and wore a knee-length, navy blue jacket. He looked unsure in his approach, but Dominic nodded him forward.

"You'll want to meet this guy," he said quietly, "and he most definitely, you."

Fae had no interest in meeting anyone at the moment. "Who is he?" But Dominic was already making the introductions.

"André de Boer, meet Fae Norris-Peeters."

André de Boer . . . the name scratched her memory like sandpaper. By the recognition in his eyes, he didn't have the same association delay. He nodded stiffly in greeting, but he kept his fists in his jacket pockets.

"Fae, you may remember André from—"

"Adrien Jandreau," Fae finished for Dominic, remembering the man's name now. "You were the one who went into la Rue with him."

"I'm not the lucky one," he told her firmly. He had a humorless face that reminded Fae of her high school soccer coach. Her eye caught a logo on his jacket which said he was, in fact, associated with a club in Ghent.

"Were you on la Rue for the Eve like they say?" André asked.

Fae looked at Dominic for direction. He gave a slight nod of approval, and she suspected then the true purpose of this meeting. She nodded.

"I remember that Eve," he said. "People said that our visitor that year was outside the basilica the whole night."

"Not the lucky one," Fae confirmed.

"André," Dominic spoke up, "tell Fae what happened."

André looked back and forth between Dominic and Fae, assessing if Dominic was serious. Then he glanced toward the hallway where his fellow villagers were disappearing.

"There's still time," Dominic told him.

André shifted his weight, began to speak, then stopped and looked at Fae like he wanted to say something but didn't know where to begin. Or how to begin. Or even how truthful he could be. Fae knew the struggle.

"Have you heard the ghost story? About Adrien?"

Fae nodded. "From a busker at the Christmas market."

André frowned. "I've told him to stop. But I don't live here anymore, so what can I do?" He shrugged and Fae could only imagine what it was like having someone making pocket change off his trauma. "He does tell the story pretty accurately," André admitted. "Adrien had been teaching me some of his parkour tricks that morning. It's a cool thing, running up walls, jumping over roofs. He'd been getting really good at it and was talking about going competitive. We were coming home and saw la Rue's gates open. I wanted to get out of there, but Adrien said we shouldn't leave them open. He convinced me to go with him to see if Monsieur was in there first. We were dumb kids and the idea of bragging about it at school was a strong motivator, so we went in."

"Did you record it on your phone?"

"His phone. No one would believe us otherwise. I stole it back from Iakob afterward, which wasn't hard. The poor guy was as big a mess as I was after everything happened. I smashed it with a hammer and threw it into a fire."

Fae probably would've done the same.

"Nothing happened while we were on la Rue, so we went all the way to the end and found the black door. It was cracked open too. I don't know what was going through Adrien's head, but he went in. I told him Monsieur had to be in there, two doors aren't randomly opened if no one hasn't gone through them, but he had to make sure. I really wanted to get out, but I couldn't just leave him, and he'd already gone in. That's when everything happened."

André looked at her as if to ask if she wanted him to continue. She nodded.

"There was a girl inside, a couple years older than us, probably the most attractive woman I've ever seen in person. She looked surprised to see us, like we were the ones who'd startled her."

"Had you seen her before?"

"No." André again shifted his weight and restuffed his hands into his pockets. "We asked her what she was doing in there. She laughed like a girl flirting does, and said she liked us. Then she came over and kissed me. When she was done, she smacked her mouth like she was trying to taste something, then went and did the same thing to Adrien. Then she took both our hands and led us into an adjoining room that looked like a cave."

André paused. All of Fae's memories of the place were coming back to life. She could imagine each step he took, smell the earthly smells, feel the anxiety . . .

"I know what's inside that space," Fae said, trying to help him. "The gravel pit, the hive ceiling, the little path around the edge."

He shook his head in disbelief. "The gases?"

"Those too."

"She kept me in there until I almost passed out from them, so I don't remember much. It was really dark in there except for this dull, green light. It was the only way I could see anything. I know she messed with us for a while, but I don't know if it was mental or if it actually happened. Adrien was bleeding. I don't know why, and my brain hurt like I'd just written a five-hour exam. At some point Adrien handed me his phone, asked me to charge it for him. I remember she'd jumped down into the pit while we were sitting on the edge of it. She'd grabbed onto Adrien's ankles and pulled him down into it with her. I don't remember what she did to him. I just remember the sound of him panicking and gravel being kicked around. I was so high on those gases and the lighting was so bad, but . . ." André paused to cough, though nothing about the cough made Fae believe it was genuine. "I swear I saw hands come up out of the gravel. She, umm . . . she told me then it was time to go, so . . . I left. I left and I . . . I just closed the door behind me, shutting Adrien in. Back out on la Rue, everything was so . . . undisturbed, like nothing was wrong. Apparently, I was found wandering the streets, but the next thing I knew, I was lying on a bed in the clinic."

Fae found herself nervously fingering the vial in her pocket. *Ask him the girl's name,* she told herself. Fae didn't want to ask this tortured man anything. *Ask him.* She really didn't want the answer. *You know you have to ask because you already know the answer.*

"Did that girl ever tell you her name?"

"Yeah. It was Charlize."

Fae slowly closed her eyes, clenching her jaw. Nefas could've picked any name in the world but he gave them that one, a calling card he knew she'd recognize. He'd once called himself Charlie for her. Was Nefas trying to impress her with his game?

"That . . . that means something to you?" André asked, more than a little surprised.

"I wish it didn't."

"I know it was *him*," André said. He looked like he was going to say Nefas' name but decided against it. "I knew it as soon as my brain cleared. I was inside the basilica that night you were here, so I didn't see you or anything that happened. People who saw him said he had no face, that he was just a black shadow. No one had seen him before you came, and no one has seen him since, so I didn't know . . . How were we supposed to know?"

The poor man was starting to ramble. Fae wondered if it would help or make it worse if she told him that Adrien was almost certainly not dead. "It was him," Fae confirmed, meeting his eyes again. "André, you're not the only one Nefas has taken from. He set his trap and he just happened to want Adrien rather than you. You won an evil lottery, and there's nothing wrong with that."

André sniffed sharply, set his face, then curtly nodded. "Merci." He stuck his hand out in a firm handshake and then excused himself. Fae watched him as he disappeared through the hallway, mentally tracking him to where the steps would take him down to the crypt with the others. For him, she didn't imagine a lemming. A piece of her went with him though, as he was the only human in the world who could truly understand what she'd been through.

"You don't know how much you've done for him," Dominic told her.

Fae forced herself to clear her throat, not wanting to dwell on the fact that she'd just met and then lost the one person she'd been needing to talk to for most of her life. "You'll have to excuse me if I don't revel in the warm and fuzzies right now," she said. "Adrien is alive."

Dominic nodded. "Yes. He is."

Fae went back to people watching, Dominic's earlier reference to a bridging relationship between her and Nefas hanging between them. She didn't ask him any more questions; ignorance was easier than facing more bad news.

Soon, Dominic tapped her on the arm and drew her attention to the young bartender from last night coming their way.

It took everything she had to not let her unhappy emotions show as Max shuffled through the pew ahead of them, a friendly smile on his face. He wore a leather jacket over a hoodie, and he looked more than ready to start the night in high holiday spirits.

"I see you and Dominic have connected already, that's great." Max said as he got close enough to be heard. He knelt down on the pew, facing them.

That shocked Fae. Someone else who knew Dominic by name? And a kid who didn't even live here?

"He's a great guy, this one," Max continued. "I'm looking forward to tonight. All these people"—Max pointed toward the thinning line of people headed downstairs—"where are they going?"

"I've never been here when this has happened," Fae told him honestly. She paused to allow for Dominic to contribute to the answer. He didn't. "You could follow them if you wanted," she said, thinking of the bouncer at the entryway, "but standing in lines are for government services and coffee."

Max laughed. "I can agree with that. So, this singing goes all night, is that right?" Fae nodded. "Are we expected the stay the whole time, or is there is nap room, maybe some food?"

This time Dominic jumped in. "Whatever you need, we can find it."

Fae hid her surprise. She wouldn't say it out loud, but Dominic never struck her as the strongest in the area of hospitality. More of the, I'll-see-you-on-the-sparring-floor-then-an-espresso-after kind of guy.

"Great," Max smiled as he stood up. "Well, I'll see you both again soon. There's someone I want to see. And, Fae, I believe you're up again." Max nodded to the back of the basilica where a woman who had to be Chantal had come in with Katie. Katie easily spotted Fae and she and Chantal navigated their way through the singers directly to her, slowly though, as Katie was caught looking at everything as she came, her head turning every which way.

Dominic excused himself with Max. "We'll be back shortly."

Dominic had better be back, Fae thought. He'd given her every reason to entrench herself in this pew, and every expectation that that wasn't going to be enough. As for Max, she'd decided he must be one of the choir members, his familiarity coming from an otherwise forgotten memory. He had to be a fighter like Dominic, otherwise he'd be wandering around singing too; so, she hoped for his return as well.

17

Katie found Fae sitting in the pews talking with two men and pointed her out to her host, Chantal, as they headed up the aisle. It was brilliant how fantastical this church looked with its fire torches and dim electric lighting, almost unfamiliar compared to the church she walked through yesterday. There were a dismal number of people who'd shown up for the concert, unless Chantal had brought them early and the choir was still warming up, which would explain why they were walking around and a few people were rushing down the hallway at the front.

The two men Fae had been speaking with left as Katie and Chantal approached, and it didn't take much to see that Fae was heavily distracted. Katie didn't take it personally. They made small talk, Fae constantly checking her watch making Katie absently rub her own naked wrist wistfully.

The longer the choir sang without breaking, the more Katie started to clue in that they weren't warming up but were already performing. They were unconventional, then, and Katie liked it; they were as fun to watch as they were stunning to hear, making them the perfect cap to her day.

When she'd asked Frédéric from the hotel for things to do today, he'd told her about a retired dog musher who adopted retired racers and was always looking for people to help exercise them. She'd been instantly sold on the idea and had driven the thirty-minutes out to his property. She'd gotten along really well with the musher and ended up staying most of the day until it was time to return to the hotel to meet Chantal.

Katie had waited for her host in the hotel lobby with an older gentleman who sat staring out the window. He'd acknowledged her only to ask the time, and with her answer he'd cryptically mumbled, "Less than twelve hours to go." Katie hadn't paid him any more attention and had taken a seat until Chantal had arrived shortly thereafter. Chantal was middle-aged, but she gave off an easy, relatable vibe, and was quite chatty though her heavy accent sometimes made it hard to follow everything she said.

"What do you know about tonight?" Chantal had asked her as they drove away from the hotel.

"Fae promised I can see her hall and whatever it's storing short-term. And there's a concert."

"Short-term storage?" Chantal had asked with an amused laugh. "I 'ave never met Mrs. Peeters, but now I know her sense of 'umor. I will tell you everyt'ing when we arrive. It will make more sense there."

Chantal had talked about something called the Gift, but as for explaining her comment about Fae's sense of humor, details were still short. Sneaking a peak at Fae's watch as she checked it again, Katie saw it was about 10:50 and she instinctively smothered a yawn just as someone slid into the pew beside Chantal whispering furiously to her. The choir drowned out any chance Katie had of picking out any words, especially because an attractive Indian man with an impressive baritone was strolling by two pews up. Katie didn't need words though to see that something required Chantal's immediate attention. To avoid talking across her, Chantal got up, slipped into the pew behind, and began the same furious whispering into Fae's ear.

Fae checked her watch again, looked over at Katie, then down the hallway on their left, now clear of people, then looked back at Katie.

"Katie, there's someone I have to speak with. I don't know how long this will take, but Chantal will start your site visit downstairs shortly, OK?"

"No problem."

Fae gave her a grateful smile and disappeared to the back of the church. Chantal began whispering to herself and Katie wondered if she was praying. Was this a Catholic church? She hadn't even thought to find out.

As promised, Chantal soon enough indicated that it was time to start the tour. Katie followed her out of the pew and down the same hall everyone had been going into earlier. At the end was a gated stairway that wound its way downward in a shallow turn. High wattage light bulbs shone from the low ceiling with the kind of brightness that suggested overcompensation for the gloominess it was trying to chase away.

The crypt they exited into was made from mostly plain stone except for the weight bearing pillars, which were decorated with pretty mosaic tiles; they stood out against the unadorned walls and flagstone floors. Warmer, weaker light filled the crypt from naked bulbs set in the walls. This light wasn't enough to chase away the shadows from the corners or from behind the sarcophagi, and it was barely enough to show the existence of a short flight of stairs at the far end.

"How many people are interred down here?" Katie asked, surprised at the number of sarcophagi laid neatly in rows among the pillars.

"Per'aps fifty."

Chantal let her take her time reading inscriptions as she fancied, though Katie fancied only a little. Priests, clergy, and people with enough money to be buried inside, it was the same as with any church. But she did come across one sarcophagus that was empty, the lid placed on a temporary table behind it. The stone looked new and had pictures carved on all four sides. She didn't know much about sculptures, but it showed a battle. Some figures were men with swords and were trampling others. Some figures had horns and tails like how medieval pictures depicted demons. The lid singularly featured two men standing side by side, one with a lowered sword, the other holding a tall pole with three medallions affixed to the front. Each medallion held someone's profile: a man, a woman, and a girl. Family members?

"Chantal," Katie called her over. "This one is empty. Is it being restored?"

Chantal looked confused as she wove her way through the grid of stone boxes. "I do not know," she confessed. "I 'ave never seen this sarcophagus before."

Chantal continued to lead on, their destination obvious thanks to a thickly muscled man standing guard at a drab, gray painted door. It made Katie hesitate. An unidentified door leading to a hall hidden in a basilica's crypt, guarded by a bouncer? What kind of short-term storage was this? Katie could only imagine that someone was stealing skeletons from the sarcophagi for the black market. But then Katie wouldn't have been invited to witness the illicit business. Unless, by watching that video in the library, she had stumbled on something she couldn't be trusted with and she had become a loose end . . . What if they were going to murder her and harvest her organs? What if *she* was going to be the one stored inside the hall?

It was a stupid idea, but down here there was a ring of possibility to it. Graveyards and crypts had a habit of setting the imagination loose, but telling herself that didn't make her feel any better.

Arriving at the door, they waited as the big man opened it for them. He smiled politely at her, and Katie wondered what his reaction time would be if she should try to make a break for it. If they were going to kill her, kidnap her at best, it would explain the last two days perfectly: the ease with which Maël let her off once he'd figured out that she'd seen the video and then introducing Fae to distract her, Chantal who was the henchwoman, Fae joking about the villagers trying to kill her…

"Relax," the big man told her as he held the door open, his smile more personable this time. "With us, you're safe. It's your own fear that can hurt you."

His words had an instant calming factor to them, and Katie tried to relax. But the very real fear of the absurd had disrupted her internal equilibrium and she couldn't shake the unsettled feeling she was left with. Nevertheless, she followed Chantal through the door.

"Behind 'ere is Fae Peeter's hall," Chantal began, a second door directly in front of them. "Please, no pictures, video, sound recording, paper, pen, or computer."

"What is this place?"

Chantal wasn't going to be rushed. "You 'ave been allowed to see what is on the other side. I will explain what I can, but you must see for yourself to understand what I am saying." She tucked some hair behind her ear. "What is sin?"

"Uhh . . ." Katie felt like that was supposed to be an easy question, but like asking what AC and DC current stood for, she struggled. "Something religion doesn't want people doing?" Katie had no idea.

"Sin is anything t'at puts you further away from our God, the love and the light of our world. Without light, life dies. Without love, people die. So, sin is death. We say, 'Sin deceived me, and t'rough the commandment put me to death.' On the eve of every Noël t'e one who is sin, who is also death, uses our people to show the world his power. He uses t'e bodies of my friends to show you what your soul looks like in a life with him. He thinks they look perfect. We do not."

"What's through that door?" Katie asked again.

"A safe place."

"Who is behind that door?"

"My friends. My village. It is where t'ose with the Gift come for the night."

"The Gift . . . you've mentioned that already tonight." Katie recalled their conversation while driving here. "It's like a gene, or pathogen that this place carries, right?" By Chantal's worried face, Katie knew she hadn't quite gotten everything right, but maybe now she would explain it a bit better.

Instead of saying anything more, Chantal opened the second door.

She led them down a curving hallway just wide enough for two. The hall had been painted in warm, earthy colors, and daytime-simulating lights and vaulted ceilings made it feel open and nonclaustrophobic. Softer lights were placed at the bottom of the floor, and for a second time, Katie thought that the lighting was trying to overcompensate.

"So, why underground, and why the guard? Is everyone being kept in, or are others being kept out?"

"Bot' reasons. During the Eve, my village will try to damage you."

Damage her? Was that a translation error?

They didn't actually have to go far until the tunnel ended abruptly, a mirror and fake floral arrangement marking the end. Chantal stopped just short of what looked like a viewing area, and judging from the change of color reflecting off the back wall, there were a lot of Christmas lights on display. That would make for a much less dark interpretation of Fae's short-term storage joke.

Chantal was talking again, explaining something Katie was trying to listen to. But, with no disrespect, she sounded like a guide on a haunted tour, and Katie's attention was snagged by the mystery of what lay behind Chantal. She'd only been waiting two days to find out.

Chantal seemed to notice and wrapped up her introduction, moving aside for Katie to eagerly walk into the viewing area.

"What the ffff—"

She couldn't even finish the word as it froze on her lips. There were four tall, narrow windows looking into the hall, just small enough so that a child's head couldn't squeeze through. A low-ceilinged area the size of a ballroom was supported by a forest of pillars. The entire room was covered in rubber floors and thick padding, but these observations were secondary, tertiary, even quaternary.

Katie inched closer to the window, fascinated and horrified at the same time. Maybe a thousand bodies were packed into that hall, all looking like they'd been buried then exhumed. Some were mummified, some were decaying, most were in some state of both, and they all stood lazily bumping around, clouded-over gray eyes twitching this way and that. Through their paper-thin skin Katie could see a green light emanating from their chests, tendrils of it twining around their bones and into their shrunken muscles. The illumination power of that green light was what lit the hall in its entirety and, eerily, the observation room as well.

Why would the village have this? Were the windows TV screens and this was all just CGI? "Chantal? What is this?" Katie cautiously reached out and tapped the window.

A body stumbled into the glass, and Katie jumped, its shoulders carrying it down out of sight, leaving a smear behind. Katie backed away in disgust, unable to tell if it was sweat, mucus, skin, or some other bodily fluid.

"T'is is what I was telling you about before we came in," Chantal told her gently, and Katie instantly regretted not listening closer. "It is what we call the Gift. On the Eve, it does t'is to everyone born in our village. It is real."

Katie adamantly shook her head. If it wasn't some kind of video effects thing, then makeup and prosthetics could've created this gory scene. But what kind of resources were needed to transform this many people? And still, why? Chantal spoke of sin, and religion, and showing souls, and weird religious stuff, which would make this one bloody-intense dramatic sermon. An art exhibit then? But why here, in the middle of nowhere? What if this was one of those elaborate practical joke shows, and she'd been set up for someone else to laugh at her expense?

"Can I go in there?" Katie asked, testing her last theory, hoping the answer would be no. "Will the actors stay in character?"

The look of shock on Chantal's face was all the answer she needed. "T'ey are not actors." She went to the window and pointed through the narrow glass at a corpse wearing an orange jacket and a beige scarf. "See there? Frédéric from your 'otel." And then she continued to point out other bodies by name that Katie might've run into, impressive since so little identity remained outside of the clothing.

"Where's the cameras then? You can show me, I'm not going to scream, so if you have someone else you're going to bring down to scare . . ." Frédéric was watching her, his milky eyes fixed on her. She side-stepped and watched as he tracked her. "Now that is creepy."

"T'is is no trick. T'is is no show," Chantal restated.

"Do you smell . . . must?"

"Oui . . . t'e smell of mold is new," Chantal said slowly as she took a long look at the mirror.

Just then another body crashed into the window, this time face first as though it was trying to get out. Katie jumped in surprise and noticed that the rest of the corpses in the hall were becoming more animated as well. Where before they were like a herd of grazing cattle, now they were looking more like a prowling pack.

"T'ey are waking up," Chantal half said to herself. "Nefas is inside of t'em. T'ey know we 'ave come."

She was speaking nonsense. "I don't understand," Katie said, fighting to stay as calm as possible. "In like, one sentence, tell me, what is this? Because I think I'm done here."

"Sin and Death, whose name is Nefas, comes to our village one night a year to show you what 'appens when you listen to his voice, when you live his life. Nefas believes what you see now is nice and is proud of it. T'is village is a living warning to not live t'e life Nefas wants you to live."

More eyes started fixing on her, and more bodies began crashing into the glass. It escalated quickly. Within seconds a mob of them were pressed up hard against the window, squishing the ones in front. Skeleton hands poked through any free space, pawing at the window. Their fingers looked like green glow sticks, and their green light created deep, black shadows in their mummified faces. She saw someone's wool jumper get stuck on an earring stud. The shirt was pulled, and the stud easily ripped out. A slow ooze of what looked like black bile followed.

Katie looked at Chantal speechless, unable to put words to her thoughts. It was getting harder to breathe in here; her chest was heaving, as was Chantal's. Katie started quickly backing away toward the exiting passage.

My beauty in your soul.

Katie startled and looked around for where that voice had come from.

"Tell me what this Nefas is, again?" Katie half-demanded, half-asked.

"Not 'what' but 'who,'" Chantal said as she also searched the room looking for something.

"Yeah, that's what I mean."

"Nefas is Sin and Death. He is the one behind everyt'ing you're seeing."

That was enough. Katie didn't care how real this all looked, it was straight-up cult, and she was not hanging around. She turned to leave.

Katie, open your eyes to see what I see. My beauty in your soul.

"Can you tell them to turn the speakers off? It's really not necessary."

Touch them to know they're real.

"What did he say?"

"You didn't hear it?" Another corpse was loudly squished against the window, the press of the corpses behind it preventing it from dropping. "My beauty in your sou—" Katie stopped short pulled out her phone, and thrusted the pictures she'd taken the day before into Chantal's face. "That's what it's saying."

"T'is is not right." Chantal looked over her shoulder to the mirror again and Katie could see her face blanch. "T'is not supposed to be possible anymore. We must leave," Chantal told her firmly. "Tis hall is outside t'e walls of Notre-Dame du Seigneur. We are not safe."

Katie looked around Chantal to see the mirror.

"No, don't!" Chantal leapt to block her view, but it was too late.

Katie screamed and jumped back but the image in the mirror didn't go away. There were two reflections: Chantal's, and a rotting body that moved when Katie moved, screamed as she screamed. It looked just like the bodies behind the windows. Its lips had shriveled up taking half the cheek with it so that she could almost see the nasal cavity. Its ears were brown and black and glistened with rot.

"*What* is going on?" Katie demanded as she turned around, walking away as fast as her pride would let her. She fingered her ears to feel that they were still there and normal.

"T'e Gift, le cadeau, is what is 'appening," Chantal said, right behind her.

"I thought that was the Gift?" Katie said, jamming her finger behind them where the constant thudding of bodies could still be heard and was eating away at the last of her nerve.

"Yes, but it used to 'ave many facets. The corpses were supposed to be the only part remaining. The fog . . ." Chantal let her sentence hang as Katie looked down and saw that they were walking through a growing layer of green fog on the floor. "Jésus."

They both started running at the same time.

The guard was waiting for them, a paragon of calm and control. Two others had since joined him. One of them, who wore a leather jacket over a hoodie, Katie had seen with Fae earlier.

"Nefas is being released," the guard told Chantal preemptively. "And so is the everyone else."

"Mon dieu . . ." If Chantal's face had been white before, it was ghostly now.

"Katie, waste no time. Up the stairs!" Chantal ordered.

She didn't have to be told twice.

Katie and Chantal came back into the sanctuary almost colliding with one of the singers. Fae was quick to meet them, the second of the two men who'd been with her earlier, the white-haired one, stood beside her. He didn't say anything, so Katie ignored him.

Between her heavy breathing, Katie blurted out, "Fae, what the—" But she didn't finish her thought, thinking better of her vocabulary in church. It was obvious from Fae's body language that all was not well, and Chantal dismissed herself to find out more. The peace of the choir was gone, and an obvious buzz of commotion was going on. "Fae, what did I just see down there? And tell me who Nefas actually is, and why were you so bloody scared of him in that video?"

Fae Peeters, this woman of success and esteem, respected by her peers, this woman Katie had learned to so admire, looked like she was breaking apart. What had happened in the last twenty minutes?

"We had a plan, Katie. We had a plan for tonight, but we couldn't have known to plan for this. Nefas is the source of everything wrong with the world. This village used to be his parade ground until he was restrained. But now he's being let out, and he's coming."

18

The hurried message Chantal whispered into Fae's ear was enough to send Fae's thoughts scrambling. A girl with a toddler stuck outside the walls desperate to get back in before the Gift took her over, her uncle who went to bring her in but had never made it back, the hurried debriefing of the girl as she was rushed into the hall to join her father—it was like watching a high-speed train rush by; it was impossible to make anything out other than a blur.

Fae excused herself numbly from Katie's innocent excitement as she and Chantal waited to go downstairs and went to the back of the basilica, ignoring the looks of everyone still sitting in the pews wondering where she was going in such a hurry. Trying to find a sense of calm, she toyed with the glass vial in her pocket running the news over again in her thoughts. She had nothing to do with any of this. This wasn't her village or her struggle.

But she was related to Monsieur Maël Dupont and was the one who had survived a night with Nefas, so that apparently gave her a sort of seniority that automatically involved her.

At the back of the basilica, the choir had discreetly formed themselves into a privacy screen, and they parted for her as she approached. She nodded her thanks to the two women who let her through. A small, distressed group was huddled together near the door. Dominic hovered nearby, detached but observant. A younger woman clutched a set of car keys in an iron grip, no doubt the same ones taken from the girl. Which likely made this woman the mother, which meant the keys belonged to the uncle, the woman's brother.

Fae had no idea what she was supposed to do.

An older woman from the group saw Fae approach and fell into her. "Our son, Henri," she cried, wrapping Fae in a hug that forced her to catch her balance. Having no words to give, Fae could only hug the woman back. The husband came, a tall, thin man, and he laid his hand on his wife to try and coax her away.

"I know who you are," he said to Fae. "We weren't living here yet, but the story of the young woman who spent a night with Nefas is still known. If you survived, then our son can too."

Fae wanted to tell this family that it would end well, that their hope would see Henri through, but she didn't know what Nefas had done to Henri. Or if he had a praying grandmother helping all the Dominics of the world to bring him back alive. Or how Nicholas still figured into this drama that had been curtained off for so many years. He was the only one who could truly give this family what they were looking for.

"You know what you have to do," was all she could tell them.

Slowly the mother relaxed her grip on Fae and the husband eased her back into his own arms. Fae exchanged sad smiles with Henri's sister who stood a couple feet away.

"My daughter, she'll be OK," the young girl's mother offered, nervously fidgeting with the keys she was holding. "She's with her papa in the hall."

A rush of cool air made Fae turn to see that Dominic had exited, the door closing behind him. She also saw Max slipping through the choir's screen making straight for the exit, following after Dominic. That made Fae nervous.

The two of them returned inside after only a few moments speaking intensely with one another. Their backs were turned, but by their actions, Fae would've guessed that they were having an argument, something Fae didn't feel comfortable witnessing. Who was Max to argue with Dominic? And what could they possibly be discussing so intensely?

It was time to meet those two Texans.

Fae invited Henri's family back to the pews to sit down. No matter what happened with their son tonight, they may as well be sitting. It would be a long night. Henri's family just needed someone to tell them what to do next, and as they came back to the seats with Fae, the choir's screen melted away.

The Texans weren't hard to find. The woman was the only one standing with her hands raised in the air swaying gently back and forth. Fae excused herself from the grieving family, but as soon as she did the choir wavered in their song. And they didn't just waver, they missed notes. For a couple of bars, they were an amateur group struggling to know what song they were singing, and it was disturbing to hear. It took the choir director and her mentor grabbing a nearby soprano and helping her find her place in the song to get it back on track. The generationally flawless choir had momentarily imploded, and not a single person didn't notice.

The reason for it was revealed almost as soon as the choir recovered: the normally discreet singers couldn't help but give their attention to the back door. Fae, and everyone else, followed their gaze to where Dominic, whose steely expression said more than it covered, was standing next to the exit. The door was flung open and in strolled a young man, with dark, wavy hair and a cocky smile.

"Henri!" People cried out his name, and his family and friends stumbled through the pews to rush him. Henri was looking around as though he were seeing this basilica for the very first time; seeing it, hearing it, and not liking it.

Unless Henri was an arrogant idiot strolling in after pranking everyone with a story of being caught by Nefas, he shouldn't be strutting around like he was. Dominic stayed close to him and Fae watched him carefully. It was when Henri opened his arms to welcome his family that she saw it. The parasite in his fingers ready to inject them all.

"NO!" Fae shouted, pushing her way back down the aisle. "Don't touch him!"

Everyone stopped but Henri kept coming, his arms open to embrace his mother, father, and sister. And then they saw it too. His mother smothered a yelp with a louder sob and his sister grabbed hold of their mother. The father pushed everyone behind him and looked back to Fae for help, but Fae was focused on Henri.

It wasn't only the parasitic fingers that were the problem. Henri's full condition, at first hidden because of his winter clothes, became apparent as he moved. His skin shimmered with the parasite like light on the water. Through the shimmer his bones could be seen—in his hands and wrists, and his neck when he turned his head. When he stopped moving the condition receded. It didn't look like the parasite was crudely controlling him like it did with the corpses, and Fae guessed that meant the parasite was joined with Henri making them as one, rather than one being a slave to the other. Henri was equally fascinating and repulsive, and in that way, he was like Nefas.

Henri, seeing his secret exposed, stopped in his tracks, and his skin gained back its opaqueness. Fae watched as the parasite in his fingers also disappeared back inside his body.

A shiver went down her spine as she looked at Henri, for in him she saw what Nefas had wanted for her. Nefas had failed because he'd needed her to have a semblance of independent will long enough for her to choose to hand over Nicholas to him. Apparently, that was not of concern this time. Which meant that Nicholas was either not Nefas' objective this year or Nefas had another plan to acquire the baby.

A circle of spectators was forming around Henri and Dominic, and Fae was only too happy to let them push her to the back. "I need to talk to someone," Henri said, his first words as confident as the triumphant grin he'd strolled in with. "Someone who can make decisions."

There was an awkward pause and shuffle as everyone looked at each other until, by all their shuffling, Fae found herself no longer at the back of the crowd but at the front, everyone's focus on her.

"What's your name?" Henri asked, like he was granting her the grace of his audience.

"Your new owner didn't tell you?"

"You mean *our* boss?" Henri smirked as he eyed her up and down.

"No." Fae was in no mood. "Yours."

"He doesn't agree." Henri paused just long enough for his words to land heavy. "For the sake of diplomacy, entertain my ignorance."

"Fae. Norris-Peeters."

Henri scoffed and turned away. "He did tell me your name. You're for later."

And with those words, Fae's fragile shelter of confidence collapsed.

Max casually stepped into the circle, taking Henri's attention, and Fae watched numbly as Max and another choir member who must've had some authority escorted Henri to a back corner. There they quietly continued the conversation, Dominic staying close. Fae looked back at Henri's family. They were all supporting each other to stand, staring vacantly in Henri's direction.

You're for later.

Henri's words rang coldly in Fae's ears and her world fell away into nothingness.

The barrage on Fae was almost immediate. As she was one of the few who were expected to have answers, the visitors who had zero idea what had just happened targeted her with their flurry of questions.

"Who is this Henri? Who is he representing?"

"I don't know. It's a long story. Ask one of the choir."

"Are we in any danger? Where are the police?"

"Not if you stay inside. Ask one of the villagers."

"What kind of sick Christmas trick is this?"

"It's not a trick. Ask one of the choir."

"We want to go back to our hotel."

"The basilica is the only safe place."

"This is unacceptable. We're leaving."

Fae didn't even bother answering. There were two serious looking men who'd taken guard at the door. Anyone who wanted to leave could take it up with them. Henri's pronouncement was still the only thing Fae could hear echoing in her thoughts, and she threw out her hands to silence everyone talking at her. The Texans saw their chance and caught up to her as she walked up the side of the nave to get away.

"Ma'am?" The man called after her, his wife next to him. "Isaac Granger," he stuck out his hand for a hefty shake. "And my wife Jenny." Jenny's hair was perfectly curled, and Isaac's was short and minimally gelled. A perfect Dallas couple, they even had the perfect little twang in their accent. "You seem to know something about this place, and I wanted to ask you, that young man who just came in here? There's something spiritual about him, if you know what I mean?"

Fae knew exactly what he meant, and she took a deep, calming breath. She'd once made the mistake of trying to explain this village to a trusted Christian friend and had quickly found out that the church's theology didn't allow for Nefas, or the Gift, to exist. She resolved to do her best with this conversation.

"No," Fae confirmed, "he's not normal. Not anymore. You two are Christians, right?"

"Yes ma'am, we are. A prophet of the Lord told us there was a darkness here, and we've come to do our part."

"Good. Come with me. I need to introduce you to Henri's parents." Fae turned back around and set off to where Henri's family were huddled together, but Jenny jumped in front of her, curls bouncing down her back.

"Mrs. Fae, we believe in the spiritual realm, and that young man over there, he's setting off alarms in me. I've seen a man possessed before, and we chased that devil out of him—"

"Henri isn't possessed with a demon, and you don't 'chase' Nefas out," Fae told them as calmly as she could, her thin patience stretching.

"As soon as he walked in, I saw a demon with his claws dug in his mind and in his heart," Isaac told her with conviction.

"Sounds like a possession to me." Jenny smiled confidently. "The Lord brought us here for a reason, and I'd cross the world to save just one person."

"Maybe the Lord did bring you here for a reason," Fae told them, "but please realize that you being here is not about coming to save the day. Nefas is not a demon." They were nice people. She wished they could've met under different circumstances.

"What is he then?"

"An anthropomorphization."

Jenny wrinkled her forehead and looked to her husband for help.

"It's when people take ideas, or objects, and give them human attributes so they can worship them as false gods," Isaac explained. "The Greeks did it with all their gods an' the Apostle Paul came and told them that their unknown god, so named because they didn't want to miss one, was really Jehovah, the one true God, greater than Apollo or Zeus who were nothing more than evil spirits leadin' 'em astray."

"Yeah, wow. That's good." Jenny was deeply feeling what Isaac was saying, nodding her head like he was giving a life changing sermon. Fae was rolling her eyes on the inside. As if Jenny hadn't heard that story at least thirty times before. It was like watching someone being told about the power of microwaves for the very first time, even after using one their entire life.

"It's not just Henri either who's going to be set free from evil spirits," Jenny said, her eyes lighting up, "but this whole village. I saw a figure standing in the middle of this place that was so large his stance spanned the whole width of the village. I heard the Lord tell me he wants his territory back."

"My wife is a prayer warrior for our church," Isaac explained. "The incredible miracle stories she can tell you . . .whoa, man, they'll get me saved and dancing like King David every time! We've been fastin' and prayin', and we believe that principalities and darknesses are under our feet. The Word of God is our sword. Last year we did a whole study on the armor of God and it changed our lives. The Devil can't steal from us no more!"

Fae said nothing and just kept walking, her patience gone. She couldn't handle these people tonight. They followed after her.

"You're not allowed to leave this basilica until the sun comes up," Fae told them bluntly. "No Jericho marches, no speaking to the buildings or the streetlamps. Do what you have to from inside these four walls. That's the greatest word of wisdom you'll hear all night."

"But Mrs. Fae," Jenny said, "We have nothing to fear. Perfect love casts out fear. We *will* do what we've been assigned to do."

Fae's response was practically leaping off her tongue, but she held it long enough to look these two in the eye. She spoke slowly for their benefit. "You're nice, genuine people, I'm sure, but people who love their religious culture more than they love their God. You talk of fasting and praying, and calling out demons, but you have yet to mention your God as the authority who actually lets you do that. If you go outside, you will be taking on more than you can understand, and all your Bible studies will be useless because the one person who could save you, that can save this village, that can save *me* tonight, is the one person you have yet to mention. To Nefas, your efforts are annoying, not intimidating, and he will break you."

The two of them looked at her stunned; like she was a faithless heathen. It was a look Fae had been used to all her life. Right now, she almost welcomed it. "You want to do what you were assigned to do?" Fae beckoned for them to again follow her and she led them to where Henri's family had huddled around each other, a group of their friends with them. "Meet Henri's family. Use all your prayer powers to help them get their son back. Henri, the real Henri, is somewhere inside that body, fighting to make the hardest choice of his life. Don't stop praying until the sun rises, and you'll do this village a bigger service than anything else you had in mind. He's your one person to save."

With a nod to Henri's family acknowledging that they were now the recipients of the Texan couple's energies, Fae left them. She saw that the negotiation in the back corner had broken up as Max and the other choir member were headed toward the hallway that led down to the crypt. Henri stayed where he was, watching them, and Dominic moved up the side aisle, the shadows of the pillars keeping him away from attention.

Fae tracked Dominic and intersected with him where he stopped, a place where he could discreetly observe everything unfolding: the confused and concerned villagers talking among themselves; the disgruntled visitors circling; the choir faithfully singing; Henri watching, his shimmering skin coming in and out of opacity as everyone shunned him. Fae wondered how Katie and Chantal were faring downstairs.

"They're going to want answers," Dominic said as she stood beside him, taking in the fallout.

"I don't have answers. They need to stop thinking I'm someone important to them."

"You're everything to them, Fae. Nefas didn't just wait for your return, he planned for it." Dominic comfortably crossed his arms.

Fae swallowed hard. "What just happened?"

He looked over at her. "Why do you need to know if none of this is your problem?" He arched an eyebrow in question before resettling his arms. "In Henri, Nefas created your opposite. You were Nefas', then were freed, and now you stand with Nicholas. Henri was once free and stood with Nicholas but is now Nefas'. Because Henri is both human and Nefas, he can go where Nefas can't, like in here, and make Nefas' demands."

"Like an ambassador," Fae said, linking their earlier conversation to this one.

"That makes you both pretty big deals."

"Then I deserve to know what Henri wanted."

Dominic nodded. "To release the villagers. And to release Nefas." A fire in his eyes flashed and she didn't have to ask what his thoughts were on that, or to wonder any longer if he and Max had been arguing earlier. But Dominic wasn't done. "To guarantee that you'd meet Nefas."

She stared at him in horror.

"Don't fear. It will kill you," Dominic quickly reminded her. "You were never a negotiating point. Both he and the villagers are being released. Nefas will come looking for you, that couldn't be stopped."

There was no more dreading the unknown. No more suspicion. Fae's head swam and she began to think about where her gloves were and how she didn't want to be outside with cold hands this year.

"I'm not leaving this basilica," she said, as though to convince herself that that would be enough to avert Nefas' efforts.

As though Dominic could read her mind, he tipped his head and guided her back to her seat where she'd left her gloves. Katie and Chantal were just coming out of the hall, back from their visit downstairs. Katie looked like she'd just been slapped: both shocked and angry.

She might need her gloves too, Fae thought dismally.

19

Katie looked blankly at Fae. They couldn't have known to prepare for this? This what? Everything about everything was going over Katie's head quicker than she could pretend to keep up.

Fae had barely finished delivering a helpless apology when some of the choir nearby stopped singing and began asking everyone who wasn't already sitting on the far side of the church, away from the hallway going to the crypt, to move there now. The request increased the buzz of questions, heightening the nervous energy. The bouncers at the back door also started corralling those trying to leave back up and into the pews, noticeably, the two families with their kids. Katie recognized them from the hotel. The three kids didn't look like they'd noticed the tone of the room yet, and their parents were too busy demanding answers to settle them, probably looking for the same information Katie was hoping to overhear.

As requested, Katie and Chantal moved along with the handful of others. Fae was still dazed from her own news, but she came, guided by her friend, jacket and gloves in hand. She sat adrift with him, barely blinking as she responded to whatever he was telling her. Katie tried to remember that r28 video as what were once insignificant details were now very relevant ones, but the image of those decaying and mummified bodies was blocking any memory from before ten minutes ago. She turned to Chantal, whose eyes were as big as a nocturnal animal's.

"What's everyone saying?"

"Le cadeau, the Gift," she said, struggling. "T'e corpses, his family, t'ey are all to be released. Nefas is released."

"Are we safe?"

"Oui. Inside the basilica. Nefas cannot come inside, and his family must go out. But Katie, after so long, Nefas must want more t'an freedom from his pit. We do not know what he wants, and t'is is why we are scared. The villagers cannot be allowed to be seen as they are right now, not by outsiders who do not know what le cadeau is. T'is is also why we are scared. For them."

Once everyone had been brought together, the rest of the choir left their roaming ways and formed themselves into a protective circle around them, as well as lining a path of travel from the hallway down both the main and far aisles. Katie glanced behind her to where the three tourist kids were noisily standing up on the pew to get a view over the men and women standing shoulder to shoulder in front of them.

As soon as all the singers were in place, they ended their song, the echo of their voices carrying through the church into near perfect silence. No one moved, or shifted in their seat, or coughed. Katie tried to get a better view. Her line of sight wasn't great through the human wall, but she did see the leather jacket and hoodie fellow and his partner coming out of the hallway, checking that the preparations were satisfactory. There wasn't time to do anything if they weren't as a release of chilled air from the hallway pushed past them, flickering the candles in the chandelier above. As the only sound in the otherwise silent church, the sputtering flames were loud.

Ominously, noises of thumping and groaning started to grow from the tunnel. It was slow, and it was a rumble of pain and effort and bone crunching on bone. Green light lit up the hallway like an advance warning, the three restless kids now looking more scared than excited.

"Chantal," Katie leaned back to speak without having to take her eyes off the hallway. Chantal was definitely praying this time. "Are these singers going to be enough if one of those . . . dead people, wants to attack us again?"

"T'e singers are strong, t'ey will be enough." Chantal whispered back. "Do not let the corpses touch you. Their green parasite will enter you, and it will not come out easily."

The villagers slowly poured out of the hallway in a mass of limbs, and teeth, and eyes, every noise they made resounding twice as loud in the acoustics of the church. Katie stood up to get a better view as did a number of others. Of the three kids, only one of the boys was still interested, the other two were hugging their parents.

The villagers dragged themselves down the two aisles toward the back door, a mob of barely distinguishable decay—the tall, the short, those with hair, those with none. One wore a scarf, another a pink ski jacket, but there was little else to differentiate the old from the young, the mothers from the sons. The rot on their faces was nothing compared to that green light inside them, pulsating their withered muscles and mechanically pulling and releasing their joints. There was no way all this was costumes and makeup. Katie looked around her. There were a couple others, like her, who weren't praying a Hail Mary. But everyone looked disgusted or scared; everyone was taking this seriously. Her being freaked out over this felt warranted.

The sound of two disapproving voices speaking clear English caught Katie's attention through the whispered prayers being offered, and her ears perked up. American accents.

"On Christmas Eve too, Jenny. A parade of death through God's church."

"These people have been deceived if they think this celebrates the birth of our Savior. Pray with me strong, Isaac, that their eyes will be opened to the truth."

Katie tried to tune them out, though it was hard as the sound of their quiet conversation was still louder than everyone else's prayers.

A loud gasp helped distract Katie from the Americans. It came from a young adolescent girl and Katie followed the girl's attention to a shorter corpse wearing a Manchester United jersey dragging itself by.

"Yves?" The girl called out. She was quickly shushed by an adult next to her, but it was too late. The ManU youth and one other diverted into the pews. The girl was instinctively pulled back by the adult, and the human-shield unceremoniously redirected the bodies back into the river staggering by. Katie looked back over her shoulder at Fae. *Short-term storage?*

Katie, open your eyes to see what I see. My beauty in your soul. The memory of that voice from the observation room exploded so clearly in her mind that it was almost as if she was hearing it again. *Believe your eyes and ears. Touch them to know that they're real.* It'd been a creepy voice then and it still was now, but objectively, it wasn't an irrational idea. Fear came from the unknown. Her unknown was these rotting, walking . . . bodies, so knowledge lay in her ability to touch one and find out once and for all. Did that green substance feel like a jelly? Or was it as untouchable as a ray of light? She'd be lying to herself if she didn't think it was as terrible an idea as it was logical. Then again, what if she should be following the locals? Maybe she should be praying too?

Touch them.

"Where are they going?" Katie asked Chantal quietly.

"To Nefas. He waits outside to be reunited with t'em. It has been many, many years since t'ey were together for the Eve."

"Outside, like outside the village walls?"

Chantal shook her head. "Corpses do not leave our walls."

As time ticked on, more and more people decided that they'd seen enough and sat down to wait. Katie was one of the few who couldn't stop watching until the last body hauled itself out; the old man she'd given the time to in the hotel lobby was another. It wasn't until the door's handle clicked into place in a final echo against the silence of death's march that the choir dispelled from their guard duties. They smoothly returned to wandering, filling up the empty spaces with their bodies and the ceilings with their voices. The song was strikingly beautiful coming after such a stiff reminder of mortality.

Katie didn't relax though, for as the choir dispersed, she noticed a lone man standing at the back of the church. He was about her age, had dark hair and a roundish sort of face. Not so attractive that he belonged to another league, but not so average that he blended in. He didn't sing, and he didn't wander, but he hadn't been penned into the pews with the rest of them either. He just stood there. Patiently. Like he was waiting for someone.

He looked in her direction and caught her staring. He gave her a friendly half smile and started coming over, like he knew her. Maybe it was someone beside her? Katie glanced around but she was the only one left standing. She took the opportunity to sit back down but didn't stop watching him. As he came closer, slipping and weaving through the choir's movements, Katie quickly realized why he stood apart. His skin shimmered with threads of that same green light that the corpse bodies had, and she could see his muscles flexing underneath translucent skin, and sometimes even the bone through that. Unlike the corpses, he was kind of bizarrely cool.

Touch him to test the theory.

Chantal leaned over and whispered into her ear, "I was familiar with t'is young man," she said cautiously. "Nefas has enslaved him. See how he looks like a corpse but is not? Stay away from him, and don't listen to him. He will only speak lies like Nefas."

Waving to people he knew sitting in the pews, he stopped just short of her in the middle of the aisle. No one waved back. He began to address them all, but he had to speak loudly to be heard over the choir.

"A bit of an unconventional way to start t'e evening, don't you think?" He spoke good English, but Katie was surprised he wasn't speaking French. Maybe he didn't want to exclude anyone? "It's been an incredible Eve already. Our families, our friends have been set free from their prison." He was genuinely happy, but he got no response from his audience. That didn't affect his winning smile. "You're all looking at me like I'm no longer one of you, but I'm not any different. I'm t'e same Henri who has shared every Christmas that I've been here with you, sitting in these pews, listening to this choir." He waited but still no response. "I'm still your son," he said, turning his attention to a couple who had to be his parents. "Elena, I'm still your brother, and Veronique is still my niece."

"Don't you say her name," Elena snapped.

His eyes flickered and his smile grew flat. He moved on. "We've been taught to be disgusted by the sight of t'e corpses, but we all have bones and muscles. What's disgusting about that? God himself didn't fear death but overcame it, found the beauty of it, the light in the darkness. This year we should overcome our fears. Come outside and see your friends and family. Christmas is for being with friends and family, yes? It is perfectly safe if you stay on the steps. It's a natural boundary. Come with me."

The now fearless kids turned to their parents and Katie watched as a typical yes-no, child-parent debate broke out. The only other person who made any motion to accept Henri's offer was that same old man from earlier. He calmly and confidently rose from his seat and stood with Henri.

"No one but us can be on t'e stairs," Henri said. "It's not even very cold out tonight. C'mon, see how your village looks on Christmas Eve—alive and full of beautiful color!"

"You need to stop talking now."

The voice of Fae Peeters giving such a command caused everyone to turn and see the woman who'd found it in herself to acknowledge the world again. She was standing tall and was focused only on Henri.

"I thought I said you were for later." He sniffed, his pleasant demeanor evaporating.

Fae eyed him. Henri eyed her back, and Fae slowly closed the gap between them.

"You did," Fae agreed. The choir conveniently lowered their volume, and now Fae could easily be heard. "If anyone wants to go with you, that's their choice. But remind them that even if the corpses can't come up the stairs, Nefas can. Remind them that they're not safe from him anywhere outside this basilica."

"Nefas hasn't left the pit yet. There's nothing to be concerned about."

"That's a lie," Fae shot back quickly, evenly.

Henri gave a quick shake of his head like Fae had no idea what she was talking about and turned away from her. "Sit 'ere all night, or get some fresh air," he said, throwing the offer back out. He gave Katie a wink and nodded his head for her to follow.

The kids won their argument and even though twenty minutes earlier they'd been scared, they bravely joined Henri and the old man, two parents following behind as guardians. The American man wasn't far behind, and Katie decided to give in to the voice egging on her curiosity and to round out the group. Safety in numbers. She got up without announcement and left the pew, stepping out just in front of where Fae stood.

Katie leaving the pew broke Fae's single focus on Henri, and she lunged out and grabbed Katie's arm.

"No! Don't go out there." Fae tried to let her eyes plead her case. She knew the luring feeling, that unrelenting need to know, to experience. It was so innocuous and natural it was impossible to resist.

Katie stopped but in a way that showed acknowledgement rather than a change of mind. "This is all a bloody freakshow," Katie said with a nod, "but I don't want to question for the rest of my life if I'd been suckered into believing some silly black magic." She gave a quick check over her shoulder to the little group leaving. "I just want to know what they feel like."

Fae didn't hesitate. "An intense freezing that burns like a scorching fire."

The quickness of her response seemed to take Katie off guard, and Fae could almost see dots starting to connect for her. Katie followed up on her last question. "That green light, or green blood, or, what . . . what is it?"

"It's a parasite. It'll leave their body and jump into yours if you get too close." Fae didn't break eye contact, willing, hoping—dear God—praying that Katie would abandon Henri's invitation. She tried not to be distracted by more villagers leaving, those who obviously had to learn the hard way. They trickled out and every time that heavy wooden door shut with a dull *thud,* she felt it. She'd warned them that they weren't safe. This was their choice. But Katie . . . Fae was still going to fight for her.

At last Katie gave in, and Fae invited her to sit back down.

"I wouldn't have asked you to delay going home if I hadn't thought it'd be better for you to stay," Fae started. "Nefas singled you out, and this basilica is the only safe place from him," she said, doing her best to explain herself. Or, to start building her defensive testimony. "The risk from Nefas would've been higher if you'd gone home. You have to stay inside this basilica tonight.

No matter what happens out there, the danger will be over in the morning. I just . . ." Fae trailed off not knowing what to say next. Her heart rate spiked every time that door opened and closed, fearing that Nefas was going to be there waiting for her.

Katie still looked like she wanted to leave, her temporary deference expiring. The same need for answers that was pushing her out the door was also keeping her here. Fae only hoped she could give enough information to satisfy.

"Can you explain those bodies?" Katie asked, raising an eyebrow. "How were they, um, made?"

Fae nodded, grateful for a question to focus her thoughts. "From now until sunrise, you have to believe your eyes, not your head," Fae began. "This village is like an intersection between worlds, a place where the unseen and the seen collide, so that the unseen can be made visible for a single night. This village has something called the Gift. It's called that because these people were gifted with the ability to show what a soul looks like when it belongs to Nefas. Those corpses are all the villagers who were born in this village; they were born into this Gift from birth. Nefas also will use them to infect anyone like you and me with a bit of himself, which is that green blob; the parasite. It will put you under his control."

Katie did not look impressed. "Who is this Nefas?"

"He's the center of it all. He is Sin, and he is Death, and he is everything that's wrong in this world."

"Like the Grim Reaper. Or Lucifer?"

Fae shook her head. "He's the by-product of Lucifer, if you will. All the darkness and all the motivation of Lucifer, that is Nefas. Nefas is your professor," Fae told her point-blank. "He's the one who caused that mirror trick and messed with those pictures you took."

"Nefas is the professor?" Katie sounded offended by Fae's accusation. "The professor's a scholar, a nice man. There's no way . . . I mean, he doesn't even look anything like the blondie in the picture."

Fae bit the inside of her lip, seeing what she'd done wrong too late. She needed to keep the professor out of this, at least for now. Putting Katie on the defensive wasn't going to help. "There are two sides in this world." Fae tried again. "Light and dark. Nefas is the dark. The fact that you saw yourself as a corpse yesterday in the mirror means you're in Nefas' world and you're free game for him to mess with. I know because I was where you were twenty-eight years ago."

Fae could practically see Katie's mind cogs turning. *Please understand, please.*

"OK . . . but why? Not that I don't believe you, but you're talking spiritual, theological stuff. If you want me to believe that a philosophy has been given corporeal life, then . . ." Katie trailed off.

The extraordinary level of suspended belief Fae was asking Katie to show might be more than what she had. The answer to the question of why was going to take more time than Katie was probably going to give. Wasn't Chantal supposed to have gone over all this already?

The door closed again with a dull *thud-click*. Another one gone. That made twelve.

"This may be a bit personal, but . . ." Katie paused, giving Fae a chance to object. She didn't. "You and Nefas . . . know each other from before? Like, in a bad way."

"Yes."

"If you two have such a bad past, and he is pretty much the Devil, why are you here?"

"Because . . ." Fae wasn't sure how best to answer that. From where she sat, she had a full view of the exit door. Henri was inside acting as the porter and he looked their way expectantly. "Because the one who saved me from him needed me to be here. I know him by the name of Nicholas. You'd recognize him as a baby in a manger. I know, I know," Fae said proactively. "This village makes the unseen, seen, right? If you can accept the existence of one of them—Nefas or Nicholas—then you're better off accepting the existence of both."

"Is Nicholas here now then? Why isn't he stopping Nefas breaking out and taking these people outside?"

Fae didn't have an answer. Her life literally depended on having an answer to that question, and she didn't. She blinked away the burn of tears springing up and felt a brave tug of a smile trying to help the cover-up.

Katie nodded sympathetically, but Fae didn't need her to be sympathetic.

Fae shook her head at Henri. He narrowed his eyes, and for a brief second his whole body became translucent showing all his bones and shimmering green muscles. Maybe it was a sign of his anger, or maybe it was him losing control over the parasite, but he left, slamming the door behind him, which made the nearby candle flames flicker and sputter, wisps of black smoke streaming upward until they recovered.

Of the twelve people Henri had managed to lure out, four were villagers. Their families joined Henri's and they huddled together. Fae was glad to see Jenny, the Texan, was still with them, and Chantal had migrated there as well.

"How long has this Gift been going on?" Katie asked.

"Longer than anyone knows."

At that moment, the choir transitioned to a song that was definitely not Christmas inspired. It took a couple seconds before Fae placed it as a lament, and it sounded like the falling of tears.

Fae braced herself for what was coming.

The screams came quick and sharp. Even the weeping lament couldn't quell the sounds of surprised panic. Katie jumped up to run outside to help but Fae grabbed her back. "You can't help them."

Katie's eyes were wide, and she was looking at Fae like she was mad. Chantal was wrestling Jenny back the same way, while the two remaining EU parents of the kids ran to the door but were blocked by the two stern-faced men. It was for their own safety. The shouting and screaming was confused and erratic and was quickly getting weaker. There was no doubt that Nefas was out there. Right now. So close. And if Nefas was outside that door, that meant her time had also come. Henri promised it. Dominic confirmed it. And regardless of what Nefas wanted, it was her single best opportunity to get him to leave her alone once and for all.

As suddenly as it had begun, the screaming stopped.

Nefas had never liked screaming. Or crying.

"Katie," Fae said so serenely she almost scared herself, "Katie, I have to leave." She stood up and took a couple of steps into the aisle. "Promise you won't go outside this basilica until sunrise."

"Where are you go—" A light of understanding went off before she could finish her own question, and Katie did a double take between her and the exit. "If I can't leave then—"

"Chantal will be here." Fae nodded to where she was with the others. Fae's feet found their strength and she almost backed up into a young woman from the choir with gorgeous fiery hair. "Don't give Nefas want he wants. Don't give him you."

Thud, thud, thud, thud, thud.

The knocking on the door was heavy enough to be a battering ram. The deep sounds of it reverberated throughout the cavern of the basilica, off the stone walls and fat pillars, and across the ceiling.

Fae felt exposed in the middle of the aisle, too easy to spot if that door was to suddenly slam open. People were watching her, and she couldn't give them any more reason to fear than they already had. She wanted to be as little a distraction as possible, so with her voice choked up in her throat, she walked away from what remained of their little group and slipped into the side aisle, resting against one of the stone pillars; it was the best barricade she could find.

Dominic met her there and Max came with him. She didn't want Max there, but she couldn't tell him to go away.

Thud, thud, thud, thud, thud.

Dominic gave a short nod. "Nefas has come for you."

20

It had taken Henri less than an hour to accomplish more than Adrien had his whole life. The blonde girl Nefas wanted, well, Henri would have to come back for her, but the night was still young. With Nefas' family now freed and some extras thrown in, Nefas was sending Henri to look after Adrien, who was being given the opportunity to prove that Nefas' investment into him wasn't wasted. Adrien was currently at the North gate getting himself ready for his big moment, and Henri would be there to ensure it happened.

Descending the basilica stairs, Henri shouldered his way through Nefas' family, captivating creatures that were about as useful as Adrien. They were all struggling for the chance to get their fingers on one of the people he'd coaxed out of the basilica, and it made getting through them difficult. As he pushed his way through though, he glanced behind him and saw Nefas overseeing nearby, smiling at the sounds of those people screaming, and as he smiled, so did Henri.

The family were still heavily concentrated around the basilica, so once Henri broke through their throng, the streets were empty. He made his way down the middle of the vacant street toward the gate, the naked Christmas lights strung from one side to the other making his path bright, and almost happy. There was an aura of green cast over the village, caught in the foggy night. The curious eyes of the world—any of the drones and satellites, whatever was out there—would be drawn to this dome of green light in the middle of nowhere. And then the rest of the world would see and know.

For the first time in a long time, Henri was content walking these streets because, for the first time, the Gift was no longer something to be feared. He had the power to free this whole village, to free them from the ties of secrecy that kept them here. All they had to do was accept this privileged life they were sampling tonight, and he had Nefas' essence in him to make that life a permanent arrangement. Their current, rotting look wouldn't last past tonight, but as the saying went, it was what was on the inside that mattered. The essence was a power flowing through him, and he flexed his muscles imagining the sweet moment when he'd be able to share this with Josie. They'd never have to see the inside of these walls ever again.

Without warning a blinding pain gripped him at the base of his skull, instantly dropping him to his knees. He yelled out with the spasms, his spine feeling like it was being crushed, squeezing everything into his brain. He buried his eyes from the lights above as a migraine exploded into his head. He kept yelling, trying to relieve the pressure, trying to hold together everything that was breaking inside of him. What was happening?

I told you it would hurt. Is it not worth it?

Both his palms were squeezing the back of his neck, which had gone so tight the muscles felt like bone. He was seeing stars and flashes of light in front of his eyelids, and the sounds of pain escaping his mouth was the only thing that told him to keep fighting.

Your soul must die to the light before you can know all of me. I've contained him inside you. He wants out. He must die.

A second Henri. A piece of him broken off inside blocking his path to knowing Nefas perfectly. He couldn't let this severed piece stand in his way. *He will die*, Henri determined through the pain.

Inner Henri bolted up and found himself in near utter darkness. The only exception was a large spot of white light beaming down onto the floor next to him. He tracked the beam upward to a tiny pinprick far, far above.

Where was he? There was a wall behind him, that much he knew, so he cautiously stood up, not knowing what lay around him. He last remembered being with Nefas in that dark alley, afraid out of his mind, but *here* was definitely not *there*. With his hands out and using the small circle of light on the floor as his reference, he palmed his way across the wall feeling the space out. It was a circle of maybe two and a half meters across and made completely of packed dirt. There were no doors. No tunnels or holes. No metal or wood, or straw, or buckets, or even evidence of rats. Nothing. Not even a noise to be heard.

Henri walked around the floor a couple more times hoping he missed something. He found nothing though, and sank back to the dirt floor, taking another look upward. That pinprick was so small it had to be kilometers away. He was, by all conclusions, imprisoned at the bottom of a silent, earthen cylinder. There wasn't any point trying to shout for someone's attention.

Henri lay down and tried to will himself to sleep. In sleep he could forget. Forget how he'd ended up here, that he was even here at all. He closed his eyes but instead of blocking his memories, he saw the outside world perfectly clearly: The stone streets of his village and someone's bad parallel parking job. He was walking past the Ski and Outdoor shop and he looked down and saw his shoes, then his hands. He wiggled them around in front of him. He could see his hand bones and every green shimmering muscle . . .

Henri gasped hard as his eyes flew open. He scrambled on his hands and knees to the spot of light and shoved his hands into it, wiggling his fingers as he'd just done, but there was nothing to see. His hands were perfectly normal, just a little dirty. He cautiously closed his eyes again, and exactly like the first time, he saw his village, and he wasn't much further from the Ski and Outdoor shop than he was before. He was bent over, he heard himself yelling in deep pain. His hands came into view again and he still saw his bones and muscles through his green shimmering skin. He willed one hand down to shove up the sleeve of his jacket, then the bottom of his pants. The green shimmer was everywhere . . . Henri jerked his eyes back open, the darkness greeting him like a relief. What had Nefas done to him? Why was the Henri outside in so much pain?

Kill him!

The echo of a whisper entered into the hole, demanding. It sounded like Nefas. Somehow Henri didn't think he was talking to him but to the other Henri, the one on the outside. Which would make this earthen cylinder not so much a prison as an execution chamber. But if he died then there was nothing holding Nefas back from finishing taking him over, and there'd be nothing of himself left. Did the other half of him realize that?

Kill him!

A thin green vapor began rising out of the dirt. Henri tried to jump away, but wherever he went, the vapor rose beneath him until the entire floor was pumping it out. It was growing fast and thick, rising upward. It smelled of mildew and sulfur, and it physically squeezed him as it rose, like a snake wrapping itself around its next meal.

"No, you idiot!" Henri shouted, covering his mouth and nose with his shirt. "Henri! You out there! Stop it!" He coughed, gagging as the vapor rose and burned into his airways. "I AM you. You kill me and we both die!"

The vapor stopped rising, though it kept squeezing him.

Coughing, Henri doubled up his shirt over his face, angry, waiting. Slowly the squeezing pressure eased off and the vapor receded back down into the dirt. Henri paced around the small space waiting for it to disappear altogether. Finally, when it was safe to do so, he slumped down to the ground. He had to get out of here somehow.

He leaned his head back to look up at that dot of light so far away. He was so deep in this hole, even the angels probably couldn't even fly down here. Wherever "here" was.

How was he going to get out? He wished for a nice, spiraling staircase, or even a knotted rope hanging down. He was still breathing, still alive, so there had to be a way. *God,* he thought, *how do I get out of here? How do I not die down here?*

The pain passed nearly as quickly as it had come, and Outside Henri took a moment as his body pulled itself together. He could feel Nefas' essence pulsing therapeutically through his shoulder and neck muscles, relaxing them and working to straighten his bent body. It took a moment, but his body and mind quickly enough reasserted itself over the pain of the fight inside.

That inside part of him had to die, had to be euthanized. He wouldn't be able to have Nefas' mind, he couldn't be perfectly united with him, if his essence and his void had to share real estate with his inner self. And there was too much on the line to fail.

With a shaky breath, Henri assessed himself as recovered enough and then wiped off his knees. Standing back up, he headed off again. He passed a darkened, glass door and stopped to see what his new, essence-infused reflection looked like. He moved this way and that to catch the different angles of himself, and as he got familiar with his new look, another figure slowly faded into view behind him. Henri stopped and watched the figure materialize in the dull mirror: a dry-boned skeleton draped in the brown robes of a monk. The long sleeves of his robe cascaded down in front of him, and his toothy, fleshless grin clacked ceaselessly to the rhythm of words that had long ago died along with him. The monk was one of four, an extension of Nefas. Henri knew this inherently, and he was insulted by his presence. Henri had just delivered more people into Nefas' hands at one time than this monk ever had, and he was still being assigned a babysitter?

Henri cautiously turned around, meeting the skeleton monk face to face. The time for checking himself out was over. With a glare into the black holes that were the monk's empty eye sockets, Henri continued on to the gate, and to Adrien, where he would deliver to Nefas an even greater success.

The monk followed silently behind. It was unsettling; like having the chill breath of death breathing coolly down the back of his neck. Henri was sure the monk wouldn't be with him for long though. He wouldn't be needed after Adrien opened the gate.

"Where's Nicholas?" Fae demanded of Dominic.

Beside her, Max answered. "Nefas isn't looking for the baby tonight. That baby grew up."

"He grew up?" It was a natural thing for babies to do, but not this one. This one ended the Gift every Christmas morning. Took the parasite out of the villagers. This one couldn't grow up. "That still doesn't tell me where he is."

Thud, thud, thud, thud, thud.

Fae abandoned her question as she looked around the pillar to the door. She didn't have to leave the basilica, she reminded herself. She'd have Dominic beside her the whole time to protect her. Nefas' taunting questions from her past rose to her memory: *What happened to Dominic? Where did Nicholas go?* She set her jaw. The past was the past, and Dominic was beside her now.

"There's more going on tonight than just you," Max was telling her, instructing her.

She managed to tear her eyes away from the door to meet his, bright and alive. No longer was he just a friendly, young bar tender; he was serious and focused, and she recognized in him the same kind of strength she knew Dominic possessed. But at this point, that was only mildly reassuring.

"Nefas has a couple of loose ends he wants to tie up before morning," he said. "You're only one."

"And the other loose ends?"

"Aren't yours to deal with." Max fished out the necklace from beneath his shirt and let the small vial swing in front of her. "Mine doesn't look like yours by coincidence. I know you have the other one. Cuvelier didn't think to unpack it a couple days ago on his own. You needed to have it for tonight. Keep it close and do *not* let Nefas know you have it."

"What is it?"

"Something he's wanted longer than you. Don't worry about what it is right now, just know that he'll go to incredible lengths to get it from you and that makes it very valuable."

Thud, thud, thud, thud, thud.

The knocking was more demanding this time and Fae knew she had to go. She only had to tell Nefas what he already knew she was going to say and then close the door on him. It was that simple, she lied to herself. She conjured up an image of Bailey and Jordan and the life without the shadow of Nefas over it that they deserved.

With jaw clenched tight, Fae forced herself out of the security of the aisle and the protection of the pillars, Dominic and Max walking tall on either side.

"Mrs. Fae!" Jenny rushed up to her, long curls bouncing. "Let me go with you."

Fae slowed her walk but didn't stop. "I need you to stay with Henri's family and the others."

"Isaac went out there, Mrs. Fae, and we came to chase away the power of darkness, not be overcome by it. I know what the Lord assigned for us, and—"

"And I'm telling you how to do it," Fae snapped. "Ask God to tell you I'm right, unless you're so wrapped up in your 'assignment' that you forgot to bring him with you." Fae kept walking, leaving Jenny behind. She wasn't sorry for what she'd said, but maybe for how she'd said it.

An arm's length away from the wooden door, Fae faded to a stop. What was she doing? Nefas was out there. She could feel him on the other side, just like how a reformed drug addict could become hyperaware of their favorite powder across the room.

Nefas knocked again, gentler, more civilized, and Fae knew he could feel her too. *Knock, knock, knock.*

"Fae?" Nefas spoke her name. That perfect voice, which had endlessly haunted her dreams, passed through the door, speaking life back into all her fears. It was just deep enough to be like warm honey, gentle enough to make Nefas' lies convincing. "Fae."

She let out a long, shaky breath. *You bastard.* She just had to tell him to go away. Her hand found the metal of the door handle, the cold seeping into her fingers. The next thing she knew, she was opening the door.

There was one lone man standing outside on the porch, made to look all the more alone by the richness of the architecture and reliefs framing him. He was all she could see, all she was aware of. Dominic and Max were forgotten; the choir, no longer heard. Jenny, Katie, Henri—they all belonged to a different life. Nefas stood there, matured to match her own maturity; but like a Hollywood silver fox, the added years only served his advantage. Salty blond hair, muscled frame, secretive smile, black jeans and a midnight blue button-up shirt—he was still perfect.

"I've missed you so much, Fae," Nefas said with an honesty that sounded real. He held out a thorned rose to her. "I'm sorry."

21

"Fae, I'm sorry," Nefas said again. "Forgive me. As you were once forgiven?"

Fae wasn't sure what to say. What was he doing? *Forgive* him? He didn't know what that word meant. There was no forgiveness in him.

"I need you to give me what I don't have." Nefas offered the rose again, and Fae nervously stepped back. This was not the reunion she'd imagined. This was Nefas, but not the stalking, hate-filled, manipulator she remembered.

"Say something, Fae. It's been so long since we've seen each other." He held the rose between them, it alone breeching the doorsill. He was playing dangerously close to his threshold, and Fae became aware of Dominic and Max again, still beside her, watching the action closely.

She found her tongue, and it felt thick, and weak. "You've never left me."

"That's hardly the same thing. We used to be like an Italian sonnet, you and I." With a charming smile Nefas offered her the rose a third time, but she still didn't take it. Didn't even acknowledge it. If she took her eyes off him, it would be a mistake. But maybe so was not taking her eyes off him.

Her hands were starting to shake. She clenched them tightly so Nefas wouldn't see. "I don't want you anymore. You have nothing to tempt me with."

Nefas lowered his head slightly and gave a sideways grin. "Are you so sure? Despite our long separation, I still know you perfectly; I still know what you want. All those presents I gave you in the void are still waiting, unopened."

Fae swallowed a thick lump in her throat. He looked so sophisticated. It would be so easy to convince herself that he wasn't responsible for any of the horrible things she'd blamed him for. Which was exactly why she shouldn't be standing at this door any longer. Her shaking was spreading throughout her body, and her shoulders were tightening in a vain attempt to keep herself calm. He was going to notice.

"Don't ever come near me again. In any shape or form. Nicholas earned at least that much for me, and you will respect that." Fae was barely breathing. No one demanded anything of Nefas without living to regret it.

"You still trust him?" Nefas looked surprised. "That selfish imp has never shown up to enforce that imaginary restraining order. Why do you think he's going to now?" He flashed a half smile. "If you really want to never see me again, forgive me. Do it to free yourself, to stop poisoning yourself with unforgiveness. Forgive me, and we both get what we want. Take the rose, Fae." He gently tossed it down into the basilica and it landed without sound.

She couldn't do this much longer.

"Nicholas did his job that day."

"Don't cover for him like his b—"

"You have nothing to do with me anymore. Remember that." Fae sharply grabbed the edge of the door to close it hard and fast, but Nefas saw the action coming and spoke quickly.

"I have a number of people outside who are in my possession."

"Their *choice* to leave this basilica has nothing to do with me."

She grabbed for the door again, but Nefas was still quicker.

"What if your choices have everything to do with them?" he asked, a familiar coldness replacing his humble persona.

Fae stalled. "No, you can't do—" His eyes flashed, but he covered it quickly and the old need to not make him angry pulsed through her. "...that."

He didn't like being told what he couldn't do either. This was more like the Nefas she expected. It was getting harder to breathe.

"If you close that door before we're done," Nefas said calmly, "I'll play with my new friends so that their screaming will keep time for all the disgusting noises coming from inside this animal barn."

This was getting out of control. "Dominic?" She called to him to make sure he was still there. She couldn't do this. Those people out there weren't her problem.

Dominic answered, "Fear will kill you."

She let her eyes drop down to where the rose lay across the doorsill, and within a blink, the perspective of her surroundings changed. The world looked like a stretched elastic, and Nefas, the basilica door, the rose on the ground, lay dozens of feet away. Whichever direction she looked, everything stretched out before her, and disoriented, she could feel herself losing her balance. She reached out for Dominic, but he looked far beyond her reach and her searching arms couldn't find him. She called his name, but if he said anything, she didn't hear him. Her ears were ringing. She had to close that door and lock Nefas out. She reached out for where she thought it should be, hoping to touch anything she could orient herself with.

Someone grabbed her shoulder. She tried to see who it was. The distortion of her view provided no answers.

"You should've taken the rose from my hand," Nefas said. In that instant, her vision returned to normal, but it was too late. She'd stumbled outside the protection of the basilica walls, and it was Nefas' hand on her shoulder.

"Fae," she heard Dominic beside her. He'd followed her out. "Even though you're among death, fear no evil."

Because the Lord is with me, she thought. The words of her grandmother's favorite Psalm. *Run back inside, finish this where he can't hurt you.*

Nefas let his hand glide down her arm, and she shirked away, letting her feet carry her backward toward the inside. But her back hit the cool stone of the outside wall instead.

"Don't," Nefas warned, his voice gently authoritative. He didn't move from where he stood, and he let the distance between them stand. "Don't go back inside until we're done."

A breeze rose up, shifting his stiff shirt so it folded around his body, and for a moment she became just angry enough to push aside the fear. "I told you to leave me."

Nefas shook his head. "You told me to stay away." He motioned behind him as though beckoning someone forward. The corpses were milling about, wandering restlessly, and they were starting to find their way out of the plaza. "This religious life"—he nodded toward the basilica—"isn't you. It never was. Places like this are daycares run by selfish children. I've wanted to teach you how to rule men. Why are you letting your idealized image of your savior baby keep you with the toddlers?"

Before Fae could say anything, she saw over Nefas' shoulder who he'd summoned. The corpses were shuffling out of the way to make room for three hooded monks who were emerging from the crowd. The light of the corpses' parasites reflected dully off their skulls peeking out from beneath their brown hoods, and they were herding their recently acquired victims…prisoners… hostages, whatever they were, in front of them. The hostages looked to be in a state of drugged fear, jumping away from things that weren't there, their eyes darting erratically about. Fae could only imagine what kind of combination of the void and the parasite was working in them. It was the three kids that stirred her the most though. The oldest couldn't have been more than thirteen.

At the sight of the hostages, a commotion of gasps, swears, and the sobbing of religious phrases told Fae that a crowd had come to the door to watch, like this was some sort of a spectator show. She picked herself off the stone wall, her anger flashing again. Glancing behind her, she saw that none of the older villagers were there—those who knew better. Katie was though.

Nefas indicated with his finger again, never taking his attention of her. One of the monks pushed the nearest person forward, a young man with a patchy scruff for a beard. A couple people behind her worriedly called his name, Jean.

"Come with me, Fae, and I will show you how to rule."

She shook her head. She wasn't going anywhere with him.

Nefas didn't even blink. A corpse standing close to Jean grabbed and laid into the young man, pumping the parasite into his veins. Jean jumped from a sedated, stupor to frozen agony, his mouth locked into a silent scream. Fae wasn't interested in Nefas' games. There was nothing she could do for these people. They'd made their choice.

Nefas was watching her closely. He nodded slowly. "But how many people will you let suffer?" Even as Jean was still being injected, a second monk grabbed the next person by the shoulders. This time it was Isaac.

"Come with me and I'll leave him alone."

"Isaac!" Jenny screamed from behind Fae. Nefas quickly snapped his attention to her, a gleam picking up in his eye. "Devil, I cast you out!" Jenny stormed out of the door, but Fae twirled around on her before she got more than two steps out. She grabbed Jenny by the shoulders and threw her back inside the basilica, harder than she expected. Jenny stumbled backward, the crowd catching her before she fell. "Stay inside," Fae commanded. "Help your husband by doing your thing in there."

"And what are you doing?" Jenny said back, finding her feet. It was a sharp comment, and it struck a nerve. Fae said she could do nothing, she'd washed her hands of doing anything, but here Nefas was torturing people to get her to do something.

She turned her back on Jenny without answering.

Nefas had the unmistakable creep of a smile coming on his face as though he knew what was coming next, and it made Fae's next words even harder because she didn't want to give him the satisfaction of knowing her so well.

"I'll go with you," she said. She didn't say it boldly, or strongly, but she said it. "*We* will go with you." She nodded toward Dominic and Max. She didn't know if Max came with the deal, but she was dragging in Dominic regardless. Between those two and the threat of Nicholas, wherever he was, that came with her, she'd have enough to at least keep her alive. "Not to forgive you, or to learn anything you think I should know, but because I want Henri back. And Isaac. And those kids, and everyone else here. And I want you to leave me the hell alone."

Nefas' creeping smile bloomed. "How I've missed you."

He swept wide his arm, inviting Fae to follow him, but Max stepped forward first, dangling his necklace between his fingers. Nefas' smile instantly disappeared, his eyes narrowing. The younger man wasn't intimidated.

"Fae sees the morning alive," Max dictated.

"Who are you?" Nefas growled into Max's face. "And where did you get that?"

"If you kill Fae, you will never, ever see this vial again."

"*Who* are you?"

It was a question Fae would love to know the answer to too, but how did Nefas not know?

"Next time we meet, Nefas, I'll make sure you know who I am."

Nefas worked his jaw, trying to keep his composure in front of his audience. A roll of iridescent green fog was appearing.

"Not even my friend Dominic here is as bold as you."

Max smiled a slight, devious little grin. "I know what you want, Nefas."

Max was going to get them all killed, vial or not, Fae thought with alarm. Nefas' muscles were bulging beneath his fitted shirt and the fog was expanding rapidly, snaking its way up and around him, spreading across the landing and down the stone stairs. Whatever that dust was, its value to Nefas really was high.

Nefas shifted his focus back to her. "We suddenly have so much more to talk about."

Turning sharply, Nefas stormed down the steps and past the monks holding their hostages. Fae followed as she knew she had to, Dominic coming with her though Max stayed. She wasn't entirely sure what had just happened or what was going to happen next, but Max had changed Nefas' game in the same breath that she'd agreed to leave with him in exchange for the hostages. She wasn't going to thank Max for that anytime soon.

As Nefas stormed past the hostages, he barked an order to his family and three nearby corpses surrounded Isaac, eagerly laying into him with their parasite-ridden fingers. As the parasite forced its way into Isaac's veins, he cried out in agony. Jenny screamed for him from the top of the stairs, Max restraining her from running out.

Sandwiched between Nefas and Dominic, Fae could do nothing except walk past Isaac, locked in the monk's iron grip, as he struggled for his soul. She couldn't even look at him.

Henri was happy to see that Adrien had been a good boy and was waiting at the gate like he'd been told. Adrien had lost his trapper hat and sunglasses, and without them Henri had the chance to see what Adrien Jandreau, the real-life ghost, looked like, taking into account that it'd probably been a long time since he'd last stolen a shower. His unkept ponytail was his most distinct feature with his hair being a heavy mix of gray with brown. Only fine lines etched his face as he hadn't had the chance to develop users' creases. Cleaned up, he could look like anyone's father. Just, one who could still run up walls and jump across roofs with a smooth finishing summersault.

Adrien wasn't acting much like an adult at the moment, though. Sitting in the middle of the road, the street lamps around the gate creating something of a lit stage for him, he was tying and retying his shoe laces together as though to play a practical joke on himself when he stood up. It was no wonder Nefas needed someone else; mentally, Adrien was still a teenager.

As Henri and his monk escort approached, Adrien looked up and he redid his laces one last time, properly.

"He sent you."

Henri wasn't sure to which of them Adrien was referring, and he didn't ask for clarity. He stopped in front of Adrien, who looked up at him with as much life as a fifteenth century portrait.

"You have a job to do. Let's go."

Adrien stood, irritatingly slowly, and led Henri to the guardhouse, taking the key for it out of his pocket. He also took off the rose-gold watch he'd been wearing and held it out for Henri. "This belongs to the English girl. I took it from her room. Nefas said you'll need it."

Henri zipped it up safely in his jacket.

Adrien unlocked the guardhouse, empty for the night as the village gates were closed and the danger they were to protect against was supposed to still be locked underground. Adrien went in but Henri stopped short.

"Adrien," he said, nodding down to where a Communion setting was problematically placed at the threshold.

Adrien looked down at the Communion and shrugged as though he didn't know what to do with it.

"Move it. I can't get in with it there."

Rolling his eyes, Adrien bent down and picked up the bread and cup and tossed them into the garbage before heading directly to the file cabinet, where he opened and closed drawers in rapid succession. Henri came in but the monk remained outside, his toothy-jaw clacking away.

Finding what he was looking for, Adrien loosely flapped a user's manual in Henri's face.

"This is for that," Adrien said, pointing to a single button with a key switch beside it. "That button controls the gate once I unlock it."

"And the key?" Henri asked pointing to the empty key switch. "Where's that?"

"I did parkour, not pickpocketing. I couldn't get it. And neither, apparently, could Nefas, for all his talents. But that's why I get to climb up to the top of the gate to try and short circuit it open," he said flatly. "Considering I didn't even get to finish secondary school, you should be impressed. Did he tell you who my lucky backup is if I get electrocuted?"

Henri tossed the worthless manual aside. He didn't like the way Adrien was talking to him.

"Was it a beautiful summer morning that day Nefas took you?"

Adrien paused. "I don't remember."

"Do you ever visit your old house and stare at the blood-stained floorboards?"

A nerve twitched at the side of Adrien's eye, but other than that, he barely reacted. He really was dead inside. "He asphyxiated them with carbon monoxide. There's no blood."

"So, you have gone back," Henri confirmed, "otherwise you wouldn't know for sure."

Adrien's eye twitched again.

"To your old bedroom? Does it bother you that everyone thinks you're just a ghost story? That your life never did, and never will, matter?"

Adrien slammed shut the last metal cabinet drawer. "You need a heart to care. Mine stopped bleeding a long time ago."

"You cared enough to apologize for introducing me to Nefas."

Adrien shook his head, shouldering his way past Henri to go back outside. Henri followed.

Shedding his coat and leaving it where it fell, Adrien positioned himself directly beneath the overhang of the low roof. With a quick jump, he leapt up, grabbed the edge, and deftly pulled himself up, rolling into a stand.

The guard booth was built into the natural corner created by the gate and the protruding gate tower, and it was this corner that Adrien was going to have to shimmy up to get to the electrical system that would unlock the gates. It was a shallow corner, less than an arm's length deep, and it was also about twelve meters straight up. Henri hoped Adrien had been training.

Adrien backed up to the very edge of the guard booth and sized up the task before him. He cracked his knuckles, his neck, loosened up his shoulders. A couple deep breaths, and then with an explosive burst, he sprinted toward the corner. Leaping up onto one side, he bounced off it to the other side, back and forth propelling himself up higher and higher. Doing what he was doing demanded incredible strength and energy to keep up the required momentum, and if Adrien didn't make it, Henri thought ironically, he'd simply fade away. No one mourns a ghost.

Adrien did make it to the top, astonishingly. Henri could see his chest visibly heaving even from twelve meters below, and Henri continued to keep an eye on him as he took a moment to get his breath back before standing up and looking out over the village.

"The corpses are coming."

"Then get that gate open," Henri shouted.

"What?" Adrien didn't wait for Henri to repeat himself. "It's going to take a couple minutes. Wait inside for my signal!" Adrien backed away from the edge and effectively disappeared into the foggy night.

With nothing left to do, Henri went back inside, trying to ignore the monk, to wait for Adrien's signal to push the "gate open" button. Simply pushing a button didn't feel like a monumental contribution to the night, but it would finish what Henri had already started. Just like how Nefas couldn't enter the basilica, he also couldn't open the gate. It wasn't his village, so it'd been up to Henri to be Nefas' voice, and now his hands as well.

As the guard booth was really only employed during December, it was both expectantly sparse and interestingly decorated with trinkets shared by the two guards. A mini-Nativity was beside the monitor screen. Two characters from the Asterix comics had places next to a daily checklist, and someone was working on a cheap pen collection. Uninterested in any of it, Henri moved his attention to the filing cabinets Adrien had been searching through. There was a not-so-secret stash of alcohol: a bottle of unopened red, and a barely drunk bottle of brandy. He pocketed the brandy.

The top drawer was empty except that on the bottom of it *In Case It Gets Out of Control* was written in marker and there was a white outline around a cannister of Velcroed pepper spray. Apparently, the guards were prepared for some extreme encounters. Behind the spray can was written *In Case It Gets REALLY Out of Control* and there was a white outline in the shape of a hunting knife. The pepper spray was still there. The knife was not.

Henri slammed the drawer shut and stormed outside. "Adrien!"

It was at that moment that that sharp stabbing pain at the top of his neck returned with a vengeance, dropping him to his knees. He grabbed the back of his neck, squeezing it to try and stop the crushing pain, trying anything to stop the explosions tearing his brain apart, to quiet his own yelling. His vision was on the verge of blacking out.

It was his inner self trying to fight back again against Nefas' essence. "This time you *will* die!" Henri growled through heavy breaths.

Stuck at the bottom of his earthen prison, Inner Henri was enough of a realist to know the top of the hole was out of his reach, but he also wasn't so short sighted that he believed "up" was the only way out. Considering how far down he was already, digging even deeper wasn't his best choice, so he'd gone horizontal, hacking away at his prison wall with his heel, loosening the dirt and scooping it out with his hands. The process felt slow, but he also had no real concept of time. So far, he'd managed to dig a tunnel the length of his body, creating a pile of dirt occupying much of his precious floor space, and he hadn't even come across a rock to suggest he was going the right way.

He lay flat in his cramped little tunnel, scooping dirt with his fingertips, perfect darkness leaving him only with his sense of touch to guide him forward. With another handful of dirt tossed behind him, he wondered if this tunnel was a waste of time. Memories of life coaches and enthusiastic preachers shouting to "keep going! Your goal is on the other side!" now sounded like nothing more than the hot air of someone who simply knew the right things to say rather than the honest thing to say. Sometimes, stopping while still somewhat ahead was even better advice.

Face to face with his earthy reality-check, Henri decided that he'd be digging like an earthworm until he died if he kept this up. There were no other prison cells to connect with, no one else for him to dig his way to, so he wiggled himself back out. He shook the dirt out from his hair and sat back on his haunches, taking in that little beam of light, relishing it for everything that it was. His failed digging experience left him tired, but he didn't want to close his eyes to see the outside. He had no control over when he did or did not see the outside, and he didn't feel like risking seeing it again, not now. He didn't want to see everything Henri Meyer got to still enjoy. But his eyes fell shut on him anyway, the need to sleep overwhelming.

Scenery of the village filled his vision. The Henri outside was bent over in agony, holding his head, trying to force himself to keep his eyes on the village's wall. A skeleton monk stood in sentry nearby not trying, or wanting, to help. Outside Henri cramped down again, pain spiking beyond what he could absorb. As Inner Henri looked through his own eyes to the outside, his vision started to black out. He blinked hard to clear his eyes, but the encroaching blackness didn't go away. It kept growing, blocking out more and more of his sight. He was panting for breath like he was brutally out of shape.

"Hey, stop it! No!" Henri yelled at himself. "We've been over this already!"

He was sucking in air, but it wasn't enough to satisfy. The air was becoming increasingly oxygen deprived.

"If I go," Henri threatened himself breathlessly, "We're both dead."

Henri's vision to the outside was almost blacked out, his lungs were screaming for something to get in.

"Give me air!"

Henri knew he didn't have a lot of negotiation time left. "Please . . ."

Nothing happened.

Henri fell to his side, squirming, gasping.

Then, from nowhere, a puff of oxygen-filled air came, and Henri greedily sucked it in, filling his lungs. The rich air kept coming, and Henri shook his head.

He had to get out of here. Next time, Outer Henri might not lose the nerve before finishing the job.

Catching his breath, Henri sat back up and reassessed his options. Going up was the only way. He had no rope, or lucky flood waters to push him up and out, but he did have one quasi-skill. He could climb. And this time he wouldn't have Levi telling him to harness up. He'd rather die from an exhausted fall, which he probably would, than be suffocated by a body hijacker.

Henri pulled off his belt and wrapped it around his hand, holding the buckle between his fingers to act as his digging tool. He'd carve steps into the earth and work his way up, and hope that he didn't die trying.

23

Nefas stalked through the sea of corpses like a god amid his creation. The corpses got out of his way like they were being repelled from him, a four-foot dead zone being cleared on either side. Fae walked behind him feeling both like his prisoner being paraded and his honored guest, and the two were not mutually exclusive.

Fae didn't know where they were going. She tried to keep her thoughts empty; they'd only be fuel for her imagination to go off in a thousand terrible directions. She kept glancing to Dominic for reassurance that he hadn't left her, and she was always rewarded seeing him half a step behind, straight faced, eyes locked on Nefas' back.

Nefas said nothing as he led on, never checking to make sure she was still following. He was effectively ignoring them, and the tactic wasn't lost on her; he was giving her time to get used to being near him again. Acceptance was always the first step to recovery.

Nefas chose the major roads for their route rather than the maze-like streets of the inner village, and it didn't take long to see that they were headed toward the outer wall. It was almost impossible at that point to stop herself from believing that he was leading them to his pit. Regardless of what Max had threatened, Nefas was going to try and finish what he'd started with her all those years ago.

They didn't go to his pit though, and when they arrived at an undistinguished section of the wall, it was both too soon and not soon enough. The wall felt like a quiet monster that was not meant to be disturbed, and yet, Nefas didn't hesitate to do exactly that as he stopped in front of one of the wall's many watch towers. Only wide enough for a staircase and a small platform on top, the towers were more architecturally balancing than anything else. The stairway door looked like it hadn't been opened since it was built hundreds of years ago. Nefas walked right through it. A moment later the door slammed open from the inside, small pieces broken off flying through the air. Fae ducked, and when the debris settled, Nefas was gone, the ascending brick steps disappearing into the darkness. Fae was supposed to follow, she knew, but Nefas could have anything in there: traps or jump scares, corpses, the void revived . . . Dominic gently took her elbow and guided her in.

"C'mon," he said.

She held onto Dominic's arm and followed him up the stairs, each step going against every internal warning she had.

The exit door was similarly blown open, and a chill air ushered them out and onto the roof. Nefas was waiting for them, his cut figure dark against the night. His back was to her as he slowly strolled around the small platform. He looked like a country nobleman taking in the view before retiring for the evening.

"Fae, come here." Nefas invited her over. His first acknowledgement since the basilica. Hoping to get this over with quickly, she cautiously went, her feet crunching against built-up gravel and bird poop. She heard Dominic right behind her.

Nefas was looking over the village. It would've been a pretty sight, given a different situation. The basilica's red and white spires piercing up between the steep roofs layered one behind the other; streetlamps and strings of lights drooping across the roads outlining the maze below. It was a whimsical view, wasted; the veins and arteries of the village were coming alive with the slow creep of the corpses' green light. The corpses had spread out from the basilica's plaza in the heart of the village and were slowly filling in the outlines of the streets and alleys, seeping outward. The bulk of the corpses were headed north, toward the gate. Nefas wanted out.

"I want you to see the life you're meant to have," Nefas said suddenly, turning to face her. His face was relaxed, but on it was written an invitation for more, and Fae that keenly felt it. She didn't want to see how human he looked, and no doubt felt, so she kept her eyes fixed on the village and watched as its streets were illuminated by the corpses.

"You deserve a life where you're appreciated for who you are, no hiding, and no shame." Nefas continued, inching a little closer. Fae tried to concentrate even harder on the village. "I chose you. What is unfolding before us is the birth of my kingdom on earth as it has never been known before."

His eagerness was growing and he sounded almost genuine, as though he was trying to reign in his excitement. He inched closer still. Dominic's feet scraped against the roof, which was enough to halt Nefas from coming any closer. His eyes were hot on her, and she couldn't help but steal a glance at him; he was the image of refined sophistication.

"What did the start of the universe look like?" he pondered quietly. "How did it feel when it all exploded into place? What did the first inhale of air sound like?" He let his voice fade out—either from memory or longing, Fae didn't know—but he quickly spoke again with a new thought. "I'm envious of the place you occupy in history."

Turning away from her, he looked out over the village, sharing her view. "I didn't just miss you all these years, Fae," he said, confessing. "I raged at your very memory."

Despite his words, his voice was as smooth and melodic as it had ever been, and she inched away, feeling acutely unsafe. Nefas stepped behind her, holding her between himself and the parapet.

"You've been my morning sickness every day, and yet here I am with you while your Nicholas sent his proxy to bodyguard you." He dropped his voice low and all the feelings of his enslavement and all the memories that came with the sound of him flooded back, alive and on fire. "You don't have to love me, Fae, but you should understand the value of a mutually beneficial partnership. I told you once that you would be my queen. I haven't forgotten."

Fae's heart pounded and she willed herself to disappear. She didn't want this, couldn't trust herself with him. She'd told them bad things would happen.

She stepped to the side to get around him, but his moves matched hers.

"I'm not going to be your anything," she whispered.

Nefas paused.

Fae held her breath.

She'd made him angry.

Suddenly and crisply he backed off, giving her her space. He leaned back against the parapet flashing a quick grin, as though he had all the time in the world.

"I understand. We left on poor terms. I've tried all these years to remind you of what a powerful pair we are—"

Fae almost choked on her own breath. "You've haunted me and hunted me," she whispered.

"Trying to *save* you!" He stopped, controlled himself, then looked back over his shoulder, out into the village. "They cast a beautiful light, don't they? My family?"

"How many satellites are out there watching right now?" Fae asked. "How long until these people are locked up?"

"You're thinking too linearly," he said easily. "They'll be celebrities. Viral, marketing magic, and Henri and Katie have all the skills I need to make it happen; even if they don't know it yet." Nefas gave a self-satisfied grin. "Of course, I have backups in case either disappoint." He beckoned her to follow him to the other side, but she didn't move, her nerves crawling and her heart pumping too fast from his closeness.

"It's OK," Dominic said to her with reassurance.

"I can't do this."

"It's OK," he said again. This time his calmness reached her.

Feelings were controllable, she told herself. Emotions could come and go. Fae took a deep breath and nodded, and together, she and Dominic took the few steps to where Nefas stood, now looking into the Belgian countryside. The moon escaped the clouds just long enough to light up the rolling landscape in a dim, silvery light before hiding away again. A couple lights from homesteads dotted the land through the fog below, but otherwise there was nothing to see but darkness.

"I wouldn't trust me either," Nefas said, noting Dominic's lead. "I still know what you want." He gave a smile. "But rather than baiting you with it, I'm going to give it to you. Right now."

Nefas waited for her to say something, but she didn't know what he wanted her to say. No matter how she responded, it would begin something she didn't want to be a part of.

"Not even curious?" Nefas finally teased, seeing she wasn't biting. "I'm not going to inject you, if that's what you're so afraid of . . . though I could." He stretched out his fingers releasing a look in his eyes that belied his desire. Dominic scuffed his feet, clearing his throat. Nefas relaxed himself.

"I'm going to give you the ability to remove my essence, Fae, to undo the work of my zealous family if you don't agree with it." He raised his eyebrows in expectation, the extended silence between them taut.

She was a mess right now, but she wasn't stupid. "That'd infect me."

Nefas chuckled quietly. "No. Such a deep pleasure is reserved for me alone. You'll draw it out, and it will come directly back to me."

"I don't believe you."

The space between herself and Nefas had all but disappeared again and the weight of his presence was increasing, not oppressively, but authoritatively.

"A queen needs power." He raised an open hand, green fog sitting thickly in his palm. With a little puff, he released it twisting and swirling before her eyes. She was ready to turn away, not about to subject herself to his manipulations, but he grabbed her arm and held her in place. She found Dominic's jacket and held tight.

The fog thickened and expanded in front of her, creating in itself a scene that became infused with all the color and clarity of real life. She watched as the corpses were let out of the village gates. Like a nest of disturbed ants, they seemed to multiply out of nothing and scurried across the countryside, then the cities. They kept spreading, faster and faster through the entire country, then the continent. They crossed the English Channel and the oceans until the whole earth was giving off its own green glow. She could see the people of earth as corpses, everyone she passed on the street, in the drug store, in the parks, and sleeping in their beds. They took over government buildings, theaters, cafes, and overran every religion's holy places. No one was disturbed by the introduction of Nefas' parasite; it was no more of an occasion than a new flavor of the month.

The scene dramatically changed and now Fae found herself in the middle of a hippodrome, designed by her own hand, and larger than any that had ever been built before. She was walking down the middle of it in procession, accompanied by administrators and attendants worthy of her position. Hundreds of thousands, maybe a million or more, parasitic corpses flooded the seats to capacity, their combined glow easily lighting up the darkness. They were as independently animated as she'd ever seen them, cheering and celebrating. Their roar of approval was for her, and the feeling of perfect command over their attention was electrifying. She was their queen.

She met with Nefas there, in the middle of the rolling adulation, never feeling more secure or more important than now, the two of them specks in the middle of the massive arena. Nefas was wearing Max's vial around his neck, a symbol of his status, and Fae was seeing Nefas in a different light. Partners. They could make this work . . .

"No!" she shouted, dispersing the fog and its imagery with waving hands. He was selling her the dream of a coup by a desperate reprobate.

She regripped Dominic's arm, grounding herself back in reality. The feelings of raw power and driven purpose were electric. She'd seen Nefas powerful in the world, worshipped . . . glorious. And she'd been there at his side, embraced just the same. Able to remove parasites, she could be the check and balance to his power, the insider, working to free those he'd enslaved, turning the tide from the inside.

"This is as true as any future I've ever shown you," Nefas said, dipping his head lower to hers. "I know that stirred something inside you." He let his observation rest between them. "This is why I need you to forgive me. It's an opportunity for both of us."

"It will always be an opportunity for you and prison for me," she said carefully, conscious of her tone. His thin patience could snap in a breath, and she extracted herself, moving away from him to put Dominic between them.

"Tonight isn't going to end like it has before," Nefas said, straightening himself. "The Gift is leaving; I'm gifting it to the world. You're not like anyone else on this planet, Fae. I made you who you are, and I'm the only one who can bring you to your full potential. You've been isolated and suppressed, clinging to the memory of a baby you haven't seen or heard from since. Don't you remember?" He looked deeply at her. "You need to die to leave alive."

Fae licked her dry lips.

Nefas nodded to himself. "You need to experience what I'm offering in order to understand. Back down the stairs."

Neither Fae nor Dominic moved.

"*Down* the stairs."

Fae looked to Dominic who was staring hard at Nefas. They traded stares until Dominic finally gave her a subtle nod, then led her back down the dark stairwell. Nefas watched them leave, and then was waiting for them as they exited at the bottom. He set out right away, though this time, he didn't lead like a god, but walked with them.

Fae tried to walk slower so that Nefas would get ahead, but he matched her pace. He walked with an easy stride and Fae had to keep reminding herself that she was only with him to bring those hostages back and not because she wanted anything from him, or because he had anything she wanted.

They came into a neighborhood of houses, all similarly skinny, though each had a unique color with some painted earthy red, rusty yellow, or foresty green, while others let their natural brick show. An urge spurred her to hold the vial hiding in her pocket reassuringly, so she slipped her hand down into her pocket. Dominic must've seen the motion as he lightly bumped into her to get her attention. "No," he mouthed. She returned her hand to her side.

Without warning, Nefas abruptly pulled up, cocking his ear as though having heard something. He walked a little further up the cobbled street, and Fae stayed put until at last he stopped a dozen feet ahead. He was flexing his fingers, balling them tight then releasing them, staring intently ahead. He was waiting like an aggressive father for his son to come home, and the similarity wasn't lost on her.

"Dominic, we should go," Fae said, quietly.

"Where would you go?"

"Anywhere but here."

"ADRIEN!" Nefas shouted, hollering into the night.

"Dominic," Fae pleaded.

"NEFAS!" A responding shout echoed out, not as strong as Nefas', but it was the sound of someone who had nothing to lose.

Fae saw the hopeless man at the same time as Dominic pointed him out. Three houses down, he was standing precariously on the side of a steep roof.

"That's Adrien," Dominic said. "That's where the Jandreau family used to live."

Adrien Jandreau stood completely naked, feet staggered on the rungs of a roof ladder to prevent him from sliding down the sharp incline. Only a glinting knife was gripped in his hand.

"NEFaS!" Adrien's voice cracked. He grabbed his ponytail in one hand and with a couple quick, sharp swipes of the knife, cut it off. Throwing the fistful of hair to the ground two stories below, he shouted at Nefas, who was watching the hair drift down. "You took everything from me!" he yelled. "You murdered my family. You made me the living dead, why? FOR WHAT?"

"For my pleasure," Nefas snapped, slowly getting closer to the house. "Your mother birthed you for my use, and your worthlessness is cemented in your failure to open that gate."

Adrien cried out, the anguish of his life escaping him. His feet slipped on the ladder rungs and he fell hard, sliding down a couple feet before stopping himself in a naked heap on the ladder. The sound of his dying heart carried across the rooftops, all the more tragic because there were so few ears to hear it, and even fewer that cared.

The sudden sound of heavy feet running fast made Fae tear her eyes away from Adrien to where the sound was coming from behind her. Not only did she see the corpses' green glow growing, announcing their soon arrival, but also Henri racing toward her. He was running fast, his shimmering, translucent skin as evident as ever, yelling Adrien's name with the anger of someone who'd just been duped. A brown-robed skeleton monk was coming hard on Henri's heels, the monk's smooth strides somehow enough to match the speed it needed to keep up. Fae grabbed hold of Dominic and hoped the monk didn't see her; those monks were Nefas' enforcers and she'd rather not be noticed.

Henri slowed to a halt when he saw her and Dominic, his eyes rapidly searching the road, the houses. He landed on Nefas standing behind them and his expression quickly turned to surprised horror. Fae inched her way out of being caught in the middle of the two of them as Nefas wheeled on Henri hard, eyes blazing.

"Speaking of failures."

"Adrien was already on top of the wall when he ran," Henri said, sounding like he was trying to defend himself, but Nefas didn't give him the chance.

"Remember why you came into my service, Henri."

Adrien was struggling to stand up again, the cold no doubt numbing his exposed skin. "Henri," Adrien yelled, his voice carrying down the street. Henri looked past Nefas to Adrien on the roof fighting for his balance, the hand holding the knife flailing behind him as he tried to find his footing on the ladder rungs. Henri didn't look any happier at having found his lost charge.

"If you survive this," Adrien yelled again, "forgive me. I had no choice. You'll understand."

"Henri," Nefas snapped, grabbing Henri's attention away from Adrien's conscience-clearing confessions. "You lost Adrien. He's mine now. Get back to the basilica and finish your job. The gate is still waiting to be opened."

With a final glare at Adrien, Henri jogged off, taking the monk with him, and as the monk left, Fae eased up her grip on Dominic.

With Henri gone Nefas turned back to Adrien who was urgently looking every which way, as much as his precarious balance allowed. "Max!" he shouted.

Fae shot Dominic a questioning look. Max? Dominic gave a single nod as though that was explanation enough. Maybe Max was to Adrien what Dominic was to her?

"MAAAX! Where are you?" The hopelessness of his voice matched the tears bleeding into his cry. "I recognized you. In the bar, I knew who you were! I know you knew me too. I couldn't . . ."

Nefas let Adrien continue shouting as he surrounded himself in a swirling vortex of green fog. As the vortex grew all encompassing, Adrien's shouts faded, and a silence heavy with dread filled the air. An identical swirling vortex formed next to Adrien on the roof, and Nefas left the street and stepped down beside Adrien. Adrien clumsily scampered down the ladder for extra distance, but there was nowhere for him to go. Nefas looked so calm, so reasonable, beside Adrien, who was naked, shorn, and losing his motor skills.

"Everything I've done for you . . ." Fae could still hear Nefas' voice clearly even though he wasn't shouting. "I can't let you die looking like that."

Nefas made a quick snatch for Adrien's arm, the parasite glowing bright in his fingers. Instinctively, Adrien tried to wrestle away, but he was no match for Nefas, who held him in an iron grip. Almost before Fae could realize what was happening, Adrien plunged the knife up and into his own chest, his last stand over.

Nefas wasn't bothered, and he kept his grip on Adrien's wilting body. The process of infecting him with the parasite was quick and mean, Adrien's will to fight it literally bleeding out of him. With Adrien's depleting veins being replenished with the parasite, Nefas ripped the knife out of his chest, letting his blood stream down his body. Nefas tossed the knife to the side and dropped Adrien back onto the roof. With a forceful kick, Nefas pushed Adrien over the edge. His body was barely airborne before it landed hard with a sickening thud.

Fae was stunned. Even though the sounds of the approaching corpses were growing louder, she couldn't take her eyes off Adrien's lifeless body. He was just . . . laying there. Motionless. Silent. The village ghost, bleeding out.

Dead.

Fae startled as Nefas suddenly, smoothly, stepped in front of her line of sight, filling her vision with himself, hiding Adrien's body behind his own.

"I had wanted a different death for him," he said sympathetically.

Fae doubted it would've been a better one.

"You need to let go of the hostages now," Fae said, her hollow voice unsteady.

"Why?" Nefas asked. He noticed then that he had some blood on his fingertips and he rubbed them together until it started to dry and roll off. "Whatever you *want* me to do with them," he said, looking up at her from his finger cleaning, "it can be done from anywhere."

"I . . ." Fae didn't know what to say next. She was still hearing the sound of Adrien hitting the stone paving, still seeing him plunging the knife into himself, the screams for Max echoing in her ears. *Jesus*, she thought, *please don't let me have to yell for Dominic like that.* "I came with you," she said. "You've shown me why I need to forgive you. Those were the conditions—" Fae stopped short as she watched Nefas' mood darken. She'd been down this road with him before, long ago, reminding him of verbal agreements, and it hadn't ended well. She forced herself to finish, trusting Dominic's protection. The formulaic words Lars Drechsler had once shouted at Nefas to hold him at bay found their way out of her memory and onto her tongue. "By the blood that never dries and the flesh that never rots . . ." She inhaled. "You owe them their choice between you and the baby. They know both sides of the story now."

She took another deep breath waiting for the consequences of her demand. She couldn't look at him. Nefas drew close to her, his exhaled breath next to her ear like an excited war horse.

"You're not Maria Peeters, and you're not Lars Drechsler. You never were."

Fae flicked her eyes up to his midnight blue shoulders and the white-jacketed arms of Dominic placed warningly on them. Nefas pulled back, or was pushed back, and he fixed his black eyes on her. "You can't play their part. You never belonged in their world. But you do have a place in mine."

Nefas took a step back and nodded down the street to where the first of the corpses had arrived, maybe thirty of them. They were shuffling and staggering, a glowing mob of rotting and decaying bodies, headed straight to where Adrien's body lay. Nefas joined the corpses and flicked his finger for Fae to come too.

"Fae, he's going to give you a choice," Dominic told her as he slowly led her over. "Remember the baby, remember Nicholas, and know that Adrien's body will be properly cared for."

Fae nodded and tried to find the anger that had helped her at the basilica. *Fear will kill you.* Her anger was nowhere to be found as she stopped at Adrien's twisted feet, Nefas standing at his head.

Dark rivers of coagulated blood had found their way from Adrien's heart and cracked head into the seams of the cobblestone pavement. Preserving his dignity, Dominic took off his jacket and placed it over Adrien's exposed body just as the first corpse arrived. One of its crisp white shoes had been lost leaving only a sock hanging off its mummified foot.

"Adrien hasn't been gone so long that my essence can't pump oxygen back into his brain and wake him," Nefas explained, the challenge in his voice unmistakable. "Before I give you the hostages you need to understand what I've made you capable of."

Fae wanted to tell Adrien she was sorry for whatever Nefas was going to do to him next because of her, that she couldn't play his game. But Adrien was dead so he couldn't hear her, and sorry wouldn't be good enough anyway. Without Nicholas here to thwart Nefas' efforts, and no Communion in hand to command his attention like she'd seen Drechsler do before, what did she have? Adrien's body lay between her and Nefas, and Fae felt all the responsibility without any of the power.

Nefas crouched down and began massaging Adrien's temples. "Adrien," he called gently, as though waking him from a soft sleep. The parasite that Nefas had infected him with on the roof lit up inside his chest. "Adrien." As Nefas called him out of his clinical death, the parasite found its heart-beating rhythm, and at the same time, it pooled at the head and chest wounds, plugging them.

"Nefas, you are death," Fae said, staring down at the body twitching to life. "Keep him." She didn't want to see Adrien come back. She couldn't imagine living the life that he had and finally finding release, only to be dragged back into his living hell.

Nefas smirked, dark pleasure cracking his lips. He stopped the massage.

"Adrien!" he called sharply.

Adrien blinked, and his palpitating facial muscles gave away his consciousness. His body shuddered and tears fell from the corners of his eyes.

He pulled his face down into his chest, curling onto his side in the fetal position. "No," he whimpered. "Just let me die."

"Welcome back, Adrien."

At the sound of Nefas' voice, Adrien cried.

Nefas reached over Adrien's curled up body and tossed his arm aside, placing his fingers over his heart and began pulling the parasite out. It retreated from Adrien's veins, going back into Nefas' fingers, leaving behind a body barely surviving. Adrien's kickstarted circulation was fast running out of momentum, and with the parasite removed, his wounds were seeping again. Pitiful crying barely escaped his deep groans, and Fae knew the extraction process wasn't painless. She too had once known the nearly insufferable burning of having the parasite push itself into her body and then have it forced back out. Watching the same process in Adrien, the old entry wound on her leg began to itch and burn.

"Nefas, don't do this to him," she said. She saw the corpse with the one shoe edge closer, its dead, white eyes fixated on Adrien, its own parasite-swollen fingers waiting at the ready.

Nefas locked eyes with her as he stood up, the parasite disappearing into him. "You wanted to be like Lars and *save* people? I've given you a gift, my queen. Only we have the power to take my essence out."

Nicholas needed to be included on that list too, Fae knew, but she kept her mouth closed.

The one-shoed corpse awkwardly leaned down and grabbed Adrien's raised shoulder. Immediately the parasite began pushing its way back into him, and Adrien's helpless crying picked up as soon as the oxygen started to reach his brain again.

"Take my essence out of him, Fae. There's no safer time to try it than now, on the guinea pig."

"Let me die," Adrien croaked.

"You can give Adrien the final death he's earned," Nefas urged her.

"Dominic," Fae looked to him, "do something. Where's Max? He wanted Max."

"This is about you, Fae, not Adrien," Dominic said, unable to hide his anger. "Remember whose side you're on. Nicholas is always with you." He glared at Nefas. "He knows it too."

"Dominic can't do anything," Nefas said, with no little bit of satisfaction. "*You* have to do something." Adrien's body was shuddering, the parasite having plugged his injuries again. "Take it out," Nefas urged again. "I won't give you the hostages until you try. I won't let you refuse this perfect gift until you've tasted it."

"Let him die, Nefas."

"Adrien isn't going to die until *you* let him."

"Fae," Dominic said, "take your eyes off Nefas. He only lies and manipulates."

"Do I?" Nefas snapped, his eyes flaring. "I once promised that I would break you, Fae, and I did, didn't I."

Fae went cold. He had broken her. And he really was going to refuse Adrien death. But what he was asking of her . . .

As though to further his point, Nefas shoved the corpse off Adrien and put his fingers back on Adrien's heart, dragging the parasite back into himself while locking eyes with Fae.

"Nefas," Fae managed, a massive lump stuck in her throat. "I command you with the blood that never dries—"

In a growl of frustration, Nefas used his free hand to haul Adrien to his feet, holding him up by the arm like a marionette, the parasite still being drawn out. It was more than the limp Adrien could bear and he cried out, weakly scratching at Nefas' arm.

"and the flesh that never rots—"

"Symbols that mean *nothing* to me!"

"Lars Drechsler used them to order you—"

Nefas dropped a weeping Adrien to the ground and crossed the distance between them in one stride. Dominic stepped in closer. "You're the girl I *broke*." Nefas blindly grabbed a corpse from behind him, and threw it to the ground beside Adrien, its boney fingers all too eager to do their job. "You're the girl I *owned*, and you're the girl who's been trying to run, but here you are, back with me. Because I *still own you*." He stepped in even closer, but Dominic's arm barred his approach. "It pains me to see you like this when I know your potential. Give Adrien what he wants, be the leader you are, and stop this!"

Adrien was sobbing, crying, both curling up in ball and trying to escape the corpse in a pathetic crawl. With his brain being starved of oxygen in stops and starts, injured from the fall, Fae had no idea what he was able to process. She couldn't do what Nefas wanted her to do, but what if there *was* a bond left between her and Nefas that Nicholas hadn't been able to break? What if that's why she hadn't seen the baby since . . . ?

But she did have the vial that Max said Nefas would do almost anything for.

Dominic intercepted her hand going for her pocket, wedging himself between her and Nefas to cover her. "This is the test," Dominic said, as though she hadn't figured that out. "Fae, you can do this," Dominic encouraged, "but not his way. The wine and bread are only symbols of—"

"How long are you going to be able to watch this?" Nefas asked.

And that was it. She couldn't watch anymore.

"Just let him die!" Fae pushed past them both.

The corpse let Adrien go, its task over. Adrien was left shuddering on the ground, his arm stretched out as though to pull himself away, and Fae quickly dropped to her knee, readjusting Dominic's jacket over him. She didn't know how this worked, but she did what she'd seen Nefas do, and put her fingers on Adrien's clammy, bloody chest, over his heart.

"It's over," she told him, "go home now."

"Nefas," Adrien said, "he's in me . . . I can't . . . get him out."

"It's OK, Adrien. It's OK." Somehow, she began pulling the parasite out of Adrien's chest. The parasite seared as it crawled its way up each of her fingers, and she bit the inside of her lip so that she didn't let out the sounds she was trying to hold in. As Nefas had promised, the parasite crawling up her fingers evaporated into fog and wafted back into him directly.

"I need Max." Adrien was twisting around on the ground trying to look around him. Fae noticed that his heart and head wounds were starting to flow again, slower this time.

"Max is here," Fae said, hoping to God that he was somewhere nearby.

"He's here just like you asked. It's OK. Go home to your parents. Your sister. Think of this place no more."

"Max . . ."

His voice was so weak as he lay limp on the ground. He stopped shivering. Then, at last, Adrien slumped and breathed no more. One last tear slipped from beneath his eyelid and slid down the side of his nose.

Fae fell back on her heels.

"You did it," Nefas said, with calm congratulations, but Fae felt like throwing up. She didn't take the hand Dominic offered to help her stand as she struggled to get up. She couldn't even look at him. "She is your queen now," Nefas announced, addressing the corpses surrounding them. "Listen to her. Together we will bring your destiny."

Fae withered on the inside. Nefas had said she only had to try the power he'd offered her, not that it represented her acceptance of anything . . .

Hello Fae.

NO! Any exhaustion and self-loathing Fae had just earned herself was instantly replaced with deep horror. It was the Voice, that deep, warming disembodied sound of Nefas. She hadn't heard it since Nicholas freed her; it had gone wherever she'd gone, speaking directly into her thoughts.

"Get away from me!"

Nefas was standing across from her, lips not moving, but there was buzzing all around her. Why was it back? It shouldn't be back!

Lucky girl.

Fae grabbed the side of her head and screamed, "Get away!"

Nefas laughed and winked at her, the creases of his face getting deeper, his black eyes swimming and churning with delight.

"No! Nefas, no!"

I've missed you.

"You made me do this! I didn't choose you!"

Nefas smiled ironically. "You took my gift and used it. That *was* your choice."

"I only need Nicholas!"

Nefas raised an eyebrow. "As queen, I think you're going to want to see what Henri is up to now. Our trip to the gate is going to have to wait until it's been opened." With a nod, Nefas walked away. "I'll be waiting over there."

You're not ready to handle me on your own.

Fae was shaking her head, backing away, trying feebly to get that voice away from her, wanting nothing more than a dark hole to hide in. Dominic grabbed hold of her shaking arms and safely folded them up in front of her, holding her tightly.

"His voice is back. I let him . . . I tried what I knew with the Communion, it didn't work. He's back, he's—"

"He's playing your fears," Dominic told her, smoothly, calmly. "He doesn't own you, you're not his, but he's going to keep trying to make you believe he does until its true. You're still under Nicholas' protection and only you can leave it."

"I want back inside the Notre-Dame, Dominic. I can't win against him." Fae shook her head, pleading with him. "He's going to kill me." Her eyes drifted down to the body of Adrien laying coldly on the ground.

"He's not going to kill you," Dominic assured her, "Nicholas won't let him. You're a matter of lost pride, and he won't risk trying again if Nicholas won't let him finish. Those people you came out here to save? They still need you."

The corpses were thinning out as they resumed their slow walk to the gate, past Fae and Adrien, and Fae noticed near the edge of the crowd Max and another man. He'd come. She hadn't lied to a dying man after all. Max put up a finger for her to stay silent and both he and the other man slipped into the shadows of the housing, coming toward Adrien. They must be here to take care of his body like Dominic said.

It was all too much for Fae. Secure in Dominic's protective hold, she cried.

25

Time meant nothing inside this earthen hole, Inner Henri had concluded. As he dug away at the dirt, carving out one hand hold after another, slowly scaling his way upwards, he determined that the relationship between how time passed in here and how it passed on the outside was inconsistent. And, he had even less control than earlier over when he could see the outside. No longer were his visions limited to random luck when he closed his eyes, but now they happened when his eyes were open too. He'd be digging and suddenly he'd see through the other Henri's eyes for a couple of seconds, or for a minute, and then the vision would be over as quickly as it'd begun. The only reliable measure for the passage of time in here was how many handholds he carved out. Ten handholds might reveal that the Henri outside had barely run a block, while two could mean ten minutes has passed on the outside.

In his last glimpse, he'd seen Outer Henri entering the basilica. That was a good thing, the basilica was safe. But he could also feel his hatred and embarrassment, and then that glimpse had ended and he was left alone again in the darkness, hanging onto the side of the shaft by his fingers and toes wondering what was happening out there.

Henri began scraping out the next hold above him. The sooner he finished it the sooner he could step up and switch sides, giving one leg and arm a rest, and punishing the other. The handholds were shallow, and he'd already broken through enough of them. The darkness left him no gauge of how far he'd climbed, and the piercing bolt of unwavering light was unchanging no matter how high he went. The pinprick was still a pinprick far above him, and the spot on the ground remained a spot.

He distracted himself from straining muscles, broken fingernails, near falls and the tedious, numbing digging with two repeating themes: getting out, and Josie.

God, get me out of here. I don't want to die in this place. Can your angels even fly this deep?

He pushed himself up another hold switching his belt buckle to the other hand and began scraping, letting the dirt fall onto his head and down his arm. He couldn't see anything anyway, so he kept his head down to stop dirt falling in his eyes.

Josie, this won't be the end. I'm going to need serious therapy after this, but I promise I'll be waiting for you in the morning.

God, get me out of here.

A trembling of the earth caused Henri to freeze. An earthquake? It escalated quickly into full shaking as dirt fell on him, and he could hear it shaking loose, falling down the shaft. He shoved his digging hand as deep into the unfinished hole as he could, struggling to find someplace for his unsupported leg to go. The quake wasn't letting up.

His digging hand was the first to lose its grip, his fingers having clawed themselves to the edge, breaking through the bottom. He felt his foot about to break its hold too.

He madly tried to re-grip his fingers as the tunnel continued having its seizure. This was Levi's gym all over again, security literally slipping through his fingers. His loose hand swiped out and found something solid and he gripped fast, pulling himself hard against the wall, holding it for all it was worth.

The shaking stopped.

Henri was panting, as much from relief as from the physical exertion, and despite his tenuous grips, he took a moment to relish the fact that nothing was moving or shaking beneath him.

He was grabbing something that felt like a root, thin and tough, and it was solidly anchored. If his muscles had been complaining before, they were in full protest now.

His vision jumped to the outside world. He was looking at a reflection of himself in a bottle of open brandy, and he could see in his eyes that he was both determined and scared. Two Henries looking through the same eyes.

"Hello, old friend," he heard himself say. "Lucky grab." Outer Henri looked up from the bottle to where a young woman with shoulder length blonde hair was taking a sloppy drink from a chalice. They were inside the Notre-Dame du Seigneur. "Please die now."

"Not a chance. Without me, you're dead, not freed."

"You're not going to want to be around for what I have to do to her," the other Henri said looking at the blonde girl.

"Don't do it," Henri warned. "Don't—"

The root he'd been holding onto began slipping through his fingers.

"Henri!" This time, he knew, he was going to fall. "Henri!"

As his outside vision was cut off, the root slipped away entirely. He fought to find something else to grip, but his foot broke through its hold and he fell into the empty blackness, his shouting loud in his own ears. The rushing air was the only guarantee that he was actually falling.

The ground met his back with no mercy, knocking the air out of him. He was left struggling, gasping. His feet were tingling oddly, and his arm was bent awkwardly beneath him. His pain receptors hadn't even kicked in yet. He couldn't move.

God, I don't want to die down here.

There was a lot that Katie didn't really, fully comprehend, to put it politely. She understood the words, but not the picture they painted. In the time since Fae Peeters had left with that man, spirit, Death-person, Chantal had tried her best to fill in the gaps, but the language barrier wasn't helping. Chantal's explanation was a giant, convoluted mess of good and evil, angels and demons, or not demons, and possession and exorcism . . . Katie decided that whatever Fae had told her was enough. Outside bad. Inside good. Nefas bad.

What Katie did understand was enough to convince her that this little, non-entity of a village, hiding in a forgettable corner of an overlooked country, was the center of perhaps the most ridiculous thing to ever be encountered on Earth. She'd grown up with her family bouncing between agnosticism, atheism, and Protestantism, and she considered herself to be somewhere, uncommitted, in the middle. Her experiences within the last forty-eight hours and the narratives of Fae and Chantal, however, only made sense if both the experiences and narratives were real and true. So, she believed that Sin and Death had a face and that there was a good side opposing him. Katie only wondered if she'd still believe it all in the morning.

The Henri bloke had also returned since Fae's departure, and it couldn't have been more obvious how unwanted he was. He'd strolled into the sanctuary with his head held high and he was ignored or glared at. He made little children cry and prompted people to pray for his soul. To these people, Henri was the enemy.

Chantal explained that Henri was an ambassador of Nefas, having been *begotten* of him; using such an archaic religious word, Katie had to wonder if Chantal even knew what it meant. Henri was both the victim and the enemy, making him unpredictably dangerous with his ability to infect others with the green parasite light that Chantal managed her best to describe as a virus-like blob, which closely enough matched Fae's description.

Despite the viral-parasitic descriptions, with the way Henri's body moved in and out of transparency and shimmered like the feathers of a flashy bird, Katie was still drawn by a desire to touch him. She watched him as he came into the church, dodged the wandering choir like any respectful person would try to do, and acted quite like a regular person. He didn't make a scene or protest the nice looking Black man who'd left the choir and walked with him when he'd come in. The man seemed to be acting like his guard—though he was still singing contentedly to himself— and Henri didn't try to do anything provocative. Maybe, Katie thought, the villagers' past experiences with the

Gift were making them unnecessarily rude.

Henri continued strolling around the church, looking around, observing. If there was any hope for him to get out of the bad place he was in, then someone had to bring that hope to him, Katie thought, and if no one else was going to be that person, Katie could. When she was growing up, the "Be a Friend, Save a Friend" campaign was popular in schools, and assessing her personal situation to be safe, thanks to being inside the basilica and that fellow guarding Henri, Katie decided to take the risk; she just wasn't so naïve that she was going to forget that Henri was still solidly on the other side of the line that separated those possessed with the Devil and those not possessed with the Devil. So, when Chantal excused herself to the washroom, Katie got up from her seat and crossed the aisle to the other side, caught Henri's attention, and nodded for him to join her.

Henri met with her by one of the stone columns, and he voluntarily gave her a healthy berth of personal space. The fiery glow from the flickering torch above played with his dark hair, and the emerald light shimmering off his skin gave him a godly air of mystery. Possession never looked so exotic.

"Joyeux Noël. Merry Christmas," Henri said with a friendly smile. He held out his hand in greeting.

Katie looked at him apologetically. "I hope you understand if I don't."

He shrugged. "I'm not offended. I'm Henri." He paused, dropping his hand. "How did you find yourself 'ere? You are a . . . London girl?"

"Katie," she offered, finishing the introduction. "From Reading, actually. A bit west of London. Are you originally from here?"

He smiled and Katie breathed a bit easier. "My parents come from a small village in Switzerland and moved to this village when I was very young. Not much of an upgrade."

Katie smiled. Henri smiled. It was typical, awkward small chat as both fished for something that could justify their continued conversation. Katie went straight to the one thing she guessed they could have a remote chance of having in common.

"Do you know Fae Peeters?"

Henri smiled again, but this time it was more personal, and she knew she had struck the perfect note.

"I suppose it depends on what you mean by 'know.' And what do you want to know?"

"What's her relationship with Nefas, and what happened between them?" Katie cut herself short realizing she sounded a bit too gossipy, and that the only answer to that question probably lay with Fae herself. She was being daft. Three hours ago, she'd started hearing voices from another dimension and was terrified that her organs were going to be harvested. Two hours ago, she'd seen the woman she'd quickly come to admire and respect sacrifice another human being to evil incarnate to try and prevent having a date with him. And now, Katie was trying to befriend his henchman with anti-bullying curriculum. "You know what, never mind. It's none of my business. There's too many elephants in the room to make this easy."

Henri gave a half smile and reached into one of his coat pockets pulling out a bottle of amber liquid, giving it a little shake. "We both need t'is, I think." Unscrewing the cap, he lifted the bottle and took a heavy gulp. The almost painful look on his face as the alcohol burned its way down his throat provided an easy laugh. He screwed the cap back on and motioned he was going to toss it over to her.

"This is a church," she said, hyperaware of everyone who could see them right now.

"What makes wine any different? Bot' are alcohol." He shrugged. "Communion could be taken with rum. Or beer?" Henri tossed her the bottle, and her reflexes made her grab it out of the air. "We deserve it. After everyt'ing we've been through tonight."

Katie had to admit, a drink would be amazing right now. But it still felt wrong.

"You do not 'ave to drink," Henri said. "But what else are you going to do tonight? The choir will sing until the sun rises and not'ing else will happen until then." Henri made the universal sign of going to sleep, and she grinned. He held his hand open to catch the bottle and she readied to toss it back over, but hesitated. One drink. She knew her family at home were enjoying some holiday cheer tonight, and Henri was right. She had earned it. Katie undid the cap and took a swig, gulping down the burn, then tossed the bottle back.

Henri easily caught it. It was incredible to see his green-laced muscles work. The alcohol settled nicely in her stomach, warming her insides.

"You know," Henri said, "I regret not'ing about tonight." He raised his shimmering and semi-opaque hands to show what he meant. "This means I'm becoming more like Nefas. Have you seen *Fight Club*?"

Katie nodded. "Yeah."

"Only people who are in fight club really know what it feels like. It hurts, becoming more like Nefas, leaving your past behind. It is a physical pain, so deep. But like fight club, it is worth it."

"What . . ." Katie hesitated because she wasn't sure if she was really qualified to get personally involved, or if she wanted to, so quickly. But, that's why she was here, standing across from the outcast in the first place, wasn't it? "What's worth it?"

"Killing the part of me who is resisting the process. He's fighting, and it 'urts. But if he lives, I can't think perfectly like Nefas, can't act perfectly like Nefas. And if I cannot do that, well, maybe Fae Peeters will change her mind and take my place wit' him instead."

Henri opened the bottle and took another drink, then tossed it back across to Katie. Should she? One drink leads to another . . . Henri shrugged his indifference to her choice and Katie resigned. To Hell with this absolutely ridiculous place; she was doing this. She took another drink then tossed the bottle back. The liquid rushed to her head as it started to work its magic. She'd never been a big partier and had done very little drinking in the last two years; she needed to be careful.

"What do you mean by Fae 'changing her mind'?"

"Ah. This I do know about my village's favorite trivia question. When Fae Peeters was much younger, Nefas offered her the world. He gave her his spirit, his gifts, his essence, but she refused him. And now Nefas is giving her a second chance. That's why she had to go outside."

"What happens if she doesn't take his offer this time?"

Henri shrugged. "Nefas is death. Death always comes after life, and death is stronger than life. My advice to you? Make friends with Death."

Katie thought back to the pictures from yesterday and the mystery man who showed up behind her. That was Nefas. And that message he'd written on the wall had always been for Fae. Katie motioned for the liquor again. Henri held up a finger to tell her to hold tight and he slipped away down the aisle, leaving the bottle with her. His guard, who was tapping out the current song's beat with his fingers, tailed him.

She leaned back against the cool stone pillar and slid down until she sat on her heels, all the pieces falling into place. She'd gotten herself in the middle of some crazy stuff. And the only reason why she was even here was because of the professor . . . who Fae insisted was directly associated with Nefas. She just couldn't see the similarity.

Katie swore, reached over for the bottle, and took another drink. She really wanted to be home right now.

"You know you're not supposed to trust a boy who gives you too much free alcohol?"

Katie startled, and looked up. The same woman she'd seen at the Christmas market looked down at her, her eyebrow cocked in question. She wore a beautiful leather and turquois bead choker which stood out against her black hair and bright, black eyes. Katie set the bottle down and pushed it across the stone floor out of reach. "I'm fine. But thanks for the reminder."

"You should go back and sit with Chantal and the others," the woman told her. "He doesn't have anything good in mind for you."

"But he can't hurt me in here, right? That's why Fae told me to stay inside."

"Hey!" Both Katie and the woman looked up to see Henri coming back up the aisle tossing a pewter goblet back and forth between his hands, his guard right behind. Henri was looking directly at the woman, squinting his eyes in challenge. "You're missing your part in the song, choir-girl. Katie has *chosen* to have a couple shots with me to pass the night."

The woman didn't look intimidated or impressed. Katie used the pillar behind her to help her stand.

"I'm OK," Katie reassured her. "This is a public space." She smiled her thanks to the woman. "I'll be careful," she added, and meant it. She nodded to Henri's guard, but the woman didn't look convinced.

"My name is Skye. I'll be nearby." Skye gave her another long look, exchanged a confirmation with the singing guard, and took her leave.

Henri watched until Skye had backed off sufficiently to his liking before pouring some of the alcohol into the goblet and setting it close to Katie's feet. He took a seat on the floor in front of his pillar and invited Katie to do the same. She studied the goblet suspiciously, already nervous about the possible sacrilege of drinking hard liquor inside a church, never mind out of a holy element.

"It's a spare," Henri assured her, guessing her thoughts. "I've seen Cuvelier using it to water plants. You're fine."

She was still wary, and no less about the liberality of his pour, but she slid back down to sit across from him.

"When I was a child," he began, "emm, maybe I was ten, I began to play handball. I played for t'ree years or so, and then I broke my hand. It scared my maman, and she wouldn't let me play anymore. She told me she didn't want me to become disabled when I was still so young. But I'm no good at football, road biking bores me, and we 'ave no pool nearby to swim. I did not play any more sports until university, but by then, my strength was more in my brain than my body. I think t'at if I still played sports when I was younger, I wouldn't be so restless today. T'at I wouldn't try so many stupid things."

"My mum," Katie responded, "loved gymnastics when she was growing up. She didn't have the body for it though, so she enrolled me in it and lived her dream through me. And I loved it as much as she did . . . until I was about thirteen and began to get bullied. It got pretty ugly before she finally let both our dreams die. I got into softball after that for a couple of years, but I don't do much anymore. The balance beam was always my favorite," Katie said. "I wish I knew back then how to be stronger than the bullies. They make you ashamed of who you are and of who you aren't."

Henri's expression changed as she told her story, like she'd triggered something inside him. "I would give anyt'ing for a second chance too." He gained a look of almost pained determination, such a rapid change from his cool confidence seconds before. "Do the angels even know I'm down here?"

Katie gave a short laugh, not entirely sure how to respond to such a dramatic response to her story. "Um, maybe? If you left them a memo?"

Henri gave his head a quick shake, and the cool confidence came back. He grabbed the bottle again, nudging the goblet over to her with his shoe.

"I know now why we are both here, Katie," he said.

Keeping her eyes on him, she bent forward for the goblet. "Because we both had something taken from us?"

Henri's eyes shone with an excited sense of adventure. "Because we both have something to give."

26

Katie didn't remember emptying her cup, but as she studied the bottom of the silver goblet, she couldn't help but laugh at the absurdity of this whole affair. She used to have alcohol in there. And now she didn't. It was a magic trick! She'd just done magic!

"Henri!" Katie turned her head to where he should've been, but she found empty space instead. "Henri? Henri." She rolled herself in the other direction and almost rolled on top of him. "When did you get from over there"—she pointed sloppily to the pillar across from her—"to over here? You're not going to try and possess me, are you? Because I have to go home tomorrow. Hey, did you see my magic trick? Look!" She held out the goblet, but it was already upside down and the last little bit of alcohol was in a small puddle on the floor. "Oh. I guess I can't show you anymore."

"I t'ink," Henri said, pushing himself up off the floor, "I gave you too much. You need to walk this off."

He turned to his guard holding held up both his hands for inspection. "No green in my fingers, see? I'm not going to 'infect' her. I'll behave." The guard nodded his approval and Henri leaned down and hooked his arms under hers, helping her to stand.

"And, pop! I'm up!" That's when Katie saw Chantal sitting nearby, watching her, the unmistakable look of worry on her face. Henri's parents, the American woman, and nearly all the others had spread themselves out into huddled groups, but the dark rings around their red eyes and the nervous fidgeting still grouped them together.

"Didn't I say," Katie addressed them all, loudly interrupting the choir's song, "nothing bad happens inside the basilica! Henri is fine. I'm fine. Everyone outside is probably fine. MERRY CHRISTMAS EVERYONE!" Katie enthusiastically threw her hands up in the air twirling about and immediately felt herself toppling over. "Whoops!" Thankfully, Henri was there to steady her. She rebalanced herself and grabbed the edge of the pew. "We should go for that walk."

Katie might not have remembered drinking all her brandy, but she did remember that Skye had come back a second time, and with Chantal. They'd tried to get her to sit back in the pews, but she was having a brilliant conversation with Henri about chips and they sounded a bit naggy. Chantal told her that Henri should be treated like he was in quarantine until the morning, but Katie was so done with her weird talk. When that approach didn't work, both women tried to get Henri to leave instead, which made him angry. Katie didn't want to see him left alone, so she stood up for him, and that's when Chantal accepted defeat and went back to her seat. Skye stayed close though and was hovering nearby even now.

Henri was helping her as she struggled down the length of the basilica between the pews and the pillars. Her world was unstable but her trusty legs didn't let her down. She grabbed a singer by the arm as they crossed paths and asked, "Do you take requests? I would dearly love a cheery rendition of 'The Holly and the Ivy.'"

Henri kept them walking.

"Why aren't you drunk?" she asked him.

He shrugged. "The night is young."

They came to the end of the pews and Henri kept leading her toward the door. Katie balked.

"No. I can't go outside. Fae told me not to go out there."

He shifted her weight against him, and Katie focused on keeping herself upright. "Fresh air will be good for you," Henri told her. "I'll open t'e door and you can stay inside."

Katie could agree to that. She'd been at the door earlier without problem.

When they got to the door Henri let her go and pulled it open, a rush of chill air filling her lungs and her brain. She took a deep breath and smiled. "Yeah. I needed this."

She took another deep breath, taking the time to enjoy the truly lovely holiday sight extending in front of her. All the stores circling the plaza were decorated with coordinating evergreen swags and red ribbons hanging on the windows. The flats in the floors above had their Christmas trees poking into view from behind shutters and curtains. A handful of corpses were still milling around like grazing cows.

She giggled at the idea.

Taking another deep inhale, a metallic gleam at the base of an arch outside caught her eye and she gasped as she immediately recognized the metal lump. "My watch!"

Katie ran outside to scoop up her lost watch, lost and now found. She'd almost given up on finding it and she enthusiastically strapped it back onto her wrist feeling like a complete person again. She proudly lifted her wrist to show it off to Henri, but when she looked for Henri she realized something. She was outside of the basilica.

"KATIE!"

Sweet Jesus and Mary mother.

Fae Peeters came yelling around the corner of the basilica along with the white-haired man. Nefas stood nearby in the plaza, watching, his midnight blue shirt still partially unbuttoned. What was happening?

"Get back inside!" Fae yelled at her as she ran up the steps on the far side. Bloody wasted or not, Katie knew this was bad.

The door clicked shut and the sound of the choir was instantly muted. Henri stood with his hand on the handle.

"Jesus," Fae said. Katie couldn't tell if she was swearing or actually meant it religiously. "Help her."

Fae came to a halt, quickly looked her over, then immediately turned her attention to Henri who was standing with his head cocked and a smirk of success locked in place.

"You had to get her drunk?" Fae accused him, and Katie watched as Henri sized Fae up. "Let her back inside. Now."

"Henri," Katie said, "I can't be outs—" Katie's heel slipped off the edge of the stair. She spun her head around to look behind her, but she did it too fast. She lost her balance and felt herself going down.

Her world spun and twisted as her shoulder hit first, her elbow, her ribs. The next thing she knew, she was looking up into the night sky from her back. "Bloody hell," she groaned. Pain all over her body was yelling at her. She took a moment to self-assess, then rolled onto her side to stand up. Her shoulder dropped out beneath her in a flash of stabbing pain. "Ahh!" She screamed. Fae grabbed her before she could hit the ground again.

Fae's face was taunt as she delicately pulled aside Katie's shirt from her neck for inspection.

"I think you've broken your collarbone."

Katie swore.

A sound of distant buzzing bees was something Katie dismissed as an aftershock of the fall, but Fae seemed to hear it too. The sound lasted only a second, and the older woman's face grew even stonier than it had already been.

"What did the bees say?"

"Nothing. He said nothing," Fae said sharply. "We need to take care of you."

"Can I go back inside?" The pain was starting to set in deeper and she didn't have a coat on. She leaned forward, cradling her arm close. With the same tenderness of petting a butterfly, Katie fingered her broken bone and found a swollen lump between her neck and her shoulder.

"Dominic?" Fae called for her friend. "Let's get her inside."

But instead of that faint British accent agreeing to help, the incredible voice of that creature of a man, Nefas, spoke and Katie heard his shoes tapping closer. "It's never that simple, Fae."

Fae stood up. "I won't let you take her."

"Someone help me inside, please," Katie moaned. She was getting cold. Wiggling her legs beneath her to prepare to stand up, she screamed in pain and doubled over. Stars flashed before her eyes and the blackness of consciousness spun her around. Someone with warm hands came behind her and steadied her.

She saw Fae's shoes twist back around and face her direction. "Don't," Fae threatened, and Katie figured it was Henri who was holding her. She tried to straighten up so she could see what was going on, but the stars and flashing blackness forced her to stay bent over.

"Don't possess me, please," Katie told him. "I need to go home tomorrow, remember?"

"Katie," Henri spoke to her. "I can set your bone. You'll feel better."

"Stop talking to her," Fae demanded. "With the blood that never dries and—"

"Shut up!" Henri exploded, inadvertently jerking Katie at the same time. Her bone shifted and she screamed, "Do it! Set the bone. Do it now!"

"Katie, no," Fae was right with her, crouching in front of her to look her in the face. "He'll use the parasite. He'll possess you."

"Do you have any idea how much this hurts?"

"Do you want to go home tomorrow?" Fae asked and then added, "Get away from her."

"Focus, Fae" Dominic said calmly. "You're not alone in this. Nicholas is with you."

"I don't care who it is, just someone do something!" Katie shouted, the pain of each syllable vibrating the bone making her desperate.

Henri held her from behind again, his green, glowing hand hovering over the swollen bulb of her collarbone. "You will have no regrets, like me," he whispered into her ear.

Fae yelled something, but Katie couldn't hear it over Henri's own cries of agony as an aura of green light flared up from her shoulder. Something was being injected into her from his fingers and it burned like fire and froze like liquid nitrogen. She knew she was screaming, and only Henri's hold on her kept her from collapsing.

The green light was reaching into her brain, freezing and burning its way up. She wanted it to stop, but she couldn't find the words through her yelling. Flashing, bright lights were blinding her optic nerves. Sounds of nails scraping down chalkboards and cats caterwauling filled her ears and then, in sudden and complete blackness, there was nothing more to see. And there was nothing more to hear, except one single musical voice that sent a shiver down her paralyzed spine.

Darkness stirs and the mind abandons itself in servitude. Katie's chapters are closed and mine begins.

"With the blood that never dries and the body that never rots—"

"Henri can't hear you, Fae," Nefas said annoyed, like she wasn't getting it.

"He can hear me! The Communion isn't useless. It worked for Lars Drechsler—"

"You're not Lars," Nefas snapped. "You're Fae Norris-Peeters."

The parasite flowing through Henri's fingers was pushing itself into Katie, who'd fallen unconscious on the ground. Henri had been pulled down beside her, and he was comatose too, his eyes rolled into the back of his head.

"By the blood that never dries—"

"You're wasting your time," Nefas said, stepping beside Henri. "Katie is just like you when we first met, without any loyalties to slow my essence down. But unlike you, I don't need her to retain independent thought or choice. She's only getting my essence, for now, which you can take back whenever you're ready."

Fae glared at him. She was kneeling beside Katie, shaking her good side, calling her name.

The removal process gets easier every time, the Voice whispered to her.

"Shut up!" She needed Katie to wake up so she could change her mind about letting the parasite in. "Dominic, I need your help." There was no answer. "Dominic!" Fae looked around, but Dominic was gone. He'd promised she'd never be left alone; that Nicholas was always with her. Maybe they traded places . . . but then where was the baby? Had Dominic meant "with her" in that useless kind of "in spirit" way?

"C'mon Katie, wake up." Fae thought of pressing down on the broken bone, now bound in a parasite sheath glowing through her skin, but her memory flashed with warnings about marrow entering the blood, and she tried to think of something else.

She quickly took another look around. "Dominic! Nicholas?"

"When will you learn?" Nefas said. "I am *ever* the only one who won't leave you."

She desperately looked around the plaza for that telltale white head, the baby, or Max even, but there was no one other than the corpses dragging themselves toward her, attracted by her yelling. She swiveled her head around and her eyes ran directly into those of Nefas, bent down to her level, his gaze locking hers, and in that exact moment, he had her.

Let me bring you back to where you belong.

His eyes were dark pits that could be filled with anything: hope, confidence, possibility. She couldn't look away.

"Katie," Fae's voice trembled, "wake up."

In her peripheral vision she saw Henri kneeling across from her starting to come to life, his chest heaving from exertion. She was out of options. Fae let her fingers find the lump on Katie's collarbone.

Nefas didn't blink, and he kept Fae locked into his stare.

She had to do it now. With a grimace Fae leaned down heavily on Katie's broken bone and not even the parasite could prevent the inward bend. Fae felt the bone grinding beneath her, and Katie shot up with a screech of pain.

"Katie!" Fae yelled, still unable to break away from Nefas' eyes. "Tell the parasite to leave!"

Katie was crying, gasping in pain. Henri was trying to figure out what was, or wasn't, happening. The corpses were coming closer, and Nefas now had

Fae's head cupped in his hands, holding her in the darkness of his eyes. Fae was losing herself in them, the outside world becoming weaker while his eyes were coming alive. In their endless, enticing darkness were the gaseous nebulae of beautiful colors, each one holding a gift to her. The void. It was the void that waited for her in his eyes.

"Nefas, please, don't . . . not back in there."

"Welcome home, Fae."

"Katie. Tell it to lea . . ."

The world around her went out of focus and all the unplumbed depths of Nefas' being swelled out of his eyes and filled her vision, the memories of the void she had thought dead coming back alive.

There was perfect stillness and complete emptiness all around her. The warmth of Nefas' voice guided her.

In my endlessness you are alone. You're falling, you can feel it, but there is no direction. No matter how far you fall in the void, there is still an infinity beyond that. Your brain is growing heavier and heavier as your thoughts sink deeper and deeper. There is nothing in this place except what I give you. Dark presents to color your soul. Void of light, yet filled with color.

There, in the distance. The nebula of yellow and green, dotted with sapphire stars. It's beautiful, like you. Don't fall anymore. Go toward it. The knowledge inside will help you navigate this place on your own. You've always adapted and survived better when you've done things your own way. It's who you are. Why did you let them change you? That baby may have saved you once, but do you really believe lightning will strike twice?

Yes, step into the nebula . . .

Fae gasped as though she'd been holding her breath this whole time, snapping the hold Nefas had on her. There was green light still around her. Had she left the nebula at all?

Nefas was smiling at her, age creases wrinkling his skin at the mouth and eyes, jowls starting to sag. She shivered, though not from the cold. She was standing on solid ground, and she moved to get away from him but bumped into a corpse instead. With its tongue shriveled up, it let out a huff of stale air, and Fae jumped, almost bumping into another one. She took in everything around her and saw where she was: alone with Nefas in the middle of an eerie green circle of corpses. They'd drifted to the edge of the plaza away from Katie and Henri, and the basilica, just the two of them and the sweet taste of shameful pleasures reawakened dripping off her lips.

The void.

She imagined herself again standing at his side in the middle of a hippodrome large enough to hold a city, the world her oyster. High on the pleasures Nefas had for her, she had the power to take parasites out while remaining free of it herself. She was above life itself, a savior to those infected . . . if she only gave him everything in exchange.

Like a warm shower, you never want to leave me.

"Let Katie and the hostages back inside the basilica," Fae told him quietly, the necessity of the words carrying them more than her conviction. She took a breath and said even more carefully, "You must give them that choice."

"You, my dear Fae," Nefas said gently, as he circled her slowly, "can lead the hostages anywhere you want."

He was lying, but she wanted to believe him.

My void is alive in you again. I know what you want. Only I can give it.

The bright glow from the corpses was waxing and waning on his face, shadows growing and dying as he circled around her. "Henri has taken Katie to the North gate, they're not your concern. The hostages are yours to command; they're on la Rue. Fae, create your own legacy. Not of Maria or Lars, but of Fae Norris-Peeters. See what I see in you."

Your own façade has been cracking for years. You left the Bible people behind for a reason. They've always thought you a bit heretical, haven't they. Pot blessing, hallelujah, God gives and takes away. They're not your people. They don't make you feel safer. Only you can make yourself feel safer. Take control.

The Voice creeped over her shoulders and down her arms, and she tried to block it out. The faces of the rotting dead were staring at her, a background to the greater beast circling around her. Her thoughts were still stuck in the nebula she'd walked into, and she was scared because she was feeling desperate to go back in. Only Nefas could give her more.

"No, no," she murmured sharply to herself. She was quickly failing to resist him. She started backing away, needing to get away from him. She needed help.

Nefas was staring at her intently; she could feel his eyes through the shadows. The shifting shadows, lights, and wisps of fog coming off him created an image completely mesmerizing.

An eager corpse behind her caught her wrist, and Fae jumped forward trying to jerk her hand away, but it was too strong. Before Fae could even try to fight, Nefas was beside her, his own hand firmly grasping the wrist of the corpse defensively. "They were told not to touch you," Nefas told her. "This one didn't listen. You can teach it a lesson."

Fae looked down at the corpse holding her wrist, and Nefas holding its wrist in turn, then she looked at Nefas. They were so close to each other. He held her gaze, encouraging her to take the next step.

She could do it. She could hurt it, break its wrist for touching her, and it'd never threaten her again.

There is so much more power you can't even imagine.

"The parasite is you," she said, her dry throat scratching. She pushed through it. "You control it. It can't disobey you." She easily broke her wrist free.

Nefas paused, then cracked a smile. His presence settled like a warm, disease-riddled blanket. Only the ignorant could embrace the comfort.

"You always were my favorite." He snapped his arm sharply, and the offending corpse was pulled to the ground, its chest and face cracking against the unforgiving paving stones. "Precedents." Nefas placed one foot on the corpse's head, and with a heavy foot, stepped on, then over the body. He came behind her, brushing his hand over her shoulders as he passed around. "You're so strong, so smart on your own."

He came back into view in front of her.

"Don't . . . don't touch me."

Fae's eye caught sight of Max standing behind Nefas' shoulder on the other side of the corpses, and she felt her cheeks flush. How long had he been standing there, watching them? He was interrupting—No, he was the help she needed.

Nefas noticed the shift in her eyes and shoulder checked to see what had caught her attention. Fae took the opportunity and darted into the ring of corpses to get away, to get to Max, ready to fight the corpses off, but not a single one raised a parasitic finger to infect her, not a single one tried to stop her, and she easily passed through them. Beside her, Nefas was breaking through the ring of corpses too, and they emerged from the ring together.

Fae quickly separated herself to be closer to Max.

"Where's Dominic?" Fae looked right at Max, then asked again, louder, to make sure he heard it. "Where's Dominic? Where's Nicholas?"

"Your Nicholas is where he needs to be," Max told her in a hushed voice. Then louder, "Dominic was needed on la Rue. He did what was asked of him."

"Those people are for Fae alone," Nefas said threateningly.

Fae understood then what Nefas meant. It wasn't just the right to be their tour guide back to the basilica that Nefas was giving her, but the care of their fragile souls. "Nefas, I don't . . ." she began to urge him to rescind, but he ignored her.

"My queen, let's see what a little power will reveal of your true nature."

Nefas already knew her true nature. She'd given into him for the hostages, then for Adrien. The Voice was back, and now that she was reimmersed in the void with all its flirtatious temptations, Nefas had every reason to be confident that the hostages were at little risk in her hands.

She wanted to melt away. This isn't what she'd meant when she'd asked for the hostages.

This is your destiny, the Voice said. *You can feel it. Don't fight the truth. It will set you free.*

"As for you," Nefas quickly changed his tone, looking at Max. "You have something of mine."

Max looked at Fae. "Go to the North gate. Now. Skye's there with Katie and Henri, she'll help. I'll catch up with you shortly. Dominic is with the hostages keeping them safe. They'll get dealt with later."

"Max, I don't think—"

"Remember who's on your side. Trust yourself and don't give Nefas what he wants," Max instructed succinctly. "Go."

Fae felt like she was leaving something important behind, but she trotted off looking behind her to where Nefas and Max were squaring off.

Only I am always with you.

Fae jogged faster, gladly letting the curvature of the street put the plaza out of sight. She jogged past a large wicker stag draped in lights and a large plaid bow. She stopped, staring at how pretty it was. It mocked what this night had become.

Nefas had so far set up this night perfectly; he'd also gotten her exactly where he wanted her: listening to everything he said.

All her pent-up emotions boiled to the surface, and she punched the stag as hard as she could, yelling into the night.

Don't give Nefas what he wants. The last time she was told that, he'd almost killed her.

28

The village had been foggy all night, but a new fog had fallen, and it was thicker than what Fae had ever seen before. It complemented the angry tears she was still crying as she powered ahead, leaving behind the abused wicker stag. She'd seen weather like this before, a number of years ago when she'd been on the East Coast for business, but what was sitting in the streets now rivaled, if not beat, that dense Maritime fog.

And it was eerie. Every sound carried clearly but was disembodied. She could hear a lost corpse shuffling in the distance as clearly as she could her own breaths. Streetlamp lights hung suspended in mid-air without a pole to be seen. Edifices were birthed out of a dream-like state with a corner here and a balcony there. Lights were scattered into particles artificially turning the black night into a brownish-gray one. The landmarks she desperately needed to guide her way were teasingly, slowly revealed as though she were a phantom in a phantom's dream. Her world was a blank canvas, and it begged for an artist to create in it. It was everything Nefas needed, and Fae knew, it was only a matter of time before he began.

Fae was left navigating by hunches. The compass of the basilica's spires was smothered, but she knew that if she could make it to the village hall, the street running in front of it would lead her straight to the gate, if there wasn't a village's worth of corpses between her and her destination. The corpses letting her pass through them untouched wasn't something she would expect again.

Somewhere nearby she heard a hard hitting *thumpf* and she stopped.

The noise sounded familiar and she didn't like it. She liked even less that whatever had made it could've been five feet away or thirty, in front of her or behind. It could've been anything or nothing.

She decided to go with the "nothing" option. It was better to claim ignorance.

She started walking again, but as soon as she did, she again heard the hard hitting *thumpf,* and this time her memory clued in. It was the sound of Adrien's body falling two stories and hitting the ground.

It couldn't be him, though. Her memory had to be replaying that time-frozen moment and the fog was amplifying it. She stared in the direction of the sound and the fog seemed to disperse, revealing the outline of what looked like a body on the ground. Had she found herself back in Adrien's old neighborhood? She thought Max and his friend had taken care of his body?

"Max . . ." A weak voice came from the body.

Oh my god, she thought. "Adrien?" Fae hesitantly called out. She blinked hard and strained her eyes to see through the fog. The body seemed to get swallowed up again in the brown-grayness. "Adrien."

"Max . . ." He was so weak he was barely audible.

But Adrien had already died. She was there when life left him, when all his muscles had relaxed with no fight left in them, when the pool of his blood on the ground was more than he could live without. She'd betrayed herself to ensure he was given that final peace. He had to be dead.

"Adrien." She took a step forward. "Adrien, go to sleep. You're free."

The fog shifted just enough to make out the body-like lump again.

"You came back?" he asked, gurgling the question through blood and phlegm choked airways.

"Adrien, stop fighting," Fae told him taking a few steps closer. "Max came and took care of you. Like you asked." This was a ghost, she told herself. After all these years of being called a ghost, Adrien really had become one. But what if . . . Fae had no idea what was possible or not anymore. "Adrien . . ." Deep, bubbling gasps came as he fought for breath, and then the fog took the body away again. "Max!" Fae panicked. Unable to sell herself on ignorance any longer, she ran into the fog in the direction of the body. "Help him!"

She ran to the spot where the body was, but it was gone, dispersed into the moisture or scattered into her memory; there was nothing on the ground. Where did he go?

You've become like your hero: too late and ineffective, the Voice told her.

"That wasn't Adrien. He wasn't real!"

And what about this one?

Something to Fae's left startled her, and she came face to face with the silent screaming of the young man she'd so easily let Nefas infect at the basilica. Jean. He was supposed to be with the other hostages on la Rue. She jumped back, his contorted body expressing the anguish his locked-open jaw was trying to verbalize.

Fae yelled, and at the same time, she started to lose her balance. The earth was shaking beneath her. She stumbled back and forth, and somewhere above her glass fell and shattered. As quickly as it'd begun, the ground settled and calmed, and an earth-shattering screech took its place. High pitched, it ripped through the air, and with horror Fae heard the rage filled cry of Nefas coming from the direction of the basilica where Max had stayed behind for a private discussion.

What had Max said? What had he done?

She forgot about the ghosts of the past and ran.

She ran wherever the streetlamps led, praying she was going in the right direction. She ran until she needed to catch her breath and then came trotting to a halt. She needed to orient herself to the gate, needed to know what Max had done that had made Nefas so angry, but her focus was washing away. She felt like a shipwrecked survivor alone and adrift in the middle of the fog-laden sea, both wanting to be found and wanting to stay perfectly hidden, unsure of what kind of person would find her. For the moment, she felt hidden, and so she felt lucky, on borrowed time, if not completely abandoned. As she caught her breath, alone and unwatched, waves of dammed-up shame, betrayal, desire, and everything else she didn't have the facilities to identify welled up and demanded her attention, and she struggled to shove everything back down because it wasn't helping.

But one memory escaped. It was five years ago that the European Union's Art and History Centre had had its grand opening. She'd never been so damn proud of anything in her life: the importance of the project, its scope, her team. Everything had been done right. When the ribbon cutting finally happened, she'd been sitting on the temporary stage set up in front of the steps of this world icon she'd helped give life to along with the rest of the project's team, members of state, and other top dignitaries. In the crowd were more dignitaries, world media, enthusiasts, and Jordan and Bailey, and Fae remembered almost none of it. Her memory of that whole ceremony focused on one man in a blue suit sitting in the VIP section with eyes only for her, a man she knew was Nefas. She couldn't think of that ceremony without remembering him first.

She could never escape him.

She'd spent so many years trying to build up a cold shoulder to Nefas, battling him inserting himself into her life, and tonight he'd expertly undone almost thirty years of effort within . . . two hours? Breaking her back down so that once again all she could see was him. Dominic kept telling her not to focus on him, but Nefas was waiting for that slip-up, and then he'd pounce. Just like with the rose. She knew what was coming: the moment when he'd pull all his strings to reel her in.

Her priority should've been thinking about what she was going to do when that moment came, or how Katie was going to be protected, or what she was supposed to do with the hostages. Nefas wouldn't have given her the authority to control the parasite unless he knew he could control her in turn. And that terrified her cold.

Instead, Fae's brain settled on rerunning the image of Nefas kicking Adrien off the roof and his naked, bleeding body meeting the ground. Over, and over again. She replayed the moment she walked away with Nefas while Isaac was being injected behind her, Jenny screaming, and Henri's face while he injected Katie.

Fae was just a ghostly shade shrouded in the fog, someone better forgotten. She sniffled, the sound of it carrying far past herself. A week ago, she'd been a career woman with a past left behind. Tonight, she'd watched people get tortured and a man die. She'd tried channeling the bravery of Lars Drechsler, but so far she'd shown herself to be a better accomplice than a defender.

The one thing, the *one* thing, she'd known she could do was keep Katie away from Nefas. She simply had to do the opposite of what had happened to her all those years ago: tell Katie the truth and tell her why she needed to stay inside the basilica. And Nefas had still won.

Then she had Max telling her to go to the North gate. To do what? "To do what?" she asked aloud, biting each word. A half sob escaped, and she held her arm up against her mouth, pinching her eyes closed.

What could she do once she reached the gate? Charge through the thousand villagers packed there and drag Katie back to the basilica? Use Nefas' gift again to take the parasite out of her? Be Nicholas when he wasn't there to do the job himself?

Yes.

Fae choked on the sob she couldn't hold back. She swore at him between breaths. "Get *away* from me."

She picked up her feet and continued trudging up the street. In the sound of Dominic's voice, she thought, *Remember whose side you're on. It's not your own. This isn't a solo fight.*

I thought I knew what that meant, she responded to herself.

She'd get to Katie and Henri, and just try to not make things worse.

It wasn't much longer until Fae somehow, miraculously, arrived at the village hall. A row of glass-sheathed lights hung between the first and second stories of the building extending into the fog, a perfectly straight line of glowing orbs. She'd made it this far. She could make it to the gate.

She walked up the middle of the empty street, her shoes making soft *clicks* as they hit the stone paving, her thoughts torturously churning over the last hours of her life. If she ever got home again—and that was foreign world away—she'd truly be without understanding. She could never tell Jordan what she'd done, or seen, and there'd be no Women's Conferences full of flowers and warrior-princess marketing that could merge her world with theirs.

"Fae."

Fae jumped. Standing on the top step of the village hall stood Nefas, looking down at her, half shrouded in fog and backlit from the dispersed light behind him. Adrift in the ocean, she'd been found by the wrong search party.

He was wearing a leather jacket and hoodie over his shirt. She recognized that hoodie and jacket combo.

You know exactly who used to wear this jacket. The Voice. *He had no need of it anymore.*

Fae barely nodded. Resigned acceptance of her darkening reality was a wet blanket on her anger, frustration, and shame. She'd interpreted Nefas' screech wrongly. It hadn't been indignation. It'd been a victory cry.

A cool wave of moist fog swept across her face and she shivered. To either side of her, brown-hooded skeleton monks emerged and formed a path from her up to Nefas, who stood regally with his new trophy jacket. Four monks. Four men caught between their faith and their true master; four men unable to escape either. The monks had always spoken non-stop, though with no tongue or vocal cords, their mandibles clacked with a foreboding rhythm. This time, their jaws didn't move and they made no sound.

As the monks took their places, hundreds of shuffling and scraping corpse bodies came up behind her. Where they came from so quickly without hinting to their presence seconds earlier was irrelevant. Nefas could do what he wanted. The corpses closed in, their telltale iridescent glow enveloping her. Forming a hedge around her, they joined with the monks to create an inescapable funnel from her to Nefas.

"Fae, stand beside me," Nefas commanded.

This was the choice she knew was coming. Fae looked up at him at the top of the stairs and eyed the open spot beside him. He was the envy of the world. The fascination of the universe. The only constant of the dimensions. Death. Lightlessness. With him, she could belong and never feel alone. With him, she could control.

And still, there was a little baby somewhere that was better than even him.

Who from a distance, wherever he was, could still scare Nefas.

"No."

"My dear Fae. I don't play games, remember?"

Fae's jaw twitched. "I remember."

His presence fell hard, and she immediately struggled to find enough breath as her lungs fought to inhale against his weight. She kept her eyes on him, his green fog melting and mixing into the night, blurring the hazy lines between where his body started and ended.

"Then this won't be a surprise."

The corpses pounced on her. Their hands and fingers, swollen with the parasite, grabbed her, yanking her into their roiling mass of hungry madness. She struggled to fight back, yelling, kicking, and elbowing; but there were too many of them. They grabbed fistfuls of her hair, were tearing at her jacket. They managed to hold back her arms, she couldn't protect herself. She was drowning in them.

"Dominic!" Fae screamed out, trying to raise her voice above the groaning mob. "Nicholas!"

"We're alone, Fae. Together with our future."

The corpse faces were moving too fast and close in front of her to make sense of them. Snaps of skin and rot. Teeth and nasal cavities. Darkness and parasitic light. The corpses scratched at her throat and face and held onto her hair, gripping her legs and rendering her immobile. And then they began forcing the parasite into her. Ice cold fire forced its way into her arms and chest, through her neck. Searing, white pain, it pushed its way into her with an incredible, agonizing strength. Fae screamed as she wrenched her body every way trying to free herself, but it was a vain effort. She was screaming, fighting, struggling. She was losing. She felt the parasite slither into her brain. And then everything was over. Blackness.

Trust me.

Fae's eyes snapped open.

The corpses were back to quiet attention, still walling her in. The monks stood guarding the way up to Nefas. Fae was in the middle of them, unmolested. She looked down at her jacket and found it untouched. Her neck wasn't scratched. There was no parasite in her. Looking around, everything was exactly the same as it was a minute ago. Everything had been reset, except that Nefas had pulled the hoodie down low over his head hiding the decaying toll his own darkness was having on him.

"Fae," Nefas said, from atop the stairs, "stand beside me."

This was more than just déjà vu.

Wanting to put extra distance between her and the corpses, Fae slid forward, though it did nothing to make her feel any less vulnerable. Adrenaline was pounding through her.

She numbly shook her head. "I can't."

"Your loyalty is noble," he said, "but it's bringing so much pain to everyone around you. To yourself." He made a hand gesture beckoning forth human forms from the mists behind him. The ghosts came, and the fog thinned so that the back lights could reveal their identity.

Fae didn't want to believe it.

Looking straight at her, unapologetically, was Adrien, fully clothed and relaxed; Lars Drechsler stood with conviction with his beaked cap and trimmed beard, the man who'd risked everything to save that annoying girl who knew nothing; her beloved grandmother who'd been everything to her growing up held out an inviting hand. They all looked at her grimly and nodded in encouragement of her capitulation.

"I am the only constant, Fae," Nefas continued. "All of your saviors are either missing or beside me now. This is your place." Nefas indicated to the open spot at his side. "I am forever. Open your eyes. The light will fade away, saviors die, but I never will."

It couldn't be true. Her grandmother, Lars, they knew Nefas for everything that he was, they knew the baby—Nicholas—for everything that he was. Fae shook her head. Max had given Nefas the ultimatum not to kill her, but if Nefas had neutralized Max? Had he taken Max's necklace too, fulfilling her vision? Would he still do anything to have hers?

She started to reach for her pocket then remembered Nefas' first reaction to seeing Max with his little vial: he'd been murderous at Max for having it. If she could die with a secret Nefas wanted, then that would be her gift to the world.

"No," Fae said resolutely, knowing exactly what was coming next.

This will always hurt you more than it does me.

The distance she'd given herself from the corpses didn't make a difference. Their boney, cold hands found her as quickly as before. Survival instinct forced her to fight the inevitable, and she tried to claw and force her way out of them, but their voraciousness was even wilder than before. She desperately stuck out her hand out to find someone's heart to pull the parasite out, not caring about the method through the madness.

Smart idea. But no.

Adrien, Drechsler, and her grandmother watched impassively only feet away as she was torn into. The corpses' green-glowing fingers latched onto every part of her as the parasite forced its way into her again. She screamed in agony. It hurt, oh God, it hurt!

Everything went black.

To keep my gift, you must stand at my side.

The darkness suddenly gave way to life again and she was back, standing in front of Nefas. The corpses were gone. The monks had backed away until they had nearly disappeared, their presence now more like a subtle reminder than a bold statement. Only Nefas remained on the stairs. Just Death and his girl.

Everything was quiet. Calm. Except that Fae's body was on fire and throbbing. She twitched and trembled against the residual, lingering feeling of decomposing skin touching hers, of icy fire being pushed into her. She knew she was crying. Breathing in shivers, she was having trouble keeping her head lifted.

"Fae. Stand beside me."

She couldn't look up at him anymore. She couldn't bear to see his confidence right before he gave the silent command again. He'd said before that only he would have the pleasure of infecting her. She wondered why he hadn't. Unless he wanted his to be permanent.

It's OK, the Voice washed over her like a healing balm. *Shhh, now. The choice of life and death is in your hands. Remember this?*

"Fae," Nefas said, his smooth voice not without compassion. "No one is around to see what we do now. Come up here, and I will show you what is yours."

She couldn't. It'd mean slavery. And refusing meant death, or wishing for death. She only had to say a single word to refuse him, but her tongue seized in protest and her lips froze shut.

It's OK.

"Is this what you want your legacy to be for your daughter?" Nefas asked gently. He stepped one foot down. "The woman whose selfishness came before not only her own fall, but of how many others already, and counting?" He waited a moment while the single word of refusal planted firmly on her tongue melted and she found it in herself to look up at him again. "Stand beside me. Confident. Empowered. Is that not the true legacy you want your daughter to know? You can leave if you don't like what you see up here. If you don't like what you *feel.*"

Nefas dragged out the last word, letting the deepness of his voice serenade like a lapping ocean wave on a twilight beach. There were more colors fanning out around him now. Gold and red joined the green. It was like one of the nebulae had come out of the void and it continued to grow, swallowing them both, a damp, dense fog of rich color.

In the void every choice is hidden.

The first step up the stairs was easier than she'd expected. As was the second, and third, and by the fourth, Nefas took her hand and helped her up the final step. She took her time turning around, the red, and green, and gold of the void swirling around with her.

She stood at Nefas' side, hyperaware of him. There would be no more pain. Looking out into the foggy village before them, she saw the four monks close ranks. All the corpses that had disappeared were back, packing the street and stretching out in both directions.

Nefas lifted her hand up to his shadow-covered lips. "Choices can be hidden," he said, "but they are still made." And then he kissed it. She could feel him smiling, could see it even through the dark shadow covering his face. He'd won.

A very human movement at the base of the stairs arrested Fae's attention.

She pulled her hand away from him and looked to the intruder. At the front of the crowd of corpses, in the exact place she'd just been standing between the monks, was Max. He was still wearing his jacket; Nefas didn't have it after all.

The colors of the nebula . . . This whole thing had been in the Void, but one not confined to her mind, one more real than she'd known was possible.

Max had been standing here with her this whole time.

And her choice had still been made.

In an instant the swirling colors of the nebula disappeared. The monks vanished, the corpses evaporated, and Nefas was gone. Even the denseness of the fog lifted, and Fae was alone at the top of the stairs, bathed in the dull glow of the village hall lights.

There was nothing of the bartender kid left in the Max standing below her. He was a young, fearless man who bore a look that told her she had no need to explain why she was standing where she was. He wasn't judging. He just knew.

Fae licked her dry lips. Her voice cracked. "Nothing stays hidden in the void," she managed to say hoarsely.

"Do you like the view up there?" Max asked, simply.

Fae didn't know what to say. There was no room to lie and she had no desire to. Exposed on the stairs she had nothing to hide. She'd warned them that something like this was going to happen, but there was no satisfaction in being right.

"No." She shook her head.

Max gave a subtle nod.

"Did you take care of Adrien?"

"We did," Max confirmed. "There was a sarcophagus prepared for him in the Notre-Dame du Seigneur. His body lays there now." Max came up the stairs and met her there, on her level, his eyes looking her over, worried. "How are you doing?"

She began shaking again, her nerves taxed to their limit, tears of relief and shame beginning to fall without inhibition. "I'm not."

Max leaned in and wrapped her in a hug that reached deep into her soul.

"You weren't brought here to fail, Fae," he said into her shoulder. "There will be a Christmas morning. It will be beautiful. And you will see it with your own eyes. Nicholas is always with you."

29

Henri had brought Katie to the watch tower nearest to the North gate. After hearing her talk of her gymnastic background, he'd figured out how to get the gate open without Adrien. Or, maybe he was starting to tap into Nefas' mind and he was following Nefas' plan. Regardless, he took it as validation that this time he'd managed to kill his inner-self, though he reserved a margin of error in that declaration. His inner-self felt like having someone locked in a wooden box in his bedroom. While the box was impossible to ignore, it was easy to forget someone was in there until they started banging around, making noise and being annoying. He could feel his inner-self intruding sometimes, looking through his eyes, or his voice escaping through his lips, but he hadn't felt anything from him since drinking with Katie. The box had been noticeably quiet.

It was with this assumption of success that Henri gripped the rusted padlock that held shut the tower's gate between both hands and squeezed down hard. It was pretty cool seeing his muscles contracting through his skin, feeling the essence working through him, weakening the metal under his pressure. The lock buckled and with a couple of tugs it easily dropped off. He handed it to Katie. "Un souvenir pour toi."

He pushed open the old door.

"After you," he said.

Katie dutifully passed him into the darkness of the staircase. She hadn't spoken much since they'd left the Notre-Dame du Seigneur. From the proper angle her skin took on a semi-transparency where Nefas' essence could be seen running through her body, but it was definitely less impressive than his own; she only had Nefas' essence though, not his void. Her broken clavicle had helped sober her up, but he still worried about her. Katie was special to him; she was the first one he'd had brought into the family.

Katie was also someone Nefas didn't want to lose, and Nefas had made it clear that if Henri didn't return her to him with the gates open, it would not be good. How Henri was going to ensure that dual success was a question that plagued him the whole way here. There was still a lot of risk management in this situation that eluded him.

Katie reached the exit at the top of the stairs and pointedly rattled its lock, its clanging echoing down the stairs. Henri trotted up the rest of the way in the pitch darkness, trusting in the stairs' uniformity. He picked up the lock in his hands and squeezed. He felt the metal buckle, and then snapped it free.

Henri had never been at the top of a tower before. Not many people bothered to break locks and steal up to the top of something they tried to pretend didn't have to exist. The view was nice though, particularly tonight. The entire village was packed at the gate below, waiting to be released, and they bathed the wall in green light. It danced and ebbed against the stones like flickering hot coals.

"Do you know what you need to do?" he asked Katie.

She nodded, apprehensively eyeing the path before her. She'd have a short drop down onto the rounded top of the wall and then a challenging walk across the top of it to get to the gate; a dangerous thing to do when the conditions were dry, but those domed caps were wet, if not icy. The fact that Nefas' first option was for Adrien to parkour his way up rather than to try this crossing said something.

"If I fall, does Nefas have another backup plan?"

"He has as many options as t'ere are failures," Henri said, guiding her to where she'd let herself down. "You don't forget the kind of balance you learned in gymnastics. Like riding a bike." Katie looked down and across to the gate no less worried. But then she nodded determinedly, and Henri could see her concentration kick in. She set her eyes on her final destination and began a few balance warm-ups.

"I'll be with her too." A woman's voice emerged from the stairway and Henri looked around to see that nagging witch, Skye, arrive. "To help."

At the sight of her, Henri growled and stepped forward to give her the greeting he'd been wanting to all night: a fist to her meddling mouth and a broken nose as a bonus.

Henri's fist was fast, but Skye was faster. She slipped his punch and was behind him before he even realized she'd moved, locking his arm behind his back. She pushed up on it threatening to dislocate his shoulder.

She spoke in French. "Don't give up, Henri. Your family are fighting for you. You don't have to die down there."

"He's dead," Henri growled back. How the hell did she dare talk to him like that? "I won."

She yanked up on his arm, and he yelped, leaning backward to try and lessen the pressure.

"Nefas used Josie to get you to listen to him," she said. "He knows you'll follow him so long as he has Josie. Find her before the gates open and don't lose track of her."

She released him with a shove and walked over to Katie, who eyed her approach with distrust.

Henri watched their interaction from a distance, gently rolling out his shoulder, glaring knives into Skye's back, but he let her step in. She'd be the guarantee he needed that Katie would get the job done, and he'd deal with Skye once her guardianship diverged from his purpose. He was Nefas' representative in the world now, and he'd make sure Skye learned what that meant.

"You're too full of the parasite for me to stop you from doing this," Skye told Katie in English, speaking with an American accent, "but I can keep you from falling. Come on."

With an impressive, controlled strength, Skye carefully helped Katie over the edge of the tower, Nefas' essence working hard to keep Katie's bone from shifting. She lowered Katie the meter or so down and gently placed her onto the rounded top of the wall.

Henri watched the delicate operation, but his thoughts were stuck where Skye had stalled them: on Josie. She hadn't been far from his thoughts all night, but he felt separated from her in a way that made him feel cold. It was a feeling he'd never known before, and he didn't like it. He knew that if he could just get Josie to meet Nefas, then that feeling would go away, so he'd kept his eye open for her all night. Skye telling him that he needed to find Josie was redundant, but her warning that Nefas was going to use Josie bothered him because he didn't think she was wrong. Nefas knew what Josie meant to him; if he were Nefas, he'd leverage her too. So, he had to find her before she got lost in the mass exit, and then he would bring her into the family, permanently, like he had Katie.

He had to. Before Nefas kept her from him.

Katie was finding her balance on top of the wall, stretching one arm out wide to balance while her broken one twitched at her side, doing what it could to help. Half her body was painted with the green embers from below; the other half was shadowed in the blackness of the night. Skye lightly dropped down behind her with barely a wobble.

"Katie," Henri called out, not so loud as to startle her. She turned her head toward him as best she could. "You'll 'ave to figure out the workings of the gate to unlock it. Adrien understood it, so it can't be very hard. You 'ave your superhero there help you figure it out."

"Are you sure about this, Henri?" Katie asked. She made the mistake of looking down and teetered.

"Focus," Skye sternly told her, ignoring Henri's comment about her.

"I am sure," he told her. "I'll be waiting below for your signal t'at it is open."

Katie nodded, and once she recentered herself, set off, one foot precisely placed in front of the other. It only took a couple of steps before she seemed to find a level of comfort with the surface, and in her confidence, she flared out her good arm as though having completed a perfect dismount, suggesting that she was still a little too drunk. Skye waited patiently. Katie looked back over her shoulder and winked at him before more seriously taking up the crossing.

Confident that Katie was well on her way, Henri made his way back down the tower's steps to head to the guardhouse one block over. The block held mostly administrative offices, the non-descript kind that people tended to forget existed except for those who worked there. There were a couple of tenants which stood out, like one of the two barber shops and a vintage store that sold old paperback books and hard copy music. It was a good place that always had people in it, but not many people buying. Somehow Otto made enough to keep the place open, and Josie always said she'd be sad to see it go if it ever closed.

Nefas' family milled about the streets leading up to the gate, mostly the strays at first, those detached from the crowd. They were as good a place as any to start looking for Josie. The first group he came to was five adults: one definitely male, and all definitely not Josie. Then there was a larger group who were all beyond identification. They mostly all ignored him, which annoyed him. He was a leader among them. They should be giving him deference.

He purposefully walked through another group, pushing them aside with a wave of his arms. They sluggishly moved out of his way and he continued down the block, keeping an eye on Katie's progress high above him while scanning the rapidly growing crowd for Josie. The reality that he didn't know what Josie looked like in this physical state was playing hard on his mind, and when the crowd became too dense to visually scan each of them individually, the size of his task almost became overwhelming.

"JOSIE!"

He was trying to find one body in a mass grave. A hundred of the nearest bodies gave him their attention, their gray, empty eyes staring at him, unblinking, and Katie gave a short yelp as she fought to regain her balance. With Skye helping, Henri didn't worry about her, and he pushed on as best he could in the thickening crowd. "Josie!"

What if she wasn't even here? Henri wondered. What if she was one of the few lost ones who hadn't arrived yet? And if she was here, would she hear and recognize her name? For the first time all night, he felt the lid of the box holding his inner-self open, and the strength of two voices united as he called out again, "JOSIE! Josie!"

"Josie!" Inner Henri shouted out her name, an overwhelming urge forcing it out of his mouth. His shout absorbed into the earthen walls he was clinging to—having begun his climb up again from his fall—but there was a strength behind his voice that he hadn't felt since he'd first woken up in this pit. Something had changed outside.

"JOSIE!" He called her name again and now he saw the outside world. Corpses were everywhere, pressed in tight. The night was afire with iridescent green radiating out of his friends' chests. As soon as his voice faded, so did his vision of the outside, and he found himself again in the darkness with a single shaft of light. "Josie!" The outside world came back, then faded out. He called her name a couple more times, each time with the same result. Henri cracked a small smile. The other Henri just lost some control. And that was hope.

Clinging to his earthen handholds, he began digging and climbing with a fresh vigor. The mystery guy who'd gotten him back up after he'd fallen was going to be right: he was never going to see the bottom of this shaft again.

And it was because of that mystery guy that he was back up here at all. He remembered falling after he'd lost his grip, of being terrified not knowing where the bottom was and when to brace himself for impact. But then his memory went from falling to waking up comfortably curled on his side. The smell of earth had been in his nostrils and he stretched his toes out against the inside of his shoes. The leather belt was still wrapped around his knuckles, the scratched metal buckle resting depressingly underneath his hand. And someone else was in the pit with him.

That "someone" had been sitting in the middle of the light shaft with one leg folded beneath him, the other leg propped up in front. To say he looked stern would be unfair. Self-assured and laconic maybe. He sported a fashionable haircut and had icy blue eyes that looked almost clear with the light shining through them. He somehow locked eyes with Henri hidden in the darkness, and it was like seeing into the heart of the universe.

"You've been mended," he told Henri, shuffling himself over, sliding his feet and knees through the dirt. "You would've died. Your parents, your sister, your friends are fighting to keep you alive. You can't get out of here with the strength of your arms."

"I can get out then?" Henri asked, not hoping too deeply. The guy nodded. "Is there a faster way than this?" Henri pushed himself up and looked down at his belt digger which was really worse for the wear.

"The fastest way out is to know that you can't get yourself out."

"Why did it take so long for someone to come?"

The guy didn't answer right away. His intensity was intimidating, but rather than being rattled by it, Henri wanted to emulate it.

"It took you this long to realize that there's no way out on your own. And my map was outdated."

Henri gave a weak laugh. "So, you're going to help me."

The guy stood up. Fashion jeans and a designer button-up shirt matched his haircut. The way he held himself hinted at strength, though Henri wasn't sure if his strength was a product of his confidence or by his evident athleticism. Maybe both, but from a photograph he would've been easy enough to underestimate, so maybe it was more of the former. He went to where Henri had been digging and ran his fingers around the amateurish handholds.

"If you stand back up and climb once more, you will not see this bottom ever again." He turned and looked back down at Henri, his icy eyes piercing him.

There was no question or doubt. Henri put one hand on his knee and pushed himself up, charged with a new strength. Was it hope, or was it this guy rubbing off on him? As Henri returned to his earthen stepladder, the guy caught the hand Henri was holding the belt buckle with. Rewrapping it, the guy securely positioned it in a more efficient way.

"Like this," he said, demonstrating how to better use of the makeshift tool. He gave a curt nod, flashed a quick half smile, and boosted Henri up the wall to give him a head start.

That had been a long-way-down ago, and Henri hadn't fatigued yet. He assumed his new ally had stayed at the bottom for now as he hadn't heard from him. *God, help me get out. I'm not going to die down here.* He no longer asked if the angels flew down here.

"Josie!" He shouted again, and even though the sound of his voice died in the dirt in front of him, he felt it carry into the outside where again he saw clearly. Outer Henri was pushing his way through the densely packed villagers. The same blonde-haired girl he'd seen before and another woman were balancing on top of the wall, not far from the gate itself. Were they . . . were they really going to try and let everyone out? Even if the satellites and drones of the world had caught their Christmas light show by now, the Gift would be over in a few hours . . . Henri stopped digging.

Satellites and drones.

Nefas didn't care what type of attention the Gift got, just that it did, Henri thought, putting the pieces together. The Gift had become useless to Nefas, so he was going to take the Gift out of the village. The endless search for the next exciting, edgy sensation would explode the Gift worldwide, and all Nefas needed was the right person to see a couple minutes of it for it to go viral. It would be the easiest return Nefas ever had.

Outer Henri must've realized this in relation to how it would affect Josie because he was afraid, Henri could feel it. He wanted to find Josie before she got caught up in this great exodus and became exposed to the world, before Nefas got hold of her.

Another eruption of Josie's name was forced out of his mouth, and he didn't fight it. "JOSIE!"

Henri looked up at the pinhole of light above him; he was no closer to the top now than when he'd been at the bottom. "God, get me out. I'm NOT going to die down here. Josie will be found in time."

As he scraped at the wall, dirt dusted down on top of him, and he used every toe and finger muscle to help him hold tight and dig faster.

"Josie!" He cried out, wanting to see what was going on outside. He saw himself throwing corpses to the ground, piling them on top of each other. Three were down already, their parasites trying to get them back up.

"Stay down," he heard himself snap, kicking one in the head, breaking the eyeglasses that had managed to stay on its face until now. He was hauling another corpse down, a hefty man even in this state who reminded him of the bank manager. Henri's vision started to fade.

"Josie!" Their united voices carried, and time skipped as Outer Henri was now balancing on top of the pile of corpses looking over the heads of everyone in that green mass.

His sight to the outside faded away and Henri dug faster. "Get me out of here!"

"How much further do we have to go, do you think?"

Henri startled, managing to keep his body close to the wall without losing a grip. He skillfully snuck a peek beneath his arm. Those icy blue eyes of his ally looked back up at him.

"How long have you . . . Where . . ." Seeing that he hadn't been alone this whole time, his thoughts stalled. "Why haven't you said anything?"

"You weren't saying anything I wanted to talk about."

That was fair enough, Henri thought.

"And you need to dig more than talk."

That was also accurate.

"How much further, then?"

Henri made a show of looking upward even though he knew. "A couple kilometers."

"That's not right. Look again."

What did he mean, that wasn't right? Henri brushed him off. "Less talking."

"Look again."

Henri decided to indulge him. "Depends how big the hole is that's letting the light in." He craned his neck up again. "Two, three kilometers away?"

"No way."

"Does it even matter? I'm getting out of here no matter."

"It does."

"If you don't like my estimate," Henri said, trying to keep his voice light, "give me yours." He completed another handhold and pushed up another foot.

"How long have you been climbing? Kilometers away doesn't seem right."

It didn't seem right, and it never did. He was climbing and digging, getting dirt in his eyes, straining every muscle in his body for no gain. Thoughts of a treadmill had crossed his mind more than once.

"The answer isn't going to change based on how many times you ask if we're there yet." Henri peeked back down at the man who cocked his eyebrow.

Henri looked upward one last time.

Unsurprisingly, the pinprick of light was far, far, far above them.

The shaft of light flickered. And then the pinprick of light started to grow larger, closer.

"Mother of a fat goat . . ."

"A classic illusion trick," the man explained. "How far away are we, Henri?"

Henri could hardly believe it. "Maybe fifty meters."

"That sounds better. You're talking too much. Get back to digging. Once your other half finds Josie, he's not going to need your voice, and he's determined to lose you next time."

Humans were wobbly to stand on, Outer Henri discovered, even when they lacked elastic skin and slippery muscles; Henri's feet kept slipping off shoulder blades and knees. It only increased his impatience as he turned in a circle calling out Josie's name, hoping to catch something that could identify her from the mass. Her coat was the only thing he knew could help differentiate her, but the strength of the green glow and the press of so many bodies made searching for a single coat a waste of time even from his heightened perch.

He glanced up to the wall again and saw that Katie and Skye had made it to the end and were working out how to get off it and onto the gate itself. Behind them, hovering in the sky, were the blinking red lights of a drone. So then. At least one curious onlooker so far had found them. Nefas' plan was working.

Henri hopped down from the stack of bodies, eyes scanning. It was a sick noise the family made, the sound of their tissues breaking down, and combined with the constant hum of their groaning, he worried that his voice wasn't getting across like it needed to. He had to get higher, and the only place he could do that and still be in position to hit the button when Katie finished her job—if Skye didn't interfere—was the roof of the guard booth.

"JOSIE!" Another wall check: Katie had made it onto the gate. He was running out of time to find Josie.

He elbowed his way through the musty smelling bodies toward the booth, shoving them if they couldn't make enough room for him to squeeze through.

"Josie!"

A heated argument from on top the gate echoed down, Katie angrily shouting at Skye, something about helping or getting out of the way.

There were only two bodies left between him and the booth, two women with strands of stringy hair hanging grotesquely down their gray and rotting faces. Seeing him, they moved out of his way and he came face to face with his brown-robed monk and a single villager waiting beside him. Henri stopped hard.

The glowing essence was radiating brightly from her chest, clearly seen through her shirt as her jacket hadn't been zipped up. Nearly unrecognizable, her eyes were heavily sunken so that the glow barely reached their cloudy grayness. Half her nose had rotted away, her lips had dried and curled back revealing most of her teeth. Her hair hung dead and matted, and he could see through her neck like looking through tissue paper. She looked like King Tutankhamen, only standing upright and with a jacket four sizes too big hanging off her shoulders. She was nearly unrecognizable, yes, but not entirely.

The monk had found Josie first.

30

Josie swayed unsteadily beside the monk, her body language showing no recognition of Henri. The monk's long sleeves draped nearly to the ground, covering most of his fingerbones, which were folded neatly in front of him while his empty eye sockets were fixed on Henri. Henri felt the fool for acting on Skye's advice; of course Nefas wasn't going to let him win the race to find Josie.

"You found her." The monk's ceaselessly clacking jaw grated on Henri as he greeted the monk with a nod of forced appreciation. The monk's jaw stopped, silencing the clacking, and Henri's ears picked up Katie's raised voice still arguing with Skye about getting the gate open. "Leave Josie with me," he instructed. "Katie sounds like she needs help. You should go help her."

Henri exchanged a long stare with the monk until the monk opened his jaw again, and this time a gravelly, cracking voice came from his mouth. "Now we are five. The youngest brother does not give orders. He fulfills them."

Henri frowned. Brother? "What orders am I fulfilling?" he asked. He was Nefas' ambassador, his prince. There was no "younger brother" in the equation.

"Hello, Henri." From the crowd behind him Nefas emerged, his face covered by a low tilted fedora. Stepping out, he edged himself in between Henri and Josie, halving the already tight space, hiding Josie behind himself. "You're too easily distracted."

Henri drew in a shaky breath as he straightened his shoulders.

"A brother?" he asked directly.

Nefas lifted a hand and ran it through Henri's hair, his fingernails gently scratching over his scalp. "My queen is all but standing at my side," Nefas said with a deep sense of satisfaction. "You've earned yourself a place beside your brothers. As soon as you finish with your inner self."

"It won't be long," Henri promised. He swallowed hard, irritated, not wanting to be reminded of that outstanding assignment and Fae's change of heart in the same breath.

"I gave you everything of me," Nefas said as he reached for his fedora and smoothly slid it off. Free of the concealing shadows, Henri saw what Nefas had been hiding: his face falling apart; his skin wrinkling and pulling, sagging loosely around his eyes and showing only perfect blackness beneath rather than the expected muscle or bone; and his eyes, which were so perfectly void they seemed to consume all light that came near. Henri didn't know how to react.

"So very, very few get to know me like you do," Nefas said, leaning in closer. As he spoke, it was as if his voice became like water bubbling into a boil, rising-up over Henri, consuming him. At the same time, he was being drawn down into Nefas' empty eyes. Drowning. His vision shifted and he saw Inner Henri, plastered against an earthen wall, purposefully climbing toward a single source of light.

"Your inability to do this one thing raises questions, Henri. Fae commands my family better than you can command yourself."

Nefas slipped his fedora back on and the vision ended. With his face again covered, Nefas was nothing but a mysterious gentleman in a foggy night.

Henri bit the inside of his mouth, pinching it both painfully and invigoratingly, trying to shake himself out of the drowning feeling. Nefas was running his hands through Henri's hair again and he bit down on his cheek harder until his pain reflexes forced him to unclench his jaw.

"I still have Josie," Nefas said. "Until you get rid of your other half, you don't have the right to even see her."

Nefas reached behind him and picked up Josie's skeletal hand in his, leading her back into the crowd, the packed corpses managing to make a path for them.

Once Nefas had gone from sight, the monk restarted his rhythmic teeth clacking and Henri went inside the guard booth slamming the door behind him. Stealing a look at the monk through the window, Henri tensely wondered how long ago Nefas had brought him and the other three monks into his family. Did they still have their own minds, or were they little more than marionettes?

He needed to have Josie. He needed to bring her into the family; he had to kill his inner self once and for all.

Taking a seat, he looked to the top of the gate and saw that a man with a fedora had joined Katie and Skye. Skye wasn't going to be a hindrance for much longer.

Deep pangs of a migraine pounded its way to the front of his brain, and he knew this round with his inner self was going to be a painful one.

"What do I call you?" Henri asked the man hanging on below him. His companion had again been mostly silent throughout the last leg of the climb, making only a comment here or there. The pinprick of light that had been so far away now filled his entire vision when he looked up.

"Slobodan."

Baltic. Henri could recognize it now in his features, especially his nose.

It had been a while since Outer Henri had called Josie's name. The last time Inner Henri had tried it, he couldn't see outside and that worried him, losing that control. He told Slobodan and was flatly told that the outside world couldn't be his focus right now. But that was the exact opposite of Henri's reality—the search for Josie was absolutely his entire focus—but he didn't argue. He just kept digging, going a little faster.

Less than four meters from the top, Henri felt like his toes were going to bounce off his feet and his heart was going to pound into his throat. He was so close. Digging and scraping carelessly, his hands were shaking, not from exhaustion, but from expectation of his upcoming escape. The grips he was carving were becoming shallower.

Three meters.

What was it going to be like when he finally made it? What was up there? Would he pull himself over the edge and instantly be united with Outer Henri? Would he be able to take back control of his body?

Two and a half meters.

He could no longer see what he was doing, the light hiding everything not in its beam. He was scraping furiously, blindly, adrenaline shooting nervous energy through his every nerve.

"Slobodan," Henri called down. He had nothing to say beyond that, he just had to say something to someone.

Less than half a meter!

There was a short ledge to the hole, something he could pull himself onto. Unable to wait any longer, Henri found the best grip he had the patience to find and leapt upward, grabbing onto the ledge. His legs were swinging in empty air as he struggled to pull himself up. Shimmying himself up and over the ledge and into the brightness of the light, Henri left the dark, hopeless pit behind.

A laugh of pure euphoria exploded out of his mouth as he jumped into the air, shamelessly shouting. He pounded his chest in victory and danced in mockery of the hole that tried to defeat him until his sense reminded him to help Slobodan out.

Slobodan, though, had already found his way out and was pushing off his knees to stand. Laughing and grinning madly, Henri came to hug him in celebration, but Slobodan wasn't sharing in the hard-earned victory of escape. Rather, he remained unaffected as he took in the sight surrounding them. The excitement of the moment quickly died, and Henri let his eyes wander to follow Slobodan's gaze.

The light, though bright like a noon sun, was void of heat and was as comforting as fluorescent tube lighting. They stood on a circular floor maybe three meters across with the dark hole they'd just left occupying the middle. The darkness from that hole formed a beam which stretched upwards and beyond sight. Familiar, featureless dirt walls surrounded them and extended up until they merged with the beam of darkness into a black spot far, far above. With the exception that this shaft was a bit wider, it was the perfect opposite of the one he'd just spent everything trying to leave.

"Henri?" Slobodan called to him, but Henri couldn't answer. He stood dumb, motionlessly staring upward into the brightness that ended in a pinprick of darkness. His heart was sinking lower and lower, his mind draining of all thought, all feeling.

"I lose," was all that he could say.

––––––––

"ARRRGH!!" Outer Henri's fist smashed into the wall breaking through the drywall. His knuckles throbbed but it was a secondary pain. His head was exploding, and a warm trickle of blood was dripping from his nose. His insides were erratic, his heart was beating irregularly, and he felt like he was being ripped into two. Tears poured down his cheeks, dripping off his chin. His hand was bright red and swelling.

The Inner Henri was finally dying and Henri's monk brother was outside the door waiting for him to just get on with it and be done.

31

Failure was heavy.

It was one of the mysterious things about emotion that Fae had never understood. How could the infinitesimal mass of emotion-causing chemicals weigh so much?

Max had let her out of the hug. She had no will to stand up on her own, so she'd let herself sink onto the cold steps. Their edges were rounded, like her back. She was unable to reconcile the pride of living with her failure. Her eyes heartlessly fixated on the village's Christmas tree on the other side of the street. It stood prouder in its death than she was in her life. The tree was supposed to be spotlighted with floodlights, but the lights weren't working, so the tree—with its oversized bulbs and plastic icicles—was as ghostly as the rest of this Christmas nightmare.

Max took a seat beside her.

Every failure is a success waiting to happen. Positive people get positive results.

The patronizing sound of the Voice wasn't even insulting enough to stir her. Was depression synonymous with failure? Or could they be two separate things?

She had to assume that Nefas had had his way with everyone he could by now, which meant that Katie was his. Henri, the hostages, and the kids—his. Every parasite she removed with Nefas' graces linked her that much closer to him; she couldn't help any more people. Max promised a beautiful Christmas morning, but she knew better than anyone that all those people's lives were ruined. She should've taken the risk and sent Katie home.

The guilt bowed her head even lower, and she closed her eyes to the dark world around her. Memories of the void greeted her, and she had to open them again.

"Fae," Max said, "why did you become an architect?"

He shifted his weight, ruffling his clothes, but to Fae's hyperactive senses, it sounded like a corpse making a grab for her, ready to force the parasite into her. She twitched hard and jumped away.

He didn't look bothered by her reaction.

"Why did you first pick up that colored pencil?"

I like Dominic better too. There's a gift inside our void that will help you get rid of this kid.

Max tried again. "Your first design. It was a house that was entirely a kitchen, wasn't it?"

Fae lifted her head just enough to see that Max wasn't even looking at her. He was playing with the cuff of his jacket, looking out as though gazing out to the horizon.

"It was a three-story kitchen-house," she said with effort. "That's where we had the best times as a family. I designed it to give my mother a place to be happy all the time, after I realized the reason she didn't always get out of bed wasn't just because she was tired."

"Reminds me of those Eataly grocery stores. The ones with multiple levels of endless food and wine, active kitchens you can order from."

Fae sighed and she let the silence sit between them as she worked up the motivation for more words.

"A friend who knows that story asked me to consult for him on a redesign Eataly wanted for their London location. They tell me that one has the most home-like experience."

"You don't think so?"

Fae went back to staring at the gray tree in front of her. "Scott did a good job leading that project."

Perceived or real, the sound of movement made Fae jump and twitch again. A flash, and she could hear the sound of her scream tearing the night apart, feel the burn of injection points all over her, the pain. Her arms jerked to fight off the invisible attackers, and she almost fell off the stair. Max caught her arm and she instinctively tore it away before she came back to her senses.

She shook her head in apology, and Max waved it off, sliding a travel-sized pad of paper and a pen over to her. She tracked it without interest.

"Nefas was very invested in getting you back here," Max said. "*How* he was going to bring you back it's best you never know, so it's a good thing Dominic got through to you first. You damaged Nefas' pride, so for revenge, he wants you at the head of this jail break he's put into motion tonight. Giving you the ability to take out the parasite is a Trojan Horse."

"I know. His Voice came back when I took the parasite out of Adrien."

Max nodded. "We needed you back here too, for the exact reasons Dominic told you. The hostages Nefas took weren't a surprise, and neither is the role Henri is filling. We needed Henri's opposite."

Fae didn't want to talk about herself. "What's Dominic doing?"

"Three monks went to la Rue with orders to put the hostages in the pit until you got there. Dominic is delaying that order." Max paused, then nudged the pad of paper. "A bad place inspired that kitchen-house and launched your career. This bad place can take you further too. Draw."

Reluctantly, Fae picked up the pad. The pen felt foreign between her fingers. She wasn't sure what she was going to draw, but she let her emotions speak through the pen, just like how she used to do when she was younger. But her emotions didn't want to speak this time, and the simple drawing was finished almost before she began. In the middle of the page was a large cardboard box shelter surrounded by a clear-cut forest. The shelter was alone and out of place in the middle of the heartless destruction.

She handed the drawing back to Max, happy to get rid of it. He took the pen out of her fingers and started to add to it, sketching for a couple seconds before showing it to her. He'd added a couple of stumps beneath the cardboard shelter for it to sit on. Then he kept sketching, longer this time before showing it to her again. This time he'd re-engineered the picture. The cardboard shelter had become a castle, and the stumps all around were now hillocks for villages and smaller castles. The picture showed an entire little domain secure within the confines of a ring of dense forest. There was a path that led beyond the distant trees, and on it was a woman walking away, leaving. That caught Fae's attention, and Max smiled seeing where her eyes rested. He flipped the page over and continued drawing.

A couple minutes later he presented Fae with a new sketch that picked the trail up on the other side of the trees. It led to a cliff that looked out over the land two hundred feet below: a sprawling vista of trees and a mirrored lake, birds and the sun on the horizon. Standing on the edge of the cliff was the woman, now surveying the vastness before her. Even though Max had only been quickly sketching with a pen he'd still managed to capture the details and shadows surprisingly well.

Max began to take the drawing back, but Fae stopped him. There was an entire world in that picture, another reality alive beneath those pen strokes. If she could stare at it long enough, maybe she could muster the will to enter it and leave this place behind.

"You're never as trapped as you feel," Max explained. "This girl had to learn it just like you."

"Who is she?"

Max smiled. "You're never alone. Remember that Nicholas is always with you."

Fae let the drawing go. "You and Dominic keep saying that, but living in the past isn't helping my present."

"You're right." He gave the notepad back to her and she took it for the sake of the girl in the drawing. "But remembering what happened once gives you the courage to see it happen again. And that is what is going to get you through this." Max looked at her intently. "You weren't left alone with Nefas. After my conversation with him in the plaza, I found you pretty quickly, but he made you fear, the fear strengthened the void, and you saw only him. Though I walk through the valley of death, I will not be afraid?"

Max was putting this on her? She glared at him, and in doing so, she *saw* him. She saw him sitting with her, *being* with her, and her anger died. There was something about Max that made her understand him over her pain, and for the first time, she was OK that it wasn't Dominic beside her. Max wasn't blaming her; he was coaching her. And that could only mean one thing: there was more to come.

"What did you say that made Nefas so angry?"

"Spoilers." Max suppressed a small smile. "If what I told him made him that mad, it can only be good for you."

A fresh sheet of paper lay in front of her. Fae slowly closed her eyes, inhaling deeply, letting the incoming air stave off the void pressuring to invade her mind's eye. She let the pen work freely. This time, she knew exactly what she was designing.

The hippodrome came to life easily. While her first sketch had been apathetic, this time her fingers found their purpose guiding the pen around the architecture of the building. Columns carried the structure almost three hundred feet into the air, practically double the height of the Roman Colosseum. Regularly placed glassed-in arches gave the structure its strength while external stone staircases were as functional as they were striking. The pen etched quickly, her creativity flowing. Carved stone decorated the bottom third, a living wall of greenery took over the middle section, while a waterfall cascaded down from the top levels. A retractable awning stretched across the top, covering the million—Fae sucked in her breath and her pen faltered— the million corpses sitting inside.

"I'm still going to the North gate, aren't I."

Max gave a curt nod. "*We* are, yes. And we're going to have to leave really soon."

"What's inside the vial?" The pen hovered over her drawing. It wasn't finished yet. "You told me not to worry about what it was, just that Nefas wanted it. I need to know."

Max stood up, shaking his legs out to get the chill off them as he answered simply, "The remains of Nefas' first two victims."

His first two victims? Fae's thoughts whirred into overdrive as they scoured her memories for why that statement sounded so familiar. Dust, victims, remains . . . She remembered the story. She'd been told the origin of the Gift her first Christmas here. It was of a young couple who hosted a dinner party for an intriguing stranger but were tricked. Instead of joining the stranger on his next traveling adventure as he'd promised, they were locked into the back of Death's wagon until they'd died and decomposed into dust. When Nefas finally stopped the wagon to collect their remains, a wind carried them away to let them warn the world about the danger of entertaining Death. It was a fable, an origin story, one that had an eerie similarity to her experiences at the time but . . . that was it.

"He's a collector of his victims, and you never forget your first," Max said.

"There's not enough ashes for two people in these vials."

"We have all that's left. I will tell you when the time comes to show Nefas yours," Max promised. "Until then, don't give Nefas any reason to suspect that you know what's in mine, much less that you have your own. He wants nothing more in this world than to have possession of them, and he'll do anything to have them. Unless you follow my lead, more people could get hurt."

To emphasize his promise, Max pulled out his vial from beneath his shirt and let it rest openly on his chest, plainly visible. He raised his eyebrows in question, and Fae nodded, swallowing her apprehension.

Regripping the pen, she turned her attention back to her drawing and quickly added three people walking on the floor of the hippodrome, not to scale. Herself between Dominic and Max with Nefas nowhere in sight. Max was part of her little support group now.

She closed the notepad and swore, painfully pushing her heavy limbs up to standing. Max took the pen and pad back.

"Whatever happened between you two back at the basilica," Fae said, "he's dancing a much finer line with my life. Courage or not, don't leave me for even a second, or I'm done."

Max stuck out his hand and Fae weakly shook it. With a determined nod, Max set off down the street at her pace, the weight of failure belaboring her every step. But at least now she had someone to help carry that weight.

They walked the streets to the gate in silence and alone, the parasites' green glow burning over the rooftops long before Fae could see either the gate or the wall. With every step she was one step closer to finishing this nightmare. That was what kept her going even as they approached the wall of corpses packed from one side of the street to the other, blocking the way to the gate, bathing her and Max in green light.

You're almost here. The Voice's words snaked smoothly down her back, underlying what she was walking into. *I'm waiting for you.*

Fae stopped fast in the middle of the street. Max stopped with her.

"Maybe . . . maybe you should take my vial and add it to yours."

Max shook his head. "It belongs to this village, so to you by proxy. And honestly, I can't wait to see Nefas' face when he sees you with it."

"What's going to happen, Max?"

Max frowned and nodded. "Nefas wants to lock you down into the place at his side and for you to keep using the gift he's given you. Once Katie and Henri open the gate, Nefas will give Katie the chance to make her choice; at that time, he will put pressure on you again."

He turned as if to begin walking again, but Fae couldn't move her feet. Their next steps would take them into the crowd of the dead, a graveyard awoken to their master, and *he* was waiting for her in there. And Katie. Her two greatest failures . . .

"Hey," Max turned around. Her eyes flicked to the side where one of the corpses began to take notice of their presence. "Hey," he called her attention gently back to him. His face was earnest, a deep reassurance coming off of him. "If you don't go to the gate, he will drag you there. Let's go on our terms. Don't fear. "

"It will get me killed," Fae rasped, her voice suddenly raw.

"It will get you killed." Max agreed.

Fae nodded with growing determination.

Redemption from your failures can only be granted by the one you failed against. Our conflict can fuel our greatness, the Voice whispered into her ear, and Fae pursed her lips. Fuel our greatness . . .

"Don't fear," Fae said, staring hard at Max, wanting to block out the Voice. "And it's the hardest thing to do."

"Nicholas took everything from Nefas, including you. That's permanent unless you choose otherwise," Max said, his eyes dancing with purpose. "Now. Nefas agreed to leave you the hell alone a couple hours ago. Let's start finding out how he plans to do that."

Fae wanted to laugh, wanted to feel strong and brave, but she didn't.

Max picked up her hand and began to lead her into the crowd, but Fae took the lead instead, keeping her hand tightly in his. "I'll go first," she said. She could be that brave, at least.

There was a general shuffling and agitation of corpses as they made an opening for her, and it felt like navigating a crowd at a music festival. Fae set her focus ahead trying to block out as much of her surroundings as possible. *Don't fear,* she told herself. *Do not fear. Though I walk through the village of Death, I will not fear.*

The smell of mildew permeated every breath, she could taste it in her mouth. The sound of cracking bones was like a haunted forest of creaking trees. Corpse shoulders brushed against hers; their decaying fingers touched her fingers. Fae's nerves made her twitch with self-preservation at the smallest unexpected bump or irregular movement, but no corpse gave her a hungry look, or even raised a finger with parasite in it.

The Voice spoke. *You are my beautiful one.*

She tried to swallow but her mouth had gone dry. Regripping Max's hand, she glanced back and saw that he was passing through the corpses as easily as she was. Was it because he was with her?

It was slow going, and neither Fae nor Max said anything as they bumped and skirted through the living dead. At any moment Nefas could have them fold in on her and she'd be buried beneath their bodies. *I will not fear.*

Fear is what will keep you alive, the Voice countered.

You guide me and comfort me, Fae continued.

I am your guide. The Voice surrounded her in warmth, and she shook her head as though that would be enough to get it to stop.

"Nicholas is with me." She broke open her dry mouth, speaking determinedly to herself. "I will not fear."

Max lightly squeezed her hand.

The gate was now in full view. Clashing human voices echoed down from the top of it, the punctuated snaps of a British girl predominately, which told Fae all she needed to know. Katie was fighting someone and it wasn't the parasite. A short man in a fedora was on the gate with her—the professor—confirming that the professor was Nefas' avatar for Katie. And there was another woman on the gate as well, probably Skye. Katie had both a devil and an angel up there with her on either shoulder, and a parasite inside her not giving her much choice whom to follow.

Fae could hear Katie demanding that the woman respect the professor, to help or to bugger off. The woman was holding Nefas at bay, trying to help an uncaring Katie differentiate between the parasite's urges and her own, telling her not to fear, while Nefas simply talked. Fae couldn't make out what he was saying.

Seeing him again so soon, even in the image of the professor rather than the Nefas she knew, still filled her with shame, with dread. Her labored breaths became loud in her own ears.

"You can't do this to me anymore. I won't let you," Fae muttered.

The professor instantly stopped what he was doing. He turned toward her, locking eyes with her even across the distance.

She gripped Max's hand tighter. She'd spoken too soon. Her words were bolder than she was.

That choirboy has made you forget your place, the Voice said so tangibly that she could almost feel his breath on her skin. *Remember where you stand.*

The blackness of the void pushed its way into her vision. She was back in the nothingness, tumbling forward, weightlessly, without orientation, her head spinning. Outside of it all, she felt arms holding her body steady.

"Nefas!" Max snapped fiercely. "Stop it."

The void vanished just as quickly as it had come.

Get rid of him.

The professor turned his attention back to Katie. "Open the gate," he yelled at her, loud enough for the order to carry. Katie gave a screech of pain as her hands went to her head and she disappeared from view.

"Fae," Max tugged at her hand, "when those gates open, we can't be in the middle of this mob."

This gate opens and our kingdom is birthed. It's the beginning of our new dawn.

Nefas was really going to do this. That future he'd shown her . . . this was how it started.

"Fae," Max prompted her again, "we have to keep moving."

Max didn't wait and he pulled her toward the side of the street, not caring that he shouldered corpses out of the way or snagged their clothing as he pushed past them. "The corpses leaving the village was part of the negotiations Henri brought when he came for their release," Max explained over his shoulder. "What Nefas didn't know was that as a result of them leaving the gates, the Gift had to end. That's one of the things I told him at the plaza." Forcing his way through the compacted mass, Max pointed up into the night where the small, red lights of a drone were hovering overhead. "The same website that brought the EU families here brought whoever is behind that drone. Nefas is going to show the world."

"Hold on," Fae demanded behind him. "The Gift is over?"

Max didn't have a chance to answer back as Katie yelled out, cutting off any clarification. "HENRI!"

Katie was waving her hands for attention, stirring up the green fog around her. Fae followed her motion down to the guard booth maybe only twenty feet away. There was a monk standing eerily on guard outside it.

There was a moment when nothing happened. Then, the sounds of hard wood and aged metal grinding creaked the gates to life.

Max dragged her the rest of the way, urgency propelling them through the mob. Reaching the edge, they plastered themselves to the wall to avoid being dragged back in, and watched as the gate swung inward, sweeping away any corpses in its path. Those caught behind it didn't have a chance.

As soon as there was room to squeak through the gap, the first corpses began to leave. Filing out first one at a time, then two, then as a group, and finally en masse, the villagers who'd done everything they could to protect themselves and their Gift abandoned all of their security measures and were protected, in the end, by nothing. The bath of green light danced beneath the stone archway as they stumbled and pulled themselves through. It was like watching a stagnant river come to life, and every now and again Fae could see one of the corpses get stuck in the current of their own movement and disappear beneath the churning feet. The drone followed their journey out.

"Max, what did you mean that the Gift is over?" Fae asked over the sounds of crunching bones and wheezing breaths. She turned her eyes away from the flowing mass of people long enough to glance at the young man beside her. His blank face gave her no clues to what he was thinking, and it was even harder to read with the iridescent light ebbing and flowing across it. "What happens to these people?"

"So ends the Gift as it has been known since beyond recorded history," Max uttered as though in eulogy. He took a deep breath and reset himself. "After tonight, the demonstration of this village is over. The drama played out here is done. After this Christmas morning, these people will return to normal and will never again live through the Gift."

"How?" Fae demanded, not caring that the question sounded harsher than Max deserved; her question was overdue for an answer. "If the baby isn't here, there is no reset in the morning. The Gift ends *with* Nicholas taking away the parasite out of everyone who didn't chose it, it can't be the end of the Gift *without* the baby."

"The baby isn't here, but no one said Nicholas wasn't," Max said. "His name is whatever it needs to be."

Max gave her a small sideways grin and Fae felt like she'd run into a brick wall. He turned back to watching the mass exit, but Fae was frozen in revelation, all of Max's mystery aligning into a clear picture. Different times called for different measures, and this time, a baby was not what was needed. Nicholas—Max—hadn't not shown up. He'd been days early.

Fae cast a quick glance up to the gate to see Katie, Skye, and the professor who was proudly watching his family pass beneath. Did Nefas know?

"My meeting with Nefas was full of surprises," Max said, answering her silent wondering. "His violence against you was part pent-up frustration and part urgent need to secure you away from me as fast as possible."

Fae gave a small nod. The full impact of what he'd just revealed was more water on an already saturated sponge. She watched as a corpse got stuck against the wall near the guard booth. Soon, a couple more got trapped too, creating an eddy in the river.

"These people will be free to live life," Max continued, "but the parasite is still Nefas' to spread, now to whomever he likes, wherever he can. He's no longer bound to the yearly timing of the Gift to infect people." Max looked directly at her again. "The big difference is that there's no more demonstration through corpses, no more glowing, which undermines his viral marketing idea."

Fae looked back up to the gate and found that the professor wasn't up there anymore. Nefas was going to be freed into the world? With all the focus on corpses being outside the walls, Fae hadn't clued into that detail. Her tongue stuck dry in her mouth, her insides tightening.

"Max, if he's free to go wherever he wants, whenever he wants, even if . . ." She shook her head. "Even *when* we break him off me tonight, he's still going to be released, no need for avatars. It's going to be worse."

"Hey," Max soothed. "*We* will cut him off, yeah? Follow my lead, OK, and trust me that this is going to turn out."

She nodded but only felt marginally better. Her failure still hung too heavy, and the wretched anticipation of waiting for Nefas to appear muted everything else.

"As for the villagers," Max picked up his answer to her question, "Nefas' parting gift to them is the fame and exposure that drone can provide. In the right hands the footage will go viral like he wants it to. Henri and Katie are intended to help take advantage of that fame, but without the Gift around anymore, the story and video will be forgotten soon enough. Anyone from this village is at risk for all the associated fallout, and Maël is going to be given instructions on how to get the village through the next couple of years." Max looked back over at her. "But that's not your problem."

"Nothing about this place ever was."

They continued to watch the remaining corpses lumber and drag themselves by, those casualties trampled and left behind slowly being revealed in the thinning torrent of the corpses' release. Soon only the last remaining corpses were dragging themselves through the gate, and Max carefully pushed himself off the wall and nodded toward the guard booth. "I haven't seen

Henri yet. C'mon." But he stopped before he even started.

Nefas was strolling toward them from the direction of the gate. His midnight blue shirt was buttoned up now, and he'd kept the professor's fedora. It was tipped low to keep his face hidden, and he looked like a classic uptown man of mystery, but one that radiated as much arrogance and darkness as his cracking body could allow.

Do you like the hat?

"My queen," Nefas said as he came closer. "Are you ready to stand by my side again?"

Nefas came to a slow halt, ignoring Max as completely as he could.

If it wasn't for Max's arm separating Nefas from her, she had no doubt that Nefas would only have to wave a parasitic finger and the thin ragdoll frame of courage she'd pieced together with Max would break. The memory of the pain he could bring was too fresh. The feeling of what it was like to have millions of people fear and revere her as she stood untouchable by his side was too real. She licked her lips to hide her struggle.

"My queen, it's time to give Katie and Henri's girlfriend their choice."

Nefas turned toward the guard booth and Max let him lead the way before reassuringly taking Fae's hand in his.

"Remember Nicholas," he said.

Fae was glad he said it like that. Max might be Nicholas grown up, but Nicholas would always be the baby who had saved her.

32

"Henri," Slobodan spoke calmly, authoritatively. "Henri. This isn't the time for being a butterfly."

Slumped forward like a forgotten marionette, Henri was slipping away, down deeper and deeper, sinking into a body already sunk. His body was cooling. He wasn't being melodramatic; despair doesn't kill within minutes.

"Henri, my friend, I'm going to help you, but you have to hold on because I have to leave for a couple minutes. I'm headed to the Notre-Dame du Seigneur to get everyone to work a little harder, and then I'll be outside for a bit. If you can keep breathing, we stay in business, OK?"

Henri had no response.

Slobodan patted Henri's leg. "OK."

Slouched deep in the shallow chair of the guard booth, Henri inspected his hand, slowly twisting it first one way, then the other. His knuckles were swollen and hurt less when elevated. It was fascinating to watch how his bruised tendons reacted to each of his movements when his skin's opaqueness faded out.

In the background his brother stood at the door. Henri had decided to call him Friar Laurence, and he'd stayed silent ever since Henri had ended his inner self. Behind Friar Laurence was the nearly empty street; only a couple of the slow starters and those who had to pick themselves up off the ground remained. He thought one looked like Veronique, but it was hard to tell.

He was eager to get outside the gate to witness the future, expecting the hillside to look as beautiful as the Lantern Festival in China, except that no lanterns would be floating away here. He wanted to congratulate Katie first though, owing it to himself, so he decided to wait until she got back from the gate before heading out. She and Skye were almost finished coming back across the wall. Seeking to trade the warmth of the booth for a little extra leg room, he got up and opened the door to go outside, keeping his injured hand above his heart, but Friar Laurence stood in his way.

"Move."

Nothing.

"Then come with me." Henri went to go around him, but he walked into the Friar's piercing grip snapping around his throat. Henri gagged and tried to swipe his arm away, but the sharp finger bones didn't dislodge. Glaring into the Friar's empty eye sockets, Henri settled in to win this confrontation one way or another.

"Henri." Striding into view, Nefas called his name.

The Friar let Henri go and stepped out of the way, Nefas taking his place in the doorway.

Nefas was eyeing Henri over as though looking for any remnants of his inner self, but Henri barely noticed the assessment. Even though Nefas still wore the fedora, the shadow it cast did nothing to hide what was beneath, and Henri was caught staring into Nefas' face, his *real* face. There was no covering mask for it this time. Henri was looking into a crystal ball reflecting humanity, and he felt his blood go cold.

Nefas' face was made up of hundreds of unique, semi-translucent faces superimposed on top of each other in an endless layer: young and old, men and women, girls and boys, thin and obese, every shade of skin color and grade of complexion. One face would dominate, then another would fade into its place, all the while keeping the same translucency which allowed for all the layers to be seen at the same time. As Nefas grinned or frowned, so did every one of the hundreds or even thousands of faces. He wasn't beautiful or wonderful, and Henri began to feel extremely uncomfortable; he may as well be looking into the face of a terrible god.

"You've done well," Nefas said, as he firmly took hold of Henri's limp, injured hand. Henri was speechless as Nefas cupped his hand between his own, roughly massaging it, feeling out the bones. Henri bit his lip, grimacing as Nefas found the injury and pinched down. After a long second, Nefas let him go, and when the screaming nerves settled down Henri wiggled out his hand, testing it. There were no sharp pangs. There was no pain at all. But Henri couldn't stop staring, caught in the web of Nefas' true face. Nefas smirked.

"Now you see me for who I really am. I keep my promises." Nefas stepped out of the doorway revealing behind him Fae Peeters, that choirboy he'd negotiated with earlier, and Josie. Not corpse Josie, but conscious, aware, living flesh-and-blood Josie, blinking rapidly as though coming out into bright sunlight and disoriented as if shook from a dream.

Henri flexed his hands, welcoming the essence flowing into them. Josie was a sight for sore eyes, and she'd be even prettier with shimmering green skin.

Josie quickly found the context to her surroundings, and as her eyes fell on Henri, they grew wide and her mouth set firm. "Henri, what happened?"

Henri couldn't stop smiling. She was amazing in every way. "Nefas happened." He nodded his head in the direction of the looming figure. "He took you out of the Gift."

"That doesn't happen. That . . ." Josie was searching inside the little guard booth, then beside her, seeing the group of strangers she'd found herself part of. "Henri? What's happening?"

"It's OK." He took a step toward her wanting to put her at ease, but she held him off with upraised arms.

"He's the shadow-man from the Gift's nightmares," she said, quickly glancing at Nefas. "And you're . . ." she struggled for words. He could tell she didn't like his new look. "The gate is open in the middle of the night. This is all still a nightmare in my head."

"This *is* the real world." Fae quickly jumped in before Henri could speak, grabbing Josie's unfocused attention. "It's not morning yet, but—"

Henri cut her off. "Nefas saved you. He took you and the rest of the villagers out of the Gift. That's why the gate is open. There's no need to keep it closed. You're one of the last ones."

Josie was backing away from him. She was going to run. "Why are you lying?" she asked incredulously. "The *gate* is open, Henri, I can see the parasite's glow; I'm not one of the last."

He didn't want to have to chase her down if she ran. She was supposed to be happy. Excited. Henri flexed his fingers, ready with Nefas' essence. The motion attracted Josie's eyes and she froze, staring at them. She had to agree to take on the essence for it to stay in her beyond the morning; he needed time to convince her.

Henri didn't wait. He lunged for her jacket to hold her put, but she was already off, sprinting down the street, shoes pounding against the paving stones. Nefas made a motion for Henri to not give chase.

"Josie," Nefas purred, "I took you out, but the Gift isn't over."

Henri watched as Josie's legs suddenly buckled on her midstride and she collapsed, hands splayed in front of her as her knees skidded and her body hit the ground. She was fighting to stand, her legs not holding her weight, but she kept fighting, trying to drag herself where her legs wouldn't carry her. Henri wanted to run to her, to help her, but he waited for Nefas' signal. Fae didn't wait though, and she rushed to Josie's side. Seeing Nefas doing nothing to stop her, Henri went after her.

The cause for Josie's fall was sharply evident as he got closer. Her emotive gray eyes were unnaturally prominent in her deathly thin face. Hollows and depressions of skin had sunk between her bones where the muscle had disappeared. Held in limbo between corpse and alive, Josie was a shell of herself.

"C'mon," Fae said, kneeling and lifting one of Josie's skeletal arms around her shoulder, "we're going back to the basilica together."

Henri leaned down and plucked Fae's arm off his girlfriend before they could stand up. "You're not going to take her away from me," he told her.

"This is my village. My girlfriend. Our life." He looked down at the older woman. "Who are you to stop me?"

Max and Nefas joined their little group, and Fae clenched her jaw, the age-lines in her face deepening. She stood up, her gaze not leaving him, and Henri didn't want to admit it, but she looked almost authoritative.

The arm Josie was propping herself up with buckled, and Henri dropped to her side. Putting his arms around her, he lifted her to her feet. She was so light, so breakable. It wasn't what Josie was supposed to feel like. She tried to speak, but with her mouth and throat half decayed, her slurred words were barely intelligible. "'Ake mwe 'oo Nota-Dam—"

"Shhh," Henri hugged her close, kissing the side of her clammy head. "I know I look different. It's OK. What you see in me is going to protect us from the Gift." Josie was finding her feet, and wanting to give her what dignity in strength she had left, he released her, though he kept his supporting arm close.

Fae spoke. "The question that really needs to be asked is, who are *you*, Henri? Nefas calls me his queen. He's given me the ability to take out the parasite. You might've stumbled across Nefas a couple hours ago, but there's been a place for me at his side since before you were born."

She stared at him without flinching, and Henri wondered if he might've underestimated her. A rush of venomous dislike boiled up in him, and he forced himself to smile to contain it.

"Who am I?" He pointed at Friar Laurence still standing at the guard booth. "I'm one of them." Fae looked to where he was pointing and didn't flinch. "And we answer only to Nefas. As you know."

Henri saw Josie starting to wander away, but she wasn't going anywhere fast. He knew where she was headed anyway.

Nefas turned to Fae, his many faces disapproving. "The girlfriend, Fae," he said, "is not yours."

Henri smirked, and he turned to bring Josie back.

"You took her out of the Gift," Henri heard Fae say. "She's a hostage if she's kept in limbo, like the others." There was a pause. "Which means she does belong to me."

Henri wheeled back around. "Josie is mine, you barking cow," he snapped. He glared Fae down as he stormed back. "This is who you've chosen over me?" Henri asked Nefas pointedly, insulted. "This scared old woman who's trying to steal—"

Nefas snapped his hand beneath Henri's jaw and squeezed, his black pit eyes drilling into Henri, his thousand different faces pinched in anger, impatient, superior. "You will never know as much as I do." Nefas shoved him off and he barely kept his feet as he stumbled backward.

Henri didn't dare massage his throbbing jaw, but he fixed his glare back at Fae. She didn't deserve Nefas' attention, and he'd be damned if he let her take Josie from him.

"The girlfriend is not a hostage," Nefas clarified to Fae. "Don't ignore Katie."

Fae said nothing.

"You still don't trust me," Nefas observed. "I wouldn't either. And you still don't trust yourself," he said with pity. "I wouldn't either. You can trust no one. That is what being queen really means."

Nefas turned his head to shout over his shoulder. "Katie!"

Katie and Skye had just finished scrambling off the wall and securing themselves safely on top of the tower. Katie waved her acknowledgement of Nefas' order.

"Henri," Max said to him as discreetly as he could, "you've lost your shimmer."

Henri looked down at himself. It was true. He no longer shimmered, and his skin was no longer opaque; he was see-through. He looked up at Friar Laurence.

You are their brother, the sound of Nefas' voice, the Voice, spoke.

Henri did another quick check on Josie. She'd made it further down the road but had stopped beneath a streetlamp with a dark-haired man. The night's fog muted the two of them but there was something recognizable about him, and a name popped into his head. Slobodan. He didn't know why, he didn't know anyone by that name, but even as he watched them, the guy began helping Josie slide and limp her way back toward them. And that made Henri suspicious.

Within minutes Katie and Skye arrived, joining the arrival of Josie at the hands of the Slobodan guy.

Nefas led Katie directly to Fae. "Give her her choice."

"And Henri?" Fae asked, her throat noticeably tight.

"Henri," Nefas smiled, "is mine. He made his own choice already. He's dead and alive to me."

"Almost dead," Slobodan corrected.

Henri angrily curled his lip back. That other Henri *was* dead! Would he be able to see Nefas' face if Inner Henri was still alive? He bit his tongue, knowing better than to interrupt.

Nefas looked at Slobodan, uninterested. "You have old information."

Josie was being released from her state of limbo and Henri took her by the arm to lead her off to the side. It was going to be just him and her and his need to convince her to willingly take Nefas' essence. But as the Gift left Josie, she yanked her arm out of his hold and backed away from him. She was shaking her head, looking to Slobodan who hovered nearby.

"We discovered how to stop the Gift, Josie," Henri told her with a lightness he hoped adequately conveyed the Henri she used to know. "It's like a vaccine. I give you a bit of Nefas to 'plug the hole' so the speak, locking him out of you. He'll never be able to bring you into the Gift again." He smiled and showed his glowing fingers as a sign of open transparency.

She kept shaking her head. "I want nothing to do with you."

"Someone had to be the distributor. I volunteered."

"You don't know the lies fed to us during the Gift, Henri." She used his name, and he took that as a good sign. "I can't believe anyone, or anything, until the sun rises. I can't and I won't. Including you. You're a walking X-ray, Henri!"

"The choir promised I'll be fine. This opportunity won't last forever, Josie, and I have no idea if there'll be another one. I wouldn't lie about something like this. Our whole village can finally be normal."

"Where is everyone else?" Josie challenged, pointing in the direction of the gate.

"You and me, we, can live normal lives."

"As you stand right now, there is no 'we.'" She turned sharply and began to walk away again, taking Slobodan with her. But the conversation wasn't over. Out of the foggy night came forth Friar Laurence, with his long brown robe hanging over his pale bones, to block her way. Slobodan held Josie back, and Henri caught up to her, taking his place beside his new brother.

"Josie," he encouraged gently, "there's a lot going on, I get it. Ignore the Friar here, but you heard Fae Peeters." Josie furrowed her brows. "*This* is the real world, and it isn't a game Nefas is playing in your head. I love you, and I really need you to make a decision. No more Gift for the rest of your life. That's not even a choice. It's everything."

Josie just shook her head. She wanted to believe him, he could see it, but she wasn't there yet. Off to the side, the sound of Katie being stolen of Nefas' essence bled over into their silence, and Henri had to fight to keep his concentration. Fae was taking away his first inductee, and that was personal.

"Josie," Slobodan said to her, "remember what I told you."

Henry demanded, "What did y—" But something about the way Josie looked at him muzzled his words. She was sad. No. She looked heartbroken. And that took his breath away.

She pursed her lips and looked doubtfully at Slobodan. He gave a short nod, and she began to sing.

Josie never pretended to be a good singer even though she sang all the time, but as she sang now, her voice cold and mystical like the night. "I wonder as I wander out under the sky . . ." she dropped off as she lost the next line but it didn't matter because Henri could almost hear the song's music carry over the pause as though she were willing the song into him. ". . . to die, for poor ornery people like you and like I. I wonder . . ."

She dropped off again and began a new song just as Friar Laurence began to move his jaw, reigniting that damn teeth clacking. But this time, for the first time, Henri heard him speaking actual, audible words.

"Nulla fuga est. Mortuus morietur ad novam vitam in morte. Nulla fuga est . . ." It was as though he were trying to talk over Josie.

The essence in Henri's fingers was starting to throb, wanting to be let out, but without Josie agreeing, it wouldn't matter.

Josie was stumbling through the song, but she didn't give up. ". . .let nothing you dismay. Remember Christ our . . ." She swallowed hard like this was hurting her and kept going. What if, Henri wondered, he injected her now to give her a taste of what was to come? Like how Nefas had done for him? ". . . to save us all from Satan's power when we were gone astray. Oooh . . . comfort and joy . . ." Josie faded out. "Henri," she said, "if you're still in there, I love you. Everyone in the Notre-Dame de Seigneur is—"

"No one inside that basilica cares about Henri now," Nefas chided, cutting her off as he came up beside Henri, all his faces tight and stoic. "He's not one of them anymore." With Nefas' appearance, the Gift began to rapidly take Josie back and Henri's chance to convince Josie faded away with her. He threw his hands forward to inject her but ended up grabbing nothing but limp clothing and a shaky skeleton.

"Fae did her job already," Nefas told him. "We have a tight schedule. You lost your chance this time."

Nefas went back toward Fae and company, waving for Henri to follow. Skye came over from Fae's group, nodding a silent greeting to Slobodan.

"Don't you dare touch Josie," Henri snapped at Skye. "Katie is yours to take care of." He stepped forward ready to fight this woman. Behind her Slobodan was shaking his head at him.

"Josie didn't choose you, Henri," Skye told him. "She's coming with me." *You're not ready for Skye. Not yet.*

Henri growled and reluctantly stood down at Nefas' bidding. Nefas had said he'd lost his chance "this time." Skye put a guiding hand on Josie's skeletal back, and together they walked away to the Notre-Dame du Seigneur.

Following after Nefas, Henri left Friar Laurence and Slobodan to do whatever they wanted, the voice of Josie singing slightly off-key caught in his head.

. . . for poor ornery people like you and like I, I wonder . . . Let nothing you dismay . . . to save us all . . . as I wander . . .

"Henri!" Slobodan crouched beside Inner Henri's bent over body, lightly shaking him. "Henri!"

Henri was breathing. He could feel that. He could feel the chilled, sweet air entering his nostrils, filling his lungs. He could feel his lungs expanding, contracting, life coming to his brain. He knew the light was going to be too bright; he kept his eyes shut. They were heavy as lead, so it wasn't hard.

"I've come back, Henri. As promised. You held on. Good job."

Henri wanted to move his toes and his knees. They were creaky and stiff. His lungs rose, then fell.

Rose, then fell.

A cheery, hardy song that he recognized as one of the Christmas songs Josie liked was dancing in his head. *Let nothing you dismay! Remember . . . let nothing you dismay! Remember . . .*

"Do you hear that song?" Slobodan asked, cautiously optimistic.

The music wasn't in his head? It was being piped in? The next time the song looped around Slobodan kept the lyrics going. He had a deep, rich voice that coaxed Henri to higher awareness. "Remember Christ our Savior was born on Christmas day." As Slobodan sang, Henri felt his body starting to creak out of its night, the weights on his limbs and joints slowly falling off. "From God our heavenly Father a blessed angel came . . ."

Slobodan was giving him a gruff shoulder rub as he sang, waking up his cold muscles. "Let nothing you dismay, remember . . ."

33

"I've shown you our future, Fae," Nefas told Fae, returning to her. Henri had just led his girlfriend off to the side to convince her to accept the parasite, and now it was Fae's turn to do the opposite with Katie. Fae had been stuck wondering what she was going to say to Katie and now her opportunity to plan was cut short.

"You stand beside me now," Nefas said. "Do what we both know you want to do."

Katie looked exhausted even as she waited obediently, her blonde hair messed and her jeans stained with mechanical grease. Fae could send Katie home to her family tomorrow, changed but not ruined. She was still so young, not much older than Bailey, her own daughter. She could reverse her failure to protect Katie. She had the power.

"Max, what does Christmas morning look like? Remind me."

Nefas motioned Katie closer. "If Max wanted to help you, Fae, he would've been there when you needed him."

Katie came as she was told, watching everything unfold with an almost tragic innocence. Skye stayed close to her.

"The morning will look beautiful," Max answered simply. "But it will be as heavy or as light as the sum of your decisions. Fae, what do you need from me?"

"She needed you at the village hall," Nefas charged. "She found me instead."

"Fae, what do you need?"

The sum of her decisions . . . Katie had asked for the parasite. That had been her choice, uninformed though it was. Was Fae really Katie's only shot at a second chance? Or had Max also retained the baby's role of taking the parasite away Christmas morning?

"Max, can you take—"

I know what you want. Nefas was hovering close.

"Answers" was what she needed to say, but her arm was rising on its own, reaching for Katie. The motion was effortless, almost like something was moving her arm for her. It wasn't until her arm was completely outstretched and practically touching Katie that Fae saw her arm was in fact resting on top of Nefas'. He was taking away all her cause for delay. All she needed to do was act. This wasn't fair. Not with Nefas so close, not with her psyche and nerves so raw.

"Help me."

She needed Max, but Nefas stole her words for himself, and her plea was no sooner off her lips than the parasite began coming out of Katie toward her outstretched hand. Was she doing this? She didn't want to be doing this!

"Max!"

The process was quick and undramatic. Katie's skin lost its sheen and she let out a loud grunt and clutched her arm. Released of its brace, her shoulder sagged unnaturally low, and Nefas slipped from Fae over to Katie bumping Skye out of the way. He gently pulled away Katie's hair from her neck and leaned down to kiss the broken bone. Fae couldn't watch.

"Nefas took that parasite out," Max whispered discreetly to Fae. "He wants you to think it was you, but I knew you were OK."

Fae almost choked on her gratitude.

Nefas let Katie's hair back down. She let out another groan of discomfort while nervously trying to keep an eye on Nefas without moving her head too much. "Fae," she whispered, a little too loudly for a sober person, "I think your stalker-guy found us."

Fae looked at Max. "Can you take the parasite out?"

"Yes," Max said. "When the time comes."

As much as a relief as that was, it still didn't change what was at stake.

Katie was not so subtly pointing at Nefas. "He's wearing the professor's hat . . . I met the professor again, on top of the gate right over there, and he told me—"

"Katie, listen to me," Fae jumped in, but Katie cut her off.

"He offered his office hours to me!"

"Katie! Shut up and listen to me."

Katie smacked her lips shut.

"After you fell down the stairs, Henri injected you, possessed you, with the parasite. Remember what I told you about it? It controls your ability to make choices so that you have to do what Nefas, your professor, wants."

"Hey, did you see me on the wall? My mum would've loved to see me balancing up there. People might even pay a couple quid to see me do that again!"

"Katie, you said before that didn't want to be possessed because you need to go home?" Katie nodded. "Then you need to say that you don't want the parasite. Right now, say it. If you don't, you're not going home tomorrow. Your body will, but the person your parents expect to welcome home won't be in it."

Katie looked like she was starting to focus, but not enough.

"Fae, you need to work on your persuasion skills," Nefas said. "You need to learn how to force a decision." Without warning Nefas snapped his hand over Katie's mouth and nose and clamped down tight. Her eyes went wide, but Nefas' grip was too strong to let her struggle. He bent down and whispered something into her ear, and she relaxed, but the fight against her loss of air was showing in her straining muscles.

Nefas looked straight at Fae. "You have less than forty-seconds to make your case."

Fae fought the urge to reach for the vial in her pocket, feeling a prick of resentment at Max for not giving the order to use it. Forty seconds to a girl still half drunk?

Imagine yourself in Katie's shoes, the Voice spoke to her. *Because this is how I'd like to see you.*

The void was tugging at her, scraping at the edge of her thoughts, calling her back in. She shook her head hard trying to clear it. "Katie, do you want Nefas' parasite again? You have to shake your head no, OK? Do it now." Katie's eyes were bulging more desperately. The call of the void was growing.

And then Fae remembered what Dominic had told her earlier. She was a bridge, an ambassador.

Katie wasn't the one she should be talking to.

"Nefas, Max has something you want," Fae said, watching Nefas' suffocating hand, almost feeling it squeezing off her own airways instead. "You're not the only one with leverage."

My queen.

Katie's struggle was approaching critical and she began fighting against Nefas' hold. Skye didn't wait any longer and ripped Nefas' hand off, Nefas holding his hands up as though he'd willingly let her go. Katie gasped her breaths, crying from the pain from her rapid, shallow inhaling.

Fae rushed to Katie's side as Skye and Max stepped in front of Nefas, holding him back. Fae took her jacket off and wrapped it around Katie's shoulders. "Walk and talk."

Katie followed, but the hesitancy in her step was unmistakable. "I don't . . ." Katie did a quick look back at Nefas. "I don't think I want to leave him. It's not a good idea."

"Yes, it is. Whatever he told you—"

"I want it back."

Fae quickly shoulder checked and saw no one but Max who was following protectively behind. "Katie, we're leaving. Skye is holding him. Max is with us. It's OK. You're safe."

"Who said anything about safety?" Katie asked. "Whatever I had crossing that bloody wall, I want it back."

"You had Skye," Fae said, speeding up their pace. "With that parasite, he owns you, takes away your freedom. You won't be the same—"

"An' I don't want to be the same," Katie countered, struggling to keep

Fae's pace. Fae slowed down but was eager to get as close to the basilica as fast as possible. "The professor, Nefas, whoever, is effing exciting. I was electric with whatever he gave me."

"A drug dealer gives you a good taste until he controls you."

Katie stopped hard in the road, almost losing her balance, and Fae knew she'd said the wrong thing. "Coffee has a good taste too and I don't call the local barista my dealer over a latte. I'm twenty-six and have nothing to look forward to except bills and a chance to sleep in. Here's someone who's going to take the world by storm, and he's asking me to be part of it."

"He just tried to kill you!"

"He's testing me! Those Halloween haunted houses, yeah? You jump, you scream, but the test is to get to the exit."

"Nefas will *destroy* who you are. This isn't a haunted house."

"No offense then, Mrs. Peeters, but you can bugger off. He's shown me my future and it's everything I want."

This, Fae thought, was how Nefas was going to win the world.

"Call it a drug, but I'm giving it a shot." She gave a quirky smile as she started to backtrack the way they'd come. "I'm still the same person, yeah? Still going home to mum and dad in the morning? You got it wrong."

Fae knew then that nothing she could say would change Katie's opinion. Katie was sinking into deep, cold waters and Fae couldn't reach down deep enough to pull her out, the liquid blackness inking Katie out as she slowly sank, a smile on her lips. Fae's promise to protect the girl sank with her.

Henri's business with Josie was done as Fae saw Skye escorting a recorpsified Josie away, and Nefas was bringing Henri back over to Katie; they were coming to reclaim her. As soon as Henri was close enough, he placed his fingers over Katie's broken bone and injected her a second time. The intensity of the parasite pushing its way into its new home almost brought Katie to her knees, but the process was easier on Henri this time, and he did the job quickly. When it was over, Katie shrugged out of Fae's jacket, and dropped it at her feet.

"The rest of my life starts now."

Without another word, and barely a second look, Katie headed toward the gate, Henri's monk guiding her out.

Max watched Katie's departure with a fired energy that said more than he was showing. The renewed weight of Fae's failures threatened to drown her, but Max was rubbing off on her, and rather than crying for Katie, Fae was angry.

Henri was also watching Katie's departure, but with a smugness that would be prime to be scraped off like gum from the bottom of a shoe. "You," Fae snapped at Henri. "Come with me." She turned on the ball of her foot and started walking. "We're going to the Notre-Dame du Seigneur. Everyone's coming outside."

Whether or not Henri came was irrelevant, but Fae suspected Nefas would make him. Fae, his reclaimed prize, independently deciding to deliver the rest of the people still inside the basilica into his hands? This was a victory Nefas would want an audience for.

"Risky move," Max said quietly, keeping up with her. "You're right to do this. Don't worry, we'll do it together."

Fae nodded as she led the march back to the basilica. She set her eyes on the gothic spires that could now be seen through the fog and followed them. No matter what happened from this point, Katie's choice was going to affect a lot more people than just her.

Getting everyone outside the comfort of the basilica was easier than Fae had expected. She alone had announced her demand as she stood at the back of the pews speaking over the smooth flowing music of the choir. "Everyone outside. Now."

Fae unwaveringly met each one of the uncomfortable looks and shocked faces; like those from Chantal, and Henri's family. The villagers had all lived by the cardinal rule she'd made a show of standing for earlier, and she was now telling them to break it with no offered explanation. Death had been tickling her with a thorny feather all night, and she had no ambassadorial diplomacy to spare. It must've shown because after her three-word demand they all started to leave their pews and go outside. The villagers and visitors were confused, unsure, and scared, but they went. And as they went, she couldn't ignore the haunting question knocking on her thoughts: where was the line between tough love and being a traitor?

What kept the question at bay was watching Max take it upon himself to help herd everyone out. She watched him go person to person, pew by pew, getting people on their feet, and she held onto that sight with everything she had to keep believing that she really was doing the right thing.

Henri was inside with her, watching, and as his family passed him by, he took on a look of expectancy, maybe hoping for some kind of filial greeting. But his mother scurried past him with barely a glance, his sister hesitated as though to say something but didn't, and his father looked nauseous at the direct insight into his son's biology. They passed with barely an acknowledgement of him. Henri just cracked his neck and straightened his shoulders, keeping his eyes fixed ahead.

Then Fae watched Jenny come. She'd lost all her southern charm, her long, blond curls having fallen flat, and all that was left of her was a wearied soul in some country boots, one who was definitely still angry at her. Fae didn't blame her.

Fae followed after Jenny outside. Nefas stood at the base of the stairs in the middle of an expanding pool of his green fog inviting each person deeper into the plaza. It made her sick and even though she knew she had to do this for the future of these people, she hated herself for having to facilitate these introductions. How many more Katies were hiding in this group?

She stood on top of the stairs and people continued to file past her, cautiously, down the stairs to the man in the fedora waiting for them. The choir continued singing, their song muted through the door. The rolling, earthy tune was unmistakably the "Huron Carol". Fae remembered learning its translated lyrics as a kid and their appropriateness now was too strong to be coincidental. *Behold, it has fled, the spirit who had us as prisoner. Do not listen to it, as it corrupts our minds, the spirit of our thoughts . . .*

Max soon exited as well, signaling that the basilica was clear, and together she and Max descended the steps, the haunting carol at their backs. There was no way she was going to mimic her experience on the steps of the village hall.

Say what you've come to say, Nefas' voice washed over her as she watched him mix with everyone she and Max had uncovered for him. He walked among them, whispering to them, making them doubt, making them believe. Each person was reacting differently to his words, which were toxic, addictive. He knew what each of them wanted.

"A couple hours ago you all had a choice to come outside," Fae began in French. She had the attention of about half of them; everyone else was listening to Nefas. One of the choir members had slipped outside to translate for Jenny. "Everyone knew it wasn't safe. Even after Henri came practically dripping with Nefas, every sign screaming at you of the danger, some of you still couldn't help your curiosity." Their eyes shifted upward to where Henri was standing behind her, above her. "The measures this village has taken over the years to protect itself did more than just protect you from the outside world; it turned you into a breeding ground of ignorance. How was I the only one who tried to stop people from leaving on Henri's invitation?" Fae let the question hang, and she started to sense an all too familiar gulf growing between her and everyone else.

"In case you haven't realized it yet, that voice whispering in your ear is Nefas."

For these people, that truth should've inspired action, a response. But it didn't. Whether they thought they weren't supposed to give a response, or maybe they were too focused on what Nefas was telling them, they all stayed in the growing pool of green fog slowly encasing them. From the back of the plaza, Fae saw Skye emerge from the street slowly walking beside Josie's corpse tirelessly dragging itself forward.

"Where is everyone?" someone from the crowd asked.

"The hostages? On la Rue. Nefas reopened it. Everyone else?" She paused. "The gate is open," she said bluntly. "The Gift is wandering the fields and the roads."

That news finally stirred the crowd and they broke into a buzz. Right away, a couple approached the stairs to talk with her privately, but she didn't acknowledge them. More were quickly descending into a frenzy. She didn't try to stop it.

You're doing well. We will control their fears.

Fae clenched her teeth, and saw Max give a reassuring nod.

It looked like Nefas had already chosen a few favorites from the crowd and was starting to focus his attention on them. Henri's father was one of them.

"Do you even know who Nefas is anymore?" Fae specifically asked the villagers, speaking over them. "You don't, otherwise every one of you would've done more to stop your friends and family going out that door. So now you need to learn, because if you don't tonight, you won't recognize Nefas later when he comes to you without any green fog to give him away. Go wander the streets for some alone time with him. Go to the gate if you want, try and stop the bleeding." Fae waved her hands trying to shoo them away into the village. "Find out how deeply Nefas really wants you. You've been so sheltered from the Gift you don't even know what it is anymore, so go!" Fae again tried to scatter them, but those who weren't occupied with Nefas' whispers looked at her blankly.

Fae had had enough, and she stormed through the loose crowd, Max following her. La Rue could be put off no longer. That's where this Christmas Eve was going to turn into Christmas morning, and that was where Nefas had always planned for it to end—on his home ground.

34

Despite Fae's determined walk, she really didn't know how to get to la Rue, and it didn't help that the village's dark, twisting streets, grown organically over generations, mixed with her memories and played with her sense of déjà vu. She relied on Max for direction, unable to trust her intuition and unable to shake the feeling that she was going deeper into an inescapable labyrinth.

"I'm not alone. I won't get lost," Fae uttered, trying to calm herself. She stalled at a three-way fork in the road. Max pointed to the left, and Fae went left. "I owe Nefas nothing."

Nefas was nowhere to be seen, but she kept expecting him to show up just around this corner or come straight toward them up that street. It was just as likely he was waiting for her at la Rue to welcome her in. Nothing about this transfer of hostages was going to be pretty, for anyone. "Max is here."

Max wasn't the only one who came. While Henri took his own route, a number of people were following her like sheep, no doubt expecting that she'd take them to their loved ones. It grated on Fae that they were all following her like she was some sort of leader, as though they'd forgotten that she'd stood by and watched as Nefas injected one of their own.

They follow the strong. They follow their queen.

In a twisted way, Fae felt better listening to the Voice than to all those helpless feet trotting after her and Max or the shrieks when one of them passed a reflective surface and caught sight of their dead soul as a corpse. It'd happened twice already, and Fae didn't wait for them. They could catch up, if they still wanted to, after coming face to face with a sample of what was to come.

Let me take you to where you want to be, lift you up to live above these people who can't understand the places you walk.

The Voice's words sowed lies and fantasies, and Fae absorbed them. Focused on them. They felt like the flagellation she deserved for all her selfishness and failures.

You are a prodigy made to feel like an oddity. That's not fair. I'll give you my eyes to see and my tongue to speak so that the world will respect who you are.

"Rip my eyes out to replace with yours, and pierce my tongue to wag as you want," Fae corrected, paraphrasing the words he'd threatened her with years ago; her mind hadn't blocked out everything. Max gave her a questioning look as if he wondered if she wanted him to step in, but she shook her head. She needed this.

Coming to a four-way stop, Max led them to the right.

Your full potential is still untapped. You're underachieving. You're special, of two worlds. You can do anything.

"Henri is of two worlds too."

He's limited, the Voice purred, *so he's been placed in a limited position.*

"We're both limited to what you want."

You still haven't forgiven me. Withholding that is a punishable offense, my queen.

"How does a queen get punished?" Fae bit her lip. She didn't mean to ask that.

The Voice chuckled. *She learns the meaning of regret.*

Fae instinctively reached for Max's arm.

"Don't fear," Max reminded her.

Tell your pig that the dust of his dead body will soon be added to the same vial hanging around his neck. The Voice swept itself around her. She didn't respond. *Tell him,* the Voice demanded. *I'm waiting for you in the void where you'll find your next gift: obedience. You'd do well to embrace that gift before I have to force it upon you.*

"Max," Fae began hesitantly, "he says—"

"I can hear him."

If Max had said that earlier in the night, she would've been ashamed, embarrassed, but it was too late for that. The Voice laughed at her with delight as though his pet monkey had just danced, and Fae snapped.

"How badly do you want that necklace?"

For a moment, the Voice said nothing, and an uneasy tension filled the silence left by her question.

The negotiation for that vial has already happened, the Voice menaced. *Your anger is misplaced. Look, everyone has abandoned you to me.*

Fae looked around, down the street, into a small park with a single set of swings, and she saw no one. How was that possible? Everyone from the basilica who had been following her, Max, they were all gone.

"Max . . ."

She spun around, looking, searching. She couldn't see him. Couldn't see anyone. The street was eerily empty.

"MAX!" Fae kept spinning around, her voice carrying in every direction. Green fog surrounded her, and she kept spinning, she couldn't stop, faster and faster like a merry-go-round. The buildings disappeared. The street was erased. The lamplight, even the fog, faded away until there was only perfect darkness, nothingness . . .

Nefas appeared before her, no hat hiding his perfect face. "You cannot threaten me."

"Fae!" Max's voice shattered the illusion, and just as quick as everything had disappeared, it all came back. Max was looking at her closely.

"How long did you see the void?" he asked.

"I don't . . ." Fae took a controlling breath, shaking her head, her brain trying to catch up. "I don't know. A minute?"

Max nodded once. "I got you out as soon as you called my name. Nefas believes he has you back and that I'm the one who won't let you go. Let him keep thinking that for now, OK?"

Fae nodded and glanced behind her taking a first real assessment of who was following her; she was happy to see Chantal hadn't. Henri's parents, Jenny, and the rest of the visitors had. The group was larger than she'd expected considering how she'd addressed them at the basilica.

"Take a minute if you need it."

Fae shook her head. "No more delays."

"Hey. Hey," Max slowed her down before she set off again. "We're close. Here." He shrugged his jacket off and held it out for her. "We're switching. You're going to need mine."

Fae really didn't care what jacket she ended up with. She fished the vial out of her pocket before making the exchange. His fit well enough, but the leather was heavy on her shoulders.

"Keep the hood up. It's going to hide your face from the drone."

She flipped up the hood and kept one step behind Max the rest of the way to la Rue, the place where Hell and Death touched Earth.

The gates of la Rue, and her façade, had been blown open. Bits of brick and building material were scattered in a blast pattern on the street leaving a black maw gaping that even the night's fog hadn't dared to cross into.

"Dear God, it does exist." Someone behind her gasped.

Fae stopped on the far side of the street. The dark significance that this place held was more than just a mere memory to sweep aside.

"You want us to go in there?" someone else said, this time, in a German accent.

"No, I don't." Fae said. "Nefas is in there, and probably his monks too. But so are the hostages, everyone Nefas took after Henri got them outside. If you come in with me to bring them back, don't assume getting out will be as easy."

Fae found Jenny standing aloof and locked eyes with her. "You wanted to pray the Devil out?" She asked her in English. "This is where you start."

Fae stepped away, navigating around the debris, Max leading the way; he crossed la Rue's threshold first. When Fae took that same step herself, she had him on the inside waiting for her.

If it was possible for la Rue to be blacker than Fae remembered, then it was. The roof that had been part of her design blocked out any natural light and she shamelessly latched onto Max's arm as he led her forward, guiding her with short comments about watching for a popped stone here or there. In turn, Jenny latched onto her shoulder, and Fae could feel the tug of at least one other person following Jenny, but she had no idea how many people had decided to come in. Other than passing along the walking instructions, no one spoke.

Max guided them around a shallow bend and was greeted by Nefas' green fog. It spanned the width of the thin street illuminating it with its hellish glow. Arms of fog stretched out toward them like slow moving tentacles, and as they walked into it, the fog wrapped around their feet and coiled up their legs before it fell away, only to do it again.

"Is this stuff toxic?" a question was asked from behind.

"No," Max said.

Fae was scanning the wall, looking for the little shrine to the baby Jesus she remembered being not far from the bend. She didn't expect it to be there anymore, but she found it, dilapidated. Cut into the bare wall, the diamond patterned glass doors had been shattered. One lay on the ground, the other hung crooked by a single hinge. Its yellow bulb of a few watts had long ago burned out, and it was only from the fog's dull glow that she could make out the tarnished metallic gold and red paint at its back depicting the baby Jesus. The painting of the Holy Child had been disfigured, vandalized by the hand of Nefas. Old man wrinkles, clusters of fly-like eyes, fangs for teeth, and a long, wart-riddled witch nose turned the once giggling baby into a horror.

Max carefully reached through the shards of glass and into the shrine pulling out a small piece of fabric.

"It's not dusty," Max observed, referring to the painting.

"To preserve the mockery though, or in devotion?"

"Defiance. Adrien risked a lot every time he cleaned it."

Fae took one last look at it, then pushed on.

Nefas was waiting for them as soon as they cleared the corner. Henri stood behind him. The two made for quite a pair, the smartly dressed Nefas with dull, green light reflecting off the underside of his hat and his face blacked out; and Henri, lit up by intertwined threads of the parasite running through his body like a skeleton and vein map. Fae knew she must've fit the part just the same, with her hood pulled low creating her own shadows deep in the fog's glow.

Nefas said nothing as they approached. He and Henri simply turned around and went deeper into la Rue, and she was expected to follow.

They went in silence, the odd scuffing of shoes or rubbing of fabrics breaking the nightmare. Fae stared dead ahead, not feeling, not thinking, letting the sounds of the people behind her constantly remind her of why she was angry in the first place.

They didn't have to walk much further before shadowy shapes materialized out the fog: four human-sized pillars and a number of low mounds all squished together in the tight space. Fae quickly pieced together that the pillars were the three monks and Dominic—the fourth monk was probably still with Katie—and the mounds were the hostages' rounded backs as they kneeled prostrated. Dominic was the furthest back, guarding the black door that led into Nefas' pit. The three monks formed a triangle in front, facing him, locked in a standoff. The hostages were penned in the middle.

"Max. Fae." Dominic greeted them through the darkness.

"Dominic," Fae said, unable to hide her sense of relief at seeing him again.

Nefas opened his arms wide as he made a show of walking into the middle of the prostrated hostages. The unmistakable sound of shuffling bodies followed him as they shimmied themselves around on the ground to continue facing him. "Fae," he said. "They're yours." He wandered back to the front of the group, and the hostages again turned to keep facing him. "As promised." As if on cue, all the hostages adjusted themselves so that they now faced her, their faces still kissing the ground.

Fae shook her head. "Stand up."

Nefas chuckled and Henri irritatingly joined in. "They worship you, Fae, as the queen of both the light and dark. I am the light, and your Nicholas is the darkness. They will never look at your face for fear of you. In fact, you've already punished that one for blaspheming Nicholas," Nefas said, pointing at a woman in the middle of the group. Henri worked his way to the woman and hauled her to her feet. Even with her face cast down, Fae could see that her eyes were solid white, seeing nothing.

"Sophia! My wife!" The Spanish EU employee rushed forward and Max quickly grabbed hold of the man to keep him back.

"Fae, you put her into this darkness, but you can just as easily take her out of it," Nefas said.

Fae was speechless. Nefas was making all this up. That he'd steal this woman's eyesight and claim that she'd done it defending Nicholas's reputation . . .

"Sophia!" the man shouted again. "¿estás bien?" Sophia didn't respond.

"Give Sophia her sight back," Fae demanded.

"She's yours." Nefas said, shrugging. He walked slowly toward her, isolating her in his attention. She could feel her heart pounding and quickly looked to Dominic, to Max, but they seemed a hundred miles away. She clenched her fists.

"Uphold her punishment, or show her my mercy?"

"You have no mercy, there's nothing to show."

"Fae," Dominic called out, pointing toward the end of the street that butted up against the village wall. "Eyes are watching." Fae hadn't heard the faint *whrrr* of the drone until now. Even though la Rue's roof forced it to fly low, she double checked that her hood hadn't fallen out of place.

"You should listen to Dominic. Be careful what you decide to do next." Nefas took off his fedora and tossed it toward the wall. Two arms popped out of the darkness and clapped it out of the air. "They're recording us to entertain the world. They arrived at the village in time to capture everything that happened at the gate before I helped them find that hole in the wall, so they could join us."

Fae was slow to ask "Who are they?"

"The right people for the job. Thank Manuel." Nefas nodded back to the hostages and Henri dropped blind Sophia and grabbed another person from the prostrated group. It was the old man who'd been the first out the door with Henri's invitation.

"I promised to take Manuel's life if he did me a favor and post an invitation online to come to this village for Christmas Eve. Sophia's son found the website Manuel made and convinced his family and his friend's family to come. This drone pilot and his two friends here also found it."

Henri dropped the old man who was still waiting for Nefas to fulfill his promise, and he crumpled back into prostration. Now that Manuel belonged to her care, Fae wondered if Nefas had any intention of keeping that promise.

Henri turned himself around and maneuvered his way through the hostages toward the black door and Dominic. "Stop blocking the door," Henri told Dominic in a loud voice. "Nefas is going to want some alone time with some of Fae's tagalongs. My papa, for one." He looked over his shoulder back at his father. The threads of the parasite tugged at the corners of his mouth, only making his words seem even more callous.

"Henri," Dominic said to him suggestively, "listen to the music."

Henri stalled, and even through the darkness Fae could see Dominic's words caught him off guard.

Nefas laughed incredulously, then abruptly stopped. "That Henri is dead. He can't hear a thing."

"Then you have nothing to worry about," Dominic said. In one swift movement, Dominic grabbed Henri and pulled him into himself, pinning Henri's arms down to his side. Henri squirmed, trying to shoulder punch his way out of Dominic's hold, but even with the parasite he couldn't match Dominic's strength. Dominic had him tight, calmly speaking hope-filled whispers to him in the dark.

Nefas growled darkly. "He's not yours."

Dominic didn't let Henri go, and he didn't stop talking to him.

"Very well then," Nefas said coldly.

Faster than Fae could react, Nefas turned on her, pushing her hard against the wall.

"This is on you, Dominic."

35

Fae's head banged against the brick, her eyes flashing between blackness and stars. "Here we are again," Nefas told her with a dark excitement. "I know Dominic still wants to protect you. But until he does, let's seal our working relationship."

She tried to wiggle out from beneath him, her head throbbing sharply. He held her tight against the wall, a thin stream of fog wafting from his mouth. It streamed directly toward her, splitting between her nose and mouth.

"No," Fae said, her hand searching beside her for Max. "I didn't—"

He leaned in closer. "What are you going to do about Sophia?"

She stuttered, trying not to inhale.

"Think very, *very*, carefully if you want to keep going," Max said in an even, measured tone, his hand reaching out, blocking the streaming fog.

Nefas slowly closed his lips.

Dominic was still whispering to Henri, restraining him; he wasn't going to stop. They both needed more time. Fae flicked her eyes to the hostages. She wouldn't use Sophia, but she did find someone else she easily recognized.

"Isaac," Fae called out shakily. "Come here."

Nefas let out a sound of surprised satisfaction and eased up on his hold, letting her go, and she knew she'd accomplished what she needed to; she'd pleased Nefas. Gently touching the part of her head that had hit the wall to make sure there was no blood, she stepped forward to meet Isaac, Nefas watching her closely.

The parasite in Isaac forced him to stand and come to her, his eyes remaining downcast. Seeing her husband, Jenny rushed to him. "Isaac, honey," Jenny called, her light and airy voice out of place.

This was the chance Jenny had been waiting for, and Fae hoped she had something to show for all her talk.

Isaac, though, barely acknowledged Jenny. He accepted her hands on his shoulder but didn't give her any attention.

"Babe? Hey, babe. We're going to set these people free, remember?"

Isaac looked over to his wife, shaking his head, licking his dry lips. "Nefas took advantage of those commands and deceived me," he said. Fae recognized the words he quoted; though slightly modified, they were the same as what was etched above the black door that Dominic was guarding. "He used the commands to kill me."

Jenny took a brave breath. She looked at Nefas and said, "Oh Death, where is your victory?"

"Jenny, don't . . ." Fae quickly warned. That was the wrong thing to say unless she knew what she was doing. And she didn't.

"Where is your sting?" Jenny finished.

"Where indeed?" Nefas mused with dark pleasure. "Let me show you."

Without hesitation the nearest monk grabbed Jenny by the arms. "Jesus in you, Isaac!" she yelled.

Nefas stepped up to Jenny, his fog coiling up around them both, bridging the space between them. The sound of the drone moving through the air for a better angle was cruel.

"I am of the royal priesthood," Jenny said shakily. "I can say to a devil 'be gone' and it will leave."

"Say it then," Nefas suggested. "Say it like sweet nothings in my ear."

"Isaac," Jenny said, weaker than before, her eyes glistening with tears, "I cast the Devil out of you—"

The low rumble of Nefas' laughter cut Jenny off, and Fae could see the tears escaping down her cheeks. The fog had shrouded her body, its swirling motions more like entangling arms than not.

"You're smarter than you sound," Nefas told her with approval. "But I have no idea who you are to talk to me like that. And I'm not a devil. I'm sure Fae told you already. You should've listened to her."

The monk holding Jenny now gripped her neck with its boney fingers making her whimper again.

"Fae"—Nefas turned back to her—"are these the self-empowering lifestylists you honestly chose to be with?"

"I chose Nicholas over you," Fae said, feeling the burn of Jenny's failure as much as Nefas' disapproval.

"It's a taunting question," Max told her.

"I've been asking myself the same thing for years." Fae said back.

Nefas continued. "This is why I gave you control over my essence. To give you what people like Jenny have lost: a place in this world."

Look at dear Isaac. Sophia.

"Look at them!" Nefas yelled, and Fae looked. Both stood facing her, and in them she saw normal people. Even though one was blinded and the other stood unmoved by his wife's quiet crying, Fae saw normal people who'd woken up that morning with the best intentions. Like her.

You could've helped Adrien. And Katie. I've given you everything you need. The baby is redundant when you can save these two on your own.

Fae swallowed the lump in her throat. "I see them, Nefas," she said slowly. Nefas was wrong. He'd never rise so high as to supplant the baby from the top of the hierarchy; *she* could never rise so high as to not need Nicholas. Fae forced a small, brave smile onto her face and stepped out from behind the protection of Max to stand beside him, using his courage as her own. "I see that they've just begun to know what life is."

"I'm glad we agree." With that, Nefas retreated into his fog and disappeared.

My queen.

The struggle Dominic was having with Henri was intensifying and no longer was Dominic simply trying to keep a fluttering bird contained, he was in a battle of wills. A rustling of bodies from the hole in the wall announced the arrival of another man who was rushing toward Dominic and Henri. Fae recognized him as the one who'd been with Henri's girlfriend at the North gate.

"Give him another minute, Dominic," the man said hurriedly. In a smooth feat of coordination, Dominic handed Henri over into the other man's arms, Henri having lapsed into something resembling a seizure. "We almost have him back."

Max spoke to everyone who'd followed them from the basilica. "You all have to leave."

"Not without Sophia."

"Yes, without her," Max said. "Corpses are blocking the exit so go to the bend in the street, where the shrine is."

A shout of excitement from the small group piloting the drone drew Fae's attention back to Dominic; Nefas had reappeared behind him having opened the black door.

Seeing Nefas focused on trying to control the Henri situation, Fae nodded to Max. She'd given Dominic as much time as she could. Now it was time to finish this Eve. She swallowed the lump in her throat.

"I'm not touching Isaac or anyone else without you," she said, keeping her voice low. Max knew exactly what she meant, and he laced his fingers through hers. She took a deep breath. Once Nefas realized what she was doing, that she was betraying his assumptions about where she stood, the end would come quickly.

With two steps, she and Max were within reach of Isaac, but the sounds of the hostages aligning themselves to her gave them away and she swore. *Dear God, dear God, dear God.* She thrust her and Max's joined hands to Isaac's heart.

The parasite came easily, painlessly, surging up Max's arm, disappearing inside him. The process had barely begun when a coldness fell on her heart, icy enough to fill even the most soulless man with dread.

"Oh, Fae," Nefas called in a sing-song voice. Leaving Henri behind, he picked his way through the hostages hovelled on the ground.

I will not be afraid. Fear will kill.

Max released her fingers. "Show him your vial. He gave up this village for mine. Make him pay for yours."

"Now you'll learn the meaning of regret," Nefas said coldly.

"Slobodan," Max quickly called out, "get Henri out of here. His fight is over."

Henri was practically slack with exhaustion, and it was only Slobodan's hooked arms that were keeping him up. Both Slobodan and Dominic had come alive with the fight they were waging, and they seemed to take up twice as much space with their presence as they had five minutes earlier. And Max, too, Fae noticed, looked no less than an equal of the three powerful figures.

She stuffed her hand into her jacket pocket for the vial; she couldn't find it.

"If you leave with Henri," Nefas warned dangerously, "you're breaking the laws. Henri is *mine!*"

Slobodan shook his head as he maneuvered himself and the barely conscious Henri away from the black door. "I told you Inner Henri was never dead."

Nefas must've found reason to believe him this time. The street began roiling and heaving with agitation, the fog covering the hostages completely, hiding them away.

"Well," Nefas said, his icy voice as sharp as a blade. "That's his mistake."

You will both learn the meaning of regret.

With no other warning the weight of Nefas' presence exploded outward, the force of it pushing Fae back into Max, and she heard the drone smash against the wall. She couldn't breathe. Deep gasps came from the hostages, and Fae thought of the kids with alarm. They wouldn't be strong enough to get the air they needed.

The monks spread themselves out. Jenny, now freed, grabbed the emancipated Isaac and, leaning on each other, they limped down la Rue as fast as they could. One monk followed after Slobodan and Henri, another stayed with Dominic. The third went to the drone friends at the hole though the sound of shouts and fast-moving feet suggested they'd finally decided to run away, back through the wall, into the countryside, and away.

Struggling for breath, Fae was digging deep in the pockets of Max's jacket for the vial, desperation making her fingers clumsy.

"Nefas," Max said, "the Gift is almost over. You're not getting Henri or Fae."

"Almost over. But not yet." Nefas snapped.

"I'm going to give you an easy exit before it starts to get awkward," Max told him, taking a step forward. Though he was physically smaller, Max stood no less Nefas' equal. The two of them only took up half the width of the street, but they dwarfed everything else around them.

Fae's hand finally closed around the vial.

"I've always wanted to be this close to you," Nefas said to Max evenly, the rage he was barely suppressing coming out with every syllable. "I will kill you and then everyone here."

Wishing in the back of her mind that she'd left a message for Jordan and Bailey, Fae took as deep an inhale as she could grab.

"You won't," Fae told Nefas, standing up straighter, "because I know what you want."

Nefas slowly shifted his head away from Max to her. "You'll wish you didn't."

La Rue fell uncomfortably still. Only the gasps from everyone fighting to breathe echoed in the small space. Already so close to Max, and so to her, Nefas loomed over her, a mountain of terrible power. Even still, she felt the draw of him, the need for him.

"What *do* I want, Fae?" He asked.

She swallowed hard.

"This." Fae pulled the vial out of her pocket with all the effort of a desperate last stand. She held it up so that Nefas could see the cloudy glass container, its angled sides reflecting the green light around them. "You want this."

Nefas let out a controlled, ragged breath. He slowly raised a trembling hand, reaching out toward the vial, but Max gripped his forearm and held it fast. Nefas' fingers were rigid with tension, his whole body seeming to tremble.

"You should've forgiven me when I asked you to," Nefas said, almost delicately. "Now, I have no forgiveness to give you in return."

Before she could register what was happening, Nefas let out a terrifying screech and lunged for her, his whole hand glowing with parasite. Max blocked him, shoving Fae out of the way. The kids on the ground began to cry despite the parasite in them. Nefas didn't like crying. Even as Nefas fought Max to try and reach her, the crying quickly turned into gagging as the parasite started to suffocate the kids into silence.

"Damn you!" Fae yelled at him with her stored-up breath. "With everything that the Communion is, stop it!"

Nefas growled and snapped at her, but the kids stopped choking. A moment later, his heavy, smothering presence lifted too, and a chorus of gasping breaths and coughing filled the small street, everyone sucking in air. Fae fell back against the wall in relief, catching her breath.

"Your lessons in obedience and loyalty will be hard to swallow," Nefas promised, Max still holding him back. "I'll always be telling you what to do."

"But that's all I've ever been to you, isn't it?" Fae said, taking her place next to Max. She teetered briefly from light-headedness. "I've never been your queen. I'm the bitch you can yank around and display. If you really knew what I want, how did you think I was ever going to give up my safety under Nicholas to play a joke at your side? Maybe you torture me into standing there, or force me into addiction, but given the choice?" She swore at him, and she could feel his frustration at not being able to reach her.

"Given the choice," Nefas countered with venom, "you gave me more souls to work with in one night than anyone ever has. I knew I could get you to give me at least a couple and you didn't disappoint. Your story with me isn't finished, Fae. It will never be."

"No, Nefas. We're done." Fae again held up the vial between them. "I know what's inside this and how badly you want it. And I know what you gave up for Max's small necklace of it." She could see her hand start to shake, her body no longer able to control itself. "For mine? You leave me the hell alone. And my family. Forever. Our story is done. Everyone in this village, including the tourists, and Henri, and their families are released from you.

Forever. We don't exist to you." It broke Fae's heart to not say Katie's name too, but Katie had made her choice.

"Fae," Nefas' voice quivered, "leave that vial on the ground and walk away. Walk away, and I leave you alone, and I give you your life back."

"You don't have it!" she yelled, ripping the hoodie off her head, no longer hiding.

"If that's what you believe." He paused. "You asked me once to show my face," he said as he reached both his hands behind his shadowed head. He began to slowly draw them over as though pulling off a mask, and as he pulled away his shadow, he revealed first hair, then an eye, then the corner of a mouth. "I don't want us to part not truly knowing each other."

Fae couldn't help her audible reaction as the shadow covering him was fully removed. It was as though Nefas' face was made up of hundreds, or even thousands of microscopically thin, translucent layers of faces. Some were in the prime of life, some were dying, and others had barely begun. They all moved as he did, reacted as he did. It was . . . horrible.

"I am all you will ever need in life, or death."

"Except," Max interjected, "you don't sit at the top, so you can never be *all*. Stop wasting time. How badly do you want her vile?"

If the glaring hate of all his layers of faces was any indication, he wanted it bad enough. Balling his shadowy hands into fists, he let out another growl and lunged at Max. Max was ready, but Dominic, who'd been waiting nearby, charged and tackled Nefas hard into the wall with a brick cracking *thud*.

"Do you agree to Fae's terms?" Max asked, coming up beside Dominic, who had Nefas pinned. Max pulled the necklace over his head.

"You'll never feel as alive as you felt with me, Fae," Nefas said, all his faces snarling. "You'll always remember this moment as the decision you regret and wonder what your life could've been."

"Do you agree?" Max pressed.

Nefas tried to push off the wall, but Dominic held him tight with another shove. The fog was curling up around Nefas, growing thicker and higher. He was going to disappear, Fae thought with a panic. Max seemed to be thinking the same thing, and he grabbed Nefas' shirt.

"There's only one way to get what you want."

Nefas tried again to push off, teeth snapping, but he couldn't get past Dominic's hold. "This is extortion," he snarled.

Max gave a little smile. "This is your decision." He stood back, the strength of who he was almost radiating from him, his body barely containing his true self. "But what we want is going to happen whether you like it or not."

"Give me the vial, Fae" Nefas ordered. "You'll get what you want. And you," Nefas said pointedly to Max, "owe me yours."

"I do." Max agreed. He took the vial swinging from his fingers and easily popped the lid off. Letting the vial tip over, he let Nefas watch his prize pour out. "This is for you to never return to this village," Max said. A breeze picked up and carried through the street sweeping the dust away into the world beyond the hole, the fine particles dancing and reflecting the green light. Nefas growled but Dominic kept him firm against the wall.

"And for Fae's terms . . ." Max handed a pocketknife back to her. She put it to the bottle's wax seal and worked it off. Lifting the vial up to eye level, she copied Max and flipped the glass upside down as she stared hard into Nefas' eyes.

Nefas glared at her hatefully as he watched her pour out the dust into the breeze, its particles glittering all the way out the hole in the wall.

Once the bottle was empty, she dropped it unceremoniously. It landed on the ground with a bounce. Nefas looked down at the bottle then back at her, his thousands of eyes swirling with the parasite, his fingers glowing with a fury. She could practically feel his hands on her throat.

"Why are you still here, Nefas?" Max asked. "There's nothing here for you anymore. It's just me and Dominic."

"This," Nefas snarled back at him, "this isn't over; we're not done. Not for all the lives and generations of this earth are we close to being done." With a final growl, he shoved Dominic off and picked himself off the wall, revealing the crater his body had left in it. He scuffed Fae's discarded vial back over to her. "Remember us."

Walking to the hole in the wall, he turned around to face Fae, giving her a smirk that could haunt a thousand nightmares. He kept his eyes trained on her as he walked backward and passed through the wall, melting into the darkness beyond. His remaining green fog disseminated into the dying breeze, taking with it its light and leaving only cold darkness.

Fae took a shaky breath. "I'll remember you like tooth decay that's been drilled out."

36

Slobodan was celebrating. It was the kind of wild celebration that belonged to Belgium winning the World Cup or when someone won an all-expenses paid trip. Something had been won against high odds, but Slobodan was on mute so Inner Henri couldn't hear what he was so excited about. Whatever it was, Henri did his best to ignore him as he sat at the coffee table in his old apartment in Antwerp, his bank account staring depressingly at him from his computer screen. This was a moment that had happened almost three years ago when he had to decide if he was going to move back home or not. He'd been without a solid job for months and only had enough money left for another month of expenses. He had to either take a risk and stay or move back home to keep trying his luck on the job market from there.

Henri rubbed his temples, wrestling with the decision he knew he had no option but to make. Anywhere but home. God, anywhere but there. It was almost a physical aversion.

Slobodan crashed into him and stood on the couch patting his shoulders like he was part of the celebration too, but Henri shoved him away, too wrapped up in the difficult decision to try and make out what his muted cheers were about.

"Don't go home."

Henri looked up from his bank account and saw himself casually strolling in from the kitchen wearing a loose tie and snacking on some bread spread with Nutella. He saw himself shrug like the suggestion was an easy, overlooked option.

"Stay here," the Henri eating the bread said. "You've already tried going home, and look how well that ended. You still have another month to find a job. If you can't, then ask your parents to help you out."

"You make it sound so easy."

"Because it is," the other Henri said, flicking a crumb off his tie, cautiously eyeballing Slobodan's silent celebrations. "You have friends you can stay with if you have to. There's so many options for you here in the city."

"The unemployment rate is almost nine percent."

"Home is where your heart is. Your heart is not in that village."

Henri looked back down at his account. One month. Maybe he could get lucky with some more contract work to hold him over. His buddy had a basement he could set up in . . . or he could go home, be a laborer for a couple months, earn enough money to stabilize again, then find a job anywhere and be gone before Christmas came.

"You know what you fear?" the other Henri asked, licking his fingers clean of the Nutella. "Is that if you go back home, you'll get stuck there."

Slobodan yanked open the sliding door to the porch and was waving for Henri to go outside with him, but he wasn't interested. The only thing through that sliding door was the Notre-Dame du Seigneur. That wasn't how he remembered his apartment view, there should've been a café and pharmacy across the street, but the difference wasn't an issue. Slobodan came over to him, trying to push him off the couch.

"Not now!" Henri snapped. Next month's expenses were going to start being withdrawn and he had to make a decision before then.

Merry gentlemen, let nothing you dismay . . .

"Hey, where's the music coming from?" Henri's ears perked up. The song was as loud as if someone were playing it there in the room.

The other Henri looked alarmed. "What is it?"

. . . To save us all from . . .

"A Christmas song."

The other Henri suddenly blanched and shot an accusatory glare first at Slobodan then at the back door.

. . . when we were gone astray . . .

"What do you see out there?" The other Henri demanded.

"The Great Wall of China. No, the Notre-Dame de Seigneur. Look for yourself."

. . . Oh, tidings of comfort and joy . . .

The other Henri reached for the sliding door to slam it shut, but it wouldn't go. His tie flapped against his chest as he struggled to close it. It looked like the door was caught on something in the track, and the other Henri glared at Slobodan with an immediate, hostile anger.

"You did this," he accused.

"What did Slobodan do?" Henri asked.

"He locked the door open!"

Henri looked beside him to where Slobodan had perched himself on the back of the couch, grinning wildly. "Why *are* you so happy?"

"You're out!" Slobodan shouted, his mute suddenly off, his hands doing as much talking as he was. "You're free of this place!" He jumped off the couch and lunged over the coffee table, over Henri's computer and papers. "Let's go. Your mother has a table full of food waiting." He winked at the other Henri, whose hand was still white knuckled on the door handle. "Be a good sport and admit you've lost."

"He was *dead!*" The other Henri menaced. "I'm a prince among peasants—"

"*Almost* dead," Slobodan said. "And you were a slave among slaves."

"If you go back home, Henri," his other self threatened, "you'll never leave and you know it! You've already tried."

"I'm just stepping into the basilica." Henri pointed down to his computer. "I can take ten minutes to see how 'free' of this mess I really am."

He followed Slobodan outside, stepping out onto the familiar cool stone flooring of the Notre-Dame du Seigneur. If Slobodan said he'd gotten out of this situation, then that was reason enough to follow him.

Nefas was gone and it felt too easy. Incomplete. Like there was more to come.

But nothing more came.

With his illuminating fog gone from la Rue, there was nothing to hold the darkness from folding back in, and everyone was lost to each other.

Fae's whole body was shaking. Her teeth began chattering uncontrollably. She couldn't stop. "D—D—Dominic," She felt for him in the darkness. "M—Max?"

"Right here," Dominic said as he found her searching hands and put them on his arm.

"I . . . I want to leave."

"Give your yourself a minute. I'd rather not have to carry you."

In no mood to argue, Fae leaned against him, holding his arm close and letting her adrenaline run itself down. She flipped the hood of Max's jacket back up, wanting nothing more than to simply disappear inside of it.

Dominic fished out a small light from one of his pockets with his free arm and turned it on, holding it high. The bright, white LED lit up the confined space. The monks had all gone with Nefas, as had the parasite. The hostages stirred as they regained full self-awareness. The four kids were the first to jump off the ground, crying and whining for their parents. Max was there helping everyone to their feet, uniting the kids with their parents. How much of the night did they remember? Fae wondered. Did they know why they were all on their knees facing her?

The old man Manuel was the first to really gain his full facilities, and he grabbed Max by the shoulders.

"Where's Nefas?" he asked as though fearing the answer. "Where did he go?"

"He's gone—"

"I can't lose him," he said with sadness. "I did what he asked. I did everything . . ." He pushed past Max and walked toward the hole in the wall. "He said he'd let me die. I can still find him." He climbed his way through the hole and disappeared into the night.

Someone behind Fae asked, "Should someone go after him?"

No one answered.

Fae let out a heavy exhale, her chattering teeth slowing down though she was still shaking. It was embarrassing. She was nothing more than a wreck of frayed nerves and exhausted strength, and she wasn't prepared for when the man known as Jean sidetracked his exit to approach her first. The side of his jaw had swollen where it'd been locked open all night.

"Merci," he said with a scratched voice. "You warned us, and yet you're still here, waiting for us on the other side." He nodded his thanks then limped off, stiff in the legs, taking another older man with him, probably his father.

"The corpses?" Fae asked Dominic.

"Nefas took everything with him when he left including his essence."

Sophia came to her next, her seeing eyes clear and bright in the white light.

"Merci. Graçias," she said, leaning in to give Fae a hug. Fae was too stiff with surprise to do much else other than accept it; it felt wrong accepting such thanks.

Sophia let her go, then went back into the embrace of her husband and kids who rapidly spoke Spanish as they left, and soon everyone was going down the cold, dark path of la Rue. The last villager to leave grabbed the ruined drone lying smashed on the ground, and Fae tried to imprint his face on her mind so she could describe him later to Maël. Max followed behind him, leaving Dominic and Fae alone in the chill emptiness. It was an unnatural feeling, being so close to the black door, so close to the pit. It was like being in an abandoned asylum in the middle of winter. Fae waited a couple minutes more before she nodded to Dominic that she was ready to leave, ensuring that there was enough distance between her and the departed group.

"Where to?" Dominic asked.

"The Notre-Dame du Seigneur. And a corner where I can be forgotten and alone."

"We can do that." He lifted high his light and guided them out and away from the cursed street. Fae walked on autopilot, seeing but not seeing, hearing but not hearing. It wasn't until they got closer to the basilica that the sounds of a celebrating crowd suggested that the villagers had all returned from outside the walls, free from the Gift.

"Do they know?" Fae asked. "That they won't have to suffer the Gift anymore?"

"They haven't been told yet, but they suspect something good has happened. You can hear it their voices." Dominic cocked his ear slightly to one side. "The sound of hope?"

Fae wished she had enough left in her to smile. She tiredly shook her head. "That's too specific a sound for me."

They walked another half block, and eventually she asked, "What will happen to these people?"

"They will learn what it means to live without the Gift," Dominic said. "Because of the conditions you and Max put on those dust remains, what happens with this village will be outside of Nefas' control. The corpses' light did catch some other attention as Nefas planned, but it will be hard to get any official, or unofficial, investigations off the ground when there's nothing to see anymore. You should tell Maël to carefully consider what he does with all the files he has."

Fae nodded. Fire was an appropriate solution. "And Nefas?"

"It was smart to release the remains into the breeze. They will continue to cry out their warning wherever they go about the danger of entertaining Death. As they do that, Nefas will be hunting down every last particle for his collection. It will take him a very, very long time."

"And he'll still try to win people over?"

Dominic nodded. "He's a vain creature with high aspirations."

"And what, what about . . ." Fae stammered as she came to a stop in front of a tailor's shop. Blue and white lights outlined the door and a simple presentation of the Communion lay at the entrance. She tried to distract herself from the question she was trying to ask with the details of the little place, how the door and all the windows were painted the same color red, how the white curtains hanging in each of the seven windows matched, and how inside the shop there was a mess of material scraps heaped onto table corners and stacks of folded clothes on chairs.

"What about Katie?" Dominic finished the question for her.

Fae sighed. "Yeah."

"She's left with the consequences of her choices. Skye is currently getting her to the doctor to set her bone."

"What about, I mean, what is she like now? She chose—"

"You should talk to her."

Fae nodded. She wished Dominic would just tell her. It was a reunion she'd prefer to avoid. Katie was likely going to thank her for a good time, and she didn't think she could handle that. "I want to see Max before I leave."

Dominic smiled with a nod. "I'm sure you'll both want your own jackets back too."

The spires of the basilica guided them the rest of the way. The crowd had become heavy and paid the two of them little attention. Everyone was too consumed in finding their friends, partners, children, or the closest bottle of Champaign. Fae and Dominic easily slipped through them all. It was how she wanted it.

Together they climbed the short flight of stairs up to the basilica, passing through the choir who had poured out and were celebrating along with everyone else, providing the soundtrack to the party. They passed beneath the detailed archivolt telling its dark story and through the iron wood door with its sweet-scented wreath hanging so perfectly, and came into the warmth of the inside.

Fae wrapped Max's jacket around her even tighter and went straight to the front pew. She dropped down into the far corner and drew her knees up to her chest. Pulling the hood even further over her head, she hugged herself close, listening to the handful of choir singers left in the basilica, their voices reverberating in perfect harmony. *What is that light so brilliant breaking? Here in the night across our eyes?* It was an old French carol she recognized, "Quelle est cette odeur agréable."

Closing her eyes, Fae's head fell heavy against her knees and let the soft crescendos of the choir carry her far, far away.

37

Warmth radiated into Henri's back. It welcomed him, forcing him into consciousness.

"It's done," Henri heard Slobodan's disembodied voice say. Someone else acknowledged the statement.

His sister.

Henri tried to will his eyes open, but they were so heavy he could only crack them a bit. He was inside the Notre-Dame du Seigneur. That much he could tell.

"Hey, hey." The soft sound of Josie spoke gently behind him. She was the warmth on his back he was lying against. "You've made it, you beautiful mess." She was hugging him close, holding his hands.

He fought to open his eyes the rest of the way, if only to crane his neck to see her. "Are we at the pillar?"

Josie let out a quiet laugh. "No, lover boy." A warm tear dropped onto his cheek from above and she wiped it off with her thumb. "We're sitting in the back row where Slobodan dumped you." She kissed his head.

He struggled to sit upright, but his limbs were as heavy as his eyes. His body was spent.

"Give yourself a couple minutes," Slobodan said, and Henri's eyes eased open all the way. Slobodan was perched on the back of the pew beside him, arms folded, watching him with a studious eye.

There was another man sitting on the other side, his feet on the seat balancing him on his narrow pew-perch. A boyish grin betrayed the mature features he had quickly grown into since Henri had last seen him.

"I know you," Henri said. "I mean, I *know* you."

"You better," Max said with a pleased grin. "We're going to have a few things to talk about after your parents see you."

"Yeah." Henri nodded slowly. "I think so."

He managed to get his arms beneath him, and he pushed himself up with Josie helping him. He looked at both Slobodan and Max. "Thank you. I . . ." Henri really didn't know what to say next, but tears were welling up. He wiped them away before they were seen. "I couldn't . . ." He tried again but still failed.

"We know." Max nodded deeply, and Henri knew he wasn't just brushing aside what he was trying to say.

"Your sister is here too," Josie gently pointed out, and Henri turned to see Elena standing patiently behind the pew.

"Where's Maman and Papa?"

"Outside. Waiting," Elena said. "Parents aren't the calmest of people." She smiled.

The sound of Elena's voice carried, which made Henri notice that the basilica was almost empty. His ears picked up the singing and bursts of laughter of the party outside, but inside there were only a couple singers left singing a Gregorian-styled chant. There were only two other people, and they sat at the very front. Their names, Dominic and Fae, popped into his head like a lucky guess, and a stab of jealousy pierced him. He didn't even know why he didn't like them, but there was part of him that was glad Fae looked hurt and alone.

"What happened?" he asked. "Is the Gift still . . .?"

"It's over," Slobodan confirmed.

"We'll answer your questions later," Max told him.

Henri nodded and their group fell silent. There were happy people and good times outside. He, however, was separated in here. People would no doubt start to notice he was missing, and there were probably already rumors spreading about him, rumors that he was damaged or tainted or something stupid like that. If he stayed inside for too long, those rumors might start to gain traction.

"Elena," he twisted around to see his sister. "Go outside and tell Maman and Papa to meet me at the back door. I don't want everyone seeing me make an entrance."

"You sure you want to go outside so soon?" Josie asked.

"I'll be OK." He forced a smile, hoping to reassure her. "I'll meet you outside too." She didn't look convinced, but she placed another kiss on his head and slipped out of the pew, leaving with Elena.

Once the door closed behind them Max looked at Henri and said, "If you block her out of this, or lie to her, you'll lose her. You know that, right?"

"Yeah." Henri stood up, battling a sudden blood rush to his head. "Yeah. I know."

"That means you can't lie to yourself, either."

"I know."

Henri led Max and Slobodan down the stairs to the crypt, not able to help the cold parting gaze he sent Fae's direction. It triggered a memory in him, a feeling more than anything. Fae had been a rival, and remembering that released a wave of other memories. He'd had brothers. He'd had leadership and authority, and there'd been a blonde-haired girl who mattered to him . . . He didn't want to remember. Henri quickly focused on the rhythm of his feet trotting down the steps into the crypt and Max and Slobodan's feet scuffing in time with his own. The faster he could get outside and be distracted, the better.

At the bottom of the staircase, Henri took a right to go to the back door, but Max pulled him to the left, into the rows of sarcophagi. "This way first," he said.

Max stopped at a newly made sarcophagus. Unlike the other simple sarcophagi, this one was busy with carvings. The lid showed two lone figures, one with a sword and one holding the images of three people on a pole. "Walk around it," Max suggested, and Henri did. He didn't know art, but as someone who knew the Gift, he could figure it out. It was the struggle of a man and his family—a very specific man against a very specific struggle.

"This is the coffin of Adrien Jandreau," Henri uttered. "A coffin for him, and a memorial for his family. You had this ready. You expected him to die?"

"Adrien wasn't going to let himself live another day."

It was uncomfortable being here, next to a coffin so recently filled. Filled with a ghost. A ghost who'd put Henri into this mess.

"People are waiting for me," Henri said quickly, turning around and leaving the sarcophagus behind.

Max and Slobodan let him exit the basilica alone, which was for the better; they'd draw unnecessary attention. Max, at least, would see him again soon enough.

The sky had begun to lighten and by now everyone had formed themselves into their natural social groups. His mother saw him first. She rushed him, bombarding him with hugs and kisses and tears, crying her love and thankfulness. His father was close behind and smothered Henri even further, and when Henri saw Veronique standing shyly between her parents and Josie, he motioned her over to join the group hug. He half expected her to refuse with teenaged offense at having been left on the side of the road, but instead she ran into him, almost knocking his mother off balance who laughed even more.

It was a happy reunion, but the more his parents, and Elena and her husband, and Ver, were focusing on him, the more he was reminded that some other person had been controlling his body and had done things that he would never have. As his father was recounting the moment when he'd first arrived at the basilica making demands, he found the story only half familiar, and he didn't want the holes in his memory filled in. Henri looked down at his fingers, stretching them out, slowly flexing them. The motion felt strong—surreal. He remembered being able to see through his skin down to the bones and his skin shimmering like sunlight off green ocean waves.

He caught Josie staring at him and he immediately dropped his hand, flashing a quick smile. What did she know? He'd seen her at some point during the night. He'd wanted her so badly, a possessive type of need that Henri had never felt before . . . but had he really seen her? She would've been under the Gift. Somehow, he knew he had.

He didn't want to be the subject of conversation anymore.

"Joyeux Noël!" he suddenly exclaimed, beaming a bright smile, interrupting whatever was being said. "There are, I believe, many more festive things going on right now that we should be enjoying. The true Gift has come to us again this morning!" He threw his arms up and around Josie, dragging her in for a quick, deep kiss to the sound of Ver groaning. Then he turned to his parents and kissed them each in turn. "Forget the past. It's dead."

"Henri!" His named was called from across the plaza as a group of his and Josie's friends found them, cheeks pink from the chill air. Antoine, Julia and Victor.

Antoine greeted Henri's parents with an exaggerated flair, kissing their cheeks in turn. "Can we steal Henri?"

"We'll have him back in time for . . . whenever you need him," Julia added, pulling the Santa hat off her head and dropping it onto his.

His mother hesitated but Henri was already pulling Josie away with him, away from the tears and the stories. "Two hours," his mother yelled after them, "and the table is ready."

"Where have you been?" Victor asked as they escaped, passing a group of preteen girls trying to outperform each other with their equally average singing. "We've been looking for you for the last hour."

"The Gift is gone, like permanently gone, you've heard?" Josie said, smoothly changing the conversation.

"Yeah, can we talk about that for a moment?" Julie asked. "How'd that happen?"

Antoine jumped in. "Do you know why they weren't letting anyone inside this year?"

The five of them found some empty chairs one of the restaurants had made available and sat down, the basilica in front of them. Its spotlights were weakening in the growing daylight, and the barrel fires that had been lit around the plaza like a vigil were already dying down. It was, by all accounts, exactly like every other Christmas morning.

Henri answered Antoine's question. "You know that woman Fae Peeters? She was outside the basilica all night, and they're giving her some space. After that, she deserves it."

Antoine was satisfied with that and took Victor to find some snacks. Julia didn't waste a breath and started asking a million questions. Did they have normal lives now that the Gift was finished? What would happen to Monsieur? How *did* the end finally come, and why so suddenly? What happened to Nefas?

It was the last question that really caught Henri's attention. What *had* happened to Nefas? He was about to press Julia for rumors, but Victor and Antoine came back with an entire loaf of sweet bread—cougnou—a steaming jug of mulled wine, and another friend, Philippe. Like Henri, Philippe didn't have the Gift and so would've spent the night inside the basilica. Henri locked eyes with him, silently pleading for his silence, whatever he might know, but he saw the way Victor and Antoine were looking at him, and he knew he was too late.

"Henri," Victor started, placing the cougnou into Julia's eager hands. "Are you . . . like, are you OK?"

Julia was confused and looked first to Henri then back to Victor for clarity, but Josie subtly shook her head at Julia. Not now.

"Why wouldn't I be?" Henri judged his words carefully, not knowing what Philippe had said.

"Why wouldn't you be?" Philippe scoffed. "Tell them why you wouldn't be."

Henri shrugged. "I don't know. Some stuff happened last night," he said with forced levity. "Fae Peeters went outside and I got involved. I did what anyone would do." At least, he was pretty sure he and Fae must've been doing something together for a while. Why else would he have reason to be jealous of her?

"Nefas had you," Philippe said loudly, and Henri bristled. "He was all over you, and in you. Are you even allowed to be out of quarantine?"

Henri could've punched Philippe; his loudness was catching the attention of people nearby. The only thing constraining him was not wanting to make things worse for himself.

"How'd you let that happen, Henri?" Philippe kept going, and Henri found the edge of his chair to hold onto. "You betrayed this whole village when you talked the choir into letting everyone out of the hall—"

"You did *what*?" Julia almost choked. "How would you . . . *You're* the one who let us out? What if someone saw us?" She struggled to find her words, and Henri was shaking his head. No. No. Josie stepped in to calm Julia down, but it wasn't fast enough. The people nearby who'd begun looking their way were staring. Those who knew him were making their way over, every type of question and disbelief on their faces.

Henri tried to remain as calm as possible. "Whatever happened, I had nothing to do with it, OK? I don't have answers. I don't know what, or how, anything happened." The problem was Henri remembered enough to figure out exactly how it had happened—Alex-Adrien, the hole in the wall, Nefas, being infected. "You don't know everything, so please don't pretend you do." He shot Philippe a strong look. "You guys were walking corpses, and you are fine now. Well, so am I."

Henri forced himself to tear off a chunk of the loaf to try to divert attention. He offered some to Josie who took half.

"So, do you know then," Philippe said, quieter but still not friendly, "what happened to that blonde girl you were getting drunk with?"

Julia, Antoine, and Victor raised their eyes in surprise, but Josie was unmoved by the insinuation. Henri's restraint against punching Philippe was quickly disappearing. The blonde girl. He had a flash memory of her being uncommonly close to him, and an incredible feeling as parasite flowed out of him and into her. "I don't know what happened to her, Philippe. But you should leave. I don't want to be around when Krampus comes to take you for being such a douche on Christmas morning."

To Philippe's credit, he left. Henri slid the whole jug of warmed wine to himself, and drank straight from it.

"He became a loudmouth in the last twenty-four hours," Josie said.

Henri set the jug down, suppressing a burp. Everyone knew the Gift was over, but did they know that Nefas was gone? Henri wasn't even sure how he knew that, he just did. There was a brief memory of la Rue packed with people swimming in green mist all focused on a man draped in shadow. Something about that memory must've held the answer. He forced a friendly, casual nod to some people who'd been watching him since Philippe's and Julia's outbursts, trying to move them along, his legs bouncing uncontrollably under the table.

Victor took a seat and helped himself to the bread Julia was still holding. "You said you were outside the basilica with Fae Peeters?" Victor asked much too casually to not give away his suspicions.

"Nefas is gone. He's not coming back, so let's move on."

"He's not coming back?" Antoine repeated with surprise. "You can't expect us to 'move on' from news like that."

"I can," Henri said with strained composure, "because in the last five minutes I've heard Nefas' name spoken more than in my entire life. He's gone, and now you're making him famous. This village is the only Nefas-free place in the world, so let's keep it that wa—" The realization hit him even as he said it. He looked straight at Josie, feeling like a sinkhole was opening underneath him. "This village is the only place safe from him," he said slowly.

He stood up fast, nearly tipping the chair over. Mumbling a quick goodbye, he walked away as quickly as he could. Clumsily weaving his way through the crowds, he stumbled past the barrel fires, needing to get away. All around him was celebration, music, and happiness. The Gift was over! Food and drink, baby Jesus and angels, and Henri wanted, needed, to get away from it all. Not just the plaza, but everything.

"Henri!" Josie called after him. "Henri."

He didn't slow down, but she was quickly beside him, not letting him out pace her. He wanted to go to Levi's and boulder up some walls, hopefully fall off and hurt himself. Fight the punching bag in the corner until his knuckles were raw and bleeding. He wanted to be at the top of the Alps screaming into the icy winds tearing at his skin, taunting them into blowing him over the edge.

He rushed through the streets, past businesses and apartments, and into a nearby neighborhood of houses. There was an abandoned lot there that had been left unoccupied for years. Its house was boarded up, and there was temporary construction fencing around it that showed intention of development, but nothing had happened in the two years since the fencing had gone up. Arriving there, Henri yanked back the fencing and headed straight to the back corner of the lot where an old, wooden garden shed barely stood, having started to crumble long ago; it was no match for his frustration.

He let himself loose on the shed, a shattered yell escaping his throat as his arms yanked at the creaky old door and his feet kicked down its rotten walls. The already broken glass windows shattered into tiny pieces beneath his feet as he tore down everything that stood.

"Henri, stop," Josie demanded when there was little of the old shed left unbroken.

Standing in the middle of the wreckage, a few splinters stinging in his hands, he looked at her in challenge. "What do you know about last night?"

"I know enough."

"What do you *know*?" he demanded.

She snapped back, "Nefas owned you." She stared at him unintimidated. "He was in you. You opened the North gate and let everyone out. You tried to infect me; you had the ability. If it wasn't for a lot of people believing that your soul was still alive somewhere to fight back, you'd be gone."

He shifted his feet crackling the broken glass beneath him. "Did I kill anyone?"

"I don't know. Nefas was controlling you."

"But he wasn't when I first met him!" Henri yelled; he couldn't help it. He balled his hands tight. "He injected me with his parasite. He breathed into me and took over my mind. Do you know how he did that?" He paused. Josie didn't take the bait. "He kissed me."

The confession tasted like vomit in his mouth and he dropped his eyes, grinding his teeth. "With *your* lips. He stuffed me into a prison and let some other Henri I don't know run my body. I fought all night to get out, counting myself lucky when I had the chance to see through my own eyes . . ."

He snorted out a puff of air and picked his way out of the shed's rubble. He kept his eyes down, focused on where his feet fell. He couldn't look at her. "How did I meet Nefas? You have to be asking yourself if it's my fault for not listening to you that this happened."

"I wasn't."

He saw her shoes and stopped. "A ghost lied to me." Henri gave a short laugh of incredulity and looked up into the sky. "A dead man lied to me. All I've wanted was to get out of this . . . *place*! To get away from the hell hole that it is, and now this *place* is the only spot in the whole world that is free from the hell hole!" He shouted the last words, finding her eyes at last.

She eyed him hard, didn't back down, but didn't yell back. "What are you going to do?"

What was *he* going to do? He snorted cynically. "Nothing. Me *doing anything* is why I'm here in the first place."

"Someone lied, that doesn't make you special," Josie said forcefully. "You can't do nothing. You'll either keep breaking windows the rest of your life and let that lie change you, or you can stop what that lie was supposed to do to you. What are you going to do?"

He could feel the anger squeezing him, kicking at his insides, demanding to be let out. With the smallest of cues, it was ready to take over, he was teetering on the edge of surrendering himself to it, to know that same power he had before. He didn't like it, it wasn't who he was, and knowing that the echo of that other Henri was still influencing him made him even angrier. He'd fought too hard to regain control of himself, so he clenched his jaw as tight as he could and said nothing. He locked his eyes onto an empty space over her shoulder and tried to stay as empty as possible.

Josie continued. "If you let what happened tonight define you, then no matter where you are, Nefas will find you again, either inside or outside this village, it won't matter on what side of these walls you're on. People are going to try and label you, Phillipe is proof enough. Don't let them."

Josie hesitated and then she relaxed just enough that Henri noticed, and he felt himself stepping away from the ledge. She pursed her lips and shook her head. She spoke again, this time, a little softer.

"I know you haven't asked for my advice, but here it is anyway." She took a deep breath. "You should leave. Make this the opportunity you've wanted and move away." She took a couple steps forward, standing on two uneven boards. "Pick a place and go. Take any job you can when you get there. A lot has changed these last few hours, and we all need to figure out what that means to us."

Her face was soft; she'd made the suggestion in kindness, and he felt his anger melt away.

"Nefas doesn't take rejection well. I can't leave."

"Can't you though?" She didn't buy it. "Henri, you're not a victim unless you see yourself as the victim. Light wins over darkness. How is that different this time? You can go anywhere you want."

He swallowed a lump in his throat, and Josie stepped off the board.

"Do you know one of the reasons why the Gift is so hard to go through?" she asked. "Because a lot of the time I stop fighting him in my head. I let Nefas win. We all do. We just don't always have what it takes to fight him, and only the true Gift on Christmas morning saves us from ourselves." She sighed. "And that's why you should leave. Because some of them are going to see their failure in you. Right after you ran off, Julia said something that she shouldn't have. Not everyone is going to welcome you back."

That news hurt. Maybe Josie was right. Maybe he should leave before the village put their sins on him and forced him out. If only Nefas wasn't waiting on the other side of the walls.

Pure exhaustion started to hit him, and he turned back to the ruins of the garden shed where a storage chest still remained. Josie followed and they sat on it, side by side.

The morning was getting brighter, and though the sky was still gray with clouds, their private little world of rubble was being given color. Across the street, a dog awoke with a couple morning barks, and the faint voices of some people leaving the basilica plaza to come home were starting to reach them.

Looking in the direction of the voices, Henri asked, "Where do you want to move to then?" He knew it wasn't fair to ask with so much else having happened, but he had to know.

She was slow to answer, and he got the feeling that it wasn't from trying to narrow down the options. He looked at her to see the hesitation he was fearing.

"You can't send me away like a fugitive."

"No!" Josie shook her head, insulted, and she turned herself so that she was straddling the box, facing him directly. "God, no. Look, I just . . . the Gift, Nefas . . . our lives, it's all changed. I need to figure out what that means for me. Just like how you need to figure out what that means for you." She looked down at the weathered wood of the box. "Wherever you go, I'll be there for you, just . . . not with you, not right away. We need to figure out who we are as individuals again first. We're not going to mess this up, OK?" She looked back up at him, her gray eyes like smooth velvet in the gray morning. "We're going to be together until the end. Not months or years, so we're going to do this right."

Josie slid in closer to hug him, and he wrapped his arms around her in turn. They listened as the people coming their way diverted up a different street than the one they were on and then disappeared.

It was time to go. To be seen as normal, he had to be seen, and it would be better if no one could associate the destruction of the shed with him on top of everything else. Together, he and Josie got up and began their slow exit.

"I have an interview in Paris," Henri offered. "I have a friend on the inside pushing for me."

"Paris," Josie repeated with an approving nod of her head, testing the idea out. "I've never been to Paris. I'd love for you to show me around."

Arriving at the construction fencing, she held it open for him, a gentle smile touching her lips.

He closed the fencing behind them and scuffed away their footprints. When he was done, Josie nodded down the street to where a house divided the road into two. Max was standing there, waiting with two hot cups in his hands. Henri let out a long, slow breath.

Max met them halfway, greeting them and offering the coffee.

Josie took hers gratefully. "I'll tell your mother not to worry if you're late," she said as she walked away. She turned her head back at him and mouthed, "I love you."

Max waited a moment then motioned for the two of them to walk on. Cupping his coffee between both hands, Henri followed the bartender's lead into the quiet residential streets.

"Well," Max started, "you're alive. And as for Nefas, you don't exist to him anymore." Henri saw him give a small smile. "So, let's talk."

38

Death

Fae must've fallen asleep at some point because she found herself jolted awake by the pew cushion compressing as Max took Dominic's place beside her. The last of the choir had left, and only the diminishing, muffled noises from the people outside remained. Dying flames from the torches flickered and grew increasingly dim, and every shift of clothing or sniff of air echoed in the nearly empty space.

Fae gingerly unfolded her stiff body, making room for Dominic to sit on her other side. She wasn't much in the mood to talk, which Max seemed to expect, so Max did the talking. He took his time explaining everything properly now that they had the time. He explained what it meant for the Gift to be over but for Nefas to be freed into the world, how the parasite was still a real threat even though no one was going to be glowing, how the dust remains had provided Nefas an illusion of choice where he really didn't have one. And he provided suggestions to give Maël on how to transition the village into its new life and how to deal with any images or videos that may find their way onto the internet. To give her the closure she needed, he told her about the sarcophagus for Adrien and his family and offered to take her to see it. She shook her head. She couldn't handle it right now.

As for Henri, Max suggested that she reach out to him in a couple days. And André de Boer too. At her request, he told her that Isaac, unsurprisingly, was having a difficult time coming to terms with what had happened. Jenny, as a result, was concerned that he was still under evil influences. They had a trying road ahead of them.

"And Katie," Max said gently, "will have a different kind of hard road. She has a pain she's never known before, and she doesn't know what it is. She'll try to figure it out, but through the guise of the professor, Nefas will make it worse. Her story isn't finalized, but, well, you know how persuasive the parasite can be."

Max talked easily at some length until a creaking door announced the arrival of Maël, who poked his head in. Seeing them, he almost backed out, but Dominic waved him back in.

"I think we're done here anyway," Max said. "Have I missed anything?" he asked Fae earnestly. She suspected he would've stayed as long as she had questions. But her mind was numb, tired, and overloaded, and she couldn't think of anything left unaddressed.

Max leaned over to give her a hug. "Tell me," he said quietly, "has the baby become a good man?"

The man whose name was whatever it needed to be. Max: the greatest. Fae nodded into his shoulder. "Yeah. A pretty good one."

Pulling back, his eyes shone. "You're never alone."

Then Max got up, and Fae watched him as he exited. He shook hands with Maël at the door and let it close behind him.

Dominic inhaled deeply and put his hands on his knees to stand. "That means I'm finished too," he said. He gave her a half-hearted little smile. "The sun has risen, and I'm not needed here anymore."

Fae nodded slightly and stood with him. "Keep an eye on me?" she asked. "If Nefas decides to break his agreement and comes back . . ."

Dominic shook his head. "He won't break the agreement."

"Just make sure I'm doing all right, OK?"

"Of course."

Dominic pulled her into a hug, and she gripped him tight, holding him like she didn't want to let him go, because she didn't. Her heart clung to him, but not wanting to drag out the inevitable, she let him go and left him standing alone. She walked down the main aisle, meeting Maël at the back, and just before she exited, she looked behind her, and her white-haired, white-jacketed protector was nowhere to be seen. Typical.

Fae knew Katie would have to come back to the hotel eventually. As much as she dreaded the meeting, she knew she had to do it. Maël waited in Elise's office and Fae sat in the lounge running a dozen different greetings through her head and hating them all. She eventually decided just to wing it.

When Katie arrived, she came gingerly, aided inside by another woman, her arm in a sling. She was noticeably pale and looked overall worse for the wear, but she otherwise appeared normal. No green shimmer on her skin or carpet of green fog paving her way.

Fae rose to meet her. The other woman introduced herself as Katie's doctor, Ingrid.

"I really need to lie down," Katie said between grunts of maximum effort, as Ingrid angled her into the lounge area.

Ingrid nodded towards Fae. "Let's get her propped up on the floor."

Between the two of them, they quickly built a makeshift floor recliner, and as gently as they could, they helped Katie down, making comfort adjustments the whole way until at last Katie let out a sigh of relief.

"This is the bloody worst," she said on exhale.

"It will be even worse on an airplane," Ingrid chastised her in her best English. She looked up at Fae with resigned disapproval. "Remind me to give you more drugs before you leave."

"Top of my mind," Katie said with another groan as her body relaxed.

Katie directed Ingrid to her room key and gave her instruction on where everything was that needed packing. With a professional level of efficiency, Ingrid took the key and headed upstairs.

Katie turned her attention to Fae. "So, you had a better night than I did."

Fae sat down on the floor across from her, nervous. So much of this conversation would depend on what, or how much, Katie remembered. She nodded to Katie's sling. "What happened to you?"

"There were some Christmas spirits being passed around. I'm told I lost my balance and fell down the basilica stairs."

"Sounds like a wild time," Fae said. "Who were you with?"

"The professor," Katie said, regulating her breathing to prevent her lungs from expanding too rapidly. "Turns out he's a doctor in sociology, and I found out his name," Katie offered happily. Fae raised her eyes to show her interest. "Charlie Fontaine."

"Of course it is." The words escaped Fae's mouth as her heart broke a little more for this young woman. By the look Katie gave her, Fae's lack of enthusiasm didn't go unnoticed.

"What is exciting," Katie stressed, pushing on, "is that he's a professor emeritus in Reading and he's opened his office hours to me."

This time Fae kept her mouth shut and managed to force a smile of congratulations. "He will teach you so much."

"For him to offer his time to me, it's . . ." Katie faded out searching the room as though the phrase she was looking for was hiding on the ceiling. It made Fae wonder if something really was on the ceiling. ". . .it's like whatever god is out there is showing me a way forward with my life."

"Hmm-hmm." Fae nodded. "You know, I remember reading once about a long-term study done among university students of three different faculties," she began, choosing her words carefully. "The researchers found that students who were being taught to be open to accepting all possibilities as valid, when later tested on the basic truths of their field, were found to be more likely to believe an opposing idea as true rather than the actual truth when compared with students of the same faculty ten years earlier. Just, remember that when the professor talks with you." It wasn't profound advice but maybe, just maybe, Katie would remember it in the future. "From one smart person to another." Fae said, forcing another smile.

"Sure," Katie said dismissively. "Thanks." She reached up to scratch an itch on her head, and Fae couldn't help but notice a thumb ring she was sporting, one she hadn't noticed before. It was a thick, platinum colored band,

and was striking for the rich, metallic green stripe running around its middle. The green stripe looked to swirl with life as Katie scratched the itch.

"Where'd you get that ring?"

"This?" Katie asked holding her thumb up. "I don't even remember. You want to see it?" Katie began wiggling it off her thumb and Fae swore she heard a deep, musical voice whispering in the air.

"No, don't worry about it. No need to move any more than necessary right now."

Katie slowly lowered her arm back down, looking at her coolly, then glanced in the direction of the stairs. "I think Ingrid will be down with my things soon. I'm headed out as soon as she comes back."

"Do you need a drive anywhere? To the airport? It's no proble—"

Katie sharply cut her off. "Ingrid is taking me where I need to go. As my doctor, she insisted."

Fae pursed her lips and gave a curt nod. This was how her best efforts were going to end.

"Thank you for your time this weekend," Katie continued. "I'll make sure to give the photos of your work not from this village the best treatment. It was an honor to meet you face to face."

Fae took her cue and stood up, making a mental note to keep an eye out for that book. "I enjoyed getting to meet you too. I wish you the best of success moving forward. And safe travels."

"Oy, before you leave . . ." Katie shuffled herself as best she could to access a pocket in her jacket, and Fae kneeled down to help. Digging into one of the pockets as directed, Fae pulled out a brown paper bag, the top folded over a couple times. "Professor Fontaine wanted to give this to you."

Fae's breath arrested.

Managing to get her legs back underneath her, she stood up, numbly unfolding the bag. The world around her faded out, her brain rapid firing her survival words, *I will not fear. He can't hurt me anymore.*

She peered inside. At the bottom was a bruised and battered rose and half a dozen earthworms wriggling and coiling at having been disturbed.

Eyes wide, Fae looked down at Katie who was smirking at her with a grin not her own. Fae shook her head. "No more."

Katie kept smirking, and a new spark flashed in her eyes. "Don't make her laugh, Fae."

"I don't exist to you."

The sounds of someone else coming into the hotel made Katie cast her eyes to the doorway before refocusing on Fae.

"Everyone else gets to wish you goodbye. I'm only doing the same—before I leave you *the hell alone*."

The paper bag fell from Fae's fingers. "There's Communion by the door, Katie. You should take it before you leave."

Katie blinked rapidly and groaned with discomfort as she shifted herself. Her eyes drifted to behind Fae where the entering people had gone straight to the stairs. "Don't you have to be religious to take Communion?"

Fae smiled sadly. "You don't, no. I'll be rooting for you. Please always remember that."

Leaving the paper bag on the floor where it was, Fae left the lobby. She called for Maël as she exited without looking back.

She'd done her best. She'd done her best, and Katie had fallen. *But she's not hopeless,* she thought as she sank into the front seat of the car. She gave Maël a long sideways glance as he started the engine.

"I'm going to need your help finding out who her parents are. Nefas wanted to use her and Henri to make this village famous. He's still going to use her for something."

Maël nodded and they drove off, back to his place where his family, presents, and general Christmas merriment waited. It was everything needed for what the rest of the world would consider a normal Christmas morning.

Epilogue

<u>*Progress Reporting & Incident Tracker of Fae Peeters*</u>

Dec. 30: Spoke with Maël who's overseeing the post-Gift transition. The hall will be properly repurposed, TBD. The pit cannot be buried for all the natural gases coming out of it, but its covering and la Rue will be demolished. Proper hazard signs will mark the pit off, leaving it a scab of exiled nothingness. Maël and Elise went to the pit to start assessing this plan and found nine bodies thrown out onto the surrounding pathway. Nefas' collection of mummies looked to represent hundreds, even thousands, of years. They'd been kept buried all this time, not allowed to die while Nefas tried to guess when his moment would come. The question became whether or not to allow scientists in on the find of so much cultural and biological data, the greatest "bog body" discovery of all time, or to give them their long overdue peace and give them a proper burial. I told Maël not to tell me what they decided.

Jan. 8: Maël managed to locate Iakob and was able to finally give him some closure. Re. the bog bodies: In this case, I suppose, hearing nothing in the news is not ignorance.

Fae capped her pen and stared at the open page of her journal. Though she hadn't planned it, it was a telling leak of her subconscious that the last word ever to be written in this journal was "ignorance." So much could be said for that.

The British Columbian night was clear and crisp with a light snow beginning to fall, and Fae looked up into it with a sense of freedom she couldn't recall ever knowing. The night sky and its white stars were being covered over by the snow clouds moving in. It was peaceful out here in the mountains, on her deck nestled in the pine trees. The gas lamps surrounding the raised fire pit were set to low, just bright enough to provide enough light to write by. They flickered in almost perfect silence. The fire itself she'd skillfully built and fed until its flames were voracious and licked dangerously at the sides of the gray flagstones, the wood crackling and snapping. She wanted it hot and hungry.

With a cathartic snap, Fae stood up and closed the journal, knotting its wooden toggle into its leather thong. Without a second thought, she tossed the journal into the fire. Seconds later a new flame erupted guaranteeing that the fire was doing its job. She watched it burn for a minute, then, satisfied, Fae reached behind her and picked up the rose waiting on the arm of the Muskoka chair. It was a sad looking flower, abused and wilted. It was exactly how she'd asked the florist to give it to her. The rose's head flopped down, too heavy for the weakened stem to hold upright.

Take the rose, he'd said. *Forgive me,* he'd said.

She chucked the rose into the fire. It landed near the edge, but even still, it was quickly reduced into an ashy, glowing shell of itself. A log soon fell on it destroying even the ghost of its memory.

It was over.

They were words she never thought she'd be able to think, much less believe.

Finding the chair behind her, Fae lowered herself comfortably into its deep seat, ready to watch the fire burn itself down into marshmallow-perfect embers. Until then, she was going to sit staring into the flames, experiencing what perfect stillness felt like. Jordan would come home soon and find her out here watching her past burn down to nothing, and together they would move on with their lives.

The future as it was now, she was not built for. That belonged to the Jennys and Isaacs of the world, even the Elises, the people who were prepared, ignorantly or not, to handle the casualties that would come with living in a world where Nefas was unleashed. She didn't doubt that someday one, or some, of those people would find her, and with eager demands for information, remind her of everything she was forgetting this night. And she would be here, in her Muskoka chair in the Rockies, with her sketch pad designing a museum or some beautiful thing to capture the light of this world, expecting them.

-3-

You Have a Voice- Use It!

Book reviews make a difference. They keep stories like the one you just read alive. What did you think about Fae Peeters' journey? Who would you recommend it to?

Help others discover Fae Peeters, the Gift, and Nefas, and leave a review on Amazon, Goodreads and/or the digital storefront of your choice.

Every review matters, and most definitely yours!

Thank you!

Stephanie M. Matthews

Acknowledgements

To everyone who believed in me and my writing, you are all the best! To everyone who took a chance and read *The Gift*, and everyone who just read *The Eve's End*, thank you. This would all be a lot of work to do for an audience of one.

To my mom, dad, and brother, you have all been awesome and your support is absolutely priceless. Steve Parolini and Emily Stewart, your editing insight and help in filling in the gaps and polishing all the rough edges has made this book into what it has become, and I couldn't be prouder of the work we've done! Polgarus Studio, once again your formatting work was excellent. To everyone who has contributed along the way, Krista Goff, Jonathan Matthews, Vanessa Racine, Jeremi Ochoa, fellow author Jennifer Brasington-Crowley, and to Aaron J. Morton for your incredible graphic skills, thank you!

Photo by Juliane Arielle Photography

Stephanie M. Matthews has always loved writing and developed an enjoyment of thriller stories early in life. She writes both fiction and nonfiction, the latter mostly related to the Ancient world. In her spare time, when she's not writing, she enjoys learning more history, experimenting with new sports, and pretending that she can play hockey. Stephanie currently resides in Ottawa, Ontario.

www.stephaniemmatthews.com
stephaniemmatthewsinfo@gmail.com

Follow Stephanie M. Matthews on Facebook and
@StephanieM.Matthews on Instagram